FINAL RETURN

A Novel

by Ron Howeth

Temecula Valley Publishing

This is a work of fiction. Any resemblance to persons, living or dead, except for Mr. Sims, is coincidental and not intended by the author.

Final Return
Copyright © 2014 by Ronald A. Howeth

All rights reserved. Except as permitted under the U.S. Copyright Act of 1976, no part of this publication may be produced, distributed, or transmitted in any form or by any means, or stored in a database or retrieval system, without the prior written permission of the publisher.

Temecula Valley Publishing
27475 Ynez Road, 145
Temecula, CA 92591
[rahoweth@gmail.com]

April 15, 2014

ISBN-10: 0-989-758028
ISBN-13: 978-0-9897580-2-4

Library of Congress Control Number: 2014937013

Book designed by Tim Brittain

This book is dedicated to all of the American men and women combat veterans who have fought, suffered and died to protect the precious freedoms we enjoy in this country. God Bless every one of them.

To Ron,
All the best,
Ron

► 1 ◄

January 1994

BJ Tanner parked in the space marked "CEO" at the Tanner Systems building in an Austin, Texas, industrial park. He stepped out into the icy drizzle and jogged the few steps to the side entrance.

"Morning, Wilson," Tanner said as he passed his executive assistant's desk. "Come on in."

"Morning, BJ," Betty Wilson replied. She grabbed an armload of documents and a note pad, then followed Tanner into his office. She closed the door, laid the packet on the corner of his desk and withdrew the first document while Tanner removed his raincoat.

Glancing at the folder, he said, "Any priority stuff?"

Betty, a thin woman in her late thirties, stood almost as tall as Tanner's six feet. "One item," she said, and handed him the document. "You need to put your John Hancock on the modified ACS proposal for delivery today. Cecil and Matt have signed off on it."

Tanner penned his name to the paper and gave it back to her. "I'm going to Dallas for a few days. Nobody needs to know where I am. Get me an early flight in the morning. Leave the return date open."

While making a note, Betty said, "Mr. Watkins from Continental Trust called again. He asked to see you tomorrow or Friday."

Tanner shook his head. "I don't have time to see him. He's trying to make a deal that'll never happen."

"Okay, next item —"

"Where's Ellis?"

"Nancy's rounding him up." Betty sat in a chair at the side of Tanner's desk. "What's happening in Dallas and where do you want to stay?"

"The Anatolle Plaza." Tanner stood and looked out the window a moment, then turned back. "I have some personal stuff going on, Betty. No one is to know."

He could see her stiffen. He never called her by her first name except when there was very good news — or very bad news.

He said, "Cecil will have more info about an IRS fraud charge against Tanner Systems. He got word of it yesterday and called me. It has to do with the foreign income on the French and German government sales. I don't know the details yet, but our attorneys should straighten that out in short order, although Cecil doesn't think so."

Tanner leaned on his desk and looked at Betty. "The Dallas thing is VA medical. I have to get more tests done with a specialist. I'm sure Cecil and Matt can take care of everything while I'm gone."

Betty was about to speak when they heard a knock and Cecil Ellis peeked around the door. "Good morning, BJ."

"Come on in, Cecil, and tell me again why we have such a big problem with the IRS."

Betty rose to leave and Tanner touched her arm. "I'll call you this afternoon and fill you in on the other thing. Don't worry. It's probably no big deal."

She nodded and said nothing, but her expression showed her deep concern.

Cecil moved into the room and took a seat in front of Tanner's desk. "That's right, BJ. They claim we committed fraud by paying the tax a year late on all three years of the foreign contracts."

"Bullshit. We cleared that with IRS before the contracts were signed." Tanner reached for the phone. "We'll get Langford and Dawson's tax guy to clear this up right now."

Cecil raised a document. "Wait, BJ. There's more."

Tanner waited, then snapped at his financial officer's hesitation. "Well, come on."

"BJ, the IRS supervisor who filed the charges . . . her name is Patricia Karney."

Tanner put the phone down. "She's in D.C."

"No, she's in Austin. Says she's been watching you for a year. The woman sounds lethal, BJ. She knows you from D.C., right?"

"I knew her a few years ago. She had issues. I guess she still does and she's trying to make this personal."

"Does Dawson know about her?"

"No need to bother the attorneys. She'll bitch for a while, then she'll go away. There's no way she can make anything stick."

Tanner reached for the phone again, but Ellis raised a hand and rushed his next statement. "A Department of Defense contract has just been awarded to Tanner Systems."

"That's a whole other issue."

"Not exactly."

Tanner leaned forward, giving Ellis a hard look. "All right, what about the DOD contract?"

"The IRS — Karney — claims that Tanner Systems committed fraud in the foreign income deal by taking deductions a year before they were actually incurred, then not reporting income until a year later. She says that when the money went into escrow it was ours, not a year later when it was released to us.

"If it were a domestic issue, it could be cleared quickly. Foreign income is another matter. We could challenge the claim and go to tax court. Dawson says we'd win easily."

Tanner straightened and raised his hands. "So what's the problem, Cecil?"

"Going to tax court will take, at the very least, five to six months."

"So?"

"A federal fraud charge against the company will put our contract on hold. If the claim isn't cleared by the time work is scheduled to start, we'll be disqualified. We'll lose more than eighteen million net before tax over the next two years on that one contract."

Tanner felt his pulse pounding in his temples. "That's extortion."

"Her offer . . ." Ellis said, "the IRS offer: refile adjusted corporate tax returns for those three years. You, as responsible CEO, pay a two-point-five-million-dollar penalty. You sign a consent decree admitting no guilt, but it disallows you any future challenge for restitution."

Tanner rose, jaw clenched. "The only way I could raise that much would be to sell controlling interest in my own company."

"If you don't, you'll lose the company anyway. We've committed everything to that contract. Our resources are spent."

"So, just because the IRS has *accused* us of fraud, DOD will cancel this new contract?"

Ellis nodded. Sweat beads dotted his face.

Tanner turned toward the window, taking deep breaths. The drizzle had turned to sleet and collected along the bottom of the window. He felt the same sinking feeling as years earlier when General Ridgewood told him he had to take medical retirement from the Corps. Again, he felt betrayed by his government.

"So what are the options?"

"Go along with the IRS demand."

"Or, fight the charges," Tanner said, "which we'd win, but Tanner Systems would lose the eighteen million and maybe face bankruptcy."

Tanner dropped into his chair. "How can she do this? We reported the international income legal and proper."

Ellis nodded. "But she can make a case that will have to be adjudicated once she's filed the charges. The way the IRS looks at the overall timing of when the revenues were applied, they claim that we illegally delayed tax payments for each of those three years. The foreign governments deposited payments to trust accounts at the beginning of each year. Although we didn't get the money until a year later, Karney's position is that we should have declared the income at the time of the trust deposits."

Tanner felt the heat rising. He took a deep breath, then looked again at the IRS document on his desk. After a moment he shoved it toward Ellis and rose. "I have an appointment."

"What do I tell Karney?"

"Tell her to eat shit and die."

"BJ —"

"Yeah, yeah, I know. Tell her I'll be back in a week. Then we'll decide what to do. But call Dave Bonner and have him work some options for me to get the money together, just in case."

As he pulled on his coat and grabbed his briefcase, Tanner stopped and jabbed a finger at Ellis.

"But I'll tell you one thing for sure. She'll never get away with it. No matter what happens to me or Tanner Systems, one way or the other that crazy bitch will pay for this."

► 2 ◄

Allie Killgore handed a stack of patient charts to Freda Goins, who glanced at her watch and sighed.

"Saint Allie, what are we going to do with you?" Goins said. "You should've been out of here a half hour ago. A twelve-hour shift isn't long enough for you?"

"I had patients to see, charts to update," Killgore replied.

"Nothing's changed since you were in the Army, has it?"

"What do you mean?"

"Honey, you get too personally involved," Goins said. "You need to learn to be more dispassionate, go by the book."

"I happen to care about patients. The book method doesn't seem to sometimes."

"The rest of us go by the book because it works. You're still out to save the world, one patient at a time."

"I'm trying to make a difference, not just punch the clock," Killgore said. She raised a hand before Freda could speak, then pointed to the stack of charts as she turned to leave. "They're all up-to-date. See you tomorrow, grouchy."

Freda grinned and waved.

As Allie approached the door, she reached into her overcoat pocket and gripped her revolver. She wrapped the coat close to her thin body, then bumped the door open with a hip. She hunched her slight shoulders against a freezing gale that Texans referred to as a Blue Norther, and she started the hundred-yard walk to her car. Allie watched for any nearby movement on the dimly lit parking lot.

She glanced at a number of the old houses across the fence ahead. They served as crack headquarters for the Dallas drug scene in the South Lancaster Road area. One evening two years earlier Allie had left the hospital as usual. Minutes later she was carried into the emergency room after being slugged and robbed.

That memory haunted her every time she left the hospital. A smiling blond teenager had stepped out from behind a van parked next to her old Oldsmobile. Before she could react, a hand slammed across her face from behind, covering her mouth. Another arm went around her waist, lifting her, holding her helplessly suspended. She could feel hot breath on her ear. "Do it, man. Do it."

The teen's smile vanished as he stepped forward, drawing what appeared to be a piece of taped broom handle out of his coat sleeve.

He's a child, she thought. *No more than sixteen, and he's going to kill me!*

A lifetime of fearful thoughts raced across her mind.

Powerful hands restrained her, easily defeating her.

"Do it, man. NOW!"

She tried to scream but could make no sound. She kicked at the blond with both feet, but he pushed her legs aside, raised the club. She closed her eyes as he slammed it down on her skull.

She still remembered the ER doctor's comments after he'd put eleven close stitches in her scalp. "You're gonna be just fine. The cut will never show after that tiny patch of hair grows back. Comb it a little different and get the red out of those blue eyes. You'll look just like Sally Field."

"I don't think so, doc. Sally Field has brown eyes and a figure."

The police officer who had taken her statement that night said, "It was a couple of kids after crack money, most likely. There's more of that happening all the time. Better not go out of here alone after dark."

Allie vowed never to be mugged again, by drug addicts or anyone else. She armed herself with the short-muzzled .357 Magnum in spite of VA rules against weapons on the premises. She knew at least half a dozen others who armed themselves as well.

She checked to be sure no one was hiding under her car before approaching. Once inside, she locked the door, laid the gun in her lap, and pressed the cigarette lighter before starting the engine. A shiver climbed her back as she listened to the engine crank repeatedly without starting. A few more turns and the motor sputtered, coughed, then died.

"Come on, baby," she pleaded, turning the key again. The engine started, shuddered, then began to rev up. She closed her eyes, said a silent "thank you" and headed toward the exit. Pulling out the lighter with a shaky hand, she lit a Marlboro from the box on the seat and inhaled a long first drag.

The exhaled smoke added a visible perception to the depth of her sigh. She could feel the heady effect of the cigarette, her first in more than five hours. With another deep drag, she felt the first minor release of tension from a day of, as Freda had said, too much personal involvement.

Another day of nursing psychiatric patients.

Another day of making it safely away from the hospital.

Another day without a drink.

Most nights Allie would be home an hour or more before she could unload patient concerns. Tonight was no different. Twenty minutes from the hospital she reached her house east of the Cotton Bowl, drove down the alley and into the garage. She pressed the remote and closed the door before unlocking the car.

Once inside, after disarming the security system, Allie took a can of diet Dr Pepper from the refrigerator, turned up the thermostat, and put down fresh food and water for the cat. Then she went into the bathroom and turned on the hot water in the tub.

God, I need a drink.

How many times had she thought that? She didn't know, but abstention often remained difficult. Would it ever be easy?

Allie turned on the portable radio in the bedroom. The howling wind rattled the windows. Lighting another cigarette, she dropped onto the bed and reached for the phone. Before she dialed, her one-eyed black cat jumped onto the bed and rubbed along her leg.

"Hello, Fletcher darlin'."

Fletcher had been a neighbor's pet until two years before when the cat had been hit by a car. The neighbor wanted to put the cat down. Allie couldn't accept that. She took Fletcher to a vet, paid for his treatment with her savings. The injuries included loss of an eye and a broken leg. He'd been living safely inside her house ever since. The foreleg hadn't healed exactly as it should have, but that didn't slow him down or keep him from jumping on counters.

Allie pulled him close and stroked his back as she dialed her work number. Freda Goins answered. They'd shared Psychiatry nursing supervisor shifts the past six years.

Allie sounded hoarse when she said, "I'm sorry I snapped at you. Anything going on?"

"I've already forgotten about it, and it's real nice and quiet, just the way you left it. You did good today." After a pause Freda added, "You all right, honey? Everything okay?"

Allie took a long drag and exhaled as she leaned against the headboard. "I should go to a meeting tonight, but I'm too cold and tired. Can you talk for a while?"

Allie saw steam rising from the tub. "Maybe a hot bath and a Dr Pepper will do it for me."

"I keep telling you, get a life and deal with something besides sick people. We need to find you a hobby, a passion, something to make your cheeks red and your hair messy."

Allie grinned. "And just what do you think would do that?"

Freda laughed and said, "Honey, you need more help than you're gonna get with a phone call. But I do have an idea. He just transferred from Houston to our MRI center."

Allie smiled and pulled Fletcher closer. "Freda, you've tried that too many times."

"Yeah, I know, but maybe that's *my* passion."

By the next morning, the norther had blown itself out. It left a dove-gray sky and an icy stillness that made Allie want to go back to bed and bury herself under the covers. With only fitful sleep, she'd be running on sheer willpower before her shift ended, and willpower had become a thin commodity.

While boiling water to make oatmeal, she remembered she had no honey. The thought of putting Equal on oatmeal seemed a sacrilege. She'd put honey on hot cereal all her life, one of a precious few surviving idiosyncrasies from her youth.

She thought about skipping breakfast, but a twelve-hour shift with no meal to start the day would be a killer, especially with so little sleep. She decided to leave early and eat in the hospital cafeteria, let someone else prepare her breakfast. She used some of the hot water to make instant coffee, then checked food, water and litter box for Fletcher. She lit another cigarette, bundled herself against the cold and took the steaming mug with her.

Early arrival at the hospital offered an added benefit. She dived into a first-row spot, no more than fifty paces from the door. It would be well lighted when she left. She locked her car and headed for the door.

In the cafeteria, Allie ordered a breakfast of scrambled eggs, bacon and a biscuit with cream gravy. She ate less than half of the food, filled a Styrofoam cup with coffee for the third time and headed down the long corridor to the Psychiatry wing.

After the elevator jerked to a stop and the ancient doors groaned their way open, Allie stepped out into a faded yellow hallway. Walking toward the nursing station, she saw Freda Goins leave a room near the far end of the corridor. Freda's huge bust swayed under a lavender sweater. One or two strands of gray hair had pulled loose from the clasp she wore.

During the past two years, since the deaths of both of her parents, Allie had lost fifteen pounds, dropping below a hundred. The first visible loss had been from her breasts. The sight of Freda's ample body had become a constant reminder.

Freda waved. "Morning, honey. You're early." She gestured toward the doctors' reception office. "Be there in a minute."

Allie unlocked the door and went inside. While waiting, she glanced at the receptionist's calendar, looking for new patient names. Five beds were unoccupied, and she wondered if they'd be put to use that day. Dr. Maroun had two appointments she didn't recognize as current patients. There may have been more, but she didn't get past the third name.

Tanner, Beauford J.

Freda entered the office, but Allie didn't notice, gone into her mind for the moment back to a field hospital in Vietnam. Freda spoke, but the words didn't register, like the drone of a radio in the background.

Allie recalled the glassy-eyed, handsome face of a young Marine officer, contorted by the burning heat of malaria fever at first, then smiling and cheerful after his fever broke. His amber eyes were alive then, glistening, alert.

She felt the heady sensation that stunned her when she saw BJ Tanner for the first time. Cropped blond hair and a round, smooth face. He'd been breathtaking to a twenty-two-year-old, small-town Texas girl. Her most worldly experience before Vietnam had been going sixty miles from home to Waco for nursing school. There hadn't been any BJ Tanners there, not for damned sure.

Beauford Jester Tanner, named for his mother's favorite Texas governor, was a Naval Academy graduate. Already a Marine Special Ops captain at twenty-five, he was destined for a distinguished military career, if he survived Vietnam. BJ Tanner would be an important leader, clearly beyond Allie's grasp.

The intensity of her memories faded when Freda squeezed her hand. "Allie? What's the matter, honey? You see a ghost or something?"

"Not yet, but I think I'm going to."

► 3 ◄

A diminutive woman stepped inside the Marble Falls, Texas, gun shop. As she walked toward the counter, she put a hand in her shoulder bag. The man with her stood a foot taller and twice her size. He scanned the store. "No changes since I was here," he whispered.

Dusty deer heads were mounted on the otherwise bare walls at each end of the room. The gun cabinets and wall cases appeared to be as old as the man behind the counter. Wisps of yellow-white hair covered his head, blending with his pale skin. On his belt, a hand-carved leather holster carried a black semiautomatic handgun.

"Ed Wilcox?" she said.

"Yes, ma'am, that's me. What can I do for you?"

She withdrew her ID. "Patricia Karney, IRS. This is Agent Palmero."

Wilcox squinted at her ID, then nodded.

Karney said, "We're here about the money you owe the IRS." She pulled papers from her shoulder bag. "We need you to sign this transfer document for your store and inventory."

Wilcox adjusted his glasses, looked briefly at the paper, then laid it on the counter. "No, ma'am. I have an agreement with the IRS. I've been paying on time for four years. It'll be paid off by the end of this year, just like the agreement says."

"That's too long for the government to wait for its money. We need to get this settled right now." She pushed the paper closer to him.

Wilcox peered hard at her, then shook his head. "No, ma'am. I have a contract with you people locked up in my safe deposit box. I'm not giving up my gun shop."

Karney glanced at the gun on Wilcox's hip. "Do you always carry a weapon?"

"Only when I'm in the store. Keep the latest model on me as kind of a sales tool."

Karney glanced at Palmero, who let his gaze move around the gun cases. He said nothing. She looked back to Wilcox. "Last chance. Will you sign the transfer?"

"No, ma'am. The debt wasn't even my fault. I trusted a bookkeeper that turned out to be crooked. He kept the payroll tax payments he collected from me. He never paid them to the IRS. Your people knew that and agreed to the terms. That's why I sold the big store in Austin and moved out here."

She put the paper away and walked out the door. Palmero followed. Once outside she said, "Visualize, Theron. Wilcox just pulled that gun and stuck it in my face. He said 'Get out and don't come back. If you do, I'll blow your head off.' You got that?"

"I don't see why we need to scam this old man. What you plan to do could give him a heart attack."

Karney pulled her coat tight and dashed for their car. An icy rain began to fall. Once in the car, she punched in a number on the car phone. "This is Karney. I need an enforcement team, right now. Another agent and I have just been threatened by an armed delinquent taxpayer. He's in a store full of guns and ammunition."

After giving more information, she disconnected the call and lit a cigarette. "There's a diner a couple blocks south. We'll wait there for the SWAT guys. I'm hungry."

"Why are you doing this, Patricia? I mean, six thousand isn't worth the risk, and he's right about the payment contract. Then there's that FBI agent, Briscoe, snooping around our building. He could be waiting for the very kind of thing you're planning here."

Karney waved his statement away. "That FBI agent is working on something that has to do with the prison system. You'll hear about it soon enough. He's no worry for us. And this business isn't about Wilcox. I don't give a rat's ass about him. He's a pawn I'll give up later to capture a king."

"I don't understand."

"Of course you don't. Let's go."

At the café, Karney ate toast and jam. Palmero left a cup of coffee untouched. They parked across the street from the gun store and sat in the gray Dodge sedan, peering through the water-streaked windshield. She lit a fresh cigarette with the one she'd just finished, tossing the butt through the small opening of her window.

She pushed long, black curls from her narrow face and checked her watch. "Where the hell are they?"

Palmero glanced at his supervisor, then tugged at his collar. "Patricia, are you sure you want to go through with this? I mean, that old man didn't —"

She jabbed a finger at his face. "Don't think. Visualize what I told you. He pulled a gun on us and told us to get out or he'd kill us."

She tapped Palmero on the temple as if he were an errant child. "Visualize, Theron. Visualize."

Through the windshield she could barely make out the words "Gun Shop" over one of the two doors into the building across the street. The other door went into an adjacent drugstore. She could see no one in there. "This is our ace in the hole to ensure a nice bonus on another case. The old bastard's too old to run a gun shop anyway."

"What does this have to do —"

"Later, Theron, they're here."

A black Suburban with dark-tinted windows stopped on the far side of the street, just past the gun shop. Another made a U-turn and stopped behind Karney and Palmero. An enforcement agent dressed in black and wearing body armor left the SUV, came up to their car and eased into the back seat.

"That's the place?" He gestured toward the gun shop.

"That's it," said Karney. "What took you so long?"

"Forty miles of sleet-covered roads from Austin. How is he armed?"

"A pistol on his right hip. Don't know about others. Hell, he may have every gun in the store loaded."

Palmero turned toward her as if he wanted to say something. Her glare stopped him.

The agent in the back seat said, "Any other employees in the store?"

"We didn't see any." He asked more questions. Karney answered all of them, not letting Palmero speak.

The SWAT agent keyed his radio. "One known target in the store. Unit Two, any visual from your side?" Karney couldn't hear the radio negative response.

Keying his radio again he said, "All units move in on me."

He left the car and ran across the street. As he did, seven IRS agents armed with shotguns, automatic weapons and handguns left the Suburbans and clustered at either side of the shop door. The street of the small Hill Country town was nearly deserted. Two pedestrians a block south moved away quickly due to the freezing wet weather.

Karney grinned as she tossed another cigarette out the window. "Wilcox is gonna be the most surprised son of a bitch in Texas."

Two of the SWAT members shoved the door open and rushed in, followed closely by the other agents. Within seconds Karney heard a volley of shots. "What the hell?"

► 4 ◄

Leaving the airport in a shuttle, BJ Tanner reflected on the call he'd received from Dr. Frankel that morning. "I want you to go to a Dallas VA specialist for more tests to determine the best treatment protocol," the doctor had said.

"I felt great until a couple of weeks ago," Tanner replied. "How could this happen so fast?"

"A man who stays as fit as you often doesn't pay attention to a minor ailment until it's well developed."

"So, back to the Dallas VA. Never thought I'd have to go there again. This is from Agent Orange."

"Hard to say, Mr. Tanner. Fast, effective treatment is what we need to focus on."

Tanner bristled at the thought of his disability retirement from the Marine Corps. It had been forced on him less than four months before he was to be promoted to full colonel. Tanner could easily afford to have the best private physicians, but he'd always demanded the best care possible from the VA as some meager payment for what the war had taken from him. Besides, the VA would be more likely than civilian facilities and doctors to use experimental treatments.

"When do you want me in Dallas?"

"Lab work at eleven tomorrow morning, then your first appointment at two p.m."

Tanner was stunned. "Tomorrow?"

"I know that's short notice, but we need to move on this right now. If I could've scheduled you today, I would have. Dr. Weiss in Oncology can't see you till three, so I've set you up with Dr. Maroun at two. I'd rather have scheduled them the other way around."

Tanner made a note of the names and times. "Why? Who's Maroun?"

Frankel paused. "He's a psychiatrist."

Tanner cocked his head. "I've had cancer treatment before without having my head examined. Why should I see him?"

"The Dallas VA can provide far more extensive diagnostics and treatment than we can give you here," Frankel said.

"You didn't answer my question, doctor."

"Just go see him. It's for your own good."

The airport shuttle van stopped at the main entrance to the Dallas VA medical center. The driver raced around to open the side door, but Tanner had already let himself out. Shouldering his travel bag, he headed toward the door a hundred feet away. A score of people huddled against the brick wall to the left of the walkway, shielding themselves from the north wind while they smoked. Patients, visitors and staff members formed tight clusters, coats pulled close, collars up.

Five men standing near the front door eyed Tanner and stepped aside as he approached, clearing a path as if they recognized him to be a senior officer. A couple of them looked fit and trim, as if they could go on duty if they were younger.

I wish the VA could afford better treatment for these guys. This country doesn't do enough for the men and women who protect it.

He gave a terse nod as he passed.

Inside the building, Tanner scanned the lobby. Fifty or so people filled the gray chairs and couches to his right, their expressions ranging from concerned to detached. Another dozen or so visitors moved aimlessly about the area like remote-controlled toys misdirected by random signals.

He crossed the lobby to the information desk, where a heavy-set, gray-haired woman smiled and greeted him in a slow drawl. "Can I help you, sir?"

Speaking in a low tone he said, "Where will I find Dr. Maroun?"

The woman gestured. "About fifty yards down that hall there's an elevator. Take it to the third floor."

Tanner rode the sluggish elevator three floors, checked the hall directory and turned to the right toward Dr. Maroun's office.

There was neither a receptionist nor patients in the waiting area. Tanner wanted to leave, but that would only delay the inevitable. He headed toward the one open door he could see. He found a cramped office occupied by a sandy-haired man in his early forties leaning back in his chair, reading a journal. "Dr. Maroun?"

"Yes. Colonel Tanner?" The doctor, an inch or two taller than Tanner, rose and offered a slender hand. He closed the door and gestured toward a chair. "Have a seat, Colonel."

"It's *Mister* Tanner now. And this meeting is a waste of time."

"Oh?"

"My problem is physical. There's nothing wrong with my mind. I've dealt with cancer before. I can do it again."

Dr. Maroun sat down and leaned back, hands resting on the edge of the desk. "I see lots of people with healthy minds, Mr. Tanner. Your doctor asked me to meet you, see if I can help set up more effective medical treatment here in Dallas."

"You're a psychiatrist. I have cancer, but it's not in my brain, so what do we have to talk about?"

Maroun shrugged. "Can't answer that till I know more about you."

Tanner squinted at the doctor, nodding slowly, feeling bored.

"You were a Marine officer, right? If your CO told you to occupy new territory and asked how you'd do it, would you answer before doing some recon?"

Tanner couldn't hold back a grin as he sat down. "Good point."

He looked at the desk, strewn with notes, papers and multicolored forms. A manila envelope with his name on its edge topped the piles. Dr. Maroun said, "You have an hour before your next appointment anyhow. You might as well give me a couple of minutes since you're here."

"All right, doc, fair enough."

An hour later, Tanner felt no different about seeing Dr. Maroun. The psychiatrist had asked questions all the way back to Tanner's time in Vietnam, about his exposure to Agent Orange, cancer treatment years ago and how he felt about the Marine Corps. Finally, he had asked about Tanner Systems and how BJ felt about running the high-tech company. Some of the questions were gentle probes. Others were direct, causing Tanner to hold himself in check rather than respond with venom.

As they neared the end of Tanner's session, Maroun said, "You have some deep-seated anger, but I don't know yet exactly where it's coming from."

"It's from the IRS, doctor. Has nothing to do with my health or my sanity. Someone on *their* side is crazy."

"Can we get together another time and talk about how you want to deal with that?"

"No, thanks. I don't need a shrink to help me deal with the IRS."

Maroun shrugged. "I have a lot of vets that need all the help they can get — from me or anybody else — about dealing with the IRS. Maybe if you're here for a while you can talk to some of them. Help them out."

"Not likely," Tanner said as he rose to leave.

"I wish you'd reconsider and spend more time with us."

"Nice meeting you, doctor, but I don't think so." Tanner headed for the hall door without looking at the people sitting in the waiting room, not wanting to be seen in the Psychiatry area.

As he reached the door, someone said, "Hello, BJ."

Tanner froze, recognizing the voice instantly although he'd not heard it for years. He turned to see her, disbelieving his eyes. The years had changed her but not so much that he couldn't recognize her.

"Allie!" he said, barely audible. "My God, it's been . . . what're you doing here?"

"I work here. It's good to see you, BJ."

He searched her eyes for the fire that had been there so long ago. He almost hugged her, then checked himself. Putting a strong hand on each of her shoulders and holding her at arm's length, he appraised her toe to head. "Saint Allie, the angel of Nha Trang. You're so thin. And you cut most of your hair off."

He glanced at her ID badge. "Killgore. You're married?"

"Ages ago. It didn't last long."

For an instant, touching her took him back to a life in another world, a time of intense feelings he'd buried in the past. "I hardly recognized you."

She put a hand on each of his wrists. "I would have recognized you all the way across Texas Stadium. You have a few minutes before your next appointment. Can I buy you a cup of coffee?"

"Hell with the next appointment. We got too many years to catch up on."

"No cutting out on the docs," she said, taking his arm and leading him toward the door. "Gonna be in Dallas for a while? Maybe have some time for me?"

The thought of time sent an unfriendly shadow across his mind. "Not near as much time as I'd like, but I'll spend every minute of it with you that I can, if that's okay."

Her hand slid from his left wrist to his bare ring finger.

Her grin turned into a warm smile that brightened her appearance, made her look more like the girl he'd known in Vietnam so many years ago. "If that's okay? You put it that way, BJ Tanner, and I won't let go of you for a year of Sundays."

Allie felt as if her shift had lasted a week and the final hour might never pass, but her friend Freda arrived a half hour early to relieve her. Allie yanked on her coat and grabbed her purse from the bottom desk drawer.

"So, how'd he look?" Freda said.

"Mighty good."

"Gonna see him tonight?"

"Soon as I can get there."

"Cooking dinner for him?"

Allie stopped digging in her purse for keys and frowned at Freda. "Now that's a dumb question from a woman that's tasted my cooking before. I don't want to scare him away."

As Allie headed for the door, Freda laughed. "Aren't you gonna brief me on patient status before you leave?"

Allie continued walking. "Some are crazier than others, but none of 'em are dangerous." She stopped, thoughtful a moment, then gave Freda a serious look. "Keep an eye on sixteen. Deep depression. I thought he should be secured, but Doc Waters said no. Watch him so he doesn't try to leave by the window instead of the elevator."

She made the trip home in three-quarters of the normal time. A quick shower, frustrating work with the curling iron, fresh makeup. Then she stood in front of the closet, hoping for the right clothes to leap out.

She settled on a pleated, dark-blue skirt and a red wool sweater. The skirt made her realize how much weight she'd lost in the past year. BJ had noticed. His comment had been the first incentive she'd cared about to improve her looks.

She grabbed her coat and rushed out the kitchen door into the garage, then retreated long enough to set the security alarm. He'd offered to call for her, but she didn't want him to see her house the way she'd left it. *God, I hope he didn't get the wrong impression about why I wanted to meet him somewhere else.*

She headed for the freeway and turned toward North Dallas. Lighting a cigarette before realizing what she'd done, she stubbed it out and opened the window a crack, not wanting to smell of tobacco.

Tanner left the rental car with a valet and went into Calafaro's Restaurant on Lover's Lane. Dim lighting, further tempered by dark paneling and burgundy linen tablecloths, seemed to mute both the light and the voices of patrons. When he'd suggested the restaurant, Allie said she'd never been there but she knew the location.

The host led him to a booth partially hidden by a large palm plant, lighted a tiny candle on the table, took his drink order and left. A moment later the waiter delivered a Jack Daniel's on ice. "Mr. Tanner, may I bring you anything else before your guest arrives?"

"No, thanks."

Tanner took only a few sips of the whiskey before the host led Allie around the palm to the booth.

He stood to greet her and drawled his words so most of the restaurant patrons could hear him. "Darned if you don't look better than you did the day you saved my life."

She slipped into the booth quickly, head down. He could see, even in the dim candlelight, that her face reddened. In a whisper, she said, "BJ! I didn't save your life."

"Sure you did. First time I saw you after the fever left, I thought I'd died and gone to heaven."

He put a big hand over one of hers and spoke softly. "Lot of miles and time from that field hospital till we met today. I sure am happy to see you again, Allie."

She smiled, closed her eyes and nodded slowly, looking as if she were about to cry.

The waiter said, "May I get the lady an aperitif? Or perhaps you'd care to see the wine list, sir."

"Coffee for me," Allie said.

"Coffee?"

"I don't drink, BJ, but you go ahead."

He studied her face, remembering their time together in Vietnam. "Not even wine?"

"Not even wine."

After a moment he gave the leather-bound wine list back to the waiter and pushed the Jack Daniel's toward him. "We'll pass on the wine.

Two coffees." When the man left, Tanner said, "You have a drinking problem?"

She smiled, shaking her head. "God love you, BJ, you never did learn to be direct, did you?"

He shrugged and smiled. "Still the same bashful boy I've always been."

She lowered her gaze to the candle flame. "When I came back to the States, the Army sent me to El Paso. Nobody out there'd been in Nam. I didn't have anyone to talk to about the war, so I found a friend in a bottle. Fooled most people for five or six years. Fooled myself a little longer."

She straightened, shaking off the memory, and went on. "I decided I better shape up when the VA took me off patient care. I went on probation. Haven't had a drink for fourteen years, but I still crave one every now and then."

The waiter returned with menus and a plate of paté-filled pastries.

Allie ordered a rack of lamb. BJ said, "I'll have your biggest New York steak, medium rare."

After the waiter complimented their selections and left, Allie said, "Where you been the last twenty years? What are you doing? I figured you'd be a two- or three-star general by now."

Tanner popped one of the pastries into his mouth and chewed a moment. "Should be, but it didn't work out that way."

"When did you leave the Corps?"

"Eight years ago."

Staring wide-eyed, she said, "You didn't even stay for twenty? Doesn't sound like the BJ Tanner I knew."

He shook his head. "Didn't have a choice. They retired me." He fought his anger to control his tone. "On disability."

He could see the questions on her face, knew she wanted to probe and wondered how she would ask. Everyone wanted to know why disability.

"You look mighty fit to me, BJ. What happened?"

"I shouldn't have kept making those nonexistent excursions into Laos and Cambodia. You know, the ones we never discussed during my first tour?"

While he talked, he absentmindedly used the points of his salad fork to make uniform rows of indentations across the tablecloth near the candle. "Second tour, I spent a few months around the Delta. Took a couple of Agent Orange showers while we were on deep recon. A few years later I turned up with lymph cancer. I beat it, but the Corps cut me loose before I did."

She lowered her voice almost to a whisper. "So, why'd you see Doc Maroun today?"

Tanner looked at her, unable to hide his astonishment. Raising a hand, she said, "Sorry, that's none of my business."

His expression gave way to a grin. "Glad you asked. I'd hate for you to let it pass and go away thinking I'm crazy."

She slapped his hand, an often-used playful gesture he recalled. "I *know* you're not crazy. That's why I'm curious."

"My doctor in Austin said I should see Maroun as part of the whole package along with the other tests."

"What other tests?"

He waved the question aside. "Nothing worth talking about."

The waiter delivered steaming bowls of cream of mushroom soup. After he left, she repeated, "What other tests?"

He pointed his soup spoon at her. "No medical talk while we enjoy this meal, okay?"

"Fine, we'll come back to it later. What've you been doing since you left the Marines?"

"Worked for General Dynamics about a year, then went to Austin and started a little outfit to build custom circuit boards under subcontract for Cordwell Computers. They nailed a super deal with the French and German governments four years ago, and Tanner Systems went along for the ride. Things have been going real good until lately."

Shaking her head, Allie said, "I can't believe you've been only two hundred miles away, and I didn't even know it." She slapped his hand again, smiling. "Why didn't you come looking for me?"

"Figured you were married with a bunch of kids. That's what you wanted, last time I saw you."

"Didn't work out that way."

"Why not?"

Her hand trembled. Her cup clattered on the saucer. "Married a high school teacher three years after Vietnam. He started drinkin' about as much as I did. He liked to party with his students. A seventeen-year-old turned up pregnant, and he disappeared. I never tried marriage again."

"How's Saint John the Holy Grocer?" he said.

Her expression darkened. "He died just over a year ago. Mom was four months before that."

"Oh, I'm sorry, Allie. What —"

She raised a hand. "Not now, BJ. I'll tell you about it another time, okay?"

He took her hand in his. "Only if ever you want to, Allie."

Their waiter refilled their cups and drifted away. "You ever marry?"

He shook his head.

"Why not?"

"Mostly because of you, I guess. Partly because I saw too many military marriages break up while the husbands were gone. That old adage about absence makes the heart grow fonder is a bunch of bullshit. It ought to read 'absence makes the lust grow stronger.'

"When the Corps threw me out, I was so pissed. The last thing I wanted was a wife to have to put up with my miserable attitude. I'd probably still be fighting the whole world if it wasn't for my company. Before I slipped all the way to rock bottom, the Cordwell contract hit Tanner Systems like a gulf hurricane. Since then I've been too busy to worry about a wife. Or about the Corps."

"So there're no little BJ Tanners to keep the future world on course?"

"Not a one. You're looking at the last train on the Tanner line."

Allie settled back, looking more relaxed, Tanner thought, than when she'd arrived. The waiter rolled a cooking trolley to the booth and began final preparations for their meal.

Tanner ate every bite of the thick steak and asparagus. Allie ate two of the five chops, claiming the sauce to be delicious but too rich. Their Caesar salads were served last. She only picked at hers while BJ ate all of his.

Two hours later, after more coffee and an awkward lapse in conversation, Tanner said, "Well, I guess we're not gonna go dancing and drinking till dawn like we did in Nha Trang, are we?"

Allie smiled and shook her head.

Raising his cup, Tanner said, "Allie, darlin', here's to the good times that helped us survive the bad ones."

Another silence, then Allie said, "BJ, I'd invite you home but it wouldn't be the way I want it."

He studied her face a moment, then nodded. "I don't want to crowd you. It's been a long time since the last time. We better call it a night. Can I see you tomorrow?"

"I ought to lie and tell you I have a real busy social schedule, but even if I did, I'd change it."

Outside, Tanner gave his ticket to the valet. He walked Allie to her car and waited while she started it. Then he leaned into the still-open driver's door. "'Night, Allie."

She looked up at him and he gave her a quick kiss, one like he'd give a sister if he had one. She didn't respond like a sister. Her closed eyes and upturned face told him he hadn't given enough. When he kissed her again, their lips parted, and he felt electricity flow from her, leaving him weak in the knees. Her hand trembled when she touched his cheek. Her breathing was strained, uneven, the same as his.

While they kissed, he envisioned lightning-quick flashes of Allie and himself swimming in the clear waters of Nha Trang Harbor. Resting on the beach under a moonlit sky. Making love quietly in her quarters in the villa occupied by Allie and seven other nurses. They assured themselves that the others didn't know they were together, not caring that neither believed it.

He rose from their kiss and took a deep breath of the cold night. "What time can I see you tomorrow?"

She gave him her hospital extension. He found no paper in his pockets so he wrote the number on his wrist with a ballpoint pen.

"Call me. I'll give you directions. I'll be home around seven thirty."

► 5 ◄

Patricia Karney heard the knock on her door. She knew it was Palmero, but she let him wait before calling him inside.

She had seen Theron Palmero the day she arrived in Austin after transferring from Virginia. She decided right then that she wanted him in her unit. She knew she would never like him. He'd be perfect.

His performance evaluations confirmed her initial assessment. He was halfway through a ninety-day probation period for poor job performance and had shown no improvement until she brought him into her unit.

His size and looks would frighten most anyone, especially with the demeanor and intimidation skills she taught him. Karney knew Palmero hated her. He feared her power. She also knew that hate caused him to bully and intimidate taxpayers.

She had saved his job and now he was indebted to her. What a perfect pawn he'd become. And what a perfect fall guy when she needed one.

Palmero pushed the door open partway and peered at Karney. "You wanted to see me, Patricia?" He stood until she motioned for him to sit. She spoke without looking up from her desk. "Has Tanner Systems agreed to our terms yet?"

"Not yet; they have till Wednesday to let us know. How did you find out about that government contract, anyway?"

Karney leaned forward with a piercing stare and jabbed a finger toward him. "You should have known about that before I did," she said in a harsh whisper. "It was in the Yellow Peril News. Start keeping track of announcements by companies in your territory. Be sure all the bragging they do turns in some extra tax dollars — and some extra bonus points."

"But, Patricia, I've never —"

"Yes, I know. You've been working small-time stuff until recently. Well, you joined the big leagues when I took you in. No more mom-and-pop stores. Now you audit businesses big enough to read about in the financial news, so keep up with them."

"I can handle the corporate stuff okay, but that situation with Wilcox —"

Karney rose and stretched forward across her desk. "That issue is closed as far as you're concerned. I'll handle the last details with the SWAT team. Not a word, not an opinion, nothing from you about that to anybody. Understand?"

She stared at Palmero. He shifted uneasily. "We're going to pull in a two-and-a-half-million-dollar penalty from Tanner Systems. That will bring you one hell of a bunch of points for your first year as a corporate auditor. Now, get out of here and get busy."

As Palmero rose and headed for the door, she added, "Call the finance officer at Tanner Systems. Ellis. Tell him we'll file fraud charges through the U.S. attorney's office Monday afternoon if we don't have their agreement by then."

"But we gave them till Wednesday. They need time —"

"They don't need another minute. That company is like my ex-husband's. They're doing sneaky stuff in foreign countries to avoid taxes, stalling for time to hide more money. Call him."

Palmero closed her door. She dialed a phone number and her daughter answered. "Hi, sweetie. How was school today?" Her voice was high and gentle. Palmero wouldn't have recognized it. She talked with her child about classes, after-school pickup and homework studies. "I have to go now, honey. There's a cheating taxpayer I have to work on." *He should be your stepdad but he screwed up.* "I'll see you at home."

After ending the call, Karney took a mirror from a desk drawer to check her makeup, add blush to her pale cheeks and brush her hair. Leaving her office, she stopped at her assistant's desk and spoke quietly. "If anyone comes looking for me, I'm meeting with a taxpayer."

"What if *I* need to reach you?"

"I'll be with my lawyer. My pig of an ex is trying to get longer visitation rights with my daughter."

Years earlier Karney had convinced herself that her ex-husband had secretly started his business and achieved success before they separated, not after the divorce. She had not been able to get his money, but she had hurt him by getting sole custody of their preteen daughter.

Now it was time to get even with BJ Tanner for dumping her when she had such big plans for the two of them.

FBI Agent Doug Briscoe, sitting in a cubicle near Karney's office, observed Palmero, then Karney leave her office. He didn't hear their exchanges, but he saw their expressions and wondered why Palmero looked so frightened of a woman less than half his size. Briscoe also wondered if he could take a look at some of her cases before he finished the Huntsville prison inmates' fraud investigation. Probably not, but it sure would be interesting to see their audit results.

He thought about why he was investigating the IRS instead of the Treasury Department. Whoever was in charge at the top level obviously wanted an arm's-length, clean investigation. Would that lead to further examination of other personnel and their operational records?

► 6 ◄

Lamar Weed struggled to breathe the winter air as he sat in his pickup at the front gate of his 700-acre ranch, afraid to drive over the cattle guard to the county road. The last time he'd crossed that line alone, over two years before, he'd been arrested for disorderly conduct.

The funeral director had driven him to attend his dad's funeral two months earlier. His mother had died three years before that. He didn't want to go to Ennis, or anywhere else, but he had no freezer meat. He'd eaten nothing but canned vegetables for the past three days. Shuffling through receipts and scraps of paper in a kitchen drawer, he found an old grocery list his dad had used. He added a few items, put on a clean shirt and headed for town, but the sight of the road had stopped him.

He rolled down the window and took a deep breath. In spite of the damp, cold February morning, beads of sweat formed on his forehead and rolled into his bushy eyebrows. Lamar rubbed a sleeve over his face and pushed back his shoulder-length brown hair. Then he eased the old Dodge through the gate and turned west on the farm road.

A mile down he passed the cemetery where his parents lay buried. He recalled that morning in December while they were repairing fences. A heart attack had taken his dad as quick as a bullet. When two deputies drove to the house the next day, Lamar had almost run for the ravine. They quizzed him all afternoon, wanting to know why he'd waited four hours after his dad died before calling for help. He couldn't make them understand his fears of the outside world, his reluctance to take his arms from around his dad.

He slowed at the gate to the cemetery, but couldn't stop. Besides his mom and dad, eight of his high school classmates were buried there. All but one had been killed in Vietnam.

Lamar still wondered how he'd survived the war, why God had spared his life but left him fearful about dealing with people. He still felt that everyone hated him for fighting in Vietnam. When he returned from the Army, he had become a recluse on the ranch, never leaving except with his dad to take cattle to market or to help load supplies to bring home.

Later, he thought of the ranch as a sanctuary. The lush, grassy pastures, hackberry windrows and giant oak trees provided a buffer from the mean world. The deep ravine across the back pasture became the one haven where he felt completely safe. There he set up targets and shredded them with the M-16 he'd bought in Dallas. He'd modified the weapon to be fully automatic, like the one he'd carried in Nam.

As he drew closer to town, Lamar felt his heart rate increase. He passed the auction barn where he and his dad had taken calves to market each year. After another mile he crossed under the freeway and came to the Wal-Mart store, his dad's favorite shopping place.

Lamar hadn't driven for years, except around the ranch. He slowed for the left turn into the parking lot, but heavy traffic flustered him and he stalled the pickup. "Dammit!"

The driver behind him honked a long blast that added to Lamar's confusion. He twisted the key, then again too soon, causing the starter to growl. "Come on, truck."

The horn blasted again, a longer wail. Lamar turned the key once more and the engine roared, but a stream of oncoming traffic blocked his turn. A second horn honked behind him. He gunned the old Dodge ahead, wanting to get away from the store, from the traffic, from everything.

A moment later, the driver behind him moved to the right lane, passed, honked and jabbed the finger out the window. "Same to you, asshole," Lamar grumbled, but he didn't return the gesture.

A few blocks later, he found a break in the traffic and turned left, planning to return to Wal-Mart. He noticed a convenience store on the corner and remembered that his dad had stopped there for chewing tobacco occasionally. Through the store windows, he saw shelves filled with grocery items, a cooler with milk and orange juice, and other things his dad carted out of the big store down the street.

Why go where it's so crowded? There are only a few people in this store.

Lamar parked and waited for two customers to leave, then went inside. He noticed the older of the two women behind the counter watching him with an uncharitable expression. The other one, a pudgy teenager, gave change to the last customer in the store, then smiled at Lamar. "Somethin' we can do for you?"

He unzipped his thermal vest and withdrew the shopping list. Unable to meet the girl's gaze, he looked at the slip of paper, then pushed his long auburn hair from his face. He handed the list to her, "I need this stuff."

She unfolded the paper, scanned it, then gave Lamar a bewildered look. "You want to buy all this stuff at Circle K?"

"Nobody else here right now. Seems like a good time."

The girl glanced at the older woman, then back to Lamar. "You know, it'd cost you a lot less to get all this at the supermarket."

Lamar patted his jeans pocket. "I got money."

The girl shook her head. "This'll run . . . Lord, I don't know how much in this store. Wal-Mart would save you a lot of money."

"Too many people down there."

She looked at the older woman again and saw her talking with two men who'd entered the store. She turned back to Lamar. "We don't have everything on your list."

"Well, I'll take what you got."

The girl stared at him a moment, then the other woman came over, took the list from her and tossed it on the counter. "We don't *fill* orders. And we don't want your kind in here makin' trouble. Go somewhere else."

Lamar raised his hands. "I'm not makin' any trouble, ma'am. I just need some groceries and I got money for 'em."

One of the men talking to the older woman, a redhead with curly hair, stepped between Lamar and the girl. He stood taller than Lamar but not as lean and fit. "Ain't they made it clear they don't want you in here?"

Lamar reached around him to take the list from the girl, but the man grabbed his vest. "Get your ass out of here before you get hurt, boy."

Lamar noticed the second man, wearing a camouflaged hunter's jacket, move behind him. Looking back to the redhead, he felt a flash of anger. Old survival instincts kicked in. He grabbed the man's wrist with one hand, twisted, and bent the fingers back, sending him to his knees. "Don't call me 'boy.' I'm older than you are. And don't ever touch me again."

The other man lunged. Still controlling the redhead with severe pressure on his twisted hand, Lamar half-turned, lowered himself and drove a shoulder into the belly of the attacker. He heard the air leave the man when they collided. Arms wrapped around Lamar, but they had no strength.

The redhead rolled with the pressure and kicked Lamar below the knee. Lamar gave the man's wrist another twist, heard a crack, then a scream. The man in the hunting jacket, still gasping for air, grabbed a can of beans from a shelf and swung at Lamar. The rancher ducked the blow, moved in close and head-butted the man in the face. Blood flew from the man's nose, and a split lip oozed a red stream down his chin. The hunter collapsed against the shelving, scattering cans and plastic bottles as he slid to the floor.

With the two men immobilized, Lamar scanned the area to find a small group gathered by the door, watching, but obviously not wanting to join the fight. The girl held a hand over her mouth, tears filling her eyes as she stared at Lamar. The older woman, color drained from her face, held a phone in a trembling hand.

Lamar lifted the hunter off of cans and bottles and lowered him onto a clear spot on the floor. Then he turned to the redhead, who tried to scoot away from him but backed up against the counter. Lamar grabbed his arm above the broken wrist and raised the sleeve to see that the skin was not broken. "Sorry about the wrist, but why the hell did you get in my face? All I wanted to do was buy some groceries."

Lamar pushed through the door as a sheriff's patrol car stopped at the edge of the parking lot. A deputy who looked to be in his early twenties, nervous, and uncertain of the situation, stepped from the car, gun in hand, muzzle in the air.

Lamar saw that his truck was blocked. He ran back into the store, bowling over the one spectator still there. The man rolled against the outside wall of the building. The older woman ducked behind the counter. The girl stood frozen.

Looking for another way out, Lamar heard another siren. He found the back door, but it was secured with a dead bolt requiring a key. No time to make the woman unlock it before there would be cops at the back of the building.

Lamar felt the walls closing in. Back in the front of the store, the redhead sat leaning against the checkout counter, holding his wrist, face contorted with pain, eyes filled with hate. The other man began to move and groan as he regained consciousness. Through the window Lamar could see the deputy crouched behind the hood of the patrol car, gun aimed toward the store entrance. He figured if he ran, even a nervous kid could get off enough rounds from the semiautomatic to bring him down.

He raised his hands and moved toward the door, wondering if he'd have a chance to explain what happened, expecting that he wouldn't.

They're gonna lock me up. Who's gonna take care of my cattle?

A deputy who seemed bigger than the football players Lamar and his dad had watched on TV unlocked the cell door. "Come on out of there."

Lamar rose from the bunk and took cautious steps toward the door. The deputy wrapped a beefy hand around Lamar's right arm above the elbow and steered him down the hall into an office. A big-bellied sergeant who looked about Lamar's age sat on the edge of the desk. His name tag read "Conyers." He gestured to a chair. His tone sounded surprisingly gentle when he spoke. "Have a seat, Weed." Conyers gestured toward the big deputy. "Take the cuffs off."

The deputy did as instructed. Lamar sat and rubbed his wrists.

"Now then, you want to tell me what happened in that store?"

"Will it make any difference?"

"Tell me the truth, it will."

Lamar ran fingers through his long hair, felt dried blood from the hunter's face. "I went in the store to buy groceries. They didn't want to sell 'em to me. 'Fore I knew it, that redheaded guy got in my face, grabbed me."

Lamar hesitated. The sergeant said, "Go on."

"I'm not real sure what happened after that. I saw the other one move in behind me. Guess I took the first one down, then butted the other one."

"You didn't go in the store an jump them?"

"I was there before they came in."

"Uh huh. You didn't tell Margaret Ann — old gal that runs the store — that you wanted her money?"

He gaped at Conyers. "Hell no. I told her I *had* money." Lamar started to stand, but a huge hand on his shoulder stopped him. "Now look, I figure I put some hurts on those two jerk-offs, but I didn't start it, and I sure as hell didn't go to rob anybody." Lamar raised his hands, exasperated. "This is why I never leave the ranch. Every time I do, seems like somebody gives me grief."

"Been a long time since you left your ranch?"

"Yeah, but not long enough."

Conyers tapped a large envelope on the desk. "I figured it might have been a while." He nodded toward the deputy. "Your driver's license expired about the time he started to high school."

Lamar studied the sergeant's face. "You ain't never gonna let me out of here, are you?"

The sergeant moved off the desk and sat in the chair. A wave of dark hair, slick with oil, dropped across his forehead. "Weed, I knew you were out there on that ranch all these years. Knew your daddy. Didn't know him well, but I patrolled East County a lot of years before I got my stripes and started holding down this desk. This is about how many stripes you used to wear, ain't it?"

Lamar nodded.

"Now, old Margaret Ann was scared shitless when you started bustin' heads. After it was over, I figure she said what Billy Ray wanted her to. He's her nephew, the one with the busted wrist.

"Georgiana — she's the youngster in the store — told us a story that sounds like yours. She's probably gonna get fired for tellin' it, 'cause I believe her, and Margaret Ann ain't gonna like what I plan to do."

He pushed the envelope across the desk. "Here's your stuff. And you're right about having enough money to buy groceries. Hard to believe you'd try to rob a store without some kind of weapon, and all that cash already in your pocket."

Conyers gestured to the big deputy. "Linden's gonna run you up to the VA hospital in Dallas."

Lamar's chest tightened. "Dallas! No way. I can't go up there. It'd —"

"Now hold on. Beats hell out of spending the weekend in jail. They'll keep you there seventy-two hours. Probably want to put you on some kind of outpatient program. It'll be good for you, help get to where you can go grocery shopping without hurtin' anybody."

"What about the guys in the store? They're gonna want me locked up."

Conyers pursed his lips and closed an eye. "Well, we know those two boys pretty well. Told 'em if they'd stay out of this we wouldn't bust 'em for assaulting you."

"Yeah, right. How well do you think that'll work?"

Conyers's belly jiggled when he chuckled. "It'll work fine. We got the video from the store security camera before Margaret Ann could erase it."

"What about my truck? And I got cattle to take care of."

Conyers raised a hand. "Now you can't drive the truck till you get your license renewed. I'll have one of my boys drive it out to your ranch.

Didn't think about feeding your herd." He pondered a moment. "I'll get Mr. Sims to help out. Won't be but three days."

"Mr. Sims?"

"He has a nice spread not far from yours, over by Bristol. He raises Beefmasters. He's a good man. I know he'll help out. Don't worry, Lamar. I'll see to your stock."

Lamar slumped back in the chair, shocked that Conyers believed his story and was making arrangements to help him, still afraid to trust the deputy, or anyone else. "Why are you willing to do all that for me, sergeant?"

"Have you ever been to the VA?"

"Not since the year I got discharged."

Conyers nodded. "I wasn't much different than you when I first came back from Nam. Met some good folks at the VA. There were lots of guys that had been over there that felt the same as me. I still get together with some of them. We pump each other up when we're feeling down. You should've been hangin' out with us all these years. You've been in some kind of time warp.

"Going up to Dallas will be good for you," Conyers added. "Damn sight better than going to jail."

Lamar sighed, feeling the tension ease. The sergeant stood and Lamar leaned forward, expecting the big deputy to restrain him, but he didn't. He rose and made an awkward gesture of extending his hand.

Conyers clasped him in the familiar style of a Vietnam brother's handshake. "If it's okay, when you get back from Dallas, I'll bring a six-pack or two out to your place. I'd like to introduce you to a couple of my friends down the road. We all fight the same devils you do."

Lamar nodded. He wanted to thank Conyers, but he felt a salty burn in his eyes and feared his voice would break if he tried to speak. He gave the sergeant's hand a last firm squeeze and whispered, "I'd like that."

► 7 ◄

Friday afternoon, following another full day of examinations, questions and more tests, Tanner dressed and went into Dr. Weiss's office. Weiss keyed information into a PC, then dispatched the data. After a moment, he said, "Long day for you."

"So, what's the story, doctor?"

"It isn't good. We can't be sure about everything until we have the results of today's tests, Monday or Tuesday."

"Come on, doc. You already have results from the test they ran in Austin. Let's hear it."

Weiss pursed his lips. "The cancer's spread from your colon. It's in your stomach lining and kidneys, and probably other areas, too. We won't know where else until we have the results of today's tests."

Tanner wouldn't let the words register for a moment, trying to fight off what he'd already perceived as inevitable. "So, what's the next step?"

Weiss, about the same age as Tanner, held his gaze with tired eyes. Tanner couldn't tell if the doctor's face expressed compassion for him or for himself for having to deliver bad news to yet another patient.

"I won't be sure till next week, but I think we have to rule out radiation protocols. The side effects would probably defeat the benefits at this point. We may want to start you on 5-Fluorouracil. 5-FU. It's a drug treatment with minimum side effects until . . . the later stages."

"What about surgery? I'm not afraid of the knife. Cut it out. Let's get this over with."

Weiss hesitated. "I'm afraid it's too late for surgery, Mr. Tanner."

"What do you mean, too late?" Tanner stood and pounded his hard belly. "I'm in good shape. Strong, fit. I can handle surgery."

Weiss shook his head slowly. "The cancer has spread to vital organs. The cancer cells spread like pollen. Trying to remove it by surgery would be like using tweezers to pick seeds out of a grass lawn. It would take days of surgery that a body can't stand. The cells are microscopic. If we missed one, we'd lose the battle."

Tanner felt the heat rise in his face. He slapped the back of the chair as he stepped behind it.

Dr. Weiss said, "I'm sorry if —"

"Three tours in Vietnam and Laos. Thirty-one months of bullets, mines, traps, you name it. I could see those things, knew how to fight them, knew when to attack or retreat. But this . . ."

Weiss said nothing while Tanner paced. "This 5-FU stuff, will it cure me? Kill the cancer?"

After a pause the doctor said, "Nothing will cure you, Mr. Tanner. The disease is fully developed. 5-FU will slow its spread, but there's no stopping it. After we get test results we'll know better what, if any, other protocols we can apply."

Tanner dropped into the chair, jaw clenched, eyes closed. After a moment he looked up. "So that's it then? I'm done? *Terminal?*"

Weiss gazed at him a moment, then nodded. "Yes."

"How long?"

"I don't know. That depends on —"

"How long, doctor?"

Weiss hesitated. "Statistically, four to eight months from this stage. It depends on treatment and attitude. You're in good shape, in terms of muscle and body fat. The drug will help you survive longer. There's no sure way to estimate longevity."

"What about side effects? They gave me chemo after the lymphoma.

I lost all my hair." He rubbed a hand over his head. "Came back with lots of gray in it."

Weiss shook his head. "You won't lose your hair. After a while you'll begin to suffer side effects like nausea, bloating, sores inside your mouth."

"What if I don't take the drugs?"

"I expect within two or three months you'd begin to tire easily, lose weight, start having stomach pains and nausea. We'd control the pain with conventional drugs."

Tanner stood and picked up his coat and snorted a cynical laugh. "5-FU, huh? That seems an appropriate name. Five months, then fuck you."

"Mr. Tanner —"

"Sorry, doctor. That was for me, not you. I'll call you next week. Let you know what I'm gonna do."

Tanner raised his face to the frigid wind when he left the building, breathed deep to clear the septic odor of the medical center from his nostrils and to erase the depression of Dr. Weiss's prognosis.

In the rental car, he opened his briefcase, removed his cell phone and punched in numbers. When Allie answered, he said, "If I had a dozen roses, where would be a good place to take them?"

"BJ, you don't need roses."

"Should have done it sooner, but I never found a florist in Nam."

She gave him her address and directions, then said, "I hate to hang up, but one of our patients thinks he can fly. I need to tie a string to him. See you tonight, okay?"

He ended the call, then punched another number. Betty answered.

"How's it going, Wilson?"

"Everything's under control, BJ. Want your messages?"

"Has Watkins called again?"

"Yes, twice. Should I —"

"What's his number?"

After writing down the digits, Tanner said, "I need to talk to Ellis."

"It'll take a while to reach him. He's gone to the Padgett rec center."

"For what?"

"Benefit for Jackie Shelton. Remember? Tonight's the first fund-raiser for his son's kidney transplant. Mr. Ellis and Kathy are checking on the facility's arrangements for tonight."

"Damn, forgot about that." He pondered a moment. "Write a check from my personal account —"

"You already did that, BJ. Five hundred dollars. Mr. Ellis has it."

"Give him another thousand."

He could hear the smile in her voice. "Yes, sir! That'll make Jackie real happy."

"Why aren't you at that benefit, Wilson? You've been helping with arrangements, haven't you?"

"I never leave till five o'clock or till I hear from you, whichever comes first."

Tanner laughed. "Get going, Wilson."

"Want Mr. Ellis to call?"

"Have him call me at the hotel in the morning. Give my best to Jackie. Tell him I'm sorry I missed the benefit."

Tanner ended the call and started the engine. He gazed at the number Wilson had given him, reluctant to make the call. He punched the numbers and listened to the ringing. A female voice answered, too perky for so late in the day.

"This is Tanner. Is Watkins already gone for the day?"

"No, sir. He's in his office. You hold on half a second. I'll put you right through."

The line clicked and Tanner muttered, "Money-hungry son of a bitch. Of course he's there."

Tanner drove north on I-45, talked briefly with Watkins, then ended the call as he turned onto Stimmons Freeway. He arrived at the Anatolle

Plaza Hotel at 6:00. Conventioneers filled the courtyard lounge in the south lobby. He managed to make his way to the bar and order a double shot of Jack Daniel's neat. He gulped half the whiskey, feeling it burn a warm trail to his stomach. He tossed down the rest of the drink. It cut through the first layer of tension.

The bartender returned with his change. "Another double," Tanner said. "Make this one on the rocks."

Except for seeing Allie, he wanted to erase the day. Forget about Dr. Weiss, the tests, Watkins, even Tanner Systems. While trying to launder his mind of reality, he heard two petroleum industry conventioneers discussing the disasters being caused by Mexican trucks driving on American roads. Their arguments made no sense to Tanner. One of them made eye contact with him. "What do you think about that, partner?"

Tanner studied the ice swirling in his drink for a moment, then thrust the glass into the man's hand. "I don't have time to worry about pointless horseshit like that. You'll have to do it without me. Cheers."

He left the two men gawking as he crossed the lobby toward the elevators. A shower and fresh clothes would shed the scent of the hospital. No more whiskey, either. It wouldn't be right to get bourbon-fortified before going to see Allie.

While driving to Allie's house, Tanner reflected on their time together in Vietnam, up until he'd asked her to marry him. "I could never marry a career Marine," she told him. "I'd die a little each day, wondering if it would be our last day."

He thought of the other women he'd known since Vietnam. None could compare with Allie. Most were faded memories. Then there was Patricia Karney. He had admired her self-assured style. She was terrific the first month, then she began to direct rather than invite him. How could she think she'd control him?

He shook his head to remove all thought of Karney and the idiotic fraud charges she'd dreamed up. He would deal with that later. He wondered where this renewed relationship with Allie would lead. Where should it lead? Should there be a relationship at all?

As Tanner parked in front of Allie's house, a streetlight revealed a thick winter-dead lawn surrounding an oak tree years older than the house. Smoke drifted into the still night sky from a chimney toward the back of her small brick house.

He walked up the flagstone walkway to the entry and rang the bell. When Allie opened the door, she stood framed by light from inside the house. For an instant he saw the young woman he'd known in Vietnam, but instead of a nurse's uniform she wore a black skirt and a gray silk blouse that felt as soft as an angel's wings when he touched her shoulders.

"Saint Allie."

Years washed away when she spoke in soft tones, the way she sounded when they would meet at night outside her quarters. "Hi, BJ. Come on in."

She closed the door and smiled, waiting. After a moment he realized he held the roses at his side. "Oh, these are for you."

"You really did bring flowers. I don't remember the last time anyone did that for me."

"Then we're square, 'cause I don't remember ever giving flowers to anybody but my mother."

She led him through the living room, furnished with matching couch and chairs in Southwestern pastels. A glass-top coffee table with a molded sandstone base held an eclectic assortment of figurines, mostly American Indian and Asian. Past the living room was a cozy den with a recliner in front of the fireplace, and a futon. Allie gestured to the recliner. "Have a seat. I'll put these in water."

While she took the roses into the kitchen, Tanner looked over the bookshelves in the den — mysteries, historical novels, medical journals and training manuals. Two photo albums were tucked into the lower shelf, one of them a blue binder he'd seen years ago.

Allie returned with the flowers in a vase as he opened the album. "I have fresh coffee and diet drinks. Can you make it on that, or do you want to go to the liquor store?"

"No booze tonight. Coke will be fine."

"Okay, then no cigarettes for me."

He thumbed through pictures of the two of them and other young nurses and soldiers on harbor beaches and around the villas. He grinned at the photos of Allie and another nurse waterskiing behind a Navy ordnance disposal team's tri-hull skiff, off-duty from patrolling the harbor for mines.

Allie put an arm across his back as she gave him the drink. "Find yourself in there yet?"

She flipped pages until a young, healthy BJ Tanner wearing cammies with captain's bars grinned back.

No gray hair. No wrinkles. No cancer. "Seems like a million years ago."

Allie turned a few more pages, then Tanner closed the album, not wanting to see more memories that would further darken the present. "What's for dinner?"

"Only thing I know how to cook. Pot roast and potatoes. But I haven't made one in ages. Hope it turns out okay. I cook a meal like this about every three or four months. I put the meat in the oven this morning. With any luck, the timer started it cooking around six."

Allie went into the kitchen. Tanner stood in the doorway and watched her prepare the meal. At first she seemed self-conscious, nervous under his gaze, then she gradually slipped into her routine. The domestic scene felt strange to him. A housekeeper took care of his condo, prepared meals he could reheat or put together easily. Mealtimes had become solitary events for Tanner, except for business lunches and occasional dinners with customers.

As he watched Allie he kept seeing her as the girl he'd known years before. He remained unable — or unwilling — to keep his thoughts in the present until she jolted him.

"You saw Doc Weiss today?"

He'd told her nothing of his condition and wasn't about to now. With his best poker face, he shrugged. "Yeah. Routine stuff. I get a checkup every year."

She looked up at him, wide-eyed, holding a spoon of green beans suspended over a plate. "You come to the Dallas VA every year?"

"No, usually go through the clinic in Austin. Guess I been a little hard on 'em lately. They wanted to see if Maroun could get me to retreat. Cut 'em some slack."

"Why have you been hard on them in Austin, BJ?"

"That roast sure smells good. Whoa, not so much for me. I don't eat like I used to."

She filled their plates, then set them on a small table in the kitchen. "Gravy's on the table. Not a fancy French restaurant, but the price is right."

"Allie, I'd trade any restaurant there is for a meal right here with you."

Tanner had no appetite at first, depressed by Dr. Weiss's prognosis, but he forced himself to eat, not wanting to reveal his despondency. A few bites restored his appetite. The roast, medium rare and moist, cut easily with a fork. He couldn't remember the last time he had real mashed potatoes, fresh-whipped with whole milk, then frying-pan cream gravy.

"What a meal. You ought to cook more often than once every three or four months. Fill out those pretty curves. How long have you been so thin?"

Allie stood and began to clear dishes from the table. "Since Daddy died. There hasn't been a lot of good news in my life for the past couple of years, till now." She leaned down and kissed his cheek. "I'm sure glad they sent you here from Austin."

After reminiscing during the meal, he fell into unpleasant thoughts of war until he realized an awkward silence had stolen precious moments from their evening. He looked up to see Allie watching him, but he couldn't read her expression.

"Want to talk about it, BJ?"

"About what?"

"Whatever it is that is on your mind."

"Probably shouldn't have come tonight. I, uh . . . had some bad news today. After I left the hospital. Business stuff. Can't get it off my mind. Guess I'm kind of boring."

"BJ Tanner, you're anything but boring. Your water runs as deep and fast as it ever did, but I never knew you to be an avoider. Or not tell the truth."

Tanner felt his face flush. No one could get away with calling him an avoider, or accusing him of not telling the truth. No one except Allie. If it were anyone else . . .

"Look, I have tax problems. If that isn't enough, some Houston outfit's trying to take advantage of the situation and buy my company for a song. I didn't think that'd make good dinner conversation."

Allie shook her head. "BJ, I work at the VA, remember? You can't come in there without me finding out why you're there."

She left the table, opened a cupboard and grabbed a fresh pack of cigarettes. "I thought maybe — at least I hoped — you might want to talk about it, let me help you."

After fumbling with the cigarettes a moment, she tossed them on the counter and turned her back.

BJ saw her shake with quiet sobs. He turned her around and hugged her, aware of how frail she seemed compared to the way he remembered her. "Allie, I'm sorry. I'd have told you, but I wasn't ready to deal with this yet. I didn't want to spoil the best evening I've had in over twenty years."

She put her arms around him, holding tight with her face buried against his chest. "I'm the one who should be sorry. Always jumping into things I shouldn't even know about. None of my business."

"Sure, it's your business. Has been since I saw you Thursday. Right now I wish I hadn't come here. Wish I hadn't seen you."

She pushed away and stared at him. "Well, thanks a lot."

He pulled her back and held her tight. "What I mean is, I don't want to hurt you. The way things are, you'd be better off if we hadn't run into each other."

"Don't you want to be with me, BJ?"

"Allie, honey, I never wanted to be without you, but now —"

She stood on tiptoes, the way he remembered, and kissed him. After a long embrace that warmed him and burned away all images from his mind, she whispered. "Stay with me tonight. We'll worry about other things tomorrow."

"If I stay, I may never leave."

She took his hand and led him toward her bedroom. "We'll take it a step at a time, but I like your attitude."

Any thoughts of gentle lovemaking were burned away by the fire of urgency when they fell onto the bed. He felt clumsy, and she seemed as frantic as he when they began. His memory of their bodies in perfect union so many years ago faded as they moved awkwardly against each other. Her once smooth and gentle curves now felt lean and sharp-edged.

He'd pushed too hard trying to get inside her at first. It had been too long for both of them. They'd hardly begun when his climax erupted. He felt embarrassed at his lack of control and wondered if his illness had diminished his ability. Allie held onto him and kept him on top of her while stroking his neck and back, her breath warm against his ear.

She helped him overcome his humiliation, and after a few minutes of her gentle hip motion under him, he became hard again. With his urgency abated, he moved slowly, causing her to coax him to go faster. Then it was her turn to explode. She locked herself about him with legs and arms, held tightly until she could breathe without gasps, then finally relaxed.

Allie fell asleep, then Tanner. Sometime later in the night he awoke when she touched him, and they started again, this time more slowly, without urgency.

Saturday morning, Tanner awoke sharply and recoiled when he felt gentle stroking on his back.

"Sorry. Didn't mean to startle you."

He rolled over to see her smiling face partially buried in a feather pillow. He slipped an arm under her neck and pulled her naked body against his. Her warmth stirred him quickly. He ran a hand along her back to an angular hip interrupted by joints, unlike the smooth, firm shape he remembered. His hand moved up and gently cupped a breast. She trembled under his touch and eased his hand back down to her waist. "They're too small," she whispered. "Almost disappeared when I started losing weight."

She put her arms around his neck and held tightly as he pushed the covers off them and rolled on top of her. They moved together more easily than the night before, finding a gentle rhythm, each seeking to satisfy the other. She felt so small beneath him, so fragile, yet she steadily moved faster, became more demanding until they both climaxed.

They lay side by side a few minutes until she covered him, went to the bathroom and showered, then headed for the kitchen.

Tanner half-dozed and half-dreamed until reality began to creep into his thoughts. He showered, dressed and went looking for Allie. From the hall, he glanced into one of the bedrooms and noticed it was empty except for an antique tiger-oak chest of drawers. Allie brought coffee to him while he stood in the doorway admiring the relic.

"That was my mother's. Only thing I have left of my parents. Wouldn't have that if it hadn't been with a furniture refinisher when Daddy . . . when he died."

"It's beautiful."

She gave him the coffee mug and kissed him. "I'm gonna run to the store for milk. Be right back, then we'll have hot cereal."

"I'll go to the store."

"I know the way." She rubbed his chin. "Besides, you haven't shaved. I'll get you a razor."

He watched her walk down the hall and through the kitchen, then heard the garage door open. From the window of the near-empty bedroom he watched her drive out of the service lane behind the house, onto the street and into the cold morning haze.

Turning back to the antique, he admired the striped wood and gently tested the chest's sturdiness. It had been refinished and probably had the joints tightened and glued. It didn't have the sway that he expected in such an old piece.

He opened the middle drawer. It moved easily without binding. He tested the narrow top drawer. Also smooth, but not empty. A handgun in an old leather holster lay on top of a handwritten note next to a stack of papers.

His face flushed when he recognized the papers, similar to the ones served to him at Tanner Systems recently.

INTERNAL REVENUE SERVICE
NOTICE OF INTENTION TO LEVY

Jesus, are the bastards after her, too?

He pulled the stack of papers from the drawer, self-conscious about his invasion, but nowhere did her name appear on the papers. The claim was against Harold St. John, dba Harry's Grocery, Corsicana, Texas.

Tanner thought of the first time he'd seen Allie, in a Vietnam field hospital after his fever broke. Her name tag read St. JOHN.

That can't be right. You're not St. John.

"I'm Allie. Allie St. John."

"You're Saint Allie as far as I'm concerned. You'll always be Saint Allie."

After Tanner and Allie became intimate, he'd teased her, calling her dad Saint John the Holy Grocer. "He'd have to be a holy man to have a daughter like you."

But she had told him her dad had died, and he saw that the papers were more than a year old.

Why would she keep this stuff?

Slipping the papers back in the drawer, he tried to arrange them as he had found them. That's when he read the handwritten note.

Allie, my sweet baby, I'm sorry. Please don't hate me. I can't go on anymore and I will not be a burden to you. I'm tired, and I want to be with Annie. Please forgive me.

All my love, Dad

Tanner slammed the drawer and paced the room, unable to focus his thoughts beyond an incredible desire for some kind of brutal revenge. The man who'd caused Allie's dad to kill himself. The ones trying to cheat Tanner Systems. The whole damned government for contaminating him with chemicals while he fought for his country, then throwing him out of the Marine Corps he'd worked so hard to serve.

When Allie drove into the garage, he met her at the kitchen door. Her smile faded when she saw his expression. "BJ? What's the matter?"

He pulled her close and held her tight.

"I know it's tough for you," she said.

"I was thinking of you, Allie, honey. Life owes you a lot of good times. God, there's so much I want to do for you."

But will there be enough time? he wondered.

► 8 ◄

Lamar Weed talked with Dr. Maroun for an hour on Friday evening, then joined an encounter group with five other men. Two were Vietnam vets, and two had been in Desert Storm. The other man, an ancient-looking Korean War veteran, still had occasional nightmares about hiding among dead bodies in a cave for two days while North Korean troops occupied the area.

Lamar connected with Ernie Castro in the group session, an ex-Air Cavalry corporal. They'd seen action in some of the same places in Nam. After a two-hour Saturday morning group session, they spent the remainder of the day together, avoiding other people by strolling the cold grounds south of the building.

Castro had come to the VA Thursday night. When he heard Lamar's story, he said, "We ought to get together. Sounds like we've been riding the same train down the wrong track for too many years."

After their Saturday afternoon group session, the two went to the cafeteria for supper. Castro, as tall as Lamar but huskier, led the way. Lamar was surprised that the Latino's dark, wavy hair showed no gray except for one small patch. He asked why Castro favored his left leg. "Bamboo spear trap my first time on the ground after we lost a helo on the Delta. If I'd taken a little longer step, I would have lost my calf muscle."

Lamar began to feel less isolated after two days of group sessions. Hearing others discuss worries similar to his own made him realize time had removed most of the concerns that plagued him. Gradually, Dr. Maroun convinced him there were solutions to his troubles and that he could learn to live in today's world. Sunday afternoon he began to worry about a new problem, one that Maroun hadn't addressed: How would he get back to the ranch?

After the final session on Sunday, Lamar and Castro had supper together. As they were leaving the cafeteria, Castro said, "You know, you remind me of my sarge. That ol' boy saved my ass ever' day for fourteen months till he bought it. Figured my number would be up right after that, but a week later they pulled my unit out of the Delta and sent us home."

"If you're from Laredo, how'd you end up here?"

Castro shrugged. "Not much shakin' down there. Made a coyote run to Dallas. Used my own van. Brought fourteen illegals."

"Did you get busted by the Border Patrol?"

"Nope. Made a clean trip. Dumped 'em at the church they wanted. No sweat. Then I spent a righteous weekend with Jim Beam and got busted for drunk and disorderly. Cops brought me here because they thought I was crazy."

Lamar laughed. "Hell, they were right. You heading back to Laredo when you leave here?"

Castro shook his head. "Nothin' down there for me. I like what I can remember about Dallas while I was sober. Figure I'll hang here for a while. Look for a job."

"Do you have a place to stay?"

Castro shrugged. "Back of my van."

Lamar waved the answer away. "That's no place to stay. Have you ever been on a ranch?"

"Yeah. I lived on one before I joined the Army."

"Did you like it?"

"Hated it. Gringo son of a bitch that owned the place worked my ass off. Damn near killed me. That's why I joined the Army."

"I've got a ranch, forty miles south of here. At least for now I do. You're welcome to stay there a while if you want to. It's better than the back of a van."

Castro narrowed his eyes. "Yeah? Why are you inviting me home, gringo? You think you're gonna work my brown ass off for room and chow? And what do you mean at least for now?"

"I can't afford to hire anybody because I'm almost broke, and I'm afraid I'm gonna lose the place."

"Did you tell Maroun about that?"

"What can he do about money? He's a doctor."

Castro shrugged. "I don't know. Maybe there are people at the VA that can help somehow. Go see him when we get back Monday." Then Castro poked an elbow into Lamar's ribs. "So you really are trying to get me to work for nothing."

"I take care of the place myself. I'm just offering while I can."

Castro laughed. "That's cool. I like the idea of stayin' on a gringo's ranch for free."

Lamar shook his head. "It's not quite free. You have wheels and I need a ride home. If I come here for more of these sessions, I'll need rides back and forth. I don't drive in the big city. Don't drive anywhere, except on the ranch."

Castro raised his hand for a high five. "I can handle that."

Lamar slapped the Latino's palm and held on to him. "There's one more thing."

"Yeah, what's that?"

"You'll have to do the grocery shopping."

► 9 ◄

Shortly before noon on Saturday, Tanner went to the hotel, checked out and returned to Allie's house. He built a fire in the den while she made lunch. They sat on the floor in front of the fire, the scent of seasoned oak filling the room while they ate tuna salad on pepper crackers and sipped hot cider.

"Never had tuna salad like this, Allie. It's great."

"My dad's recipe. He used to make the picnic lunches when we'd go to the lake. Either cold fried chicken or tuna salad. Never let Mom cook on Sunday. Said she worked too hard the rest of the week."

Her sad expression and long gaze told him she'd drifted back to another time. "Why did he do it, Allie?"

"Do what?"

"Suicide."

She pulled a pillow off the futon and hugged it, still gazing into the fire.

"Some depraved bastard in the IRS killed him. You saw the papers, didn't you? They took everything he had, everything he'd saved in seventy-one years. Mama always handled the taxes. He forgot to make estimated payments for six months after she died. They charged him penalties that God wouldn't impose on an unrepentant serial killer!

"Mr. Robnett, Daddy's attorney, didn't know about the tax claim till it was too late. He said the IRS took advantage of an old man. Scared him into giving up everything before he ever talked to his lawyer."

Tanner felt his stomach tighten, her words rekindling his anger over Tanner Systems' tax troubles.

"Robnett thinks something else weird happened, too. Said the store was auctioned within a week and sold to some Gulf Coast outfit two hundred miles away. It never was advertised in Corsicana. Local buyers never had a chance to bid. He said the store and inventory were worth three or four times what they sold for."

Tanner pulled her to him. She continued hugging the pillow as tears welled, then rolled down her cheeks when she closed her eyes. Her voice dropped to a whisper. "He was such a sweet man. Never had much because he and Mama were so generous. He gave candy to every kid in the neighborhood. Gave food to anybody out of work. Said they could pay him back when they got on their feet again, but he never collected."

Tanner could feel her shake with silent sobs. He pushed the pillow away, pulled her arms around him, then hugged her tight. They held each other until the fire faded to embers.

Monday morning Tanner kissed Allie good-bye and stood beside her vintage Oldsmobile while she started the engine.

"You'll call Dr. Weiss this morning?" she asked.

"Yep."

"Promise?"

"I promise."

She raced down the service lane. He went back in the house, poured a fourth cup of coffee and sat at the table to watch the news on a portable TV in the kitchen.

A gang-related shooting of three youths in Oak Cliff was the lead story, followed by pictures of a small plane crash with two serious injuries. The next item caused Tanner to chuckle as the somber reporter told the story.

"The Internal Revenue Service reports that almost one and a half million dollars were paid to four Texans this month as refunds to more than *eight hundred* fraudulent tax returns filed by computer. The electronic filing process, intended to speed refunds to taxpayers and simplify IRS operations, has become a major source of fraudulent activity, a Treasury Department spokesperson says. The men used Social Security numbers of inmates in Huntsville State Prison for the bogus returns. Three arrests have been made. One suspect is still at large, and less than a third of the money has been recovered.

"This story, although dating back to April last year, was only released Saturday by the IRS, the day after the shooting of a Burnet County gun-shop owner during a tax enforcement visit. The timing is presumably to cast the IRS, and not the taxpayer, as the victim."

Tanner shook his head while dialing Betty Wilson's number.

"Cecil wants to talk to you ASAP," she said.

"Put him on."

A moment later, Ellis said, "Two things, BJ. One, the top tax attorney at Langford and Dawson haggled with Palmero at the IRS, but he didn't get anywhere. The agent kept referring to their allegations that we filed the incorrect returns. We faxed him copies of the accountant's records and IRS comments showing approval, but he hung onto the issue like a dog with a bone. Karney wouldn't talk with our attorneys.

"Palmero called first thing this morning. He said they're going to file fraud charges today if we don't agree to the penalty fees. And, BJ . . ." Ellis hesitated. "She wants to hear from you personally."

Tanner slammed his mug on the table and spilled most of the coffee, stepping back in time to avoid getting it on his clothes. "She really is the mother of all evil bitches. Give me her number." He wrote it down. "You said two things."

Ellis cleared his throat. "Watkins called this morning. He . . . he knows about the IRS claim. Said it could kill the deal with his buyers if it isn't cleared quickly."

Tanner paced Allie's kitchen the length of the wall-phone cord. "How'd he find out?"

"Wouldn't say."

"Anybody else at the office know about this besides you and me?"

"Betty."

"That's all?"

"Absolutely."

"Then he didn't get it from Tanner Systems. Nothing in the *Business Journal*? Other newspapers? Wouldn't surprise me if the bitch leaked information herself, even to the press."

"Not a word that I could find."

"What'd you tell him?"

"Said I'd talk to you and get back to him. He's curious as hell about why you're in Dallas, by the way. He said he called the hotel, but you'd checked out."

"Let him wonder. You have any *good* news for me?"

"About all I can think of is that the benefit dinner for Jackie Shelton's son worked out well. He was hoping to raise ten thousand, but collected over sixteen."

Tanner stopped pacing and stared at the frostbitten shrub outside the kitchen window. *Shelton's kid needs money for a new kidney to survive. All of my money won't buy me another year.*

"That's a long way from a hundred and fifty grand."

"It's a good start. Doctor says the boy can last maybe twelve to eighteen months without the transplant. Somehow they'll come up with the money before then. Too bad his son's an adult and can't be covered on our company insurance. Oh, here's a hoot for you. Blaylock, that weird guy from our computer lab, showed up at the benefit!"

Something stirred in the back of Tanner's mind at the mention of the young computer wizard. "Des Blaylock? Hell, I didn't think he even knew Jackie."

Ellis's voice jumped an octave. "Mr. Do-Anything-For-Enough-Money got teary when Jackie's wife was talking. He even made a contribution."

"Well now, that's a first."

Ellis laughed. "Everyone around here is giving him a hard time today, calling him Robin Hood. I think by now he's sorry he made a donation."

Tanner ended the call and cleaned up the spilled coffee. Then he made a note in the tiny notebook he carried:

Shelton - Communications
Blaylock - Computers
Who else?

He stared at the note a moment, then dialed Allie's number. As soon as she recognized his voice, she interrupted. "You call Doc Weiss yet?"

"I'm gonna see him at eleven."

"Are you —"

"Allie, darlin', think you can get me in to see Doctor Maroun this morning?"

"Probably so. I'll bribe him with some of his favorite food. You gonna take his advice, BJ?"

Tanner sighed, relieved that he'd avoided her question about his cancer treatment decision. "I've been having some crazy thoughts this morning. Things I've been thinking about could get me locked up, so I guess I better see that shrink of yours."

"BJ, that's great. He'll make you feel a lot better."

He agreed to meet Allie at noon, then ended the call. He started to pour more coffee, but his stomach boiled at the thought of talking to Karney. He felt his chest tighten as he punched the numbers. A woman answered.

"Patricia Karney," he said.

"Who's calling, please?"

"Tanner."

"Just a minute."

Then, "Well, well, *Mister* Tanner." The flat tone of her voice sounded as cold as a Texas norther.

"Patricia, what do you think you're doing? You know this will never work."

"Oh, it's going to work. If it doesn't, you and your company are both going broke. You have a chance to at least save the company. Have you agreed to my terms?"

"I haven't agreed to anything. There are more than three hundred people at Tanner Systems. You're playing God with them just because you're pissed that things didn't work out between you and me."

"You used me until you hit a big contract with DOD. Then you left town and dumped me. Nobody dumps me."

"What do I really have to do to end this, Patricia?"

"You have to pay two and a half million and sign a consent decree. You better start liquidating this morning, or Tanner Systems loses that nice big contract."

"I'm going to the U.S. attorney's office at three today if you don't commit to the payment and the consent decree."

Easy, Tanner. She's baiting you.

He forced himself to remain quiet, taking several deep breaths. Karney said nothing, either. After a few seconds that seemed to last forever, Tanner said, "Your timing's perfect. I'll give you that. We both know I'd win in tax court, but I'd lose a good contract in the meantime."

Tanner felt on the edge of a tirade but checked himself. If he lost his cool, she would win. That battle would come later when he had complete control. "What's the next step?"

"You cut a check to the IRS for two million, five hundred thousand. I'll deliver an action dismissal removing further claims against Tanner Systems on these specific charges, and you'll sign consent decrees from the company and from you personally."

Using every ounce of self-control, he said, "I'll be back in Austin tomorrow morning. Send someone for the check and bring the papers at ten."

"That won't be convenient. I'll be there at one thirty."

Instead of giving her the satisfaction of hearing him bang the phone, he pushed the disconnect switch with a finger, then slammed the instrument back onto the cradle.

He stomped out of the kitchen, grabbed his jacket and went out the front door, sucking in deep breaths of cold air. The sun had burned the dark gray out of the overcast, leaving a layer of white vapor that seemed to enhance the icy chill. He walked about the brown lawn, pulled one of the few remaining dead leaves from the oak tree, studied it a moment, then crushed it.

Rage left him slowly. The dampness, or maybe his receding anger, caused a shiver. Never a fan of winter, he wished for warm summer days and having Karney and the IRS trouble behind him.

I wonder if I'll still be alive come summer.

► **10** ◄

Tanner crossed the empty reception area to Dr. Maroun's office, watching the three veterans walking out together. Their demeanor gave the appearance of healthy men. He wondered how many veterans had passed through the mental facility, shuffled across the discolored tile floor and sat in the worn chairs. He also wondered about their surviving military skills.

Maroun rose as Tanner entered his office. "Hello. Have a seat."

Tanner dropped into the visitor chair while Maroun closed the door and made his way around the desk. "Appreciate you taking time to see me on short notice, doc."

"No problem. What brings you back here, Mr. Tanner? Or can I call you BJ?"

Tanner nodded and leaned forward, elbows on his knees, studying his hands while rubbing them together. "The other day I said I didn't need to be here. Didn't need your kind of help. Guess I spoke too soon."

He looked up to see Maroun gazing at him, expressionless. "Last Friday, Dr. Weiss told me I have cancer. It can't be cured."

Maroun nodded but said nothing.

"I have a real problem, and I hate like hell to have to deal with it. Coming here turned out to be a big mistake."

"Mr. Tanner . . . BJ . . . the cancer started long before you came here. You only *learned* about it —"

Tanner raised a hand. "I'm not talking about that. Hell, I guess I knew how bad it was before I left Austin. Just wouldn't admit it to myself till Weiss confirmed it."

"Then I don't understand. What's the big mistake?"

"Running into Allie."

"Sorry, BJ, but now I'm really lost. I understand you two go way back. Seems to me she's real happy about it. Why do you think it's a mistake?"

"It'll be too hard on her. She's had too much dumped on her already. Lost her daddy last year. Her mother a couple years before that. She's dropped so much weight she looks like a POW. Now I pop back into her life when I'm about to check out. That's too much for one person. Specially one as good as Allie."

Dr. Maroun studied him. "You sound like a man talking about a life-long mate, BJ. You and Allie rekindled your friendship less than a week ago. Do you think you're overstating that relationship, maybe avoiding the real issue?"

"What real issue?"

"Your illness."

Tanner shook his head and snorted. "Jesus, doc, I'm not afraid to die. I spent too many years expecting it to happen any minute. Now it's different. That's the trouble with knowing someone like Allie. I could have turned toes-up a week ago. No problem. I didn't have to worry about leaving anyone behind. But I found her again. I've been wondering why in God's name it happened now. Why not years ago when the Corps retired me? She'd have married me then, knowing I wouldn't be in any more wars. We could have had a life, for a while at least."

Maroun shook his head. "I had no idea you two had such a serious relationship. Even so, after all these years, you seem to think it's still —"

"Doc, it never cooled for either of us. We just didn't see each other for a long time. After last weekend it's like we never were apart."

"I see. Well, you can still have a relationship. You and Dr. Weiss discussed treatment alternatives? Lots of options available today, drugs that can retard the disease's development."

"He gave me some options, but there's not much any of them can do for me. I don't think I want any treatment. I met with Dr. Weiss this morning and told him. I don't want to prolong this and turn into a stick man, a breathing skeleton lying on a bed. That's no life. I'd rather do the best I can with what I got while I can, then go see my Maker."

Maroun nodded. "I understand that alternative. Many other people with your character have done the same. How did Allie take that choice?"

Tanner pointed a finger at the doctor. "That's my problem, doc." He lowered his gaze. "God, I hate having to tell her. She'll think I'm a selfish bastard. Guess she'll be right, too. But I'd rather have a few weeks or months of good times with her than a year of her pity and causing her more pain."

"Isn't that for her to decide, BJ? You better have a talk. Let her know your choice before she hears it from someone else. Allie's strong, has a good head. She'll deal with it, and she won't think you're selfish."

Tanner sighed again. "My God, I hate dealing with this."

They sat quietly a minute, then Dr. Maroun spoke. "You said you have another concern?"

Tanner moved to the window and looked across the parking lot to a row of naked gray-white trees along the perimeter. "Yeah. I want to stay here in Dallas so I can be with Allie, but I need something to keep me busy while she's working."

"What about your business in Austin?"

"Selling out. Had an offer on the table before I found out about the cancer. The offer didn't look too good before. With any luck at all, it'll be a done deal by the end of the month."

"What do you think you want to do in Dallas?"

"I don't know exactly, but it can't be in the electronics business. Wouldn't want to do that anyway."

He turned back to the doctor. "Maybe some volunteer work. Something to help out little guys trying to get businesses started. I've never done anything like that."

"Sounds honorable and rewarding. Good way to spend your time. Why not go to the Small Business Administration and volunteer?"

Tanner nodded. "Thought about that, but I figure there's some guys here at the VA that need help. They're the ones I'd like to find."

"Sorry, BJ. That's way outside my area, but I'll arrange for you to talk to the counseling staff. I do want you to talk to Allie, though, and soon. The longer you wait, the tougher it'll be for both of you."

"Thanks for your time, doc." Tanner opened the door and stepped into the reception area.

"Wait a second, BJ. Let me run something by you."

"Yeah?"

Maroun pointed to the chair. Tanner closed the door and sat down.

"A man in one of my groups has a ranch near here. Thinks he's about to lose the place, but it sounds like he has assets. His dad died recently, and he doesn't know how to manage the ranch. Think you could give him a hand? See if there's a way he can hold onto the property?"

Tanner pursed his lips and frowned. After a moment Maroun challenged him. "You said you'd like to help the little guys, BJ. Here's a perfect opportunity. Matter of fact, you might help several men."

"How's that?"

"Join my group session Wednesday morning. There are some good men here. They need leadership, help getting their lives together."

"You may be right, doc. But I wouldn't want people thinking I'm in need of group therapy."

Maroun stared at Tanner a moment, then shook his head. "I don't believe you worry about what other people think of you, BJ. Maybe what Allie thinks, but no one else. She'll know what's going on. You'll get to see more of her. How about it?"

Tanner gazed at the floor, his feet alternately tapping a quick staccato beat. "Okay, doc. I'll be here Wednesday and meet the rancher."

Tanner stopped by Allie's nurses' station and waited for her to leave a patient's room. He saw her come into the hallway with a sheaf of papers attached to a clipboard. She walked slowly, concentrating on her notes. When she saw him, a smile softened her face, and a new energy transformed her demeanor. "Hi, handsome."

"I've been trying to get the doc to put me in one of these beds so you'd have to take care of me all the time. Which one's your best room?"

She slipped an arm around him under his jacket, steered him toward her office and drawled softly. "Darlin', you don't need a doctor's orders to get in my bed."

Once inside, she said, "How'd it go with Doc Maroun?"

"Fine, except he wants me to go to a group therapy session Wednesday morning."

Her smile faded for an instant. "Really?"

"He thinks I can help a man in the group with his ranch business. I said I'd talk to him, see what I can do." He wrapped a strong arm around Allie's shoulders. "Maroun said he'd testify to you that I'm not crazy. That's not why I'm going to his therapy session."

She spanked his hand. "I'm not so sure about that."

"You have time for lunch?"

She shook her head. "We have a couple of things happening this afternoon. I better stick close. Sorry."

"I'm flying down to Austin this afternoon. Settle a few things at the office so I can get on with selling Tanner Systems. I'll be back tomorrow evening."

"That won't interfere with your treatment schedule with Dr. Weiss?"

He shook his head, looking down and digging into his pockets, as if searching for something. "Gonna run. See you tomorrow night."

She stood on tiptoes to kiss him. "Are you bringing a bigger suitcase full of clothes to my house?"

He cupped her face, feeling the sharpness of her jaw line. "I'll be driving back so I can bring 'em all."

Tanner left quickly and headed for the elevator. He looked back and waved good-bye again as he stepped into the decrepit lift. Riding the elevator he thought about his technical staff members at Tanner Systems, and about the many veterans he had seen at the VA. His mind wandered to vengeful thoughts against Karney and others.

What the hell's your story, Tanner? You wouldn't muster a team of psychos to pull a wild-assed stunt for you — would you?"

As Tanner unlocked his car, he could hear his cell phone buzzing in his briefcase. When he answered, Betty Wilson said, "Oh, BJ, I've been trying to reach you all morning. I'm so sorry but I have very bad news. It's your uncle Ed. He's been shot in his store. He didn't survive."

Tanner gripped the wheel, shouted inside the closed car, then took a breath and said, "What happened?" Before she spoke, he remembered watching the story on TV. Ed's store in Marble Falls was in Burnet County.

"Ed's friend, Chet Travis, called here to let us know. He said a SWAT was responsible." She had no information beyond that.

"In what God-forsaken universe could our inept government send a SWAT team after Ed Wilcox?" Tanner growled.

"Are you okay, BJ?"

"No, I'm not okay. I haven't seen Ed since Christmas, and that was only for a couple of hours. He had lots of friends his age still around. He didn't expect much from me, but I should have been there for him more than I was."

Tanner's throat tightened as he continued. "Now he's dead." He wondered if Patricia Karney had anything to do with the situation.

Betty gave him Chet's number. He made the call and began making plans for a funeral with military honors. Chet asked questions Tanner wasn't prepared to answer. "BJ, I'll make the arrangements for you. I'd be honored to do it. Ed's gun shop has been right next door since before my wife died. He did all her arrangements for me. Let me take care of this for you. The VFW will help, too."

Tanner gratefully agreed.

Ed mentioned something about a video, but Tanner had already moved to new and more vengeful thoughts.

Tanner's flight from Love Field pushed back from the gate but held on the apron while a helicopter made a landing approach. He watched as the helo settled to three or four feet above the tarmac, air-taxied sideways and landed on a flat-top trailer just off the apron. A moment later his plane rolled onto the runway, gathered speed and lifted into the gray sky. The small turboprop aircraft began to pitch and bounce within seconds after takeoff. He reclined the seat and closed his eyes to discourage the passenger next to him from conversation while he pondered his business situation.

Three weeks earlier Watkins had brought an offer from his client to buy Tanner Systems. A weak bid that Tanner wouldn't even consider at the time. Then he learned about his medical condition. Next came the IRS extortion attack. Two days later, Watkins said his offer might be jeopardized because of the tax problem and reduced his offer by almost the exact amount as the IRS bill.

How did he find out about the tax claim? Not from anyone at Tanner Systems, no doubt about that. IRS claims weren't a matter of public record, certainly not before they were formally filed. Watkins's call came within hours after informal negotiations between the tax attorney and the IRS agents. How did he know?

Tanner remembered his conversation with Patricia Karney, and the thought caused him to recoil, startling the passenger beside him. He looked past the man, out the window. Off to the right through a brownish gray haze he could see the Waco skyline slipping behind the aircraft. The man by the window said, "Bad dream? Or did the turbulence wake you?"

"Nightmare." He closed his eyes again, and Allie pushed to the front of the clutter in his mind. He saw her tear-stained face beside the antique chest. Her dad's note. The bundle of papers. The gun.

His thoughts became a badly mixed jumble, like a deck of cards shuffled with some of them face up, shaking his consciousness like the turbulence slamming the airplane about.

This isn't right. None of it is right.

▶ 11 ◀

Betty Wilson followed Tanner into his office with a mug of coffee and a stack of mail. "How was your Dallas trip?"

"Went pretty well. I'm going back tomorrow."

Betty raised her eyebrows. "Oh?"

"Looks like I'll be spending lots of time in Dallas the next few months."

Before she could ask more questions, he raised a hand. "I can't explain it right now, except that it has to do with Watkins."

"But he's in Houston."

"The most critical part of the deal may not be in Houston. Or Austin, for that matter."

He could see her bewilderment. "Don't worry, Wilson. It'll work out. I'm not gonna bring you piles of work with ASAP tags on them."

"But who's taking care of you in Dallas? I haven't —"

"No problem, Wilson. Mostly informal stuff right now." He patted her arm and smiled. "I'll call when you need to be involved. And don't worry. Nobody could take your place, not even temporarily. Besides, I may need an angel before it's all over, but that won't be for a while yet."

Betty's concern seemed to vanish at the mention of an angel. Cecil Ellis entered as she left Tanner's office. "Welcome back, BJ. How was the trip?"

He told Ellis of his planned return to Dallas and gave him no more explanation. Afterward, he said, "I need you to take care of business for a while. Keep everything rolling. I'm going to be away for a few weeks."

Ellis frowned. "Are you trying to work a different deal in Dallas? That may not be a wise move."

Tanner shuffled the mail on his desk but said nothing.

"You know, BJ, this IRS thing will make it tough for you to negotiate any kind of a deal. You'll have to let the buyer know we've paid off."

When Tanner remained silent, Ellis continued. "Dave Bonner says the bank is very concerned about our position. He's mentioned it a couple of times but doesn't want us to say anything to Tom Mabry. They don't want us pursuing another deal while we're dealing with Watkins."

Tanner studied Ellis's face, then turned away. After a moment he said, "Sit down, Cecil. It's time I told you what's going on."

By noon Tanner had told Ellis the story about his illness and the prognosis. "Cecil, I'd appreciate you making a personal call to each board member to let them know. I'll be in touch with them after the drama passes."

He explained that, no, there wasn't another deal working in Dallas to sell the company. Watkins's offer stood alone. The deal wouldn't work until Watkins guaranteed no summary dismissals during the first year. That would give the employees time for fair assessments by new management.

Yes, the IRS problem would drive down the value of Watkins's offer, but the hit would go against Tanner's personal shares of preferred stock. Betty rang the intercom to ask if Tanner and Ellis wanted lunch ordered in before their 1:30 meeting with the IRS. Neither had any appetite. Immediately after hanging up, Tanner had a thought and rang Betty. "Anybody using the design shop conference room today?"

"I'll check."

A minute later she rang back. "No, sir. Most of the designers are on site at the Cap City project. Mitchell and Grover are the only ones there."

He nodded satisfaction. "Tell them to go someplace nice for a long lunch and bring me the bill. I don't want them back in their quarters till we're through with the IRS. Have the maintenance guy turn the heat off over there and open some windows."

He gave Betty more instructions, then discussed minor issues with Ellis regarding projects under way, whom Ellis should depend on to keep each project on track in the coming weeks. At 1:42, Betty knocked and entered the office. "Ms. Karney and Mr. Palmero have arrived. Nelda's taking them over."

Tanner gave her a thumbs-up, then looked at Ellis. "We'll give them a few minutes to cool their asses."

Ellis shook his head. "I don't understand what you're doing, BJ."

"Don't want them in my office. I'd always remember they'd been here every time I looked at a chair where either of them sat. Hardly ever go to the design shop. Karney hates cold weather. She'll hate it over there and want to get going. The sooner she's gone the better."

Karney and Palmero waited by the receptionist's desk until a short, stocky young woman showed them where to sign the visitors log. She made temporary badges for them, then led the way outside into a courtyard at the center of the U-shaped building. The woman wore a nylon jacket. She'd tucked her hair under a Lady Stetson to protect it from the icy drizzle.

"Where the hell are we going?" Karney asked, hunching against the cold.

The woman flashed a pleasant smile. "Conference room."

"Why don't we go around inside the building?"

Pointing to the center section of the facility, the young woman said, "Classified area back there. Can't go through without proper clearance."

Karney dashed ahead across the courtyard toward the far door. Palmero fell into step beside her and struggled to move his large body ahead to open the door. He yanked the handle, slipped and fought to keep his footing on the slick tiles. "Dammit!"

Karney huddled against the building. "It's locked. Hurry up. It's freezing out here."

Still ten yards away, the escort maintained her pace. "Too dangerous to run on this slick walkway."

Karney thought her smile now seemed insincere and she wanted to slap the girl.

Palmero hoisted his briefcase over his boss to shield her from the rain until the woman unlocked the door. His hair dampened and sagged down his forehead.

Inside, Karney unbuttoned her coat and shook off the moisture. She'd followed the smiling cowgirl several paces down a hall before she realized the building was hardly warmer than the courtyard.

"What's wrong with the heat in this place?"

"Probably has something to do with the equipment testing they do over here."

When they entered the conference room, Karney looked around the Spartan facility, sensed the cold and noted that no heat came from the vents.

"That's it! Where's Tanner's office?"

"He's in the confidential area, ma'am. Can't go in there."

"Get him in here! Right NOW!"

"Yes, ma'am. I'll be sure he knows you're here."

The woman left them in the conference room and closed the door. Palmero used a handkerchief to mop his hair. "Damn! These people must be Eskimos."

"These people are harassing representatives of the United States government. It's gonna be —"

She stopped short of saying it would be a pleasure taking Tanner's money. The room could be bugged.

Tanner glanced at his watch. "It's been ten minutes. They ought to be cooled down by now. Ready to go?"

Ellis nodded.

"You have the check?"

Ellis rose, his face grim, and patted his notebook. Tanner led the way through the building into the design area. He opened the conference room door and peered inside. When he first saw Karney, he thought she must be ill. Her pale skin seemed blue and he didn't remember her being so thin. She'd worn her hair shorter before, and without the permed curls.

Is the man with her a bodyguard? Wish the son of a bitch would take a swing at me.

Both IRS agents stood on the far side of the table and stared at Tanner as he entered the room, followed by Ellis. Tanner looked hard at Karney without speaking. After an uncomfortable silence, Ellis said, "Eh, BJ, you know Ms. Karney. This is Mr. Palmero."

No one made a move to shake hands, and Tanner didn't invite them to sit down. Karney said, "You have the check?"

Ellis opened his folder and placed the draft on the table. She reached for it, but Tanner leaned forward, the heel of his hand on the check. "You have the action dismissals?"

She glared at him, then glanced at Palmero. "Show him the decrees."

Palmero shifted his gaze to her, then Tanner, and back to her, like a man following the ball at a tennis match. "The papers. Yes, I have them right here."

He placed his wet briefcase on the table, opened it and found the documents. Karney snatched them from him and tossed them across the table.

Tanner didn't move, his hand still on the check. Ellis inspected the papers and compared them with a fax from their tax attorney. He nodded approval and slipped the paper in front of Tanner. "It's correct, word for word."

Karney glared at the small man beside Tanner. "Of course it's correct. The check?"

She reached for it again, but Tanner continued to hold it. The venomous tone of his own voice surprised him when he spoke. "Why did you kill my uncle?"

Karney recoiled but kept her composure. Palmero retreated a step and looked back as if searching for another exit.

"A SWAT team did that," Karney said. "He pulled a gun when they went in. I wasn't even in the building when it happened."

"You caused it to happen. You killed him. Why?"

"What makes you think I'm responsible?"

"You just told me, the way you and this jerk reacted to the question. You knew Ed was my uncle."

"He owed money to the IRS. I was just doing my job."

"How the hell can you live with yourself, *just doing your job?*"

"Now listen —"

Tanner turned to Palmero. "Were you there, too?"

Palmero glanced at Karney, then down to his briefcase. Tanner nodded. "So that's at least two souls you'll have to face on Judgment Day."

Palmero jerked his head back as if he'd been slapped.

Tanner removed his hand from the draft, but left it on his side of the table for Karney to stretch across and pick up. "God help you both." He turned to leave the room. "Nelda will take you back to the lobby. You'll have to sign out."

Karney tossed her visitor badge on the table. "Like hell I will."

Palmero removed his badge and dropped it beside Karney's.

Tanner shrugged. "Fine, but you'll be the first two suspects for the FBI to investigate when classified documents turn up missing." He opened the door and motioned for Nelda. "Show them back across to the lobby. Be sure they sign out and save themselves from any future trouble with Tanner Systems."

He left the room and turned toward the back of the building with Ellis close behind. He'd gone less than ten paces when Karney called out. He turned to see her in the hallway, holding the check high.

"How does it feel to give this up?"

He'd never before had the desire to physically hurt a woman. How could she be so vindictive? She seemed to want to persecute him as if they'd been lovers for years instead of dating for a few months.

Using every ounce of control, Tanner shrugged, smiled and spread his hands. "It's only money, Patricia. You know about my new contract. A few months and we'll have new revenues on the DOD contract. What's it worth, Cecil? Eighteen million? Most of it's mine personally. And I don't have to sell the business now unless I want to." He shrugged. "I can live with myself. But you two . . . you better watch your backs."

He turned and continued walking, sure that the fire in Karney's eyes would warm the hallway and burn his back before he reached the door. He expected a salvo from her, but she said nothing more.

Walking back to his office, Tanner felt as if he were going to throw up. His stomach churned and bile rose in his throat. He swallowed hard. He could feel the heat in his face, and he knew by the way others avoided him that they could see his rage.

As he passed the engineering director's office, he glanced in and saw Dave Bonner. "What's he doing here, Cecil?

"I'll ask."

"Never mind. We'll see him at a soon."

After plodding through project reviews with Ellis and laying out assignments for the coming weeks, Tanner could see that the finance officer appeared to be more depressed than he was. He decided to lighten the mood before he left. "What's the latest with young Desmond 'Robin Hood' Blaylock?"

Ellis smiled and seemed happy to segue to an amusing topic. "Still taking heat from everyone. They've added a new charge against him."

"Oh?"

"A couple of crooks filed phony tax returns for a bunch of Huntsville prisoners."

Tanner nodded. "Saw that on the news."

Ellis chuckled. "Couple of guys in Blaylock's group accused him of being the one that screwed up the IRS computer and got away with the money."

Tanner nodded vigorously. "I'd like to get into their damned computers and screw things up. And I don't mean just a few hundred returns. It's past time for somebody to take advantage of some of the IRS people for a change."

After saying good-bye to Ellis, Tanner worked through a stack of papers Betty had left with him. He returned them to her desk on the way out. "I'm going home to pack a few things. Want to be back in Dallas before the rain turns to sleet. Take care of Cecil. You two are gonna have to run the business for a while."

"You're sure there's nothing more I can do for you, BJ?"

"Soon as there is, I'll let you know, Wilson. I'll call every day."

All of Tanner's clothes fit into two large duffle bags, except for business suits and winter coats. Those items he laid across the back seat of the Cadillac.

When he looked around his condo for any personal items he might want to take, he realized how little he had in his life except for the company he'd created and loved so much. His employees were his family. He cared about them and their security. He'd filled his office with photos, mementos, and awards for Tanner Systems people. His condo held no such treasures.

This place shows as much personality as a prison cell.

The thought reminded him again of the news story about the tax fraud at Huntsville.

One last security check, then he grabbed a Dr Pepper on the way through the kitchen to the garage. A few minutes later, he joined the heavy traffic on I-35, slowed by the light rain.

A half hour north of Austin the rain stopped and traffic thinned. Tanner set the cruise control for 70. Concentrating to clear his mind, he set aside all thoughts and emotions to focus on one issue: *Can I prove what Karney and Palmero have done? Or should I just kill the assholes?*

For two hours Tanner paid minimum attention to his driving on the uncrowded road. First he fantasized about ways to physically punish the two IRS agents. Then he began to mentally stumble through a cluster of jumbled thoughts, all related, but not accurately connected. While passing through Waco, the first thread of logic tied a number of ideas together, forming a thin plan. He considered it an impossible fantasy, but by the time he passed Hillsboro, more tangled thoughts began to tie into the scheme, falling into logical order.

He dug in the glove compartment for his micro recorder and taped the string of ideas. He figured there would be holes in the plan that exposed its absurdity, shocked that he could envision such extraordinary action in the first place. But he felt even more astounded when he played back the tape.

There's a chance that this could actually work.

While playing the tape a second time, Tanner could feel his heart pounding. Could he seriously consider such an outrageous undertaking?

He shook his head, grinning as he rewound the cassette.

Long odds, Tanner. You can't do it alone. And you sure as hell can't put anybody else at risk.

He grinned at the road ahead, laughed aloud and said, "But it'd be one hell of a coup if it worked."

He left the freeway and stopped in the covered, well-lit parking area of a Dairy Queen to make additional notes while listening to the tape a third time. He dug a note pad out of his briefcase and wrote down the actions that would fill in two of the four gaps in his plan. Two other items he noted with question marks:

FIELD PERSONNEL?

TRANSPORTATION?

Tanner tore the paper off the pad, then slipped it into his shirt pocket with the recorder. When he started the car and shifted into reverse, he stopped and examined his hands, surprised to find he had sweaty palms.

That hasn't happened for years.

He rubbed both hands on his thighs, conscious of his faster heartbeat and quicker breathing. He gunned the Cadillac back onto the freeway toward the ghostly city, aglow through the rainbow-tinted mist.

By the time he reached Dallas, a frosty haze cloaked the city's high-rises. The buildings with multicolored silhouette lighting added an eerie dimension to the scene, like the aurora borealis distorted by shrouds of ice fog.

When he reached the I-30 interchange, he almost missed his turn, lost in a fantasy about the success of his scheme.

▶ **12** ◀

Tanner stood by the window next to Allie's antique chest holding Harry St. John's tax-lien papers. He'd read them again, rechecked the signature of the tax agent and stared at Harry's suicide note until he'd memorized the words.

While gazing into the darkness, watching for headlights on the street, he mentally reviewed the plan he'd worked out while driving from Austin. Each time he thought about it, more details filled out his mental picture, making the fantasy more exciting. He felt sure the strategy could work if recon visits settled a couple of issues he couldn't solve without observing the targets.

He reached for his pocket recorder to tape more notes, but headlights rounded the corner. When he recognized Allie's Oldsmobile turning into the service lane, he returned the papers to the chest and went to meet her.

While Tanner brought in more wood for the fire, Allie put a kettle on the range, then showered and changed into jeans and a bulky sweatshirt. She made mugs of tea with honey and joined him in the den. They sat on the floor in front of the fireplace, backs against the futon.

"I missed you last night. How was Austin?"

"Cold, wet and costly."

She gave him a wry smile. "Why? Did you party all night with the boys?"

"No such luck. Had to buy my way out of town this afternoon. Spent the whole trip here trying to figure how to get my money back."

"Did you work it out? Or do you need my help?" She winked while poking a finger in his ribs. "Remember, I carry a gun and I know how to use it. Show me who took your money. I'll get it back."

"I'm afraid we'll need more than one gun. These robbers are a big outfit."

Her smile faded. "What're we really talking about here?"

He waved the question away. "Business stuff. Nothing to worry about."

They sat in silence a few minutes, gazing at the flames. Tanner began to relax, enjoying the comfort of the cozy fire, and Allie nestled against him. But her next question, the inevitable one, jolted him. "You have clinic appointments tomorrow?"

This is it, Tanner. Time to tell her.

Her dark-blue eyes seemed violet, reflecting her royal-blue sweatshirt and the glow of the fireplace. He took her hand in his. "Allie, I thought a long time about my options. I'm afraid you're not gonna like the one I chose."

He braced for her reaction, wondering if it would be pain and tears, or anger.

God, please help us get through this. Don't let it tear us apart.

"I thought about the poor helpless bastards I've seen lying in hospital beds, just waiting to die. I can't do that, Allie. I have to —"

She squeezed his hand and smiled. "I know, sweetheart."

"What?"

Her eyes appeared even brighter, magnified by the tears welled in them. She nodded slowly and whispered. "I thought about that, too."

"I don't want to hurt you, Allie, but —"

"It's okay. I understand. I don't want you to end up that way either. Guess I knew all the time what you'd do."

He put an arm around her and stroked her hair while she snuggled against his shoulder. "Allie, I —"

She put a finger over his lips. "No more about it, please. We both know what there is to know." She raised her face to his. "I want to enjoy every minute I have with you, starting with this one."

He gazed at her a moment while stroking her face. "My God, I should have never let you get away the first time I found you."

"None of that either, BJ. We don't have time to waste looking back. Like I said, every minute."

The firelight gave her face a bronze glow that reminded him of how she looked so many years ago, tanned by the tropical sun. Their kiss felt soft and warm, the gentle beginning of a perfect union. No awkward feelings or urgency as with their first time the previous weekend. She lifted her hips and slipped out of her jeans as he eased them off of her, then the sweatshirt was gone. While she unbuttoned his shirt, he kissed her hair and whispered, "Want me to carry you to the bedroom?"

"No, let's stay here and keep the fire warm."

The next morning, Tanner left early for Marble Falls to attend the funeral for Ed Wilcox. Dozens of men in their sixties and seventies and older, a few women of the same ages, and many younger people attended the ceremony at Ed's church. Virtually everyone had a few words for Tanner after the service. Then most of them attended the graveside ceremony, having wrapped themselves in their coats and scarves against the cold wind.

A Marine Corps rifle squad and bugler, all in dress uniform, appeared not to notice the frigid temperature. The riflemen fired their volleys. The honor guard lifted and folded the flag and presented it to Tanner. The bugler blew taps.

Tanner wondered at the ability of the bugler to perform without missing a note when his lips must surely be stiff from the cold.

After the services, Tanner went to a restaurant with Chet and a few of Ed's close friends. They told stories of fun times, toasted his memory, and asked for blessings upon his soul.

Tanner found it difficult to see through occasional tears while driving back to Dallas.

▶ 13 ◀

Dr. Maroun ended the Wednesday group session at noon. Tanner waited at the back of the room and watched the men leave. The Mexican who had introduced himself as Castro offered to push Roscoe in his wheelchair to the Pulmonary Unit. Castro spoke to Lamar, the rancher, over his shoulder. "I'll meet you and Sonny in the lobby."

Standing near the door, Lamar waved acknowledgment but kept his eyes on Tanner.

As the other men dispersed, Dr. Maroun sat down beside Tanner. "Well, what did you think, BJ?"

"Interesting group, Doc."

"Anything like you expected?"

Tanner shook his head. "Not much wrong with most of these men. All they need is some leadership, structure and a break or two."

Maroun nodded. "Men like these — no families, no lasting support units — can use up a month's worth of my efforts in one lonesome night." He nodded toward Lamar. "That's a good man. He can be out of here in no time. He needs some help understanding bookkeeping, and a little self-confidence. You can give him all that, show him how to use his cash-flow assets. A couple of the others are staying at his place. Wish they all were. You could turn them into the men they should be."

"I don't know, doc. I haven't worked with men like that for a long time."

Maroun grinned. "Like riding a bicycle, Mr. Tanner. Come on, Lamar's excited about you helping him."

Tanner followed the doctor to the door. "Lamar, the doc says you could use help with the business side of your ranch."

"Yes, sir."

"Want me to give you a hand?"

"Yes, sir."

"Why me? I've never run a ranch before."

"Doc Maroun told me about your company in Austin. I figure you can handle anything, Colonel."

Tanner saw in Lamar's eyes a deep truth, and trust that made him want to help this man, no matter how long it might take.

"You don't have any problems with tending the livestock?"

"No, sir, none at all." He dropped his gaze to the floor. "But I should have paid more attention when Dad was trying to teach me the office stuff."

"I'll help you get your finances squared away," Tanner said. "We'll make you an expert business manager."

Lamar dropped his gaze. "There is one problem, Colonel. I don't know how soon I can pay you. I'd have to —"

"That's not an issue, Lamar. Question is, are you and your two buddies willing to put up with me on your ranch?"

Lamar stared back with resolve in his eyes. "Yes, sir, right up until we both agree that I can run the place myself."

Tanner stuck out a hand. "Deal. Give me directions. I'll stop at home, then be less than an hour behind you."

Lamar thought a moment. "I don't drive much, Colonel. Can't give good directions, but I could send the others ahead, ride with you and show you the way."

Tanner nodded. Lamar stepped into the hallway where Sonny Kruger waited and sent him to meet Castro. Then he turned to Dr. Maroun and pumped his hand. "Thanks a million, doc. This is gonna be great."

Tanner headed south on I-45, following Lamar's directions. Lamar leaned away from the window, obviously uncomfortable being so close to other vehicles.

"You all right, Lamar?"

"Sorry, sir, I'm not used to the traffic."

"Tell me about your ranch."

"Seven hundred acres of good pasture with plenty of water. Hundred twenty Beefmaster cows. Three of the best bulls in Texas."

Tanner looked at the land along the highway, flat with only a few gentle contours. "Any trees on your place?"

"Yes, sir. Magnolias around the house before I was born. Nice willow tree by the big lake. When Dad cleared the property years ago, he left some mesquites in the pastures. I keep 'em trimmed high. Good summer shade for the livestock. Pecan trees and oaks down by the range."

"The range?"

Lamar shifted uneasily. "I call it a range. It's just a gully on the back side of the place about a quarter-mile long, away from the road."

Tanner passed a long line of slow-moving traffic, then Lamar directed him to take an exit at Ennis and head east. Tanner noticed large rolled bales of hay in some of the pastures they passed.

"Been feeding hay to your stock this winter?"

"Some hay but mostly winter oats."

"Sounds like you know what you're doing, Lamar. What kind of help do you think you need?"

"I really don't know anything about the mortgage or the bank accounts. There's not much money left in the checking account. I know that Dad had some savings, but I can't find a passbook or anything that makes sense to me."

The overcast thinned while they drove along the farm road, and the early-afternoon sun brought welcome warmth through the windows. Lamar pointed out a cattle guard on the right and Tanner crossed it. A border collie lying by the fence sat up to inspect the car. When he saw Lamar, he jumped to his feet, tail wagging, and ran beside the Cadillac.

"That's Ike. He helps me with the cows and keeps possums out of the barn. You ride horses, Colonel?"

"Not for a long time."

Lamar pointed to a small pasture to the left of the barn. "Two quarter horses. The roan's mine. Dark one was my dad's."

The crushed-limestone drive ran from the gate to the barn two hundred yards from the road. The wooden structure had a steel roof and wore a near-new coat of barn-red paint. All ground and loft doors were closed and latched, and the building looked square, with no sags, uncommon for an aged facility in black-loam country.

Fifty yards to the right of the barn, smoke rose from the chimney of a fieldstone house that had a shake roof. Two magnolia trees dominated the front yard. Tanner observed that, as often is the case on farms and ranches, the barn appeared to be in better repair than the house.

A dark-blue Ford van sat in the carport at the left side of the house. Next to it was a dirty, faded-green Dodge pickup. "That your van, Lamar?"

"No, sir. It's Castro's. That's my pickup. I'll move it so you can park inside."

"When's the last time you washed that truck?"

Lamar's face colored. "I don't drive much, Colonel. Guess I need to give it more attention." He ran from the Cadillac, jumped in the pickup and backed out of the carport. When Tanner stopped his car, Lamar was already beside it to open the door for him.

"All the records are laid out in the office, Colonel. Front door's around this way."

Tanner ignored Lamar's gesture, went to the back of the house and scanned the pastures. He could see fewer than thirty cows. "Where's the rest of your herd?"

Lamar pointed to the southeast. "Feedin' in the back pasture. Good grass back there."

"How about a tour of the place? Will that pickup get us around okay?"

Lamar nodded and they climbed into the truck. Ike leaped into the back. They drove through two pastures. All the stock tanks were full from good winter rains. The fences were straight rows of cedar fence posts with five strands of barbed wire as uniform as the strings on a guitar. Off to the right Tanner could see the naked, gray top branches of trees rising from a deep arroyo. "What's over there?"

"Pecan trees. They like it in that gully."

"Let's have a look."

"Nothing to see in there now, Colonel. Only some bare trees."

"Is this the place you called a range?"

Lamar nodded. Tanner said, "Show me."

Lamar drove to the top of the arroyo and stopped. Tanner stepped out and scanned the area, then headed down the slope with Lamar behind him. He stopped halfway when he looked toward the far end of the gully and saw what appeared to be a stack of feed sacks. "That's no place to store supplies. Those bags should be out of the gully and covered."

Lamar shoved his hands deep in his pockets and looked down. "It's not feed, Colonel. Nothing but dirt in those sacks."

Tanner walked toward the stack. "What are they for?"

A few paces closer he stopped abruptly when he saw an opening facing the length of the arroyo. He turned to Lamar and said, "A bunker?"

"It's, eh . . . well, it's a place where I come to let off steam."

"How?"

"I do some target shooting down here once in a while."

"With what?"

"M-16A1 mostly. A bolt action .308 and a Browning Hi-Power side arm."

"Are you any good with them?"

Lamar straightened. "Very good. Turn sideways, I could shoot your buttons off with the .308 and never touch the coat."

"You a hunter?"

"I shoot targets. Never want to kill anything again."

"Must make a hell of a noise. Any complaints from the neighbors? The sheriff?"

Lamar shook his head. "They never hear a shot."

"Bullshit."

"No, sir. I'll show you why."

Lamar led the way to the bunker with Ike at his heels. He moved two bags to make the opening bigger, then slipped inside. "Come on in, Colonel."

Tanner climbed in, waited for his eyes to adjust to the dim light and examined the space. The interior floor was four by ten feet. The five-foot-high ceiling of heavy timbers was covered with two layers of sandbags. Halfway down the length of the space a row of bags separated it into two compartments. At the back of the bunker, Tanner could see a pile of blankets and several large pieces of egg-crate foam rubber. Mixed with the smell of damp earth he caught the unmistakable odor of sulfur.

"I shoot from back here," Lamar said. "Hang the blankets overhead and along the sides, make a foam-rubber frame around the window. All the noise stays inside. Earplugs and pads take care of me."

"How often do you come down here?"

A shrug. "Couple times a week. Sometimes more."

"Where're the weapons?"

"Locked up at the house. Not likely anybody would ever find them, either."

Tanner slipped out of the bunker and brushed dirt from his pants. "You carry the side arm when you leave the ranch?"

Lamar, hoisting one of the bags back into the opening, stopped his motion. "No way, Colonel. Like I said, I shoot for fun and to let off steam."

He put the other bag in place and they headed for the truck. Lamar drove to the back of the pasture and gestured to the weedy thicket of mesquites and scrub oaks on the adjacent land. "Hundred eighty acres in there going to waste. Daddy wanted to buy it couple years back but couldn't make a deal. Said the owner wanted too much for it."

As they drove to the barn, Tanner asked about Castro and Kruger, and Lamar described his relationship with them. "They've been driftin' too long. Need a place to light for a while."

"Are they willing to work for you?"

Lamar grinned. "Castro jokes a lot about gringos taking advantage of him, but he's okay. Kruger grew up on a ranch. He misses it. That guy will do about anything I tell him, long as he gets to stay here." He frowned, shaking his head. "I don't know how I'm gonna pay 'em. I sure don't want to sell all those cows with calves on the way."

While the pickup bounced across the pasture, Tanner studied Lamar and saw a different man from the Lamar Weed at the VA, or the one who had traveled down I-45 with him. The rancher had tied his hair into a ponytail that hung behind his hat. His relaxed position showed confidence that Tanner hadn't seen in him until they arrived at the ranch. Dr. Maroun had described all three men as good work prospects. Lamar Weed could definitely fill the bill.

"You don't look or sound like a man that needs to be in therapy, Lamar."

"Everything's fine while I'm here on the ranch. Outside the front gate's a whole other world. Nothing seems to work right for me out there." He told Tanner about his shopping trip.

When they reached the barn, Ike leaped out of the back of the truck and headed down the side of the structure, nose to the base of the wall. Tanner went inside and inspected the facility. He found the feed room swept clean, barrels and burlap bags neatly stacked, and no signs of rodents. In the tack room, two clean saddles sat on padded frames. Bridles, harnesses and coiled ropes were hung in good order.

Outside the barn, Tanner said, "You have a mighty fine spread, Lamar. Well cared for. You do a real good job. Now, let's check out your dad's papers."

Lamar sucked in a deep breath and led the way toward the house. "Sure hope you can find something that I've missed, Colonel. I don't know what I'd do if I lost this place."

Lamar insisted that Tanner enter the front door instead of going through the kitchen, leading him along the wide veranda from the carport. The stone walls had seam cracks in a few places, but every crack had been filled and sealed.

The living room showed scant evidence of the Lamar Weed that Tanner was getting to know. The hardwood floor gleamed. Two platform rockers, with doilies across their tops, faced the fireplace. The cherry-wood coffee and end tables were probably older than Lamar, as were most other items in the room.

Castro and Kruger sat drinking Cokes at the round oak table in the kitchen. They rose when Tanner entered. The butane stove and refrigerator appeared to have been in place more than half of Lamar's life. The white wooden frames of the glass-door kitchen cabinets showed bare spots from years of wear, but dishes and supplies were neatly stacked inside every cupboard.

Tanner shook hands with the two men. "You're staying here with Lamar?"

"Yes, sir," they said.

Tanner motioned for them to be seated, then he and Lamar joined them at the table. "You know he's offered me a temporary job here, too?"

Kruger looked at Castro, and the Latino said, "We heard you were gonna help out with the paperwork a few days."

Tanner nodded. "This ranch is a big investment. We want to be sure Lamar knows everything he needs to about running the place. I want to stay till he's comfortable."

Lamar smiled while Castro gazed passively at Tanner. Kruger wiped beads of moisture from the side of his Coke can. Tanner studied each man a moment, then said, "There can be something in it for you two, if Lamar approves and you're willing to work for fair compensation."

Castro squinted at Tanner. "Who decides what's fair?"

"I do, and I expect it's gonna be the best deal you've ever had. It'll be up to you to take it or leave it."

Kruger said, "So what's the deal, Mr. Tanner?"

"Colonel," Lamar corrected.

Tanner put a hand on Lamar's arm. "No need for that. None of us are in the military anymore." He turned to the others. "First, I need to see the books, then talk with Lamar. I'll let you know what the deal is tomorrow. Where's the office, Lamar?"

As they left the room, Castro spoke to Kruger loud enough for Tanner to overhear. "We better get ready to go, Sonny. Sounds like the gringo grandee has arrived."

Tanner turned back. "Is that a bad thing, Castro?"

"Has been every other time in my life."

"Don't be in a hurry to leave. I'm betting that your luck's changed for the better. Won't cost you anything to wait a day or two to find out."

Castro pondered a moment, then hoisted his drink in a toast. "Okay, Colonel, we'll hang out till we hear from you."

Tanner gave him a thumbs-up. "Good choice."

Lamar led Tanner into a small office next to the master bedroom. A gleaming rolltop desk dominated the room. A high-backed leather chair and a stool were the only other furnishings except for a file cabinet in the far corner. Tanner envisioned Lamar's dad seated at the desk, turned toward the window overlooking the open pastures.

On the wall above the desk were individual pictures of four bulls. The opposite wall held several photos of a boy at various ages, each posed with a different calf sporting an FFA blue or red ribbon. Tanner took a closer look at the photos. "Lamar, you've always been a winner, haven't you?"

Lamar's face colored, but he said nothing as he raised the rolltop. He eased onto the stool after Tanner sat down at the desk and began examining documents.

Stacks of papers surrounded two ledgers and a checkbook in the middle of the desk. Tanner found the record books to be complete and orderly accounts of seven years of purchases and expenses, cattle breeding records, and income for livestock and hay.

"Colonel, there's more of those books in the file cabinet. They go years back."

"These will do for now. You have a calculator?"

Following Lamar's gesture, Tanner opened the middle drawer to find pens, pencils, a calculator and a dozen or so keys.

After perusing the stacks of paper, Tanner said, "Where are the tax returns for the most recent years?"

Lamar opened the bottom drawer of the cabinet, and Tanner found copies of hand-written tax returns dating back seven years. "Well, if your daddy didn't bury money out in the pasture, we shouldn't have any trouble figuring out what you're worth, Lamar. This'll take a while. If you have other work to do, go on about it. I'll come find you later."

Lamar hesitated. "Yes, sir, but there is one thing."

"What's that?"

"I was wondering what you meant about somethin' here for Castro and Kruger."

Tanner stood and walked to the window. "Two things, Lamar. One is that you need help with this place. At least one man. Other thing is that I'm looking for some men to do a job for me pretty soon.

"Don't worry about paying them. I'll see that their finances work right. It'll be my money that we'll use to pay them till I find out if they're right for the job."

Lamar nodded, but his expression showed concern. Tanner put a hand on his shoulder. "I won't commit a dollar of your money until you understand and agree to everything."

By 5:00, Tanner had seen enough documents to know the Weed Ranch was in excellent financial condition, unless Lamar's dad had squandered thousands of dollars yet to be accounted for. Two phone calls to local real estate agents gave Tanner a range of value for the property. Deducting the mortgage balance from the low end left good equity. Tax statements showed substantial profits over the past seven years, but he found no savings books or investment records for money that should be there.

Tanner left the office and helped himself to a beer, then stepped onto the front porch for fresh air. A clear sky, the first in days, assured a fair sunset. The magnolia trees cast shadows to the barn, leaving multicolored patches across the lawn and driveway.

Between gusts of the cold breeze, he could hear a motor somewhere in the pasture. He rounded the corner and saw Lamar driving a big green

Case tractor toward the barn, with Castro and Kruger riding on either side of him, long-handled tools in hand.

Tanner went inside, grabbed three more beers and met the others at the tractor shed beside the barn. Lamar said, "They helped me fill a wash below one of the tanks. Don't want any erosion ditches in the pasture."

Lamar and Kruger thanked Tanner for the beer. Castro seemed more shocked than grateful. He cocked his head to one side. An inch-long triangular scar on his temple next to his right eye pinched into the shape of an arrowhead. "Grandee never brought me a beer before. You tryin' to soften me up?"

Tanner poked a finger into Castro's stomach. "Looks like you've already softened up. Lamar will help you get rid of that."

Castro sucked in his belly, and an angry glare flashed through his eyes.

Tanner smiled and shook his head. "You sure must have been dealt a lot of bullshit in your life, Castro. Your luck's changed for the better."

"I'm watchin', Colonel."

"Call me BJ."

Castro nodded.

Tanner said, "Lamar, let me show you what I've found out today. We better get to the office and talk things over so we can make these men an offer."

"Okay, Colonel . . . uh, BJ."

After they'd walked far enough toward the house that the others couldn't hear him, Tanner said, "Lamar, was your daddy a gambler?"

He didn't need to hear a denial. The expression on Lamar's face told him clear enough.

"Sorry, but I had to ask. If he didn't gamble or give it away, you must have a fair bit of money somewhere. This place has been a money-maker for a long time."

Tanner closed the door after they were in the office and pulled a single sheet of paper from under a ledger. The page was covered with his notes.

"Do you have any idea where he might have put it? Someone he might have left it with? Anything?"

"No, sir."

"Did he have a stockbroker? Invest in real estate? Buy trust deeds? Anything like that?"

Lamar shook his head, looking bewildered. "I don't know of anything."

"What about a safe deposit box?"

"We had a safe deposit box until four or five years ago. They tore down the bank. I don't know what he did after that."

"Did the bank have another branch?"

"Yes, sir. They built a new one a couple blocks away on the main street. Dad used to go in and see Mr. Montgomery once in a while just to visit. They had known each other a lot of years. Dad never said anything to me about a new deposit box in that bank. Never got a new key."

"Is that the bank that has your mortgage?"

"Yes, sir. I think so."

"Do you know Mr. Montgomery?"

"I met him a few times, but we never really talked."

Tanner closed the ledgers, turned off the calculator and slipped it back into the desk next to the ring of keys. "You go see him tomorrow. He may know something."

"You gonna go with me? I'm not sure I'm ready for that by myself."

"Have Castro drive you. Don't mention my name. Matter of fact, it's best if you don't tell anybody I'm working with you."

"What about Doc Maroun?"

"Play it low-key. Tell him everything's going well, and I expect to be gone by the end of next week."

"But BJ, I won't be ready —"

Tanner raised a hand. "That's our cover story, Lamar. I won't leave till you're a pro at running this place. Now, here's what I have in mind for Castro and Kruger."

He suggested salaries and said he would pay the wages himself for six months. "That's very generous, but why should you pay?"

Tanner's heel tapped a staccato on the hardwood floor, and his chest tightened at the very thought of the scheme he'd conceived. "I'm working on a plan that'll require help in a few weeks. I want them available to work with me, if they turn out to be the right men. Might ask you to do something for me, too."

"Anything, BJ. Just say what and when."

"Forget that for now. You get those two working on the ranch. Teach them discipline, commitment, the things your daddy taught you."

They found Castro and Kruger at the kitchen table with fresh beers. Tanner made the salary offer but said nothing about paying the money himself. "Lamar's in full agreement. He wants you to take over most of the ranch work while he learns to manage the books and take care of selling the cattle. Six months down the road, we'll see how everybody's doing. Decide where to go from there."

"I'm in," Kruger blurted.

Castro said, "We ain't even talked about it."

"What's to talk about? It's damn good money with free room and board. The ranch is in good shape. Won't be hard to keep it that way. I'm in."

Castro peered at Lamar, then Tanner. "Nobody ever offered me more than a couple hundred bucks a month for ranch work. Why are you doin' this?"

"You ever work on a ranch nice as this one, Castro?"

He shook his head.

"Good salary slows turnover. Steady hands take pride in doing good work. They stay happier. With free room and board, you can save lots of cash."

Castro didn't sound convinced. "What's in this for you?"

Tanner sighed. "I'm going to sell my company in Austin pretty soon. I'm working on another plan, but I can't talk about it yet. It involves a government deal. You two, maybe a couple of others from the VA, might be right for part-time work in my new outfit. I want to see what you're made of before I start. You'll have a chance to check me out, too."

The Latino stared at his beer can while he mulled the information. After a few moments, he looked up, and his quizzical expression melted into a grin. He stuck a hand across the table.

"I think you're right, BJ. Looks like my luck has changed." He winked at Tanner. "We got a deal, *Jefe.*"

▶ 14 ◀

Before dawn Thursday morning Tanner entered that time-distorted period between deep sleep and consciousness. He had fallen asleep while trying to recall every document in Lamar's office, wondering if he'd missed something, some key to where the missing funds could be found. In that transition time from sleep to awake, his mind seemed hyperactive, and he could see the entire process again: The ledgers, tax forms and other papers, numbers on the calculator, and finally slipping the tiny machine back into the drawer beside . . .

The memory jolted him wide awake. He tossed the covers aside and bolted out of bed.

Allie, startled from deep slumber, sat up. "What is it? You okay?"

When Tanner saw her confused and frightened expression, he sat on the bed and held her. He could feel her heart pounding against his chest. "Sorry, darlin," he whispered. "Didn't mean to do that to you. I woke up thinking about a problem from yesterday that's got to have a simple solution."

She fell back on the bed, eyes closed, lines of sleep creasing the faint smile on her face. "You know very well I'm not a morning person. Don't let that happen again." She poked him and laughed. "You might wake up the real me, and you wouldn't like that."

He turned on the hall light while he found clothes and a note pad. Then he closed the bedroom door and went to the kitchen to make coffee and work on his plan before calling Lamar.

Tanner ended a string of notes when he heard Allie turn on the shower. Outside, the inky sky had given way to a reddish gray intrusion on the southeastern horizon. He dialed Lamar's number but quickly hung up again before he heard a ring.

Better not leave a trail, in case we really try to do this deal. Wouldn't be good to have his number on Allie's phone records.

When Allie turned off the shower, he took a mug of coffee to the bathroom and knocked.

"Thought some coffee would help you get over my waking you too early."

She took the mug and kissed him. "I'd rather you'd have joined me in the shower."

Her short, wet hair had been brushed straight back, and he noticed that the few gray strands he'd seen before were not showing.

"I have to run to the store for milk. I'll be back by the time you're dressed."

"I bought milk Monday."

"It went bad. Probably sat on the store shelf too long."

He kissed her again, went to the kitchen and poured out the milk before leaving. Ten minutes later he walked out of a mini-mart with a fresh half gallon of milk and three dollars in change. He faced a nippy breeze while crossing the parking lot to a public phone. He dialed the ranch number, deposited coins and waited. Lamar answered on the third ring.

"Lamar, there has to be some connection from your dad's old deposit box to the new bank. Go look at that key ring in the desk."

After a few moments Lamar came back on the line. Tanner said, "You know what all those keys are for?"

"Some padlock keys, probably the same as the ones on my ring. Extra truck key. Couple for the house. The other key was for the old deposit box in the bank they tore down."

"Take it to Mr. Montgomery. Ask him what happened to the old box. There has to be an answer. They didn't just tear them down and scrap them."

Before Tanner ended the call he said, "One more thing, Lamar. That number I gave you to reach me in Dallas?"

"Yes, sir."

"Don't call it from the ranch. If you need to ring me, go to town and use a pay phone. I'll explain later. Good luck at the bank. I'll be at the ranch when you get back."

After morning chores at the barn and making a list of work for Kruger, Lamar and Castro returned to the house and cleaned up for the trip to Ennis. When they climbed into the van, Castro glanced at Lamar while waiting for the engine to warm.

"You look as bad as you did yesterday when we left for Dallas, but we're only goin' five or six miles."

Lamar tugged at the straps of the nylon backpack in his lap, shortening, then extending their length repeatedly. "Don't have to go to Dallas to get this way. Outside the front gate's far enough."

"You know where the bank is?"

"I think so."

"How long since you were there?"

"A few years."

Castro gave him a startled look, then laughed. "Man, that's a hell of a long time between visits to see your money."

The bank had moved to a new and larger building since Lamar's last visit. He stepped out of the van. "God, I hope this works out okay. If you see any cops coming, don't let 'em shoot me."

Lamar walked into the lobby, where three people waited in line for two tellers. A gray-haired wisp of a woman sat at a desk to his right. She eyed Lamar and the empty backpack on his shoulder.

After a moment he approached her. A name plaque on her desk read, "Ms. Simmons, Manager."

"Is Mr. Montgomery here?"

She pinched her bird-like features into a frown. "He retired two years ago."

Lamar stared at the woman, then glanced at the key in his hand, wondering what to do.

"Can I help you with something?" she asked.

"I haven't been in the bank for a while."

"I gathered as much." She gestured at the key. "You want to get into your safe deposit box?"

"Uh, yes, ma'am, if I still have one. Used to be in the other building."

Ms. Simmons lifted half glasses from the desk, perched them on her sharp nose and touched keys on her terminal keyboard. "Everything from the old vault was moved intact, so your box and its contents haven't been disturbed. I don't suppose you remember your box number."

He looked at the key but there was no number on it. "No, ma'am."

She nodded, asked for his name, punched more keys and waited for information to appear on the screen. After a moment she gave him a warm smile. "You're Amos Weed's son, aren't you?"

"Yes, ma'am."

She removed her glasses, leaned across the desk and spoke softly. "Such a dear man. We were so sorry to hear of his passing."

"Thank you."

"Now I understand why you asked for Mr. Montgomery. He used to come here and meet your daddy every couple of weeks after he retired." She gestured toward the café across the street. "They'd have lunch over there.

"Mr. Montgomery and his wife are in Europe for another three weeks. He was so sorry that he wasn't here for your daddy's funeral."

She checked the computer screen and made a note.

"It'll take just a second to check the signature card, then I'll take you to the vault." She leaned close to him and added, "Are you aware of the status of the loan, Mr. Weed?"

"Yes, ma'am. That's why I'm here. I want to get that taken care of quick as I can."

She smiled again and nodded as she rose and walked away. "Not to worry, Mr. Weed. Mr. Montgomery said that would be taken care of when he returned. He promised your daddy he would help with your accounts and such when the time came."

Lamar ran a hand through his hair. So there was a deposit box, but it had been so many years since he'd signed a card. It couldn't possibly still be in their files. Now what? Maybe BJ could figure some way to make them let him get into the box.

While wondering how to make a graceful departure, he looked up to see Ms. Simmons behind the teller line, motioning him to come to the far end of the counter. He wanted to leave; it would be easier to come back later if he thanked her and said good-bye. As he approached the half door where she waited, she opened it. "This way, Mr. Weed."

He followed her to a desk next to the vault door and she gave him a pen. "Please sign the log."

"What's this for?"

"Merely a record to keep track of who's been inside the vault."

"You, uh, you're gonna let me in the box?"

She gave him a shocked expression, eyebrows raised. "Of course."

He signed the log, followed her into the vault and watched her insert a bank key into one of the two locks in a large door on the bottom row. "May I have your key, Mr. Weed?"

He gave it to her, and she inserted the key and twisted, but it didn't move. Lamar swallowed hard.

Ms. Simmons removed the key, examined it, then went back to the desk. "Your key's a little rusty, but I can take care of that."

She sprayed the key with a lubricant, wiped it with a tissue and went back to the box. This time the key turned, unlocking the box, and Ms. Simmons removed a metal box more than a cubic foot in size. "It's rather heavy. Would you?"

"Oh, sure." He picked up the container and followed her to a booth.

"Take as long as you like. When you're ready, press that button. I'll be right back to put away the box."

Lamar stared at the metal case, anxious yet fearful of opening it. Tanner figured money was missing. Had his dad stashed it here? Why not in a savings account? He wiped his palms on his jeans, then raised the lid.

The first bundle of documents was the ranch deed and mortgage papers, dated a year before his mother died. Ownership had been changed to The Weed Family Living Trust. Lamar remembered having signed those papers as a trustee. Next was a copy of his dad's will. He decided to review that later and ask Tanner to help find a lawyer to take care of it. As he lifted the trust document he almost lost his breath. The lower half of the box was full of $100 and $500 savings bonds. "Thank you, Sweet Jesus," he whispered.

He made a quick count of the bonds in one tall stack and guesstimated at least four hundred to five hundred bonds. After savoring the delight a moment, he put everything back in the deposit box and pressed the buzzer. Ms. Simmons returned in a few seconds. He took the case back to the vault, then she locked the drawer and gave him his key. When he stepped through the counter door she said, "Very nice to meet you, Mr. Weed. Let me know if there's anything else we can do for you."

Lamar thanked her, made a quick trip to the van and dropped the empty backpack on the floor between his feet. Castro made a U-turn and headed toward the ranch. "How'd it go?"

Lamar shrugged. "Didn't have a fight or get busted."

"Looks like you didn't find a pot o' gold either," Castro said, pointing to the empty bag.

"Get me back to the ranch."

"I'm gonna stop at that Circle K. You want anything?"

Lamar stiffened. "No, and neither do you. Not there."

"What's the matter with —"

"Keep movin'. That's where I got busted."

Castro laughed as they passed the convenience store. "Man, you have to learn the unwritten rules. White guys aren't allowed to be bad asses in that kind of place."

When Tanner arrived at the ranch, he parked the Cadillac inside the barn and stood by the stall where Kruger had taken Beauty to groom her. The desert war veteran brushed the quarter horse with gentle strokes, rubbing her neck with his other hand and talking softly. Her ears moved constantly in response to his murmurs.

Tanner noticed the size of Kruger's powerful but gentle hands, his palms as wide as the oval grooming brush. Beauty's feathery winter coat gleamed, and her mane hung straight and smooth. The day before, each horse had mud caked on her legs and knots in her mane.

"Looks like you two are old friends, Kruger."

"Been around horses all my life. They trust me."

Kruger ran the brush over the mare's hindquarters, then gave her a gentle slap. Tanner watched the younger man, as big as himself but with features he'd outgrown by the time he'd become a teenager. *Hard to look at that baby face and see the hard-nosed combat soldier he was trained to be.*

A moment after Tanner followed Kruger and the horse out of the barn, he saw Castro's van turn into the front gate. He met them in the carport. "Find anything, Lamar?"

"Yes, sir."

Lamar followed Tanner to the office, told him about Ms. Simmons and that Mr. Montgomery had retired. "They're holding the loan okay till Mr. Montgomery gets back."

"Didn't you find any money, a savings account?"

Lamar's face brightened. He told Tanner what he had found. Tanner gave Lamar a wide smile, realizing how much he'd come to like the rancher in a short time. "Anybody else see the bonds?"

"No, sir, and I didn't tell Castro, either."

"I'd say your financial worries are over, Lamar."

Tanner referred to the note sheet he had created the day before, listed several dollar amounts and said, "Here's how much you'll need to cash in and deposit into your checking account tomorrow. That'll include enough to catch up the mortgage payments, too. Congratulations, Lamar, I think you're eligible to be called a gentleman rancher."

Color drained from Lamar's face. He opened his mouth but made no sound. Tanner savored what was surely the greatest moment so far in the life of the rancher, surprised at the pleasure he found in Lamar's good fortune.

Tanner grabbed Lamar by the shoulders and gave him a hard look. "Let me tell you something. Your daddy ran this ranch better than ninety percent of the best business people I know. He left it in good shape and gave you room to live as you want to."

"Thanks, BJ. I don't know what I'd have done without you."

"You would have worked it out."

Tanner opened his briefcase, withdrew a stuffed legal-size envelope and gave it to Lamar.

"What's this?"

"Five thousand dollars cash. Should be enough to buy a used pickup."

"But I don't —"

"It's for me. Don't want to drive my car out here anymore."

"Look, BJ, if you want to save your Cadillac, use my pickup. I'll clean it up and Castro can —"

Tanner raised a hand. "You'll get over not driving to town soon, and you'll need wheels starting this afternoon. I'm not worried about my car. I just don't want anybody to know I'm connected to you or the others."

Lamar looked at the money, then cocked his head, frowning at Tanner. "I don't understand. You want to tell me what's up?"

Tanner grinned and headed for the back door. "See? Your dad and I both knew you were smart. Use what you need to buy a three- or four-year-old pickup. Register it in Sonny Kruger's name. It'll be his to keep in a few weeks. Have him drive it and follow you and Castro to the VA hospital on Monday. I'll meet you there after your group session and tell you what I'm planning to do."

"Okay, but where're you going now?"

"You've given me a great idea for a business deal. I need to go to Austin for some research. See you Monday."

▶ 15 ◀

After leaving the ranch and stopping in Ennis for gas, Tanner drove west to Waxahachie, then south on I-35. Once he was on the freeway, the cell-phone signal strengthened, and he punched numbers into his car phone. Desmond Blaylock answered.

"Des, I want to see you around three today."

"Your office, or are you coming to the lab?"

"I want you to come to my condo."

"Cool. Should I bring a date?"

"What?"

"Just kidding, BJ. What'll I need?"

"Your mainframe computer expertise. I may have a major project for you in a few days. It'll be top secret. Don't let anyone know where you're going this afternoon."

He ended the call knowing he'd left Blaylock with a head full of questions, then dialed Allie. "You have all your birds in their cages?"

"All but one, and I expect to have him in my nest in a few hours. Where are you?"

"Something's come up in Austin. I'm on the way down there, but I'll be home tomorrow afternoon."

"Aren't you the boss? Make them come up here."

"Can't. Government stuff. Can't take secret information out of the building."

"I'll miss you tonight, BJ, but I like the way you say, 'I'll be *home* tomorrow.'"

He could hear a smile in her voice and it warmed him. "The weekend will be yours, darlin'. Anything you want to do."

"Promise?"

"I promise."

She gave him an impish chuckle.

He thickened his Texas drawl. "Don't plan on doin' any work Monday, darlin'. You'll be too tired, because I'm takin' you dancin' till your feet get sore."

He ended the call laughing, thankful for her understanding. Another woman might have complained and laid a guilt trip on him, but not Allie, even though he'd have deserved it.

Tanner turned his thoughts to Des Blaylock, wondering how he'd approach the man about the high-risk plan he had in mind. Blaylock, the most enigmatic person he'd ever known, continued to surprise him at every encounter, as he had with the quip about bringing a date.

At the end of his enlistment, the young black man had been referred to Tanner by a former colleague at the Pentagon. Blaylock had an uncanny aptitude for computer systems. The man's skills were everything that Tanner could want for his mission. His only concern about Blaylock would be his striking appearance. The tall, lean man dressed as nattily as a GQ model. He would be easy to remember by any witnesses if that became an issue.

He's smart, single and often says he'll do anything for enough money. It's time to put that comment to the test.

An accident on the freeway near the Pflugerville exit delayed Tanner, and he didn't arrive at his condo until 3:10. He found Blaylock in his silver 450 SL parked in front of the building. The man climbed out and headed for the front door as Tanner drove into the garage.

"Sorry to keep you waiting, Des. Come in."

Blaylock stepped in, held the door ajar and peeked out. "Good thing you're here, BJ. Cop came by a few minutes ago. He probably would have arrested me for casing the place if he'd seen me a second time."

Tanner turned to see Blaylock grinning. "Just kidding," the man said. "What's going on, government work so technical that it can't be solved?"

Tanner smiled and shook his head. "You want a beer? Something else?"

"If something else is Johnnie Walker Black or better, I'd like that."

Tanner pulled a tray of ice and a beer from the bar fridge. He gestured toward the Scotch and told Blaylock to help himself.

"New car. Thousand-dollar suits. Black Label. Nothing but first class, Des. Do I pay you that much money?"

He gave Tanner an obviously phony look of surprise. "No, BJ. Did you call me here to offer me a raise?"

"Could be."

The sardonic expression shifted to one of genuine interest. Tanner opened his beer and took a long pull. "You always say you'll do anything for money."

Blaylock shook his head. "Anything for *enough* money."

"What's anything and how much is enough?"

The response came quick and serious. "That varies case by case. What do you have in mind?"

Tanner stepped from behind the bar and sat on the barstool next to Blaylock. He took a deep breath. This would be the first commitment. The first exposure.

"I want to hack into a mainframe."

"No problem, but I'll need more than that for an estimate."

Tanner swallowed hard. *Careful. Go slow and easy.*

"I want to get into a computer network, a big network. I want to put a virus in the network that will wreck access to every record. But I want to be able to remove the virus and restore access when I'm ready."

Blaylock nodded. "Presumably to give back the records at a later time for full recovery."

"Right."

Blaylock shook his head. "It's probably doable provided we could get network access with a mirror-image server you could fully control. It would have to be hard-wired into the network without the system manager's knowledge. That would be one hell of a trick."

"You make it sound impossible."

"Not impossible, but difficult and costly. It could take a very long time. Taking a long time increases the possible exposure."

"Can it be done?"

Blaylock shrugged. "Sure, but it's high risk, unless you want to provide a throwaway system and a very cool way of secretly getting it wired."

"What do you mean?"

Blaylock explained, asked questions for clarity, then began to draw rough diagrams on a note pad. After an hour, Tanner was convinced his scheme could work with the right computers and communications facilities. The way Blaylock laid it out, there would be virtually no risk for himself, but Tanner would have to provide a computer system that couldn't be traced back to Blaylock, and it would be abandoned after the exercise.

"Now then, BJ, tell me who you want to poison with a virus, and I'll tell you how much it'll cost for me to do it."

Blaylock took a swig of Scotch as Tanner answered. "The Internal Revenue Service."

Tanner grinned at the man's reaction. For the first time in the three years he'd known Desmond Blaylock, the unflappable young black man lost his composure, sprayed Scotch over the bar and his sleeve, and he choked on the rest.

When he stopped coughing, Blaylock said, "Jesus Christ! Don't you want to warm up on a smaller target? Like maybe the White House, or the CIA?"

Tanner laughed, the comment breaking the tension he'd felt since he began thinking of the plan days before.

Blaylock wiped Scotch spots from his sleeve. "You spent all this time to set me up for a joke?"

Tanner raised a hand and shook his head. After a moment he regained control, "Sorry, but I've never seen you 'uncool,' Des. It would have been a good joke, but I'm serious."

Blaylock sat with arms crossed, fingers drumming on his elbows. "The risk factor just took a multi-magnitude leap." He began to ask questions about what Tanner wanted to accomplish and why.

After giving him answers, Tanner said, "How much?"

The man hesitated, then leveled his stare at Tanner. "You're serious?"

"Dead serious."

"Doing it my way cuts down on the risk, but still . . ."

"How much, Des?"

"A hundred grand."

Tanner studied Blaylock's face a long moment. "Why would you be willing to do this for money, Des? Yeah, you can minimize the risk, but you're still taking a hell of a chance. If you're caught, you could be locked up for the rest of your life."

"Why do you care?"

"Always want to know what makes a man tick when he's on a mission with me. I hate surprises."

Blaylock climbed off the stool and paced the living room. Twice he started to answer but stopped. Finally he dropped on the couch.

"Truth is, I hated that racist asshole buddy of yours at the Pentagon. Those white bastards rode me like a mule. They didn't know near enough about the systems they ran. I did the work. They took the promotions. My only revenge was getting out of the Army and leaving them there to try and learn what I'd done.

"When I came to Austin, I figured I'd face the same thing at Tanner Systems. Thought you'd be like the others. But you weren't. You're the first white man who's given me a fair shake and not tried to take advantage of me."

"My God, Des, you're only twenty-five, still a kid on your first job outside the Army. You haven't known enough businessmen to pass judgment on all of us already."

"I think about my parents, living on the streets in Mississippi till they died. There's nobody left but me, so it doesn't make much difference what I do. The IRS has never done anything for me but take every dollar they could. I figure you have a good reason for this little caper, and for a hundred thousand tax-free dollars, I'm in. When do we start?"

After Blaylock left, Tanner called Cecil Ellis. "I want an emergency board meeting tomorrow."

"What's up, BJ?"

"Money."

"What about money?"

"Tomorrow, Cecil."

"Just the two of us and Mabry?"

"No, I want the others there, too."

"All five of us?"

"Yes."

Ellis probed for details, but Tanner wouldn't give any. "Shouldn't take more than a couple hours. Everybody'll go away happy."

He asked Ellis to transfer the call to Betty Wilson. After talking with her about messages and mail, he asked her to put him through to Jackie Shelton.

"Is your team still working on that network installation at Southwestern Bell?"

"No, sir. We finished that over a week ago," Jackie said. "Nothing left there but a little follow-up work."

"So you still have access to their switching center?"

"Sure. We'll be monitoring the new equipment another month or so."

Tanner took a deep breath. "Jackie, stop by my condo on your way home. Leave now if you can get away."

"Should, uh . . . should I bring anything?"

"No, I just have a few questions about the phone company project. Don't say where you're going. It'll be off the record, okay?"

When Shelton arrived, Tanner gave him a beer and steered him to the living room couch. "How's your son?"

"Hangin' in there. We sure appreciate the money you gave toward his transplant, BJ."

"Forget it. When's the surgery?"

Shelton shrugged. "We're a long way from having enough to cover it. Damnedest thing, you know? If we didn't have any assets, the surgery wouldn't cost him a penny. He could go in soon as there's a donor match."

Tanner lowered his gaze, unable to look at Jackie, knowing what he was about to do would be pressing an advantage. Worse, he feared his friend and favored employee might not accept the opportunity.

"I need a favor, but you may not want to do it. If you don't, just say so and that's the end of it. No problem."

"What do you need?"

"A couple of unlisted phone numbers and addresses from phone company records."

Shelton smiled. "No big deal. Monday soon enough?"

"Yeah. There's something else I'd like, too, maybe in another couple of weeks. I'll tell you now so you can decide if you'll do it."

Shelton paled as Tanner explained what he wanted done. Finally, he leaned forward, shaking his head. "I don't know, BJ. That's . . . damn! That could be real dangerous."

"Danger for me is okay, Jackie. Is there any way they'd be able to find out you'd done the cable assignment?"

Shelton mulled the thought a moment, then shook his head. "No, there'd be no log for the maintenance terminal. Only way they could know would be if someone watched me and read the screen while I was on the computer doing the assignment."

"Is that likely to happen?"

"No way. I usually drop in after hours so I don't bother anybody. Sometimes they don't even know when I've been there if I go into the building when an employee keys the door for both of us." He took a breath and sighed. "I can do what you want, BJ, but I sure hate to. You'd be playing with fire. If they catch you, they could put you away for years."

Tanner rose and walked to the bar, giving Shelton's shoulder a squeeze as he passed.

After it's over, you'll never see me again anyhow, little buddy.

► 16 ◄

Friday morning, when Tanner stepped out of his car in the office parking lot, he found the air surprisingly warm under a clear sky. The ever-present breeze had abated, leaving an uncommon stillness for the first week of March. The thought of a new month heightened the urgency of what he would accomplish today. Every day. There wouldn't be many more days. Maybe not enough.

Inside, Betty Wilson stood in front of his office door like a sentry, blocking his way. "Mornin', Wilson. You keeping the company running all right?"

"BJ Tanner, you didn't tell me there was a board meeting this morning! How the hell am I supposed to —"

Tanner raised his hands. "Whoa. It's an emergency meeting. Didn't call it till last night."

He started to move around her, but she didn't budge. "Cecil knew about it before he left here yesterday. You've never done this to me before. Don't let it happen again."

Tanner grinned, put a hand on her arm and spoke softly. "I'm sorry, Wilson. It'll never happen again. Now, will you join me in my office . . . please?"

She took a deep breath, closed her eyes, then whispered. "Yes sir, as soon as I get coffee for us."

He watched her walk to the coffee bar and noticed the caterer's cart covered with a linen cloth. He knew that every board member's favorite pastry and juice would be served, and the boardroom would be perfectly equipped for the meeting, in spite of the fact that he hadn't let her know about it directly.

Betty returned to his office with coffee, and Ellis right behind her. Before Ellis could speak, Betty said, "What documents do you need? And how long will you be meeting?"

"No documents. No projector. Nothing. We should be done in an hour."

Tanner smiled as she gave him a look that said, "I've heard that before," then she left.

Ellis pulled a chair close to the desk. "Mabry and Bonner will be here. Don't know about Michael Phillips. I left messages with his secretary. What's going on, BJ?"

"There's nothing you can do in advance, Cecil, so let's wait. I want to go through this only once."

"What if Phillips isn't here?"

"You and Mabry can fill him in later."

Tanner entered the boardroom at 9:30 sharp. The other four board members were present. Dave Bonner, executive vice president of Knoll State Bank, sat next to Tom Mabry, president of the bank. Bonner sipped orange juice, and each time he put the glass down he carefully centered it on the coaster.

Mabry, a lean, ruddy-faced man with electric blue eyes and curly hair the color of rust, was Tanner's oldest friend and associate in Austin. He had arranged the start-up money for Tanner Systems.

As Tanner approached the table, Mabry grabbed his hand and gave it a good shake. "Where you been, ole son? I haven't seen you around for a while."

"I ran into a friend in Dallas."

"Does he treat you as good as your old friends here?"

Tanner chuckled. "No, *she* treats me a lot better."

Mabry slapped him on the back. After a similar exchange with Phillips, Tanner sat at the head of the table and started the meeting.

"I have three items to cover. First, I want to borrow two million cash from the company, secured with my stock."

Phillips froze, suspending his cup motionless halfway to his lips. Bonner put his glass down, missing the coaster, and looked at Mabry, who broke the silence.

"Why from the company, BJ? Why not the bank? And what are you gonna do with that much cash anyway?"

"The second thing is, I want to sell the company to the employees by way of a leveraged buyout."

Bonner said, "No, you can't do that!" Mabry touched Bonner's arm to quiet him.

Cecil blanched and appeared to try to speak, but no words came out.

Phillips looked at each of the other board members like a poker player reading their reactions. Mabry leaned forward, all signs of humor gone. "What's up, BJ?"

"You know about the tax situation, how we've paid extortion money to the IRS. You know Watkins represents somebody who wants to buy the company. We don't know who his client is, but he heard about our tax problem before we did. I don't like that. Nobody's leaked *this* plan to him because right now is the first time it's been said out loud."

Bonner began writing in his notebook. A moment later he removed a financial calculator from his briefcase, rapidly punched in numbers and noted the computations.

Ellis, still clearly stunned and speechless, shook his head.

Phillips said, "What kind of deal are you talking for the employees?"

"I take two mil and turn over enough of my preferred stock to the company to pay that plus interest. We vote a ten percent salary increase across the board for all employees, then apply the increase to pay for the stock. Nobody's allowed to sell their stock outside the company. Anybody who resigns or gets fired is required to sell it back at fair market value when they leave."

"No, you really don't want to do that," Bonner said.

"Why not?"

Mabry said, "You're crazy, BJ. That kind of deal would cost you personally well over a million bucks. More than that in another year, after the DOD contract starts paying off."

Tanner studied his reflection in the freshly polished table top and wondered how late Betty had worked to get the room ready. Then he looked up at Mabry. "It'll be worth it to me to know who owns my company, to be sure everybody who wants to can stay. My gut tells me I don't want Watkins's client — whoever the hell it is — to take over."

Ellis stood and paced the opposite end of the room. Tanner thought he knew his financial officer's concern. "Cecil, you don't have a worry. There won't be any downsizing, you'll get more stock, and the DOD contract is the first of many contracts to come."

Mabry put a hand on Tanner's arm. "You want to tell the rest of us why you're willing to give up a small fortune?"

Tanner gazed at Mabry a moment, then scanned the other faces at the table. "I'm not gonna be here next year."

"With two million cash in your pocket, that wouldn't surprise me. What're your plans?"

Tanner shook his head. "The friend I met in Dallas? I ran into her at the VA hospital while they were running tests on me. I'm not gonna be anywhere next year."

"Sweet Jesus," Mabry whispered. "Cancer again?"

Tanner nodded. "Found it too late this time."

Phillips said, "I can understand your motives now, but giving the company to the employees would hardly be fair to your heirs."

"Come on, Phil. You know I don't have any heirs. Now, as the board, tell me, is there any reason — aside from my personal loss — why we shouldn't do this deal?"

Phillips and Mabry looked at each other, shrugged, then shook their heads.

Bonner waved a hand over the notes he'd made. "BJ, this doesn't make good business sense." He looked at Mabry and said, "Sorry, Tom, I have to vote against this."

Tanner figured that Bonner must be responding to sentiment and not thinking rationally. *He'll get over it and see that I'm doing the right thing.*

"Anybody want to put my plans in the form of a motion?"

After a moment Mabry said, "So moved."

Mabry looked at Bonner, who always seconded his motions, but the gaunt little man said nothing.

Tanner said, "Mr. Bonner, do I hear a second?"

In spite of Bonner's declaration earlier, he spoke in a near whisper under Mabry's glare. "So moved."

The vote was unanimous.

Phillips nodded. "That avoids conflict due to your personal-gain potential." He began to make notes, recording the information, and agreed to have formal documents prepared by early afternoon. "You said you had three things, BJ?"

"Right. I want you and Tom and Cecil to be the selection committee to find a replacement for me as CEO."

Phillips and Mabry gave subdued acceptances. Ellis stared at Tanner.

Mabry said, "When do you want the money?"

"Monday. Deposit it in my personal account."

"Why the hurry?"

"I don't have much time to spend it."

▶ 17 ◀

Before ending the board meeting, Tanner swore them all to secrecy about his condition. As Mabry and Phillips left, they made awkward attempts at saying consoling words to Tanner. Bonner had already gone.

Ellis closed the door after them and turned to Tanner. "BJ, are you sure you want to do this? We haven't discussed your plans at all before today. There may be other alternatives."

Tanner put a hand on Ellis's shoulder, gently moved him aside and reached for the door handle. "Get used to the idea that I'm not gonna be around much longer. When you get past the emotional part, you'll know this is the right thing to do."

"I really don't understand."

Tanner let go of the door and turned to face him. "Understand what, Cecil? That I'm dying? That this company is all the family I have?" *Except for Allie.*

He waved an arm toward the door. "Anything I leave behind I want to go to the people in this company. They've all worked hard to get it for me. You too."

Back in his office, Tanner moved behind his desk. "I thought you'd understand that. I've had some good years with Tanner Systems, but my watch has ended. Now you have to help keep the company on track.

"Look, why don't you take the rest of the day off. Make it a long weekend. Monday things will look better to you."

Tanner left before Ellis could say anything more, stopped to tell Betty he'd be back to sign the board secretary's notes in the afternoon, then he left the building.

The March breeze had picked up and chilled the air, but the sun warmed the inside of the Cadillac. Tanner drove to I-35, then south past the Capitol and exited to the east. He stopped half a block from a long, single-story, limestone-faced office building standing alone, surrounded by parking areas on three sides. Cement steps led to a door flanked by a long, two-segment wheelchair ramp to the right. A guard sat behind a desk in the glass-walled lobby.

There were no signs identifying the occupants, but Tanner knew it was the district office of the Internal Revenue Service. Patricia Karney and Theron Palmero worked somewhere inside that building. The thought of them caused Tanner's chest to tighten as he remembered their confrontation. He drove into the parking lot on the left side and slowly circled the building clockwise. He found one emergency exit on each side and a commercial loading door at the back of the facility, but he couldn't figure out where the main computers would be.

A car entered the parking lot as Tanner approached the exit. He ducked, pretending to inspect something on the passenger seat to avoid anyone seeing his face. That plan ended badly when Tanner heard a knock on the driver's window. A man about Tanner's age carrying a briefcase stood waiting for him to open the window. "Can I help you?"

Tanner considered gunning the car and leaving without comment but thought better of it. "I'm looking for a law office, but I don't think this is it."

"This is the IRS."

"Oh, are you an IRS agent?"

"No, sir. I'm with the FBI."

"You have offices in there, too?"

"No, I just happen to be working on a project. Sorry I don't know the area better so I could help you."

"Thanks," Tanner said. "I have a phone in the car. I'll know where it is in just a minute."

He drove off the lot and headed toward the freeway, wondering what project the FBI was working on and how long they would be there.

Tanner's next stop was a cellular phone store where he purchased six portable units. While a technician activated them, the clerk let Tanner make a call on the store phone. When Blaylock answered, Tanner said, "Want to slip out for an early lunch?"

"Sure."

"Meet me at Chuck's Café. Half hour."

The clerk thanked Tanner as she handed over the new phones, each tagged with its network number. When Tanner reached the café, he noted the number of one phone and took it with him after locking the others in the trunk.

Blaylock had already arrived and taken a table isolated from other customers. He scanned the room as Tanner sat down and slid the phone and accessory case across the table. "There's a number programmed in autodial. That's the only phone you're to use to call me."

Blaylock nodded. "So we have a deal then? You really want to go ahead with this . . . project?"

"Look around for someplace where we can rent space for a couple months. Make me a detailed list of exactly what kind of computer and peripherals you'll need. I'll let you know when I've rented the space and have the equipment."

"I can do all of that, BJ."

Tanner shook his head. "No way. Nobody connects you to anything that'll be used. Only to me. I don't even want anybody to see you coming and going once we're set up." He pointed a finger in Blaylock's face. "And I don't ever want you inside the place without gloves on. Don't leave a trace. Even though the equipment will be removed within two days after we finish."

Blaylock raised both hands in surrender.

Tanner waited for a busboy to pour water and leave before he continued. "I'll have your money in a numbered account in the Bahamas next week. You'll get the account ID number as soon as the computers are linked and we've run your program."

A waitress approached and asked for their order. Tanner rose and dropped money on the table. "You go ahead, Des. I can't stay. Call me when you have a possible location and shopping list."

Tanner left the freeway in Waxahachie at 5:30 p.m. The sun had already slipped out of sight, leaving an orange halo in the west. He stopped at a Shell station, filled up, bought a drink at the mini-mart, then called the ranch from a pay phone. Lamar answered on the fourth ring.

"You get some bonds out of the safe deposit box?"

"Yes, sir, made a deposit to checking, paid the mortgage, mailed some payments for other bills. Everything's caught up with the money issues. Castro and I made a raid on Wal-Mart, so the pantry's full of food. Rest of the money's in the bank."

"How about the used truck?"

"A Ford F-150, and it's in real good shape. Castro's a wheeler-dealer. You even get some change back."

"Are you boys going out tonight?"

A long pause. "Hadn't thought about it. May let Sonny go to Dallas and see his kinfolk, but I don't think Ernie's ready for a night out yet. Maybe next weekend."

Tanner nodded. "Have Kruger drive the new pickup to the VA Monday morning, find my Cadillac and park close by. Leave the keys in the truck. I'll be in my car watching for him. All of you head straight back to the ranch in Castro's van as soon as your session's over. I'll brief you on my plans, then I want Castro and Kruger to take an overnight recon trip."

He paused, then said, "One more thing. Tell Doc Maroun I've finished working with you on the ranch. That won't be a lie. I'll only be looking over your shoulder once in a while when you work on the books."

"What'll you really be doin', BJ?"

"Maybe nothing. You might run me off when I tell you what I want to do. But if you hang in there, it'll be the damnedest thing you ever dreamed of. I'll fill you in Monday."

▶ **18** ◀

Friday evening Tanner opened the kitchen door when he heard Allie drive into the garage. He watched her climb out of the car, looking spent following her twelve-hour shift, yet her face brightened when she saw him, as if she were actually gaining energy.

"Happy to have a long week behind you, darlin'?"

She pointed a finger at him. "You better not have anything to do for two days but let me spoil you."

"How about I take you out for a light dinner, then we'll go to bed early. Tomorrow we can do anything you like, as long as we go dancing after dinner."

She bounded up the two steps, kissed him and gently stepped on his foot. "Don't you remember what it's like to dance with me?"

"We only tried once or twice. A little practice will make it right, then I plan to show you off at the high-class dance halls every weekend from now on."

She put her purse and handgun on the kitchen counter and removed her coat as she headed down the hall. Tanner studied the gun for a moment.

"You in a hurry for dinner?" she asked.

He watched her walk away and wondered if his eyes deceived him, or if she'd actually gained weight, rounding out some of the sharp angles on her body. "No, I'm in no hurry. Why?"

She gave him an impish smile from the bedroom door. "I need a shower before I go anywhere. Want to join me?"

Saturday morning Tanner and Allie toured Dallas as if they'd never seen the city. After a breakfast of cinnamon French toast and crisp bacon, they went to the Museum of Art. Allie had read about Oldenburg's gigantic soft sculptures of everyday objects, like hamburgers and ice cream cones. They enjoyed the amusing art, but Allie was taken by another exhibit featuring three of Rodin's sculptures of Rose Beuret. After reading about Rodin and his lover, she couldn't pull herself away from the images. The artist had so beautifully captured the elegance, indeed the soul, of his lifelong companion and model. Allie wiped away tears. "BJ, I wish you and I had spent as many years together and knew each other as well as they did."

Later they walked the shops of the trendy West End. Tanner gave a street musician five dollars for his efforts on a guitar and blues harp. The man made an abrupt change from a slow blues number to an upbeat song they didn't recognize, but it pleased the spectators and drew more bills and coins to his instrument case.

After driving to Las Colinas, where Tanner examined up close for the first time the lifelike images of the bronze running mustangs, they toured North Dallas and the SMU campus. By late afternoon they'd decided where to go for dinner and dancing, but instead of going home, Tanner turned west off the highway and crossed the downtown area.

"Where are we going?" Allie asked.

A few minutes later, they sat in the bar atop Reunion Tower sipping iced tea and watching the sunset. Tanner scanned the vista, shaking his head. "Look out there, Allie. You can honest to God see the curvature of the Earth."

She held his hand while gazing toward the setting sun, distorted by transparent heat waves along the Earth's surface as it enlarged and drifted below the horizon. Her smile reflected a peacefulness Tanner hadn't seen in her until that moment, and there was something else, something different about her. When he reached for his drink and bumped the ashtray, he realized what had changed. "You haven't had a cigarette all day!"

"I haven't had a cigarette since Tuesday, and I gained three pounds not counting what I've eaten today. See what kind of influence you have over me?"

He rocked the table, almost spilling their drinks when he leaned across to kiss her.

After going home to freshen up, they started the evening with dinner at Del Frisco's. Following heaps of salad, Allie had a petite filet while Tanner attacked a medium-well-done sirloin half the size of a Stetson. Later, they were surprised when the last dance was called at Peach's, both still eager to keep going. Tanner felt exhausted, but he said nothing to Allie. He held her close during the slow dance. "I don't remember the last time I had so much fun," he said.

"Last time for me was on the beach in Nha Trang, dancing barefoot in the sand. Course you were doing the dancing, holding me a foot off the ground so I wouldn't step on you."

He gave her a gentle slap on the butt. "Stop complaining about your dancing. You haven't stepped on me once tonight."

Sunday morning came late. They slept until 9 o'clock, then had Spanish omelets for brunch at the Mansion on Turtle Creek. After that they drove to Fort Worth to visit the stores in the Stockyards area. Tanner hadn't been there since his high school days.

His thoughts drifted to some of the veterans at the medical center when he saw a man with a right-arm prosthesis working in a saddlery shop. The craftsman, surrounded by handmade saddlebags, bridles, women's purses, belts, and a silver-studded saddle, worked on a beautifully tooled leather briefcase. How many men with physical and mental handicaps, Tanner wondered, could become as skilled and productive as this man if given the chance to learn?

Later, back in Dallas they went for a walk along the shores of White Rock Lake. Cloud cover drifted from the north and hid the sun. A fresh breeze brought colder temperatures and caused them to hurry back to the car. At home, Tanner built a fire while Allie made hot cocoa. She piled a mound of pillows on the floor, and they cuddled there, watching the flames while listening to an ancient tape of *Percy Faith's Greatest Hits*, a reminder of their time together in what seemed another lifetime. Later, when the tape ended, they made their own music in the warm silence between them, no longer desperate for each other, but eager, wanting to capture as much as they could of the life they'd missed together.

▶ **19** ◀

Monday morning a chilly wind howled across the VA parking lot in the early light. Tanner parked the Cadillac in the second row of cars on the north side. He and Allie walked to the door. Once inside, he gave her the key to his car.

"You sure?"

He nodded. "We need to trade in that old clunker of yours."

"That fancy Cadillac may be a target for thieves around here."

"It has an alarm and it's insured. Don't worry about it." He grabbed her arm, leaned close and lowered his voice. "And for God's sake, don't get in a damn shootout over the car. If anybody tries to take it, let 'em have it."

"Who's giving you a truck to use?"

"A man I'm gonna be working with for a few weeks. He's a rancher."

He kissed her good-bye and watched her head for the elevator, then he hurried through the tunnel to the main entrance to watch for Kruger.

Minutes later Sonny drove the white F-150 into a parking space, left the truck and walked toward the entrance to the old building. Tanner waited inside the main lobby until Sonny reached the far door. When he was out of sight, Tanner went to the truck and drove away from the hospital, going east toward the freeway. He stopped at a convenience store where he had arranged to meet Lamar and Castro. They didn't arrive for a half hour, much later than he expected, but he immediately knew why they were late. Lamar was at the wheel. Tanner smiled as the van pulled beside him.

"Lamar, did you drive all the way here in morning traffic?"

"Yes, sir, and it was a bitch."

Castro laughed, shaking his head. "He had me worried a couple of times, BJ. He's right, it was a bitch, but he did better than some others out there. He didn't bust any heads or get arrested."

Lamar cuffed him gently and Castro laughed harder. Tanner nodded approval and said, "Good work, Lamar. I'll see you at the ranch this afternoon."

By the time he reached Ennis, Tanner had become familiar with the pickup, accustomed to the engine and road noise that he never experienced in his Cadillac. After stopping at an office supply store, he went to the ranch and let himself into the house in spite of protesting barks from Ike. He set up a marker board in the kitchen, propped on a stool so he could see it from the table. He outlined events, made action lists for each man and prayed that all of them would want to participate.

Ike followed Tanner when he walked to the corral, where the horses eyed him, checking for handouts of meal cakes or apples. When he offered nothing, Honey snorted and both horses meandered away, heads down, looking for clumps of grass. He stood leaning against the fence, wondering where to find another person with the one skill missing from his plan. Abruptly Ike whined and took off for the front gate. Lamar and the others were back from the VA.

When Tanner met them in the carport, Castro said, "Lamar tells me you want us to do some recon."

"Only after you know what I have in mind. You may not want to do it. If you don't, it's okay. You still have a job with Lamar for the next six months."

He watched as they entered the kitchen and saw the cell phones on the table and the marker board against the wall. Each man removed his jacket while staring at the board.

Tanner said, "Before we talk about these plans, I'm gonna tell you about my health, then I'll explain how the Internal Revenue Service literally robbed me and my company. That'll make it easier to understand why I want to take money from the United States government. I prefer to think of it as a refund with interest and penalties."

Two hours later, Tanner had reviewed every detail and answered all their questions. Lamar had been quiet, asking only a few questions. Tanner read his expression as one of concern and disappointment. He put down the marker pen he'd used on the white board. "That's it. Comments? Suggestions?"

Castro tipped his chair back and flashed a big grin. "Damn if you don't surprise me every time you open your mouth, BJ. An hour ago I thought you'd lost your mind. You'd have to be crazy to try this. Now . . ." He pointed to the lower right corner of the marker board. "I think it'll work after we fix those three things. Me an' Sonny can take care of the first one tomorrow."

Tanner took a seat across the table from Castro. "You want more time to think about it?"

Castro shook his head. "Nobody ever looked out for me as much as you have already, and this thing hasn't even started. I'm in."

"What about you, Lamar?"

The rancher dropped his gaze to the table. "You have this great big plan, and only want me to help out for about ten minutes at the end. Don't you think I'm able to do some of the other things, too?"

Tanner felt relieved that Lamar's disappointment was not with the plan itself.

"Damn right you are, Lamar, but you have too much at stake to be involved along the way. If you were caught, you could lose your ranch."

"What about you, BJ? Big company. Lots of money. You're risking everything. If it wasn't for you, I might have lost this place anyway, so why shouldn't I be with you all the way?"

Tanner shook his head. "Lamar, I need a place where we can work together without having eyes on us. That's what you do for me now. Your biggest job starts after we get through with the IRS and have the money."

Lamar gestured to the board. "You mean —"

"No. We haven't talked about what I want you to do after we leave Austin. It'll be legal. Plenty of time to talk about that later."

Lamar shrugged. "Looks like you have it planned right down to spare shoelaces. I don't feel like I'm doin' my fair share, but if that's the way you want it . . ."

Tanner shook his head. "Lamar, you have no idea how important you'll be in the future. We have to get this part done first." Turning to Kruger, he said, "Sonny?"

"I'm thinking about the helicopter pilot."

Tanner groaned inwardly. "That's the missing key. I don't know yet where to find somebody for that part of the team."

"I might," Kruger said, "if you don't mind having a woman do it."

"Oh, no," Castro said. "I ain't ready for some old girlfriend to jump in here, get scared and run to the FBI. Forget it."

"She's not an old girlfriend. Nothing scares her, and the last thing she'd do is run to the feds."

"Who do you have in mind?" Tanner asked.

"My big sister, Becky. Used to fly Hueys in the Army."

"Where is she now?"

"Works on one of those mega ranches in Wyoming. Place where they herd cows with helos. She's a flying ranch hand. Loves to fly but hates her job."

"What makes you think she'd be willing to work with us?"

"Because of what the Army did to her. She'd jump on this job in a rodeo second."

"How do we get her here so I can talk to her?"

"Send her an airline ticket."

► 20 ◄

A light rain fell on Austin Monday evening as Kruger pointed out the freeway exit to Castro, and they turned east. Kruger sketched a rough map showing the street intersections and buildings in the area as they drove, and he asked Castro to note the distance from the freeway to the building that housed the IRS.

They turned into the parking lot and circled the building. Most of the lights were still on, but only a handful of people could be seen inside. "Six-thirty. Looks like nobody's in there but the cleaning crew," Castro said.

Castro drove slowly around the building while Kruger examined the exit doors and scanned the windows through binoculars. As they returned to the street, Kruger said, "Looks like the computers are on the right side in the back half of the building. I'll go inside tomorrow. Find out for sure."

"How you gonna do that?"

"As a volunteer."

Castro squinted at him and Kruger laughed. "I'll show you what I mean tomorrow. Let's find a motel."

"You really want to get a room here? We're only an hour away from San Antonio. I know some foxy little Latinas there that'd singe that curly blond hair of yours. We can party till it's time to come back in the morning."

Kruger shook his head. "First the mission, then the party."

Castro bunched his fingertips and kissed them. "Hey, gringo, you ain't lived till you've had a hot-blooded Tex-Mex work you over. Only an hour away."

Kruger gave Castro a hard look. "Ernie, you're working on the best deal that ever came your way. Don't even think about doing something tonight that would screw it up."

"I didn't say I wanted to get wasted, *blanco*, just played and laid."

Kruger gestured at a freeway sign ahead. "Take the airport exit. There'll be motels around there."

Tuesday morning Kruger woke with the dawn, climbed out of bed and pulled on sweats and running shoes. After a few stretches, he left the room and ran for an hour in the light drizzle that continued to dampen Austin.

Castro was up when he returned. After Kruger showered and dressed, they had breakfast, then drove back to the IRS building. Only a few cars were in the parking lot. Kruger passed the building and parked across the street half a block away. Castro said, "One guard in the lobby."

Kruger nodded while making notes. "Looked to be in his late fifties. Overweight. Left-handed. Carried a revolver. He's no problem."

"Jesus, gringo, how'd you see all that?"

Kruger shrugged. "I wasn't driving."

During the next hour they counted over one hundred people entering the building through the front door. By 8:30 the parking lot had filled. Sitting in the back of the van using binoculars, Kruger could see that everyone either presented an ID badge to the guard or signed a visitor log and waited for an escort.

A few minutes after 9:00, a delivery truck drove to the rear of the building and backed up to the commercial door. "Let's go to the back parking lot," Kruger said.

A minute later they'd parked where they had a view of the loading door. When the delivery driver came out of the building, Kruger said, "I can't see a guard, but there has to be one inside that door."

"How are we gonna get in there?"

"We'll wait for the right ticket."

Castro dozed after an hour or so, head back and mouth open, exposing a gold-crowned upper molar, but Kruger stayed alert, keeping notes on every delivery: type of truck, company name, how long they were parked. At 10:40, a truck backed up to the door, and its driver, a slight man in his mid-forties with slicked-down black hair, climbed out of the cab, heaved a sigh and headed for the rear of the truck. Blue-and-gray lettering on the side panel read, "Computer Supply Corp." Kruger dropped his notebook in Castro's lap. "That could be my ticket."

Castro sat up as Kruger opened the door. "Where're you going?"

"That driver looks like he needs help."

He ran to the far side of the delivery truck, waited till he heard the driver inside the cargo area, then stepped behind the tailgate. "How's it going?"

The driver didn't turn but kept stacking boxes on a handcart. "All right."

"Want some help?"

The delivery man turned to eye Kruger. A name patch over his breast pocket read "Angelo." Kruger shrugged. "They hired me for the day to help with a big load of something that hasn't showed up yet. I figure as long as they're paying me I might as well do something."

Angelo gestured to the boxes on the cart. "Twenty-four of these to take to the computer room."

"Got another handcart?"

Angelo rolled the full one onto the power-lift tailgate. "Sure do. Usually have a man to help when I come out here, but he's out sick today."

Kruger climbed aboard the truck and helped load the second cart, then rode the tailgate down and followed the driver inside the building. A gray-haired guard in his early sixties sat at a desk in the hallway facing the delivery door. He read a *Sports Illustrated* magazine and showed little interest in the visitors. Angelo said, "Twenty-four boxes for the computer room."

The guard glanced their way, nodded and went back to his magazine. Kruger followed the other man down a long hallway that ran the length of the building. A sign on the first door they passed read "INFO SYSTEMS." Ten yards farther along they went through a door marked "ISO SUPPLIES."

Kruger squatted and retied his running shoe, hiding his face from the attendant. Angelo put a clipboard on the counter and asked for a signature. Kruger made a fast exit while the woman read the order. He rolled his empty cart into the hallway. "I'll get started with the other boxes," he said over his shoulder.

He stopped at the door they'd passed and looked through the square safety window into the computer room. Eight blue cabinets sat along the left wall. A dozen disk drives and printer stations sat across from them. The cabinet at the far end was open, and two technicians peered inside. One of them, a heavyset man with thick glasses, held a finger on a chart and pointed to cables tied into the cabinet. The other tech, a slight woman who appeared to be in her early twenties, probed a terminal with a screwdriver. A third man with his back to the door sat at one of the three desks along the right wall.

Across the hall from the computer room Kruger saw a door labeled "Tel. Equip." He propped his handcart against the wall, tested the door handle and found the door unlocked. He took a quick look inside, noted that one set of distribution blocks was labeled "Phones," and the other "Data Circuits." He closed the door and raced toward the delivery door when he heard the driver's handcart rattle into the hall.

Back in the truck, while they loaded more boxes, Kruger asked, "All this stuff computer supplies?"

Angelo laughed. "These boxes are full of form paper. A lot of it'll be turned into tax bills and scare hell out of the people they goes to."

When they took the second load of cartons into the building, Kruger stopped near the guard's desk and shuffled the boxes as if they weren't properly stacked. While rearranging them, he examined the area around the desk, looking for wires, buttons, anything that might indicate an alarm system, but he saw only a single-line telephone.

He followed the same procedure as before, leaving the supply room ahead of the driver. This time he stopped to talk with the guard on the way out.

"Always this quiet around here?"

The guard snorted a laugh. "Nothing ever happens around here except up at the front desk. Now and then some tax cheat comes in crying because the IRS has stripped his bank account."

"Does that happen often?"

"Only once while I been on duty up there. Most exciting thing ever happened back here was when a dog ran inside while the delivery door was open. Thought I'd never get that mutt out of here."

Angelo rolled his cart into the hallway. Kruger said, "Better go for another load before the boss gets here."

Inside the truck, he put four more boxes on the cart, then tore a packing slip off one box and shoved it into his pocket.

After delivering the boxes, Kruger walked up the hallway toward the front of the building, pushing the empty handcart and looking through the small safety windows into the office areas. He could see nothing but a few heads above freestanding, cloth-sided partitions.

Two women entered the hall and walked toward him, but neither paid him any attention. He'd gone over halfway to the front when a large blond woman confronted him. "Where's your badge?"

Kruger slapped his chest as if feeling for his ID, then turned the handcart toward the rear entrance at a faster pace than the woman could move. "Must have knocked it off in the truck." Over his shoulder he said, "Thanks for noticing, ma'am."

Outside the back door, Kruger motioned for Castro to drive to the east side of the building as he tossed the handcart into the delivery truck. He leaped into the side door of the van and closed it before Angelo came out. Castro said, "What'd you find out?"

"This place'll be about as hard to get into as a public park."

He climbed into the front seat, unfolded a street map and found a "2" he'd marked on it. "Turn north on the freeway."

Kruger gave Castro directions and checked numbers until they found the address, one of the two Tanner had been given by Jackie Shelton. The building was a condominium complex. "Park down there across the street."

Castro drove slowly past the two-story brick building's main entrance and its motorized parking garage gate. "No need to stop. I veto this one."

He gestured toward the building and Kruger saw the video cameras above each entrance.

They drove to the third and final address marked on the map. The long and narrow two-story apartment building of used brick backed up to a wooded area along a narrow creek. Between the building and the woods a carport ran the length of the structure. Kruger examined the creek area and the back of the apartments, memorizing the area. "Perfect. Damn near too good to be true."

Castro drove until he found a street on the far side of the creek. He parked across from the apartment building, and they walked into the woods, checking the ground for the best path across the area. Castro sat behind a clump of bushes and scanned the back of the apartment building through binoculars, then handed the glasses to Kruger. "Looks too easy."

Kruger nodded. "Yeah, but the way the Colonel tells it, this target's too arrogant to ever expect anything like we have in mind. Let's go back to the office."

As they drove, he wrote a name on a large manila envelope, stuffed newspaper inside and sealed it.

Twenty minutes later, Kruger stepped out of the van a block from the IRS. He waited until Castro parked across from the front entry and had time to set up. Then he jogged to the building, entered the lobby and handed the envelope to the guard. "Can you call this guy to come down for his package?"

The guard squeezed the envelope. "What is it?"

"A few thousand words of really important information. He needs to pick it up right away. He'll have to sign for it."

Kruger stood at the side of the guard station and observed the security system's two video monitors while the man checked his directory, then made a call. "This is the lobby guard. You have a package here. Man that brought it says you need it right away." After a pause he added, "Yep, he's waiting right here."

A moment after the guard ended the call, Kruger snapped his fingers. "Forgot my sign-off sheet. Be right back."

He left the package on the guard's desk, went down the steps and around the side of the building, then ran across the parking lot out of sight around the next building.

Castro kneeled in the back of his van holding Tanner's camera with a telephoto lens aimed toward the guard in the lobby. He saw Kruger race away. A minute later, a man entered the lobby from inside the building. He approached the guard and took the envelope. Castro began snapping pictures. The man towered over the guard. Castro estimated the dark-complexioned, square-faced man at six feet four or taller.

"Won't have any trouble recognizing you," he muttered while snapping pictures.

The guard gestured to the side of the building, and the big man walked toward the parking lot. After a moment he headed back to the lobby, opening the envelope as he climbed the steps. He stopped inside the door, pulled out the newspaper and looked bewildered. Then he spoke to the guard, tossed the entire package on the guard's desk and went back into the office area.

Castro climbed back into the driver's seat and headed for the corner to meet Kruger. As he passed the building, he took a last look at the lobby. "Gotcha, Palmero."

▶ 21 ◀

Tanner left the ranch at 1 o'clock Tuesday afternoon and drove the short trip to Ennis. When he neared the interstate highway, he parked the pickup near a feedstore and dug the black cell phone from his briefcase. The gray one he used to communicate with the team; the black phone he used for talking to the rest of the world.

He dialed Betty's number and she answered on the first ring. "Hello, Wilson."

"Where in the world are you?"

"On the road. What's going on?"

"Call Mr. Phillips right now. He's been looking for you since yesterday. Says it's critical. Then call me back."

He rang the attorney's private number. "What's up?"

"BJ, we have a couple of problems: Watkins and Bonner."

"Bonner?"

"He's stonewalling me. Won't hand over the information I need to finalize the union proposal. He keeps disappearing. Can't reach him when I need him."

"You talk to Mabry?"

"He's gone, too, off on another one of those mega deals he likes to get into. He hasn't been able to catch up with Bonner by phone, and no one else at the bank has the info I need."

Phillips agreed to prepare everything but the final numbers, then asked, "Have you talked to Ellis today?"

"No. He's still upset. Thinks I'm giving away too much of my assets. I'll call him. Now, what about Watkins?"

"He's filed for an injunction against the employee buyout."

"Son of a bitch! How'd the bastard find out about our plan? Nobody but the board members knew."

Phillips said, "Not true, BJ. Yesterday I sent a preliminary notice of intent to the union. It must have leaked from there."

"How can Watkins do that? He has no stake, no position, nothing but a desire to buy the company himself. Hell, he hasn't even made an offer yet."

"His strategy may be to make the water so muddy the union will back off. Claims he had a verbal agreement that you'd do no other deals until you received his written offer."

"Not true." Tanner answered Phillips's questions, then said, "I want you to form two nonprofit corporations with my money. One in Austin, the other in Dallas. Be sure there's no way the money can be traced back to me."

Phillips asked more than Tanner wanted to answer, but the attorney's questions about nonprofits were finally satisfied. Then Tanner called Betty and told her where to find more information that Phillips hadn't been able to get from Ellis. She gave him messages, and he assigned them to other people in the company. After she finished, he said, "Where's Ellis?"

"I don't know. He left the building an hour ago."

"What's his problem, Wilson?"

"It isn't my place to —"

"Bullshit. Come on, Betty. What's going on?"

She hesitated, then spoke so softly that Tanner could barely hear her over the traffic noise. "He's been on the edge ever since you left. Some of the financial reports he and Mr. Bonner prepare have slipped past their due dates. He's never let that happen before. I've covered everything I can, but . . ."

"Okay, I'll call him at home tonight and get him straightened out. You hang in there, Wilson. I'll call you tomorrow."

Tanner felt a twinge over his comment about Ellis, thinking that he should have developed a better off-the-job relationship with the little man.

Tanner used the other phone to call Castro. When he answered, Tanner said, "Where are you?"

"On the way home. Should be at HQ by sixteen hundred."

Tanner felt a letdown. "Didn't take long for you to make a decision. Sure you checked all possibilities?"

"Enough to know we have two green lights. No problem."

The response stunned Tanner. He grinned and slapped the steering wheel. "Which green lights?"

"One and three. Other one's too risky."

"Well done to both of you. Put your partner on."

Kruger's voice came over the phone. Tanner said, "Have you made your Wings contact?"

"Yes, sir. Wings'll be with us Friday p.m."

"Way to go, son. See you back at headquarters."

Friday afternoon Tanner was waiting at the ranch when Lamar and the others returned from their session with Dr. Maroun. Each man reacted to the gratifying aroma in the kitchen as they entered the back door. Tanner had purchased heaps of fried chicken, real mashed potatoes, cream gravy, biscuits, and honey from a local drive-in that the national fried chicken chain could never match.

Castro and Kruger set the table while Lamar brought the food from the oven. No one seemed bashful about helping themselves to their favorite pieces. After a few minutes of silence, except for the crunching of the fried crust, Tanner said, "Ready for your trip, Castro?"

"Soon as I put away more chicken and taters. What's the occasion for this feed?"

Tanner shrugged. "Seemed better than cold sandwiches."

Castro tore off a crispy bite, pointed the damaged chicken breast and winked. "You're one sneaky grandee, BJ. You make it hard for a man to get pissed at you."

Tanner grinned, then turned serious. "You be damned careful in Houston this weekend."

Unable to speak with his mouth full, Castro nodded as Tanner continued. "You've made your contacts?"

"Yep."

"No problem getting the goods?"

"Nope."

"You're sure these people won't try to jack up the price when you get there with the money?"

Castro shook his head. "Not a chance."

"I just don't want —"

Castro raised a hand. "BJ, I've known these guys a dozen years. Saved their *cajones* from trouble in Mexico twice. The situation's under control, *Jefe*." He spread his hands. "No problema."

Tanner spoke to Lamar. "You have the stash place ready?"

"No, but it'll be done tomorrow afternoon." He gestured toward the carport. "Stuff in the back o' my pickup's to build the silo. When I'm done, nobody will know it's there, not even the cows. We can use it a little at a time, however we want to, as long as it takes."

Kruger tapped his watch. "BJ, my sister's flight's due into DFW in an hour."

"Okay, Sonny, let's go see what kind of wings we have."

Castro said, "I don't know about that, BJ. One Kruger's more than enough, let alone another one, and she's a chick."

On the way to the door, Kruger slipped an arm around the Latino's neck and gave him a knuckle rub on the head. Tanner stuck out a hand and Castro slapped him a high five. "See you Monday, Ernie. Safe trip."

They arrived inside the terminal in time to see on the status board that the connecting flight from Casper, Wyoming, had landed. Tanner followed Kruger to the gate and watched the 737 taxi into position. Five minutes later, the first passenger came out of the jetway, a tall blond in her early thirties, wearing a gray Stetson, pale-blue western shirt, jeans, and cordovan boots.

Her movements seemed like those of a rodeo rider, but when she spotted Sonny, her searching face was transformed by a radiant smile that seemed to soften everything about her. She dropped her shoulder bag and hugged her brother.

After a moment, Sonny pushed her to arm's length, then turned to Tanner. "BJ, this is my big sister, Becky."

She stuck out a hand that wasn't as big as Sonny's but bigger than any woman's hand he'd ever been offered. She stood at Tanner's height in her western boots, making him consciously stand as tall as he could.

Sonny took her bag, and she slipped on her western-style leather jacket as they headed for the exit. Tanner led the way to the parking lot, then drove the pickup while Becky and Sonny caught up on family gossip. A half hour later, they checked her into the Embassy Suites on Route 183 between DFW and Texas Stadium.

Tanner sat at an isolated table in the lobby bar sipping Jack Daniel's. As the Krugers walked to the bar and picked up beers, he noticed that Becky stood at least two inches taller than Sonny even though he, too, wore boots. She wasn't as wide through the shoulders, but bigger than Tanner would expect in a woman. They both had narrow waists, but the shape of her jeans left no doubt that she was all female. She'd left the hat in her room, and as the two of them approached he could see that, barring the few years difference in their ages, they looked enough alike to be twins. The greatest difference Tanner could see was that Becky's eyes were lighter blue than her brother's.

"Your room okay, Becky?"

She dropped into a chair, propped a foot on the one next to her and held the beer in her lap. "Beats anything around the Bighorn Mountains."

She took a pull on the beer. "Are you ready to tell me why I'm here?" She pointed the longneck bottle at Sonny. "I know it isn't because he wanted to buy me a vacation."

"Sonny tells me you're a pretty good helicopter pilot."

"He better have told you that I'm a damn good helo pilot."

"What do you fly?"

"I can handle most anything. Use a Robinson to fly the range and keep an eye on the cattle. I fly the Bell Ranger for the boss when he leaves the ranch."

"How about Army Hueys?"

"That's my favorite. I got over twenty-one hundred hours in Hueys."

"Any night flying?"

"Lots of it."

"How long were you in the Army?"

"Six years."

"Why'd you get out?"

Her smile faded and she shifted in the chair. "I did something that was considered good sport for a man but conduct unbecoming for a female officer, so I resigned."

"What'd you do?"

She took a long drink of beer, then smiled. "After a night exercise at Fort Bliss we saw a freight train crossing the desert west of Carlsbad. I flew ahead to some hills, dropped the chopper down to about ten feet above the tracks and came around a curve toward the train with my landing light on. When the engineer thought he was about to have a head-on collision, he locked up the brakes. Sparks flew from every wheel on that train. Looked like a quarter-mile-long sparkler."

Her smile soured. "Stupid thing to do, but I wasn't the first one to do it, only the first woman. The male pilots got off with warnings. I lost my wings."

Tanner gave her a solemn nod. "Double standards come in all shapes and sizes in the military. Don't always have to be a woman to get nailed by 'em."

While her brother went to the bar for more drinks, Becky said, "Sonny tells me you retired from the Marines."

Tanner nodded. "I was about as happy to leave as you were. Forced disability."

He told her of the cancer that caused his retirement, but not about his current condition. "How do you like ranching in Wyoming?"

Becky shrugged. "Not my first choice of work, but I get to fly."

She gestured toward Sonny. "Rather be somewhere close to my little brother, but he hates snow, and I can't find a job around here that'll get me in the air every day."

"Shouldn't be hard to find work in Dallas."

She shook her head. "Don't just want a job, I want to fly."

"With all your hours, that shouldn't be too hard. Maybe a flight instructor. Most of the TV stations are getting news helicopters."

"Anybody that lost their wings the way I did is never gonna get a real commercial pilot job. I'll fly on that ranch till I can't fly anymore, then they can bury me."

"How long would it take you to get back into flying a Huey?"

"About as long as it'd take to strap on the seat belt."

"How long till you'd be ready to set one down on a cracker-box roof at night?"

"Soon as it gets dark."

Tanner leaned forward and lowered his voice. "Without clearance. In the middle of a city with an Air Force base five miles away?"

Becky leaned close to Tanner, eyes narrowed. "What do you have in mind?"

"Something a damn sight riskier than losing your wings playing with trains, but when it's over, you could be the number-one ranch pilot on a real nice spread close to Dallas."

Her expression told him that she had guts and had no fear about the conditions he'd mentioned. He liked her already as much as he did her brother, and he felt he could trust her without reservation.

Sonny returned and sat fresh drinks on the table. "I miss anything?"

Tanner stood and picked up his drink. "Let's take these to Becky's room. I want to tell her more about our plans."

Sonny smiled and put an arm around Becky's waist. "All *right*, Sis. This is great. Wait till you meet —"

"Not yet, Sonny. First, she has to hear enough to decide if she wants to be part of this."

Tanner sat on the couch watching Becky while she gazed out the window. Her head moved slowly as she watched a 747 cross from left to right and land at DFW. Sonny sat at the table on the far side of the room, both heels tapping anxiously.

Tanner checked his watch as the last daylight faded from the horizon. He could see only her silhouette against the window when she turned.

"No."

"What?" Sonny blurted.

The simple word hit Tanner like a fist in the stomach, but he said nothing.

"Sorry, BJ. Do you want me out of this nice room you rented?"

He sighed heavily and climbed to his feet. "No, Becky. It's yours for the weekend. You two have a good time."

He tossed the pickup keys to Sonny. "I'll grab a taxi home."

Becky said, "Is that it then?"

"That's it."

"You aren't gonna try to convince me to work with you? Even though you know I'm the best person for the job?"

"Hell yes, you're the best person for the job," Sonny said. "I can't believe you don't want to do this."

Tanner shook his head. "Like I said, this is strictly a volunteer mission. All I ask is that you keep to yourself what we've talked about here."

"What'll you do for a pilot?"

"Keep looking until I find someone qualified that will join us."

"And if you don't find one?"

"That isn't your concern."

"Sure it is. My brother's involved."

Tanner felt nausea boiling as he reached for his coat. "If we don't get the right team, we scrub the mission. I won't go to a different plan and increase risk for anyone."

He started to slip the coat on, but she stopped him. "Look, BJ, you're probably gonna think worse of me than you do now, but I had to know if you'd twist my arm to join in on this 'project,' as you call it. I wanted to be sure my little brother hadn't been forced in either. If I haven't pissed you off too bad with my little game, I'm your pilot."

"Yee-ha!" Sonny hooted.

Tanner's heart pounded and he couldn't hold back a grin. He stuck out his hand. "Don't think I'd want to play poker with you, Becky, but I sure like your style. Welcome aboard."

▶ 22 ◀

Saturday morning they took the Cadillac through a car wash, then drove southeast of Dallas, around the back roads of Kaufman County and along Cedar Creek Lake. A strong breeze caused whitecaps to break and spray mist across the gray-green water. Along the east side of the lake they found a little café near Gun Barrel City that served fresh catfish, vinegary coleslaw and home fries. The owner, a huge woman in her sixties who called herself Mattie, made her own version of tartar sauce that included an eye-watering dose of horseradish.

Tanner and Allie laughed at each other, tears rolling every time they took too big a bite of the sauce. Mattie gave each of them an extra yeast roll to sponge the burning tartar from their palates. They both said no to Mattie's coconut cream pie, but she ignored their objections, delivered two large slices, and they ate every bite.

Later, while they walked hand in hand along the lakeshore, bundled against the chilly wind, Allie said, "I'd love to live out here."

"On the lake?"

"In the country, away from the craziness in town."

"There're hospitals in some of these small towns that'd hold community celebrations if they could hire a nurse with your experience."

She shook her head. "Couldn't leave the VA. I like working with the vets. They need people who really care about them."

"Too bad you can't take them to the country, too."

"Sure would be a good way to get 'em off the streets. Away from booze and drugs."

"How do you deal with their problems all day, then go live your own life?"

She locked her arm around his and pressed against him. "Didn't have a life till you showed up. I quit drinking because the VA was going to can me if I didn't. I quit smoking, too. You know how long it's been since I had a cigarette?"

"How are you doing without them?"

"Like I was without the booze at first. Some days are worse than others. Couldn't do it without you here to help me." She patted her stomach. "I'm gaining weight, too."

"I noticed, but that's not where it's going. Damn near thought you were a boy first time I saw you at the hospital. I don't have to worry about making that mistake again."

She gave him an elbow in the ribs and pushed him away, but he pulled her close and kissed the top of her head. They walked in silence a few minutes, then she asked, "What's on your mind, sweetheart?"

"Wondering how to get you and the vets out in the country. Seems like a good idea. I'll see what I can do about that."

She laughed. "Is that your next project?"

"Soon as I finish the deal I'm working now."

"You're not serious."

"Of course I am."

"Why?"

His voice softened. "Because I love you, Allie, and I'll do anything for you."

Lamar wiped sweat from his face with a shirtsleeve, stretched his aching back a moment, then climbed out of the square hole he'd dug in the gully a hundred yards from the bunker. The posthole digger attachment on the tractor had softened the earth, but he still had to shovel more than a cubic yard of wet loam onto a trailer to be hauled to the lake dam in the main pasture.

The afternoon sun slipped lower, and the temperature dropped as fast as the shadows crossed the ravine. He thought of quitting work for the day. There'd be plenty of time to finish in the morning before Castro returned, but he'd told BJ the silo would be finished that day.

He took a long drink of water from a thermos, then tossed the precut timbers into the hole for the flooring. After that he installed the corner posts, then assembled the side walls. Two hours later, he'd finished with the timbers, placed the access cover over the top and spread dirt, leaves and twigs over it. Satisfied with his work, he climbed onto the tractor and headed for the barn, ready for a cold beer and a hot shower.

Lamar looked over the grazing cattle as he passed, then drove through the gate to the front pasture. When he topped the rise near the field shed, his heart leaped into his throat and he instinctively stopped the tractor. Two vehicles were parked in the driveway next to the house. One was a tan Ford Bronco that he'd never seen. The other was a sheriff's patrol car.

His mind raced. What could have called their attention to his ranch? Had Castro been caught in Houston? Had he told where he was taking the goods?

After a moment, Lamar started moving again. When he reached the tractor shed he saw two deputies standing next to the Bronco. Sergeant Conyers, the deputy who'd sent him to the VA instead of jail, climbed out of the Bronco wearing civilian clothes and carrying a six-pack of Coors. He met Lamar halfway to the house. "You're wearing lots of dirt for a cowboy, Lamar. What the hell you been doing?"

Lamar looked at his pants and all the mud caked on them. "Patched a weak spot on one of the dams."

Conyers nodded. "Thought I'd drop by and see how you're doin'. Do you have time for one of those beers we talked about last time I saw you?"

Lamar felt weak in the knees, relieved to see Conyers, but wondering about the two men in uniform. "Thanks, I could use a beer." He gestured toward the other deputies. "Is this a business call, too?"

"No, couple other vets in the department. I asked them to stop by and meet you since they were out this way."

Conyers introduced them. Both were about the same age as Conyers, but trimmer.

Conyers pulled a can from the six-pack and handed it to Lamar. "Ned's place is close to the big yellow house right up the street close to Wal-Mart, real easy to get to. We're gonna grill some steaks at his place after his shift ends in a couple of hours. Wondered if you'd like to join us."

Lamar lowered his gaze. "I don't know . . ."

"If you're still not driving, I'd be happy to give you a ride and bring you home."

Lamar shook his head. "I'm driving again. One of the men in my group at the VA helped me take care of that."

Ned said, "Won't be anything fancy, Lamar. More Coors, some nice tri-tips and baked potatoes. Sure would like for you to join us."

Conyers winked at him. "That probably fits right in with what the VA docs are telling you to do. Right?"

Lamar kicked at a pebble. "Yeah, probably so. What time should I be there?"

Ned gave directions to his house, then he and Carl left. Lamar's mind raced, wondering if Conyers or the other deputies had seen Kruger and Castro, or Tanner.

Ernie Castro woke Sunday morning to the sound of an annoying, steady drumbeat. When he tried to lift his head from the pillow, he realized the drumbeat was his own pulse pounding at the dull ache in his temples, reminding him of the night before. Several times he tried to open his eyes without success.

Gradually he became aware of someone else breathing close by. He turned over slowly, eyes squinting until he focused on a tangle of long, dark hair bunched on the pillow next to his and drifting under the covers. He tried to visualize the face on the other side of the hair until he realized he couldn't even remember where he'd met her. Then he decided he might not want to see her face after all.

Castro's next thought caused a splitting pang to shoot through his head and brought him instantly and painfully wide awake.

The money!

Tanner had given him cash to buy the goods he'd come to get in Houston.

He looked around the room. It had to be the least-expensive and closest motel to wherever he'd been when he'd paired off with the woman beside him. Most of his clothes lay across a sagging chair on his side of the bed. Her blouse lay on the dresser, and other articles were strewn between the bed and the bathroom.

Easing out of bed, Castro checked his pants pockets, thankful to find the keys to his van. His wallet appeared to be intact, and some of the roll of bills he had started out with for pocket money was still there. His watch said 7:10. He peeked out the window, thankful to see the sun in the east. At least he hadn't slept the entire day and missed his appointment.

He took a fast shower, praying that he or the woman had the presence of mind last night to use protection, then he dressed and headed for the door. Thankfully, she didn't wake; at least she didn't move. If she'd shown him an ugly face, he'd have felt even more disgusted with himself. If she were attractive, he'd want to stay with her. Somehow, he figured there was little chance of that.

Outside, he scanned the parking lot and felt a twinge of panic when he didn't see his van. He hurried to the corner of the building, each step sending a jolt through his head. He sighed with relief when he saw the truck, parked squarely between the lines.

He unlocked the door and felt under the driver's seat until he found a tiny wire handle, pulled it, and a spring-loaded cover popped up under the floor mat. He pushed the mat aside and sighed again when he saw Tanner's cash intact.

Wish Kruger had been here to keep me sober last night. I can't even remember if I had a good time!

As he drove from the parking lot, the gravity of the risk he'd run the night before poured into his mind. The situation wasn't as simple as taking a load of wetbacks to Dallas. In that case, he figured if they were caught, what the hell? They'd only be shipped back to the border on a bus more comfortable than his van.

But he'd risked BJ Tanner's money. More than that, he'd betrayed the trust of three men who'd given his life more meaning in the last few weeks than he'd ever felt before. The thought made him retch. He pulled to the curb in time to avoid ruining the interior of the van.

After stopping at the next service station to wash the outside of the streaked door, he stopped at a Denny's, found a waitress with a bottle of aspirin and downed four of them. While drinking hot coffee, waiting for bacon, eggs, and hot cakes, Castro swore a silent oath to BJ, Lamar, and Sonny that he'd never drink himself into oblivion again.

At 9:00, Castro stopped in front of a rundown warehouse, killed the engine and waited. He'd been inside the building three years before when he had driven two men there who were wanted for weapons violations in Mexico and the United States. After meeting them in Reynosa, he walked them across a deserted stretch of the border, then drove them safely to Houston. They'd met their partners and paid him well. When he talked with them the previous week, they agreed to get what he wanted, no problem.

He waited ten minutes before the walk-in door opened and one of the two men he'd smuggled from Mexico, the one called Bones, moved to the van and climbed in the passenger side. Without making eye contact he said, "Hey, hombre." Looking out the rear windows, he added, "Let's go. Two blocks, then make a right."

Castro swallowed, trying to moisten his dry throat, but he said nothing as he followed the directions. Bones watched the street behind them. Castro could see nothing suspicious, no movement except for a derelict near the first corner. Two trucks passed in the other direction on the next street. Bones gestured for another right after a block, taking them to the back of the warehouse. He watched the street intently until they reached the building where a sliding door moved to one side wide enough for the van to enter, then closed behind them.

Bones lost the tense expression that had kept him detached while they drove. His gaunt features hadn't changed except for a generous expanse of gray in his thin brown hair, and more lines around his eyes and mouth. He smiled and stuck out a hand. "Ernie, my man. Good to see you, pal."

Castro relaxed as he took Bones's hand. "You too, gringo. Guess you haven't been to Mexico lately, huh?"

Bones laughed as the man who'd closed the door, a stranger to Castro, approached the van on the passenger side. He had dark-blond hair, an acne-scarred complexion and arms too thick for the extra-large shirt he wore. Bones said, "This is Tiny. We already told him about you."

Tiny nodded but said nothing. Castro glanced around the warehouse, empty except for a white Jeep Grand Cherokee. "What's happening? Business so good you sold everything?"

"We don't use this place anymore. Moved to a better one. It has more ways to get out of it if we have to. I decided to meet you here since you know where it is. What the hell are you gonna do with a handful of weapons and a piece of C-4? Blow up the bridge at Laredo?"

Bones and Tiny laughed. Castro smiled and gave a thumbs-up. "Seems like a good way to stop the tourist traffic. Clear the way for a serious businessman like myself."

Another round of laughter.

"Hardly worth coming all the way from Laredo for this tiny little bundle of goods, Ernie."

Castro shrugged, glad they assumed he'd come from South Texas. "Where is the stuff?"

Bones gestured to Tiny, who put on latex gloves, opened the rear door of the Cherokee and pulled out a tan, soft-sided sports bag about three feet long. The bag appeared to be full. He also carried a smaller pouch the size of a shaving kit.

Bones opened the sliding door of Ernie's van and reviewed the list of goods as Tiny hoisted the bags inside. "Three Uzis. Ten magazines and a thousand rounds per weapon. Three Browning Hi-Power semiautomatics, couple of two-pound strips of C-4. The primers and remote triggers are in the little bag, Ernie."

Tiny opened a green canvas bag inside the duffle and lifted out a two-inch-thick, slightly arched military-green plastic container the size of two open hands. Letters along the convex side read, "Front Toward Enemy."

"These six Claymores weren't easy to come by. You remember how to arm them?"

"That's something you never forget."

Tiny unzipped the large bag and pulled out one Uzi. It appeared to be brand-new. Castro felt for each of the other weapons, then pulled out one strip of the plastic explosive wrapped in green Mylar. Bones said, "You want to check all of them?"

"No need. You said four grand, right?"

Bones nodded. "That covers our cost. Anybody else would pay twice that much, but you're still my man for getting us out of Mexico."

Castro opened the trap door under the floor mat, withdrew the right amount and gave it to the smuggler, who handed it to Tiny without counting. He stuck out a hand to Castro. "Be careful on the road, partner. I'd stay out of the beer keg till you deposit this stuff. Be damn careful, you hear?"

Castro climbed into the van while Tiny moved toward the street door. "Don't worry, Bones. Nobody'll be around to hear this stuff when it goes off. Peace, bro. See you next time."

Bones peered outside, signaled Tiny to open the door, then waved Castro out.

An hour later, Castro had crossed the Houston metropolitan area headed north on I-45. Twice he left the freeway, backtracked an exit and headed north again. Certain that no one followed, he punched Lamar's number into his cell phone. "Filled out my shopping list. I'm on the road. Should be there in about four hours."

"Okay, but if you see any strange vehicles or sheriff's cars hanging around headquarters when you get here, keep driving and wait till I call you."

"The sheriff? You haven't —"

"No problem. It'll only be a social visit."

Castro ended the call and tossed the phone on the passenger seat.

Great! I'm on the way home with enough illegal weapons to get me hanged, and Lamar has the sheriff dropping by for a beer.

► 23 ◄

Monday morning Tanner awoke abruptly, his stomach burning with nausea. Easing out of bed, trying not to disturb Allie, he hurried down the hall to the guest bath so she wouldn't hear him retching. After rinsing the bile from his mouth and washing his face, he went to the kitchen. He found Allie standing by the coffee maker in the half-light, arms crossed.

"How long has that been going on?"

"What?"

"You know damn well what. What else besides throwing up?"

"Nothing. Get a little tired sometimes. That's all."

"Have you seen Dr. Weiss?"

"No."

"He can give you medication that'll ease the pain."

"Tums, Zantac, and Advil are working fine so far. Besides, his stuff would slow me down too much."

Her voice quavered. "Really, how long has this been happening, sweetheart?"

He hugged her, an easy way to hide his face as he answered. He was surprised how quickly his body was changing, getting noticeably weaker by the day. "It only happened a couple of times in the past two weeks."

He felt her shake with sobs and eased her to arm's length, forcing himself to smile. "Please don't worry. It isn't that bad. We have a long time to go yet."

"I'll stay home today and take care of you."

"No, Allie, you can't do that every time I have the slightest pain. Hell, it could have been something I ate. Besides, I have to go to Austin today. I'm flying down so I can be back tonight."

"BJ, I . . ."

She put a hand over her mouth and closed her eyes. A tear rolled down her cheek, visible when it reflected the faint light from the front window.

He wiped the tear and kissed her forehead. "You have people to take care of at the hospital, darlin'. I'll be here when you get home, waiting for you to spoil me."

Tanner gazed down at Lake Travis as his flight circled for final approach to Austin's Mueller Airport. He couldn't identify the inlet along the west shore where he'd rented a large house twice yearly for a Tanner Systems managers' retreat. The rental had been a good investment every time. Swimming, boating, and fishing brought the managers closer and built team spirit.

His chest tightened and he stopped searching the shoreline at the realization that he wouldn't be able to go there with them again.

Whitecaps on the water foretold the wind that buffeted the plane moments later as it descended to land. The 737 bucked and bounced like a jeep over rough terrain until a few feet above the runway, then settled gently.

Moments later he hurried across the terminal, signed for a rental van he'd arranged to keep for a month and headed for Phillips' office.

The attorney led him into a sixth floor corner suite with a view up Congress Avenue to the State Capital. Phillips' secretary served coffee and left them alone. "I've filed papers to set up the two non-profit corporations."

He slid a folder across his desk to Tanner. "Here are copies and the bank account numbers for each one. Now, you want to tell me what the hell's going on?"

Tanner shuffled through the documents and pulled out a book of checks. "These are for the Austin account?"

Phillips nodded.

Tanner noted the account number, then pushed the checkbook in front of the attorney. "There'll be a half-million-dollar deposit from an offshore account this afternoon. Send a hundred and fifty grand to University Hospital."

"Are you taking treatment there?"

Tanner shook his head. "Send a letter with the check. It'll be a donation to pay for the kidney transplant for Jackie Shelton's son."

Phillips stared at Tanner. "Is that it, then? You're gonna give away all your money?"

Tanner ignored the question. "The Dallas account will get a million later this week."

Phillips raised a hand. "Wouldn't it be a good idea to name a CEO? Have somebody in charge of the outfit before you hand over a million dollars?"

"Matter of fact, it would." He gave Phillips an envelope from his briefcase. "These are the people I want in charge and descriptions of their key responsibilities. Have your associate in Dallas interview them and make job offers they can't refuse."

Phillips, looking exasperated, raised both hands. "Hey, it's your money. At least it used to be."

"Be damn sure there's no way to trace the money back to me."

Phillips slumped back and gazed at Tanner. "BJ, are you sure you know what you're doing?"

Tanner shoved papers into his briefcase. "Don't worry, Phil. You'll be proud of me when the game's over." From the door he gave the attorney a grin. "But you won't be able to say anything because you won't have facts, only assumptions. A lawyer doesn't have to do anything about assumptions. But he does have to observe the attorney-client privilege."

Tanner left, climbed into the rental van and called Des Blaylock. "We have a location?"

"Yeah. Telemarketing outfit moved out last month. There'll be plenty of phone lines for the facilities we need."

"Where is it?"

Blaylock gave him the address and a list of computer equipment he'd need. After verifying everything with Tanner, he said, "If you buy all that stuff new, you're talking maybe three-quarter million. I made some calls and —"

"I told you not to make any contacts."

"Nobody knows who it was, and I used the phone you gave me. Triple S Corp. closed their Austin plant the end of last month. They have the kind of computer system we need sitting in their old building collecting dust. You can lease it, then let them repo the stuff after we're done."

He gave Tanner a name to call in the Triple S Houston headquarters office.

"Good work, son. You've already earned your money."

"I'd be happy to take a bonus."

"Bonuses come at the end, not the beginning."

Tanner called the realtor Blaylock mentioned regarding the vacant office listing. "Name's Appleton," Tanner said. "I'm with the Veterans Volunteer Service. We'd like to do a six months lease on the office. No improvements required."

The woman agreed to have a contract ready by 2:00. "Shall we meet at the building? You can see the space and sign the lease."

"No, my schedule's too tight. I'll have an attorney handle it."

"I've never had a tenant who was so fast and decisive, Mr. Appleton."

Tanner said, "I can hardly wait to get this non-profit started."

Next Tanner called Triple S Corporation. The information systems manager was reluctant to consider leasing to a non-profit organization he hadn't heard of, but Tanner prevailed with another offer of advance payments. He suggested that they could write off the full value of the computer as a charitable donation. Later, they'd recover the equipment when the non-profit group moved into permanent quarters after buying its own equipment.

"Our attorney will handle the details of the contract and pay in advance for the entire lease period."

After waiting next door to Phillips' office while one of his associates signed the lease agreements and collected keys, Tanner headed for the airport. He met Blaylock in the terminal and gave him one of the keys.

"Damn, you don't mess around." He looked into Tanner's' face and frowned. "You feeling okay? You look tired."

"Des, will you be able to handle the phone lines without help?"

"No problem. That is if you don't mind my running wire across the floor instead of inside the walls. All I need is the cable pair numbers to the terminal box in the building."

"Remember what I said about gloves."

"Won't leave home without 'em."

Tanner boarded his flight and it departed for Dallas. He asked for coffee when the attendants began serving. He hadn't eaten all day but didn't find the thought of food appealing. He took a sip of coffee and winced at the pain of a new sore in his mouth. He asked the attendant to take it away and give him ice water, then he gazed down on the clouds, recalling the symptoms Dr. Weiss said he would experience as the disease progressed.

Please don't be in a hurry for me, Lord. I still have work to do down here.

► 24 ◄

For the next two weeks, Texas enjoyed an early spring from warm Gulf air, but Tanner's health worsened. In spite of Allie's efforts to feed him and maintain his weight, he slipped to twenty pounds below his normal 205. His cheeks hollowed and his clothes began sagging except around his waist. His stomach felt constantly bloated, causing discomfort and self-consciousness.

Allie, in contrast, gained pounds on the healthy diet regimen she followed for both of them. By midmonth she reached her drinking days' weight. Tanner smiled, watching her one evening after dinner when she brought fresh strawberries into the den, his serving covered with rich cream. She wore Danskin shorts and a tube top that showed shapely legs, rounded hips, and bigger breasts.

She caught his expression and smiled. "What are you looking at?" she said.

"Just admiring the graceful swan that's grown out of the skinny duckling. You look terrific, Saint Allie."

When she turned away, he thought she'd been embarrassed by the comment, but he saw her wipe a tear as she went back to the kitchen. Moments later she returned to sit beside him, smiling but red-eyed.

"Sorry, sweetheart. I hate thinking about my health improving while yours . . ."

"Not something I like to think about, either," Tanner said. "But I'm more concerned about you than me."

"How can you say that?"

He put the strawberries on the coffee table, and she promptly handed them back to him. "Eat."

"We know what's happening to me, but afterward, you're —"

"Don't talk like that."

"Allie, sweetheart, you deal with this kind of thing at work every day."

"That's different."

"Yeah, but this is more personal. You can't ignore it."

He stopped talking when she put a hand over her eyes. He picked at the berries, ate some of them, then put the bowl down again. This time she left it on the table. Tanner slipped an arm around her and she cried on his shoulder.

"I can't think about after you're gone. Every day will be dark after that. There won't be a reason to keep going."

"No, Allie, that's not true. When I die it'll —"

"Stop!"

He held her tighter. "I have this vision about myself, Allie. When I die, it'll be at the end of a rainy day. The sun will come out, then I'll be gone. My spirit will be part of the sun. I'll be happy to shine on you forever to be sure you take care of yourself and live well. You can't disappoint my spirit, Saint Allie. Your happiness is the most important thing in the universe for me."

Phillips called Tanner on Wednesday. "The union's approved your proposal to sell the company. There was never a question about them supporting the deal. They merely wanted to clear it with their counsel, be sure nothing would come back to haunt them later."

"How long till it's a done deal?"

"They've seen my draft of the papers and suggested three changes that we can live with. I figure we can close the deal by Friday."

"Why not tomorrow?"

"Don't you want to see the changes they asked for?"

"Do you have any problem with them?"

"No, but —"

"Then let's do it tomorrow."

Phillips started to protest, then stopped. "I'll check with the union's counsel and call you back."

While waiting, Tanner swallowed the last three Tylenol capsules from his pocket vial. He went to the bathroom to refill the container from a large bottle. The man in the mirror had changed. His cheeks were deeper, and the light in his eyes seemed to be dimmed by a shadow, and that swollen stomach . . .

He turned abruptly from the mirror, unable to deny what he saw there, yet unwilling to accept the observation.

When Phillips called, Tanner grabbed the phone on the first ring. "They agreed to sign tomorrow. One o'clock, my office. Want me to call Ellis and the others?"

Tanner hesitated. "No, only Mabry. The three of us are enough to formalize approval. Call him at home tonight. See that he says nothing to Bonner till after we sign."

"What about Ellis?"

"I'll let him know later. He's been too damned emotional about everything since I told him I was . . . sick. Bonner's been a little off, too."

Tanner ended the call, then forced himself to eat a cup of yogurt, two bananas and two slices of wheat toast with jelly. After eating, he sat on the futon in the den, willing his body to accept the food.

At 1:00 he used his gray cellular to ring Lamar. "How're things going?"

"Real good. I drove to Dallas and back today. It's getting easier every trip. The deputy came by last night and met . . . my two friends. Everybody got along fine. Had a couple of beers, told some war stories."

"Don't let him see that everybody has their own cell phone. That might raise some questions."

"No problem, we're careful about that. Wings called before we left this morning, on the way back from the scouting trip. She'll be here tonight.

Says she found everything we need, all of the equipment and a place to store it."

Tanner smiled at the news. Becky's mission had raised his greatest concern about the success of his plan. She'd been working alone for two weeks, and he'd been anxious to hear from her. With Tanner Systems sold and no way for anyone to use the company as leverage against him, and with Becky's task completed, he could begin the next phase.

The following morning, after a bout of nausea, Tanner showered and began dressing. Allie took him a mug of tea with three spoonfuls of sugar.

"Did you weigh yourself this morning?"

"No."

"Get on the scales."

"I'm running late, darlin'."

"BJ . . ."

He looked at her stern expression in the mirror, then turned to hug her. "I'm one eighty-four. Only lost a pound since Friday."

She gave him a doubting look but didn't ask again. "I have toast and jam and bacon for you, and a protein drink from the health food store. Dr. Weiss says it's a good formula to keep up energy and slow the weight loss."

"That stuff tastes like hell."

She shook her head. "I put sugar and banana flavoring in it. You'll love it, and you *will* drink it."

After dressing, he sat down at the kitchen table and began to eat in spite of his lack of appetite. Allie took his mind off the food.

"Sweetheart, that rancher you helped out a few weeks ago, Lamar Weed?"

"Yes?"

"Doc Maroun says he's never seen anyone turn around as fast as him and the two guys staying with him. Says they really have their act together. Are you still working with them?"

"I dropped in on them a couple of times. Why?"

She shrugged. "He mentioned them yesterday while we were talking. Called me to schedule a meeting Monday. He and I are gonna see some lawyer."

"For what?"

"I'm not real sure. He asked to see Doc Maroun and me. Says he has an opportunity for us."

"What kind of opportunity?"

"I don't know."

"You're not gonna run away and leave me, are you?"

She leaned down to kiss him. "Not a chance, sweetheart."

After signing the union agreement and letters to each of the non-union employees of Tanner Systems regarding their new ownership, Tanner excused himself and left Phillips's office. From the lobby he called Jackie Shelton and arranged to meet him in the parking lot of the LBJ Library in a half hour.

When Shelton arrived, he joined Tanner in the rental car. As they shook hands, he frowned. "You feeling all right, BJ?"

"Little tired. I've been on the go lately. What'd you find out?"

Shelton gave him a page of computer-printed notes. "I located all the data circuits for the IRS computer, interfaced them to the cable pairs at that location you gave me. Here's a list of circuit numbers and user terminals. I changed Southwestern Bell's cable inventory records to show all these circuits out of service for maintenance. Nobody will mess with them."

"You sure there's no way anyone can trace those assignments back to you?"

Jackie shook his head. "Not a chance. I used a maintenance terminal. No transaction record. I wired the private line repeaters and tagged them as Air Force Base circuits. Nobody messes with military circuits without a government order."

"I don't know how to thank you, Jackie. I couldn't have done this without you."

"What *are* you doing, BJ?"

"You don't want to know. For God's sake, don't ever let anybody know you helped me."

"Like you never let anybody know who paid for my boy's new kidney?"

Tanner gazed at Shelton a moment. "That was a gift from a charitable organization."

Shelton smiled. "Sure, BJ. When do you want me to disconnect those circuits?"

"A month or less. Someone will call you at home and say 'Turn the lights out.' When they do, you get those circuits disconnected ASAP."

They shook hands again. "Take care of yourself. You look like you've been working too hard. Get some rest."

"I'm going to, Jackie, real soon."

After leaving the parking lot, Tanner went to the office he'd rented and appraised the work Blaylock had done in setting up the big computer and its peripheral equipment. Two gray phone cables ran between the utility closet and one of the computer cabinets. Dozens of multicolored wires extended from the cable onto circuit boards on the communications processor. He looked at the telephone terminal in the closet, shook his head and left the paper Shelton had given him inside the panel.

Tanner thought about Blaylock while locking up. "Thank God he knows what he's doing."

He left the office and headed for the airport.

Tanner's flight arrived in Dallas at 6 p.m. He felt weak after walking up the jetway and through the terminal. Allie would have a fit if she knew he hadn't eaten since breakfast.

After resting a moment, he went to a public phone and called Lamar. "How did everybody do with their training today?"

Lamar laughed. "Better than last time. Sonny and Becky are doing fine. She said Castro's slow at the door, but then he's okay. He favors that leg that took the bamboo spear."

"Is she worried about him?"

"Nope. Says when the time comes, she'll boot his butt to move him faster."

Tanner smiled. "How many sessions is that for everyone?"

"Five, and they're doing fine, BJ. Everybody is, including Castro."

"Watch him close. We absolutely cannot risk failure."

"Something else happened today. I hope it won't be a problem for us."

"What's that?"

"Real estate agent stopped by right after we came home. He said that land next to the east pasture sold. Anybody moves in over there, they could hear some of our work in the gully."

"Don't worry about it. We'll be done before anything can get started on that land. I'll see y'all tomorrow afternoon."

Tanner made his way across the parking area to the pickup and headed for Allie's house. While driving he placed a call to Des Blaylock on the gray cell phone. "Where are you?"

"At the office — the new office — tying down wires. Found your note."

"Any problems?"

"No. This looks like a real service order. How the hell did you manage that?"

Tanner said, "When will you have everything hooked up?"

"Couple more hours. I'll start grabbing data tonight. Give me something to work on over the weekend. I should be ready to start doing fun stuff by Monday."

"Today's definitely the right time to start."

"Why is that?"

"April Fools' Day."

► 25 ◄

Shortly after noon Friday, Tanner waited at a café on South Loop 12, two miles from the VA hospital. Castro and Kruger arrived in the van, followed by Lamar in his pickup. Tanner did a double take when Lamar stepped out of the truck. He'd been to the barber, giving up his shoulder-length hair for a cropped style that flattered him and brightened his expression. He flushed as Tanner stared at him.

"Lamar, you look ten years younger and ready for *Ranch* magazine cover. When did you decide to cut your mane?"

"I figured if I can go to town and act like everybody else, might as well look like I belong there."

Tanner shook his head. "I can't use you in my plans anymore."

Lamar stopped in his tracks, gaping. "Why not?"

"I was worried before about people remembering your long hair. Now they'll know you because of that handsome face. You're too high profile now to be part of my plans."

Castro and Sonny laughed. Lamar flushed a deeper red as they went into the café. Tanner ordered a barbecued-pork sandwich and forced himself to eat, washing the food down with a glass of cold milk. The others showed healthy appetites and no sign of nerves.

"Looks like you two are ready."

Kruger nodded. Castro said, "No problema."

"For God's sake, be careful. If anything looks like it isn't right, abort. We can delay and start over, but we can't undo a screw-up."

Kruger seemed complacent, like soldiers Tanner had known — experienced and well prepared for their missions. Castro smiled with anticipation.

Tanner said, "Don't assume this is a snap, Ernie. There's room for any number of things to go wrong. That means that usually something does. Be ready."

Castro gave him a thumbs-up.

"Either of you have any weapons?"

"No, sir," Kruger said.

Castro shrugged. "Couple of pounds of wet sand in a sock. If we have to sap him, that'll bring him down without any serious damage, but I'm betting on Sonny to bulldog him in record rodeo time."

"Don't hurt him. I don't want a mark on him."

"Come on, BJ, we been over it a dozen times. We do it clean, or we're on our way home alone."

After finishing their meal, Castro and Kruger headed for the van. Lamar, having hardly spoken while they were eating, said, "Be sure you call me before you come to the ranch. If I don't answer, don't drive in. Conyers has been dropping by pretty regular."

Then Lamar said, "BJ, you don't look too good today. Why don't you go home and get some rest?"

"No time for that."

"I think you ought to reconsider. Wait till you feel better."

"I'm never gonna feel any better, Lamar. That's why I'm in a hurry to get this done."

Lamar stared in silence. His expression seemed to say that, for the first time, he understood the gravity of Tanner's illness. "Jesus, BJ, I'm sorry."

"Don't be. Stay alert and objective."

Lamar shook his head. "But it ain't fair. You're still . . ."

"Nothing is fair, Lamar. You've been a prisoner on your own ranch for how many years? Is that fair? What about Castro and the way he's been treated in South Texas? And what the Army did to Becky. Hell, I could go on complaining all day about what's not fair, but I'd rather do something about it.

"There's a nurse at the VA I want you to meet. You'll like her. She's had the short end of the stick longer than anybody deserves. Time she had a better bite of life along with you and the others. Let's get back to the ranch. I'll tell you about her."

Castro slowed to exit the freeway in Austin before the Friday evening rush-hour traffic began crowding the streets. Kruger awoke and climbed off the mattress in the back of the van, taped two shipping boxes together and slipped the mattress inside them. "Did Becky call?"

"Yep, your sis did her job. Said she called him at the office. Turned on the sweet voice and Palmero tried to answer so fast he stuttered. Sumbitch must not have had a date in a year. Hell, he even gave her his home address when she asked if she could meet him there."

"What time?"

"She set him up for six thirty."

Kruger checked his watch. "We better get over to his place right now."

Castro shook his head. "We'll wait till dark. Another half hour."

"What if he's already home?"

"I'll call him and say I'm a neighbor and I backed into his car."

A half hour later, Castro parked the van on the street across the wooded area behind Theron Palmero's apartment building. He removed the sock of wet sand from under the driver's seat and dropped it into his coat pocket. "You have the tape and hoods?"

Kruger nodded. He took two ski masks from a pocket of his field jacket and slipped them under his belt.

Castro's heart pounded. He felt even more excited than when he'd gone for the weapons in Houston. He also felt better about himself being cold sober. Kruger's face looked impassive except for the steady flexing and release of jaw muscles.

"Okay, let's go."

After checking to be sure the street was deserted, they slipped out of the van and ran in crouched positions, ten yards across low weeds into the woods. Castro led the way, picking out vague shapes of landmarks he'd memorized across the three or four acres. They reached the creek with no problems, but the water had risen due to recent rain. Kruger leaped across the stream, but Castro landed short, in water up to his ankles.

"I told you to wear boots."

"No big deal. I've been in worse than this for weeks at a time."

They moved behind shrubs Castro had selected as a hiding place, in front of the third parking space away from the one marked "19" for Palmero's apartment. "Looking good, *blanco*. No car in his space, and that station wagon next to him will make it easy for you to get behind him."

Castro worked his toes, felt the squishy wetness in his Reeboks, then forgot about his feet when a car drove into the parking area. They ducked as the light beams crossed their hiding place. Castro grew anxious thinking about the one aspect of their plan left to chance — what if another tenant was in the parking area when Palmero arrived?

A couple stepped out of the car, opened the trunk and seemed undecided about what to do with its contents. "Come on," Castro whispered. "Get the hell out of here."

The couple rearranged items in their car, shifted things from the back seat to the trunk and finally locked the car and carried packages into the building.

A second car entered the lot and parked a few spaces away from Palmero's. The driver, a small woman in her late forties, left the car and hurried into the building.

Five empty spaces remained on the lot when Palmero arrived. As soon as his headlights were out, Kruger dashed between the second and third cars to Palmero's left, holding a strip of duct tape in his left hand.

As the IRS agent locked his car, Castro rose. Standing in the shadows, he said, "Hey, Theron."

Palmero leaned forward, peering into the darkness. "Who's there?"

Castro spread his hands so Palmero could see his silhouette. "It's me, bro. How you been?"

Palmero started to speak again, but Kruger lunged, slapping the tape over his mouth. Palmero grabbed for the tape, but Kruger bear-hugged him, pinning his arms to his side. Although six inches taller, Palmero couldn't resist Sonny's superior strength as the younger man forced him face down across the hood of his car.

Palmero grunted and snorted, unable to shout. Castro grabbed his right arm and twisted it behind his back. Kruger yanked the double ski masks from his waistband, jammed them over Palmero's head backwards so he couldn't possibly see anything. Then he pulled Palmero's left arm behind him and strapped his wrists together with the duct tape.

They dragged the big man behind the shrub where they'd waited. Palmero kicked hard, catching Castro in the shin. He choked off a scream and struggled to breathe through his nose.

Castro pulled the sap from his pocket and raised it, but Kruger stopped him. He had Palmero face down on the ground, sitting on his back.

"Get his keys. He dropped them when I jumped him."

Castro crouched and moved beside Palmero's car, feeling around the tarmac until he found the keys. Less than a minute had passed since Palmero stepped out of his car, and no one had driven into the parking area.

Kruger took a garrote from his pocket. He lifted the ski masks enough for Palmero to see the wire, then slipped it over the tax agent's head, around his neck. After replacing the masks, Kruger leaned close and whispered, "I'm gonna stand you up, and you'll walk with me without giving any trouble, right?"

Palmero nodded, breathing hard through his nose. Kruger yanked him to his feet by his coat collar, then led him stumbling into the woods. Castro scanned the area to be sure no one saw them, then followed Kruger and their captive, smiling.

Ten minutes later, they'd passed through the woods and stood at the edge of the clearing near the van, Palmero wet to his knees. Castro looked left and right. "Let's go."

"Not yet," Kruger said, untying Palmero's hands.

Castro gawked at him. "What the hell are you doin'?"

Kruger gave a gentle tug on the wire. "You're gonna be laying down quiet as a mouse for a few hours. Better take a leak if you don't want to do it in your pants."

Palmero's shirt collar was wet with sweat. He tried to speak, but the tape stopped him, allowing only a whine. He reached for the masks, but Kruger grabbed his wrist and twisted the arm back down to his side. With shaky hands Palmero unzipped his fly and relieved himself, making no further attempt to speak.

Castro noticed the man's wet collar and lifted the tail of his jacket to reveal a sweat-stained back. "Ten-minute walk in the woods and he's soaked. This dude's really out of shape."

"He's never *been* in shape," Sonny observed.

Castro and Kruger took turns relieving themselves after retaping Palmero's hands, then hurried across the clearing into the van. Kruger taped Palmero's feet, placed him on the mattress and slipped the boxes over him.

"You make one sound and I'll give a yank on the wire. If you're a good boy, when we get on the highway I'll take the tape off your mouth. It's a long way to the Gulf. We wouldn't want you to choke."

Castro circled several blocks and drove along curved roads so that Palmero could have no idea which direction they headed before turning onto I-35 north. A few miles from Austin, Castro called Lamar.

"We have a prize turkey in the bag. Get the coop ready."

Lamar's cellular phone rang again at 10:15. Castro and Kruger were passing through Ennis and called to be sure neither Conyers nor any of the other deputies were at the ranch.

Tanner and Lamar met them in the carport. After freeing Palmero's hands and feet, Kruger led him like a dog on a leash, walking him around the yard behind the house to restore his circulation. Then he took Palmero into the kitchen and sat him at the table.

Lamar rolled the masks up to Palmero's nose, then let him peel the gag from his mouth, wincing as he slowly detached the silvery tape's adhesive surface from his lips. Skin pulled away in two places.

Lamar gave him a sandwich and water to drink while Kruger stood behind him to be sure he didn't uncover his eyes.

In the living room, Tanner had Castro give a rundown on their mission and felt satisfied there were no loose ends.

"After he eats, put him in the small bedroom," Tanner said. "Tie him to the chair with his back to the door."

The task completed, Tanner entered the bedroom and closed the door. The walls, window and floor were covered with black construction plastic held in place by masking tape. All furniture had been removed from the room, replaced by an army cot and a steel folding chair. Palmero sat in the chair, hands and feet tied, eyes covered.

Tanner stood in front of him and pulled the masks off his head. Palmero blinked, then looked up. After a few seconds he focused and recognized his abductor.

"Tanner!"

"Have a nice trip, Palmero?"

"You'll never get away with this. You must be out of your mind." The tax agent's cracking voice belied the conviction of his words.

Tanner nodded as he sat on the cot and leaned against the wall. He kept his voice soft, matter-of-fact. "I probably am out of my mind. After all, you set me up to pay two-and-a-half-million dollars of extortion money."

"Y-you're a fool, Tanner. You can't fight the government this way."

"I don't care about the government. It's too late for that. I paid the extortion, then gave up my company, too."

Palmero shifted, tried to look behind him toward the door. "Th-this isn't the way to get it back."

Tanner shook his head. "Don't want it back."

"Well, if you think the IRS is gonna give you anything, you're out of your fuckin' mind."

Tanner forced a pleasant smile, then removed his jacket. "Apparently you don't know about my health, Palmero. See how much weight I've lost? Am I paler than the last time we met?"

Palmero ran his gaze down Tanner's body, then stared at the floor but said nothing.

"I'm dyin', Palmero. The IRS, Tanner Systems, all the money in the world can't change that. I don't have much time left."

Palmero's face contorted. "Look, let me go right now and I'll never breathe a word of this to anyone."

Tanner's smile changed to a scowl as he leaned close to Palmero. "You low-life pus bag. You'll never breathe a word of this anyhow. That I'll guarantee. Tomorrow morning you're going to participate in a sport you've never seen before, and you'll never tell anyone about that, either."

He pulled a hunting knife from his jacket pocket, removed the leather sheath and cut the tape from Palmero's feet and hands. "Get on the cot."

Tanner could see fear in the other man's eyes. "Wh-what're you doing?"

"You sleep on your back or on that doughboy gut?"

Palmero rolled on his side toward the wall and drew his legs up in the fetal position. He closed his eyes as Tanner put the masks back on him. Tanner whistled and Sonny came in and taped Palmero's hands together. Then he taped the IRS agent to the bed.

"Sleep if you can, Palmero. And remember, there's a bunch more men here. Any one of them would love for you to try to get away while they're on watch."

Tanner turned out the light and closed the door.

► 26 ◄

Saturday morning Tanner rose before dawn, telling Allie he had business with his client until noon. He promised to stop and eat on the way to the meeting, but she climbed out of bed and fixed breakfast for him anyway.

"I don't like the idea of you working at all," she pouted. "Much less on my time."

"This is the only day we can do what we have to, darlin'. It has to be finished this weekend."

Allie made wheat toast with butter and a thick layer of peach jam. She heated a large slice of ham in the microwave and fried two eggs. Instead of coffee, she made hot chocolate.

"I can't eat all this stuff."

"Then go back to bed. You're not leaving till you do."

That kind of meal hadn't appealed to him since he'd been a child, but he began to eat slowly, remembering a Saturday morning meal when he was thirteen. His mother had admonished him to eat well because the Boy Scout camp food wouldn't be nearly as good.

Tanner's trip to the ranch took only a half hour, thanks to light traffic on the interstate. He arrived shortly after sunup.

"Any trouble from Palmero last night?"

Lamar shook his head. "Not a peep. Looked in on him this morning. He twitched a little but didn't even try to look my way."

"You had your practice this morning, Lamar?"

Lamar took a deep breath and sighed heavily. "Yes, sir. I'm ready."

Kruger waited outside the bedroom door while Tanner went in. When Tanner poked Palmero in the back, the man recoiled and made a yappy sound like a startled dog.

"Get much sleep, Palmero?"

"Mr. Tanner, please, let me go right now and, swear to God, I'll never mention this to a soul. There's nothing to gain by what you're doing."

Tanner cut the tape and poked Palmero to his feet. "Sure there is. Like you said, I've lost my mind. Simple minds seek simple pleasures, Palmero. Today's gonna be fun . . . for me."

After securing the double hoods on Palmero, Tanner opened the door, and Kruger led the prisoner outside to the Ford pickup. Lamar drove them to the ravine and parked above the opposite end from the bunker. Kruger steered the tax agent down the hill to the trees where Lamar had mounted his targets.

"Take off your pants, Palmero."

"What for?"

Sonny pinched the right side of Palmero's neck with a vice-like grip. "Take 'em off."

The IRS agent dropped his pants and stepped out of them.

Sonny backed him against a thin ash tree and tied his hands to it, then strapped his waist and feet to the tree. Tanner removed the hoods from Palmero's face and taped his head to the trunk so he couldn't move, then backed away about six feet in front of Palmero. A board ran between them, straight out in front of Palmero at eye level, nailed to two trees. Along the board were five paper shooting targets a foot apart; they each had red bull's-eyes.

"Y-you aren't gonna kill me. You wouldn't have blindfolded me if you were."

"Wrong. We're about to play a deadly game, Palmero. It's called, 'I win or you die.' Here's how it goes. I ask questions. You give answers. Every time you don't give a right answer . . . well, you'll see as we go along."

Tanner put on a pair of clear, wraparound glasses. "First question: Why did you pull that bullshit extortion scam on Tanner Systems?"

Palmero's legs shook and his chin quivered.

"That was a . . . a routine call. We didn't know about the GSA contract. It —"

Tanner raised a hand and dropped it. The board between him and Palmero slammed against the trees with a sound like a sledgehammer, hitting squarely on its flat surface. A bullet hole just touched the red center of the farthest target from Palmero.

"Jesus Christ! What was that?"

"I heard a lie, Palmero, and you lost your first red dot. The board will take four more wrong answers. The fifth one goes in that pudgy ear on the side of your head."

"Next question: Repeat of the first one. Why'd you extort Tanner Systems?"

"I didn't extort your company, I —"

Another bullet hole appeared, this time inside the red center of the second target. Palmero recoiled from the board's movement as if a hammer blow had hit it.

"Three more wrong answers and I'll bury you right where you stand, Palmero."

"Tanner, please . . ."

"Third question: Why Tanner Systems?"

Palmero's knees gave way. He sagged against the rope around his waist and his huge belly rolled over it. Sweat beads formed on his face. He started to speak, squeezed his eyes and his mouth closed as if expecting another silent shot to shatter the board.

Tanner waited. "Well?"

"You won't kill me. I'm an agent of —"

CRACK!

A third bullet hit the board, this one just outside the red center toward Palmero's face. Wood splintered from the back side of the board and flew behind the trees.

"Now that was really stupid, Palmero. A complete waste. Only two targets left. I don't know how many thousands of acres there are on this place, but the boys figure you'd be good wolf chow after we're done with you today. You know, put some of you here, some of you there. Wolves and buzzards would clean you up in no time."

Tanner leaned forward, dramatizing his inspection of the board. "Only two more targets before you're wolf bait. Fourth question: Same as the others."

"I . . . I wasn't responsible. You have to know it wasn't me."

Tanner took a step closer, moving in front of the already smashed red spots on the board. He pulled papers from his coat pocket.

"Yeah, I know you're a pissant, a messenger."

He held the papers in front of Palmero. "But this is what it really comes down to."

Palmero squinted, and Tanner held the paper closer. "Tax lien on Harry St. John. Your signature. Your action. He was a harmless old man seventy-one years old. Made a simple mistake and you killed him, sure as if you'd put the gun in his mouth and pulled the trigger yourself."

"No, no, I didn't. Swear to God I didn't. That should have never happened. I didn't want to scam him. I was forced."

Tanner took a step back. "Why, Palmero? Why?"

"I, I can't —"

CRUNCH!

The board danced as a bullet hit the fourth target and shattered the board, sending shards of wood into Palmero's face. He screamed in a tone so high pitched that it surprised Tanner. He examined the tax man to see if he'd been severely injured.

Kruger, standing behind Palmero, waved to get Tanner's attention, then pointed. Tanner looked down.

"You just shit your shorts, Palmero. Figured that would happen. Good thing I made you take off your pants."

Palmero writhed against the ropes and tape, and began to cry. Tanner spoke in a softer voice. "You have one target left before your ear, Palmero. When it's gone and you fail the last question, I'll go down range and put the last one through your head myself. That's a promise. Now then —"

"No more, please! Oh, sweet Jesus, please stop!"

"No problem. All you have to do is give straight answers."

"Karney! It was Karney. She's been after you ever since she came to Austin. Even before that, waiting for the right time. Waited till the GSA gave you that contract. She told me when to do the audit and set up the charges against you."

"Further back. Why'd you come down on Harry St. John?"

"That was Karney, too. I'd only been in her unit a short time. I didn't know her scam at first."

"What scam?"

"She picked small businesses that wouldn't draw attention. Forced them to shut down, then had a silent partner buy the assets cheap at a quick auction. He'd sell them off, then cut her in on the profits."

"And you got a cut, too?"

"Y-yes, but not much of one."

"Why'd she go after Tanner Systems?"

"Can you take the tape off? Let me move —"

"Why'd she come after me?" Tanner shouted.

"You have to know that was just personal. She hates you, Mr. Tanner. Says you ruined her life and left her for no good reason."

Tanner stared at the tax agent, then spoke in an icy voice. "Her timing was too good. How did she know exactly when to drop the ax on me?"

Palmero squeezed his eyes closed again as if he expected the next shot. "There's someone inside your company passing information to her."

"Who?"

"I-I —"

"WHO, Palmero?"

"Bonner. Dave Bonner."

Tanner gaped at the tax agent, stunned by the revelation. "Bullshit."

"Swear to God. He and Karney knew each other in Maryland. He worked for the CFO of her ex-husband's company. Bonner tried to help her identify hidden assets in her ex's company to benefit her divorce position. The effort got him fired."

"What does that have to do with Tanner Systems? She wouldn't try to wreck a whole company just to get to me."

"The hell she wouldn't. She wanted a share of what would be left of Tanner Systems, too."

"And how did she think that could happen?"

"She and Kirk Watkins have some silent investors."

"Patricia and Watkins? You're making this up as you go along."

Palmero tried to turn his head, fearful of another shot. "No, it's true. Bonner and Watkins worked for the same accounting firm in Baltimore years ago. Watkins moved to Houston. He kind of paved the way for Bonner to move here and get positioned in the bank. He set Bonner up as a consultant and used him for inside info on good takeover prospects."

Tanner turned away, paced a few steps, then returned. "I can see that low-life bitch extorting me to get even for what she thought was a busted love affair. But she'd kill my uncle and wreck my whole company? Destroy all the people there just for revenge against me?"

"I've never known a tougher, more vindictive woman in my life, Mr. Tanner. She'll do anything."

Tanner stood nose to nose with Palmero. "Why did you have my uncle killed? You already had me to where I'd have to pay or lose my company."

Palmero's eyes grew wide, like a calf looking at a hot branding iron. "That wasn't supposed to happen. I begged her not to do it. She said it would convince you to pay up in case you had any ideas about fighting the penalty fees levied on you. Your promise to pay in return for dismissing the charges against him. When the SWAT team went in something happened. They —"

"Something sure as hell did, Palmero. You killed him. Another nice old man killed on your watch. You can't think of a reason good enough for me to let you stay alive."

"My God, you aren't that kind of man. Please, for God's sake."

"The paper said Ed pulled a gun on you and her. What really happened?"

Palmero blurted out the details of how Karney kept telling him to visualize her story. "She told me so many times that after a while I almost believed her."

"All right, Palmero. Here's your one chance. I want you to get me enough evidence to put Karney in prison."

"I can't do that. That would mean —"

Tanner stepped back again. "Wait!" Palmero pleaded. "All right, I'll do what I can. Just please don't shoot anymore."

"What kind of proof can you get to tie her to Bonner and Watkins?"

Palmero breathed hard, eyes darting side to side. "Give me a minute. Don't shoot. I can't put my hands on proof, but I know she has a trust fund in her daughter's name. That trust owns stock in Watkins's company."

"What else?"

Palmero's eyes were wild, like an animal looking for escape when there's no way out. "Watkins — and Bonner before he went to work for the bank — arranged payoffs for companies to avoid tax audits. Karney took enough of those to have a fat stash."

"Where?"

"She goes to Barbados a couple of times a year. She dropped her airline tickets one time, and I saw where she was going. Made me swear to never mention that she goes there. Probably has a numbered account."

"What else?"

"I can't think of anything. If I do I'll tell you, I swear."

Tanner took off his safety glasses and slipped them on Palmero, then stepped back. A bullet cleanly pierced the last target's red center. Tanner knew Palmero could feel the concussion when the bullet hit. The tax agent's eyes were still closed when Tanner removed the safety glasses from his face.

"Have a look, Palmero."

The terrorized man opened his eyes and Tanner pointed to the target. "Did you hear the shot before it hit the board?"

"No."

"See how all but one shot's a bull's eye? And that one would still kill you?"

"Yes."

"He can do that anywhere. So can the other men. Don't forget."

"Dear God, how could I?"

"Like I said, the game is 'I win or you die.' Today I won, so you don't die."

Palmero slumped against the ropes and heaved a deep sigh. Tanner motioned to Kruger, who put the blindfold on Palmero from behind, then untied him.

"Here's what happens now, Palmero. We'll take you home tonight. Get some rest tomorrow. We'll be watching you. Monday morning you go to your attorney, alone so there's no question of coercion. Tell him you've had an attack of conscience and want to set the record straight.

"Give your counsel a statement of the illegal things you've been involved in with Karney. Tell everything you know about her, Watkins and Bonner. Feel free to off-load as much guilt as you can. Get enough notarized copies of your statement to send three to me at Tanner Systems, one each to the Director of Internal Revenue Service, the FBI, and your congressman. I expect your attorney will go with you when you surrender yourself and deliver one copy to the U.S. attorney. Send my copies right away, but hold the others till I tell you to deliver them."

Palmero shook his head and reached for the blindfold, but Kruger grabbed his hand and hammer-locked his arm.

"If I do that, I'll go to jail."

"If you don't, I'll kill you. And you can be damned sure it'll happen soon because you'll go to prison or die before I do. You may be able to cut a deal for probation if you do what I'm telling you. Karney will take the hard fall. You have till Friday to deliver my copies of your confession.

If you try to leave Austin before then, you won't make it. If I don't have the document Friday evening, you won't see Saturday morning. Do we understand each other?"

Palmero nodded immediately. "Yes, yes! No more shooting, please."

Tanner said, "Walk him to the pond so he can wash off."

As Kruger walked Palmero up the slope to the top of the canyon, Tanner gave thumbs-up to Lamar in the bunker. Lamar jogged up the canyon, the .308 slung over his shoulder. Tanner grinned and spoke softly so Palmero couldn't hear. "Nice shooting, Lamar."

"You sure stood close to the board, BJ."

"No problem. I've seen you shoot."

"Think we scared him enough?"

Tanner chuckled. "He'll do what we want."

► 27 ◄

Castro and Kruger kept Tanner informed of Palmero's movements on Monday. They watched him enter an attorney's office at 10:30, and he didn't leave until 3 o'clock. After they followed him home and reported in, Tanner called Palmero's apartment.

"You didn't go to work today."

"Called in sick. I did what you wanted. Saw my lawyer."

"Yes, I know." Tanner read the address of the law office aloud. "Don't you feel better about yourself?"

"I wanted to finish the whole thing today, but my attorney said I should go slow, wait a few days. Be sure it's what I really want to do."

"You are sure, aren't you?"

Palmero's voice quavered. "He's having my statement transcribed tonight. We'll review it tomorrow, and I . . . I'll send copies everywhere you want them."

"Did you tell him everything?"

"Yes, except about seeing you."

"Way to go, Palmero. Keep up the good work and you may survive. We'll be watching."

Tanner ended the call and rang Betty Wilson. "Has Dave Bonner been around the last few days?"

"Matter of fact, yes. Have you put him on a project? Cecil says he's been bugging him way too much."

"We have a problem, Betty. Absolutely nobody is to know but you and me."

"Yes, sir?" Her tone reflected the concern Tanner expected.

"Lock up my office. Say you lost the key or something. Nobody goes in but you and Phillips."

"What's happened?"

"We have a traitor."

Allie surprised Tanner by arriving home two hours early. He shoved papers off the kitchen table into his briefcase and met her at the back door. "Hi, honey. What's the occasion?"

She returned his kiss, then gave him an exasperated look. "What are you up to?"

Her question took him off guard. "What do you mean?"

"Doc Maroun and I saw that attorney today."

"Yeah, and . . . ?"

"Oh, come on, BJ. You know damn well he offered us jobs."

Tanner raised his eyebrows, trying to look surprised. "What kind of jobs?"

"They want me to start working at a country retreat down near Ennis where vets can go after hospital treatment. Place where they can live, stay off the streets, away from booze and drugs, learn job skills."

He raised his hands. "Sounds good to me. You said you'd like to be out in the country. When do you start?"

She took a long breath and sighed. "Don't insult me, BJ. Some nonprofit outfit? Founded by anonymous donors, and you don't know anything about it?"

"Did you tell Maroun you thought I was involved?"

"No, I wanted to know exactly what the hell you think you're doing before I told him it wasn't gonna happen."

"It is gonna happen, darlin'. Already has."

"How? Why?"

"How's easy. I sold Tanner Systems for cash and bought some property. It'll take only a few more dollars to get it in good shape.

"The why part is easy, too. Lamar Weed and those other men are not the same people they were just a few weeks ago. They're in good condition, mental and physical. They're focused and they have their feet on the ground. Being on a real working ranch is good for them, Allie."

She surrendered on the last point. "Doc Maroun said they'd made faster improvement than anyone he's seen in the program so far."

"No reason others can't do the same. Get them off the streets. Give them structure, dignity. Teach them new skills."

"Yes, but that's not your job, BJ. You have to take care of yourself."

"How, by lying down and being shot full of pain-killers? By being a lump on a bed waiting to die? No way. We already talked about that."

She grabbed at her pocket for cigarettes that were no longer there, then crossed her arms and walked to the table. He moved behind her and hugged her. "You said you liked working with vets. Take a day off and I'll drive you out to Lamar's ranch. Let me show you what can be done."

She hesitated a moment, then nodded. "Okay, I'll ask Freda to split her shift and cover for me in the morning."

"That's my girl."

She buried her face in his chest. He stroked her hair and noticed how long it had grown in the past two months. "There're a couple of things I need to tell you before we go out there. You have to promise to keep them to yourself."

"What kind of things?"

"One's about the money for the vets' retreat. You can't tell Maroun or anyone else that you know where it's coming from."

She nodded.

"The other's about a little tax problem I have, and how I'm fixing it."

An hour later Allie sat on the floor in the den, gaping wide-eyed at Tanner after he'd explained his plan. He waited for her to speak, but no words came. "Well, what do you think?"

"I think I need a bottle of vodka and a carton of cigarettes." She climbed to her feet and headed for the kitchen. "How'd you ever convince other people to get involved in such a crazy scheme?"

"You see any holes in the plan?"

She returned with two glasses of grape juice. "Nobody can do that to the IRS."

"The sons of bitches aren't gonna get away with what they did to me. And to my uncle and your dad."

She kneeled on the floor in front of him. "You have to stop right now. Let that guy Palmero send his statement. You stay out of it after that and pray you don't go to jail for kidnapping. I'd feel responsible."

"Why?"

"Because you saw Palmero's name on my dad's papers. I think you're doing this for me, and I don't want that."

He shook his head. "Can't stop now. They'd only crucify Palmero, maybe Karney too if they find any proof of what she's done, but nobody outside the IRS would ever know what happened."

"So you're willing to spend your last days in prison to expose those two? Fine, but what happens if Lamar and the others get caught?"

The question caused Tanner's stomach to boil. "That can't happen. We've worked out the plan to perfection."

She shook her head. "Think back to your Marine Corps days. Nothing works perfectly. Maybe in theory, but not when there's a real enemy on the other side."

"We've pulled off everything so far without a hitch. As long as each person does their job, no problem. Wait till you meet my team tomorrow."

She raised her glass. "Here's to them. If they have any sense, maybe I can talk them out of this madness."

Palmero could feel sweat breaking out on his face as he approached Patricia Karney's office. Had she found out what had happened to him?

Had his lawyer called her? Told her about the confession? Should he go straight to the U.S. attorney's office and ask for protection from her?

He walked past the head-high panels of the general work area toward Karney's walled, private office by the windows, his breath growing shorter with each step. He stopped a moment before moving in front of her doorway, then leaned around to peek at her. Her face, normally so pale it seemed blue tinted, was flushed. She had squeezed her hands into tiny, white-knuckled fists on the desk.

Her narrow lips barely moved when she spoke. "Inside. Close the door."

"Wh-what is it, Patricia? Something wrong?"

She stared at him in silence until he thought he'd throw up.

"Tanner."

Holy Jesus and Mary! I'm dead.

Karney rose and came around the desk, her gaze never leaving Palmero. "I warned you. Warned Watkins, too. I can't believe you let this happen."

"I-I'm sorry, Patricia, I didn't . . . I mean there was no . . ."

She went on as if she hadn't heard him.

"The son of a bitch sold the company," she said. "Done deal. He moved as slick as if he knew what we were going do."

Palmero gaped at her, unable to assimilate her comment with his own thoughts. "I don't understand."

She paced along the windows. "He sold out, turned the company over to the employees. He took a loss. Big-time loss, but that's not enough to suit me. I wanted Watkins to get that company so I could have a piece of Tanner for myself."

She stopped and jabbed a finger at Palmero. He recoiled as if it were a gun.

"Get a Form 2210 on Tanner for two-point-five-million dollars. Do it right now. I want it signed off before my director leaves tonight so I can personally serve it on Tanner tomorrow. That'll burn another half million out of his pocket a year before he expects to pay capital gains. Move it!"

Palmero left her office without another word, afraid his knees would collapse before he could clear the door. He wiped his face with a sleeve as he walked to his desk and fell into his chair, swallowing hard to keep the contents of his stomach in place.

When he finally collected his thoughts and his pulse slowed to somewhere below the rate of a sprinter, he accessed Tanner's IRS records on his computer terminal, then he remembered that Tom Fear, Karney's director, had already left on his trip. Palmero's heart began pounding again as he dialed her intercom number.

"Patricia? Uh, Tom's already gone. Want me to set up the order for Bosworth's signature?"

"Shit!" she muttered. "No, Bosworth would ask too many questions. Carleton will be here tomorrow. Set it up for him to sign. Have it ready before you leave tonight and put it on my desk."

She slammed down the phone, adding to the pain already coursing through Palmero's head. He sat gazing across the office toward the windows, wishing he was on the tenth, or twentieth, or hundredth story instead of the ground floor.

Tuesday morning a silvery haze masked Dallas until the sun burned holes through the overcast. When they went to the garage, Tanner surprised Allie by getting into the pickup.

"Aren't there decent roads to the ranch?" she asked.

"It wouldn't be a good idea for me or my car to be seen there."

They climbed into the truck, and he told her about the deputies who'd befriended Lamar, how they dropped in once in a while for visits.

She stared at him, then shook her head as he turned onto the freeway. "My God, I can't believe what y'all are doing, BJ. It looks like your mind was the first thing to go."

When they arrived at the ranch, Ike ran to meet them at the front gate and raced along barking at the passenger side of the pickup, as if asking, who is the stranger that has come to see him?

Tanner parked in the carport, led Allie to the back of the house and through the kitchen door. Lamar, Becky and Castro rose from the table as they entered, and Tanner introduced everyone.

"This is Allie. Right now she thinks she's going to talk us out of our objective. Once she gets over that, she'll be a big help."

Castro brought more chairs to the table and held one for Allie. Becky sat next to her. "We've heard a lot about you. Glad to finally meet you."

Lamar poured coffee for Allie and heated apple juice in the microwave for Tanner, who raised his mug to the others.

"Here's to the team. Good to have you with us, Allie. You and Lamar better get to be good friends. Y'all are going to work real close together, but we can't have you working with the rest of us. While we do the fun stuff, you two will have to stay squeaky clean."

"Why should I be treated different from the others?" Allie demanded.

"Because you and Lamar have the biggest jobs, but they don't start till after we finish the fun part."

He grinned, enjoying the shocked expressions around the table.

"Guess it's time to tell y'all the rest of my plan."

► 28 ◄

Tanner brought more money to the ranch and worked in the background while helping Lamar hire contractors to clear brush, dig more stock ponds, and put up new fencing along the property adjoining his ranch. He felt proud of Lamar, pleased that the rancher had grown so much in such a short time, able to conduct business in town, no longer fearful of crowds and road congestion.

Although Tanner hadn't been present during discussions with contractors, he observed that the rancher arranged deals fair to both sides. Lamar said his dad taught him to be a firm negotiator when they hired people to work on the ranch. Tanner noted that Lamar learned his lessons well from his dad but wondered why that same father left him suffering from post-traumatic stress for so many years.

Des Blaylock called Tanner on Thursday. "I've ID'd the access codes I need. Started duplicating and storing data to create our mirror-image system. Sneaked into the central system in West Virginia two days ago. I've created a virus to plant there that'll give their memory chips Alzheimer's. If they try to replace data from file tapes, same thing will happen. There're only two ways they can restore the system. Best one is to get the codes from us. That way they could make a full recovery."

"What's the other alternative?"

"Shut down completely, reformat the system and install all new software." He blurted a hearty laugh in Tanner's ear. "Then they'd need a zillion hours of manual typing to re-enter tax records — if they have hard copies — but that wouldn't save their asses either."

"Why not?"

"Hell's bells, the way you handled the data systems access, your victim would have to go through every phone company central office in the U.S. to find where they've been breached. I could start the virus all over again."

"Are you sure their computer technicians won't know what's happened and be able to fix it?"

"Oh, they'll figure out what's been done in no time, but to figure the random codes I'll use to wreck their data will take a little longer."

"How much longer?"

Blaylock laughed. "A supercomputer would do it faster than anything else. That'd take about a hundred and fifty or sixty years to test every code combination."

"You sure you can restore the data?"

"No sweat. I'll mark where I start in their system. When you give them the random codes and starting point, they can have it cleaned up in a few hours. When do you want them infected?"

"Midnight next Friday."

After a moment Blaylock roared. "Midnight, April fifteenth. Good on you, boss. Now, that's my kind of twisted sense of humor."

Thursday morning Tanner drove to the area northeast of Dallas where his team trained. Sonny, experienced from military duty, finished early. Tanner observed Castro and Becky during their final efforts and nodded satisfaction. He called Lamar and said, "Look's like everybody's ready. See y'all tomorrow."

Late Friday morning, Tanner called Betty. "How's it going, Wilson?"

"Same as I told you yesterday. Everybody's wondering about you and what's going on. Cecil hasn't had much to say. He's staying locked up in his office most of the time; everything seems to be going slow but steady.

"There is a personal thing, BJ. Mr. Travis has called several times. He owns the building where your uncle's gun shop was. Says he has some very important information but he won't give it to anyone but you personally. Says it has to do with building security."

Tanner said, "I'll call him later. Has Mabry been there?"

"Yes, he and Phillips, but they don't know what to do. I have to tell them who to give assignments to. I don't know what to say when people ask for Cecil."

"He's screening candidates for my job. Has Bonner been around?"

"He wanted into your office. Got upset with me, but then he left. A messenger delivered a personal package for you from a law office this morning."

Tanner asked her to take it to his condo and leave it in the mailbox, then he called Sonny. "You still watching our boy?"

"Yes, sir. He's been in his office all morning."

"Go over to my place and watch for a package to be delivered by Betty around noon. Wait till she's out of sight, then pick it up and call me."

A half hour later Sonny called back. "The red ears worked. He must have thought of some things he didn't tell you. It's a thirty-four-page confession."

"Come on home. We're ready to take the next step tomorrow. You and Becky will leave tonight."

Tanner greeted Sonny on his return from Austin as the sun settled below a clear, red-orange horizon that soon gave way to darkness. Lamar broiled T-bones on the backyard grill while Castro made enough cottage fries and salad for a football team. Sonny showered and changed, then joined the others for supper. Castro ribbed him about keeping an eye on Palmero.

"You watch him all the time?"

Sonny nodded. "Knew where he was every minute."

"So how'd he look in the shower?"

Tanner allowed the jokes to run for a while, enjoying the bonding between himself, the three other men, and Becky. After they'd eaten and cleared the table, Lamar went to the fridge.

"Guess nobody gets to have a beer but Castro and me since you're all leaving soon."

Castro raised a hand. "I'll pass."

"You sure?"

"No more beers for me till this mission is complete."

Tanner had noted Castro's diminished alcohol consumption since his trip to Houston and had mentioned it to him in private, but he gave the others no indication of his pleasure about the Latino's new attitude.

Tanner checked his watch. "How long will it take you two to get where you're going tonight?"

Becky and Sonny rose. "She says two hours, but it'll be nearer three since I'm driving."

Lamar and Castro wished the Krugers well, then Tanner walked to the carport with them.

"Sonny, you've done a good job, but the last one was easy compared to what you're going for now. Be damn careful, and don't either one of you be afraid to abort the mission at any time if there's the slightest hitch."

Becky said, "I checked this plan from every angle, BJ. All we have to worry about is the first hour. After that, it's a breeze."

"You have everything you need?"

She gestured to the pickup. "Four drums of JP fuel, five gallons of oil and a used Yamaha motorcycle under the camper shell. The bike isn't in great shape, but it'll carry Sonny and me a couple hundred miles with no trouble. Sonny and Ernie lifted the other motorcycle into the hayloft with a hoist and hid it behind some bales.

"Lamar will take fuel to the relay point near Austin. Then we can head for Mexico."

She opened the cab, took a hand-held, two-way radio from behind the seat and gave it to Tanner. "It's set to the first frequency we'll use."

Tanner stared at the radio. "If anything isn't right . . ."

"Hey, there's never been a better team than the Krugers. No sweat, BJ. We'll handle it right, or it won't happen. Believe me, it'll be easier than you can imagine. Surprise will paralyze them."

"That's right, BJ. Me and Sis can do damn near anything."

Tanner shook hands with Becky and Sonny. "Good luck. Call me soon as you can tomorrow night."

Sonny and Becky drove to Fort Worth, then west on Interstate 80 for two hours. A few miles east of Ranger, Becky pointed out an exit and they left the freeway. Sonny followed her directions along a farm road, then onto an unused gravel lane that was badly rutted and overgrown. While they crept along, rabbits ran in front of the truck, froze in the headlights, then scurried away.

After a mile, the road ended at a tall Quonset-shaped tin building, long abandoned and overgrown with brush. Sonny stopped the pickup with the headlights aimed at the big sliding doors of the building.

"How the hell did you find this place?"

"Pilot I knew in the Army. His dad had a crop-duster service here. Place's been abandoned for ten years or more."

"How'd you know the building was still standing?"

"Didn't till I flew out here two weeks ago. Airstrip's shot. State built a dam south of here. It backed water up over the far end. Made it too short for fixed wingers. Come on, I'll show you what's in the hangar."

Each of them took leather work gloves and flashlights from a bag on the seat and headed for the building. They checked the ground around the outside but found no footprints or other indications that anyone had been there since Becky's last visit.

Sonny opened the lock his sister had put on the hasp, then pushed the door open wide enough to walk through. After scanning the building with a Maglite, Becky moved further inside and illuminated a steel and aluminum dolly with eight hard-rubber tires along each side of two channels eight feet long and a foot wide. A long Y-hitch attached the dolly to a Bobcat tractor.

Sonny paced the sides of the dolly, which measured eight by twelve feet. "You sure this'll do the job?"

"If those doors opened another four or five feet we wouldn't need it. I would just fly it out of here."

Sonny pushed the door wider while Becky climbed into the pickup and backed it inside the hangar, positioning it along the right side of the dolly. Sonny propped boards on the tailgate for a ramp and rolled the motorcycle to the floor. Then he hitched a torsion line from the front of the pickup bed around each barrel and rolled them to the floor.

After standing the barrels on end, he closed and locked the hangar door. Becky pulled three packed parachutes and two sleeping bags from behind the seat of the pickup.

"Better get some sleep," Becky said, "We have to be on that motorcycle by six in the morning."

► 29 ◄

Sonny awoke to the sound of his wristwatch alarm at 5:30. He crawled out of the sleeping bag and stretched the kinks from his back and legs. Becky roused and stood, smiling as if she'd spent the night on a feather bed.

"You bring anything to eat?" Sonny asked.

She shook her head. "Back to the freeway and two miles west is our exit. There's a truck stop there. Hot showers, and the food's okay."

They slipped out of their clothes and changed into camouflage military uniforms with the ranks they'd earned. At 0600, Lance Corporal Sonny Kruger locked the hangar door and started the motorcycle. Captain Becky Kruger climbed on behind him. Both wore helmets with tinted visors covering their faces.

Before going to the road, Sonny headed south along what used to be a dirt runway, now deeply grooved by erosion.

When he turned the bike to head back, he noticed that the top and sides of the corrugated metal skin on the Quonset hangar had rusted to a dingy brown that nearly matched the bare patches of earth around it.

"I thought you said this place had been abandoned only a few years."

"Yeah, but it was built before you were born. Last week I thought I'd never get those old doors to move. I used a whole can of WD-40 on the top rails. Then I replaced the rollers."

The trip along the old lane went faster in daylight. They ducked hanging branches, dodged rocks and ruts, then sped down the farm road to the freeway.

When they reached the truck stop, each headed for their respective facilities for hot showers. Afterward, they met in the restaurant for breakfast. Becky had removed the stitched name tags from their uniforms and replaced them with names from jackets she'd found in a surplus store in Dallas. The waitress looked at them while taking their orders. "Wilson and Adams, huh? You look enough alike to be brother and sister."

Becky shrugged and Sonny continued to study the menu.

After eating eggs, bacon and hashed browns, they left the truck stop at 7:30 and headed north through rolling hills coming alive with spring grass and budding leaves. Along the highway, blue bonnets formed large green patches with only a hint of the radiant buds that would soon adorn the Texas highways.

The Krugers crossed the Red River into Oklahoma at noon. A half hour later, Sonny stopped the motorcycle two blocks from the main gate of the Armstrong Air National Guard facility. While he and Becky watched traffic passing through the gate, she tapped him on the back.

"See what I mean? They don't even check IDs in the cars, much less bikers. Let's wait for a line to form, everybody heading back to base after lunch. We'll cruise right through, no problem."

Sonny moved a block closer, waited for traffic to stack up at the gate and joined the line. The guard held up a hand to stop them until Becky leaned out far enough for him to see her insignias. He waved them through and snapped a salute. She returned it.

"Okay, little brother, turn left. The PX is two blocks down. We'll hang out there a while, then go walk the flight line and check night schedules. There'll be a flight taking off around eighteen thirty."

"What if there isn't?"

"Then we'll call in a special from the XO's office."

Sonny chuckled. "Yeah, right."

"Don't laugh. I did that to make weekend flights when I was on active duty. Used to go out at dusk when sailboats were heading in off the lake and it was too dark to see my side numbers. I'd come up behind a boat, autorotate till we were about fifty feet above it, then add power and hover right on top of it. Blew them over every time."

Sonny parked the bike in an end space at the PX. "You're one bad chick for playing grab-ass in a Huey. How are you when it comes to being serious?"

"Better than you'll believe, little bro. Wait 'n' see."

They drank coffee in the canteen at the PX until they felt conspicuous, then wandered through the exchange and around the base. Becky had been right about how to get into the military facility, but they had to pass time until dark without looking suspicious or being challenged by officials.

At 1500, they went to the flight line separately. Sonny walked along the edge of the tarmac and watched four helicopters land. After the flight crews left the aircraft, Becky approached the last Huey on the ramp, the one farthest from the line shack, while Sonny watched the ground crew tend the helo at the opposite end. The enlisted man in charge of ground care for the helo that Becky approached gave her a sharp salute, recognizing her shoulder patch designating her as a regular Army unit member instead of National Guard.

She returned the salute. "How are the weekend pilots treating your equipment, sergeant?"

"Nothing is like it was a few months ago when I was active, ma'am."

"Your aircraft in good shape?"

"The best, ma'am. Even that, uh, the major and his crew didn't down it for night duty."

"When's the next launch?"

"Eighteen forty-five."

"Think your equipment can stand up to a regular Army inspection, sergeant?"

"Well, ma'am, I mean, well, it just now landed. I haven't had time to —"

Becky nodded. "I'll allow for that. I'm only checking mechanical."

She went over the aircraft thoroughly, engaging the battery and checking instrumentation, then climbing on the transmission deck to check for fluid leaks and loose or missing safety wires. She examined the engine, tail rotor, fuselage, hatches and skid rails.

Becky nodded her satisfaction. "Soldier, you have a clean and safe aircraft. Only needs fuel and oil to be ready for the next launch."

The man gestured toward the far end of the ramp. "Fuel truck is on the way, ma'am. My bird will be ready in fifteen minutes."

"Your squadron better be proud to have you taking care of their equipment."

The soldier beamed. "Thank you, ma'am."

"You working the evening launch?"

"Yes, ma'am."

She nodded. "Thank you, Sergeant . . . Macklin," she said reading the name on his uniform. "Well done. Keep up the good work."

"Yes, ma'am. Thank you, ma'am," Macklin said and saluted.

Sonny joined up with Becky as she headed away from the flight line. "Is that the one?"

She nodded. "Damn shame, really. That's a four oh aircraft and the plane captain does a hell of a good job taking care of it."

The Krugers walked the whole base before dark. Sonny thought the sun would never set. At times he and Becky would split up and walk several blocks, falling in near other groups of National Guard men and women on the move, but avoiding direct contact.

At 1800, they met at the PX and drank more coffee while the sun settled behind the gentle slopes west of Armstrong, finally leaving the air base in darkness. After checking their personal equipment, they headed for the helo ramp, approaching the opposite end from the line shack. They waited behind an auxiliary power unit at the edge of the ramp, confident that no one could see them in the darkness. Red-lens flashlights and orange directing wands were the only lights allowed on the flight line to avoid night blindness.

Sonny's chest tightened when he saw vague images of men silhouetted in the red glow of the line-shack door.

"Here they come."

Becky touched his arm, causing an involuntary muscle contraction. "Okay, little brother, you know what to do. I'm on my way."

She put on gloves and her black motorcycle helmet with the visor down partway to hide her face. Given her size and the darkness, no one would figure her to be a woman unless they heard her voice.

Sonny put on goggles, pulled his cap tight and waited for the three-man crews to walk around their aircraft for preflight inspections. He became aware of the cool spring evening and of the cold sweat beads rolling down his chest. He peered into the darkness behind the helos, but he couldn't see Becky.

When the ground crewman that had replaced Macklin for night-shift duty moved out in front of the helo and lighted his directing wands, Sonny knew the flight crew had boarded.

The first helicopter started its engine. The low hum of jets coming to life gradually climbed to a high-pitched, piercing whine.

Sonny jogged along the edge of the ramp until he was behind the ground crewman, who held the orange wands crossed over his head.

The second aircraft's engine revved. The kerosene-like odor of jet fuel drifted across the ramp in the wash of the rotors.

Sonny approached the man, then stopped as he glimpsed the profile of someone on a bicycle peddling from the line shack toward him. He crouched behind a Kidde flight-line fire extinguisher on wheels, parked at the edge of the ramp.

The third helo's engine began to turn.

The bicycle rider passed between Sonny and the ground crewman. Apparently it was someone merely leaving the flight line, heading for the PX.

The ground crewman began rotating a wand overhead, signaling for the last Huey's crew to start the engine. Sonny ran to the man and startled him by touching his shoulder. The rotors began turning, gaining speed, catching up to the rate of the other aircraft. With the noise of jet engines and rotors beating the air, Sonny had to shout to make himself heard.

"Sergeant Macklin needs you in the line shack, right now! Emergency. I'll finish the launch."

The man peered at Sonny but obviously couldn't recognize him in the darkness and behind the goggles he wore. He nodded, handed over the wands and ran toward the building.

The first helo lifted six feet above the ramp and began to air-taxi sideways toward the runway, its rotors beating the air with the distinct whop-whop sound of the Huey.

Sonny crossed his wands, signaling the pilot to hold, then placed the lights on the ground, still crossed, and ran to the helicopter. The crewman in back leaned out, but Sonny climbed around him and boarded the aircraft. When the crewman started to ask what was happening, Sonny shoved a Browning semiautomatic pistol in his face and pointed to the deck with a gloved hand. Too stunned to react, the man complied as Sonny pushed him down and put a foot on the back of his neck.

He removed the helmet from the crewman and put it on so he could hear the pilots on the intercom.

The second aircraft lifted and began to air-taxi.

Sonny moved to the opening from the cargo area between the pilots and pointed the gun at the captain's face. Using the intercom, he said, "First man to key the radio is dead."

Both pilots froze. Becky opened the right side pilot's hatch, yanked his helmet off, unbuckled his seat belt and motioned with her gun for him to climb into the cargo area, where Sonny forced him face down on the deck next to the crewman. She held the gun on the co-pilot until Sonny pulled him into the cargo area.

The third aircraft lifted and began to air-taxi. Sonny glanced toward the line shack and noticed someone running toward them. Three others headed out the door behind him.

Becky strapped herself into the pilot's seat and took the controls. Then Sonny dragged the co-pilot into the cargo area. He pulled a roll of duct tape from a side pocket of his camo blouse and wrapped the man's hands behind his back. Becky put on the pilot's helmet and shouted over the intercom.

"No time for that! Ground crew's on to us. Get them out of here. Now!"

Without hesitation, Sonny dragged the pilot to a sitting position at the hatch and shoved him out. The man hit the ground running, hands taped behind him. Sonny motioned with the gun for the others to leave the aircraft. They were gone in an instant.

The ground crewman raced to within six feet of the helo as Becky turned up the RPM and lifted the collective stick. Sonny aimed his pistol at the crewman, who stopped as the Huey lifted. Instead of following the other aircraft to the left toward the runway, Becky climbed 30 feet, then headed to the right, crossing the main part of the base, barely clearing rooftops.

Sonny scrambled to find a grip and avoid falling out of the aircraft, surprised by the move.

"Jesus, Sis, you about lost me. Sorry things didn't go like we planned."

He heard no sign of the stress that had been in her voice when she had shouted before. "Check for the other aircraft. Can you see any of them coming our way?"

Sonny peered into the sky toward the base, unable to see any lights besides the rotating beacon flashing one green and two white lights every few seconds.

"Don't see them."

"Well, there's good news and bad news."

"Yeah?"

"Good news is we're not guilty of kidnapping and we don't have to stop and put the crew on the ground."

"What's the bad news?"

"If there's one air controller in the tower that doesn't have his head up his ass, every military base within five hundred miles already knows somebody stole a Huey."

The radio had been alive with normal departure information. Now the air controller's voice changed from the confident monotone that directed routine traffic to a higher pitch. "Guard four seven, tower. Where . . . What the . . . Four seven, you're in violation of the flight pattern. Return to base and land without delay."

After a pause, the voice continued. "Guard four seven, turn downwind, return to base and land at helo spot next to tower. Stand by for duty officer. Four seven, you copy?"

Becky headed west from Armstrong, climbing to 300 feet in full view of the tower, running lights already turned on by the original crew. Sonny slipped into the left seat while she strapped her note board to her thigh. She banked to the north and a minute later switched off the running lights as she zigzagged side to side to check for aircraft behind them.

"See any of the other helos, Sonny?"

"Negative."

"Me neither."

She switched off the radio, continued northwest across the first rise, then made Sonny's stomach jump into his throat when she nosed down, gained speed and leveled off too close to the treetops for flying in the dark.

"Everything all right, Becky?"

"No, this helmet's too big, keeps falling down over my eyes."

"What? You mean you can't see?"

"Just kidding. Hell, yes, everything's all right. I finally have a Huey attached to my ass again. One more rise coming up. After we cross that I'll turn south. We can stay under radar all the way to the Red River. A few miles west along the river there's a general aviation airport on the Texas side. We'll climb out of there with the transponder on a civilian VFR code. FAA'll think we're local traffic. You see any aircraft?"

Sonny had been watching the ground, expecting the skid rails to strike tree branches at any moment. He lifted his gaze to the horizon on his side and behind the aircraft.

"Nothing, Sis. Why don't you turn the radio back on, see what they're doing?"

"If they're still on the same frequency, they aren't doing anything worth worrying about. I don't have time to look for them on other frequencies." She paused, then said, "Okay, we're gonna slow down in a couple of minutes. Some power lines ahead of us. We'll go under them."

"What the hell!"

Sonny peered ahead but could see nothing. When Becky reduced power and slowed the aircraft he still couldn't see power lines. Becky turned to the right until he saw a steel tower dead ahead. She banked the helo sharply to the right, then back. The tower, carrying megawatt power lines, flashed by within a few feet of them. He gasped, sucking in a deep breath and the intercom mouthpiece.

"Good God, you almost hit the tower!"

"No way. Flew at it till I could see the wire cradles, knew we were under them, then scooted by right next to the tower. That's where the cables hang the highest. Trust me, bro. I told you I know what I'm doing."

"Shouldn't you have night-vision goggles or something?"

"Nah, that'd take all the fun out of it."

He shook his head and mumbled. "Hope I live to enjoy some of your fun."

When they reached the river, the quarter moon caused an uneven reflection that Becky said improved her depth perception and allowed her to fly even lower, much to Sonny's discomfort. After ten minutes along the river, she turned inland over Texas.

"Okay, time to look like a civilian aircraft."

She turned on the radio and set in codes she read from her note pad while Sonny held a penlight. "We'll set in the GA code for VFR and . . . good, there's Sutter airport, but the lights aren't on. Watch this, Sonny."

She keyed the radio three times and the airport runway lights came on dead ahead. Again he felt sure the helo would hit something along the ground, but Becky banked to line up with the runway, flew halfway down its length, then climbed gently to 1,000 feet. Sonny took a deep breath, feeling as if it was the first breath he'd had since boarding the Huey.

Again Becky keyed the radio, then spoke in a higher voice and softer tone than he'd ever heard from her.

"Flight service, this is Cherokee five bravo yankee, departing Sutter for private airstrip west of Ranger. I'm VFR at one thousand, and I'm real sorry, but I forgot to file a flight plan."

She gave a fictitious name and aircraft description, and estimated flight time.

"Roger five bravo yankee. Say the name of your private airport destination."

"My daddy's big pasture. He'll turn the lights on for me and get the cows out of the way."

Becky ended the FAA call, then laughed over the intercom while Sonny scanned the sky and pointed out lights above them to the southeast.

She held a thumb down. "No sweat, that's commercial traffic heading for DFW. Sit back and relax. We'll be at our little hangar in a half hour."

After crossing Interstate 80, she slowed the Huey and dropped down within twenty feet of the flat ground of a long pasture, then stayed low as she turned toward the old crop-duster strip.

Again she used the gentle voice on the radio. "Flight service, this is five bravo yankee. I'm on the ground. Good night."

She switched off the radio and transponder. "The FAA will think some rancher's spoiled daughter landed in her backyard."

When they touched down in front of the old hangar, dirt lifted around the aircraft, momentarily forming a curtain of dust swirling at the outer tips of the blades. Sonny removed the helmet and put on goggles before leaving the aircraft. The blowing grit stung his face as he ran for the hangar. Becky kept the rotor engaged while he opened the doors. Then he started the Bobcat and towed the dolly outside.

Becky raised the collective, eased the helo up and followed Sonny's light signals until she'd settled the skid rails onto the dolly. After shutting down the engine, she hand-turned the tail rotor until the main rotor blades lined up lengthwise to the aircraft. Sonny restarted the tractor and backed the helicopter inside the hangar.

Once they'd closed the doors, he laughed and raised his hand for a high-five. "You're every bit as good as you said."

She slapped his hand. "Let's refuel and check the oil, then I'm ready for some supper."

Sonny shook his head. "We better call BJ as soon as we get to a cell signal. He isn't gonna believe we pulled this off."

She stepped onto the dolly and stroked the side of the helo with her gloved hand.

"Just wait till you see what else I can do with this sweet thing."

► 30 ◄

Tanner and Allie sat in the den watching a Harrison Ford movie she'd rented. He checked his watch so often she asked if he'd rather turn off the video.

"Sweetheart, you haven't seen a bit of this movie."

"Let's stay with it. I wouldn't —"

His gray cell phone rang and he grabbed it in a flash.

"Yes?"

Sonny said, "Howdy, boss. We have Pegasus safe in the palace."

Tanner's heart pounded and he couldn't speak for a moment. After a deep breath, he said, "Are you two okay?"

"Yes, sir."

"My God, I've been . . . You sure you're in the clear? Nobody followed? No chance that radar —"

"Wings did a hell of a job," Sonny said. "One little hitch from the original plan, but everything went smooth and fast as a bullet down a barrel."

"Can anyone ID either of you?"

"No, sir. No one ever heard Wings's voice. Never saw a face."

Tanner wanted details but wouldn't discuss it further by phone. "When will you be back to base?"

"We're about to have supper. It's been a long day. Should be home in about three hours."

Allie ignored the movie and sat watching him until her phone rang.

She stopped the VCR and went to the kitchen for her call. Tanner watched her leave, then said to Sonny, "You have it inside? Secure?"

"Boss, everything's been a four-oh exercise. Wings is even better than I expected. Pulled tricks out of the hat that would've stopped the best in the business. We're refueled and ready to roll."

"Well done, son. I hope you're having the best steaks in your part of the state. Be careful on the road tonight."

Tanner ended the call and rose, feeling better than he had for days, exhilarated by the news. Yes, they'd reviewed the plan over and over, discussed contingencies, ways to scrub the exercise at any point and escape, but they'd actually pulled it off. He could hardly wait to see Sonny and Becky and hear the details of their mission.

He paced the den, then headed for the kitchen. His excitement faded when he saw Allie's ashen face. Her hands trembled, banging the phone when she tried to put it in the cradle.

"You have to get out of here, right now!"

"Why? What's happened?"

She started toward the bedroom, tugging his arm to follow her. "That was Freda. The FBI's been looking for you at the hospital. They just left there a few minutes ago."

Tanner felt as if he'd been slugged in the stomach. He couldn't get a deep breath.

"Coming here?"

"Probably. They asked for Doc Maroun's address and phone number. It won't take them long to find out you're staying here."

"But why? How could they —"

"BJ, you have to leave. No time to pack everything. Grab your stuff from the bathroom. I'll get some of your clothes together."

He went into the bathroom and gazed at himself in the mirror, trying to figure where he'd slipped up. Not because of the helicopter. No way anyone could have connected that one to him yet, even if the Army knew who'd taken it.

Palmero!

Had to be. He'd caved in to Karney and told what happened to him. But how would he know where to send the FBI? Castro and Kruger had hinted that they were driving him to south Texas. He couldn't possibly have figured where they'd taken him in the van.

What about Lamar and his ranch? Castro? The Krugers?

"Come *on*, BJ. Go!"

He raked his shaver and other items off the counter into his travel kit. Allie had loaded a duffle with socks and underwear and grabbed clothes on hangers from the closet. She shoved a load in his arms, took more off the rack, then headed for the garage. He picked up his briefcase on the way through the kitchen.

They shoved his clothes into the pickup, on the passenger seat and floor. Allie slammed the door, kissed him, then pushed him toward the other side of the truck.

"Go, sweetheart."

"Darlin', can you find your way to Lamar's ranch?"

"Yes, now go."

He kissed her again, then climbed into the truck and started the engine. Allie went outside the garage and peered both ways along the service lane.

Tanner startled her when he jumped out of the pickup.

"What are you —"

"My phone. Left it in the den."

As he hurried through the kitchen, he saw car lights on the street in front of the house. Were they here already? Could he still make it out the back? He grabbed the cell phone and raced back to the garage, coughing and breathing hard.

"I love you, Saint Allie."

"I love you too, sweetheart. Now, get going."

He headed the long way down the lane. When he reached the corner, he turned away from the street in front of her house, resisting the urge to see if federal agents had already descended. He turned left, right, then left again without seeing a moving car. Satisfied that he wasn't being followed, he headed for the freeway, then south toward Ennis.

While crossing the Trinity River bridge he dialed Lamar. "Everything okay at your end?"

"Yes, sir, fine. Are you okay?"

"Somebody's looking for me."

Lamar hesitated a moment. "Because of Wings? They called and said everything went okay."

"No, I think our guest spilled his guts. Looks like we should have taken one more ear."

"Where are you, boss?"

"Heading your way, but I'll stay in the nearest motel tonight."

"No, sir. You'd be better off here. Call again from outside. I have a safe place for you. No sweat."

Tanner called again, a mile from the ranch. No deputies had been by, so he drove through the gate and into the barn. Castro closed the sliding door. Lamar had Honey and Beauty saddled with camping gear strapped on them.

"Why the horses?"

"Ground's a little soft from the last rain. Don't want to leave tire tracks. Besides, I doubt there's an FBI agent that'd think to follow horse tracks, even if he recognized them."

"Have to get rid of my personal stuff from the truck."

Castro said, "I'll take care of it, BJ."

Lamar gestured toward the horses. "Let's go."

Tanner slipped his briefcase strap over his shoulder and climbed on the horse. "Are we going to the bunker?"

"No, sir, a little campsite nobody could find without walking every square inch of the ranch."

They rode at a slow pace across the pastures, dark except for the faint glow of a quarter moon. When they reached the far edge of the grazing area in the back pasture, Lamar used a flashlight to find a break between shrubs leading into heavy brush. They rode into the thicket of hackberry trees and brambles near the south fence, then down into a wash about twelve feet deep. Lamar led the way along the wash fifty yards, then stopped by a flat shelf three or four feet above the bottom of the ravine.

"Anybody but me comes snooping out here they'll fall in the gully before they find you. The ground here is high enough to keep you above water in case of rain. Trees overhang so no one can see anything from the air. You'll be safe here, BJ."

They set up a six-by-eight-foot tent, barely tall enough for Tanner to stand up inside. Lamar tossed a roll of dark-green construction plastic, dull side up, over the tent, shielding the light of a lantern inside. Then they put all the camp gear in the tent.

Tanner marveled at how much preparation Lamar had done in such a short time, packing enough food and water for three days, even a foot pump for the air mattress under his sleeping bag.

From a coat pocket Lamar took one of the Browning Hi-Power semiautomatics Castro had brought from Houston. He also had two loaded magazines and a box of ammo.

"No need for this, but I thought you might like to have it while you're out here."

Lamar pulled a folding stand from one of the bags and set it up, then placed plastic bags and toilet paper beside it. "Combo camp stool and latrine." He gave Tanner a wink. "Guess we're old enough to be spoiled some in the field."

"Thanks, Lamar. A couple of days and we'll figure out what's going on with the FBI. Then I'll leave here and hide somewhere else. Don't want to put you or the ranch at risk."

"BJ, I'm not gonna sit on my ass and watch you take off by yourself trying to hide from the feds, especially when they're the ones that have committed all the fouls."

Tanner shook his head. "I'll get away from them somehow. We've come too far to let them shut us down now."

"I'll be here first thing in the morning, BJ."

Lamar climbed on his horse and led the other horse out of the gully.

Tanner chewed four Tums and downed three Tylenol. Then he slipped into the sleeping bag, turned out the battery-powered lantern and stared into the darkness.

How had the FBI got on to him? Had Palmero told Karney instead of going to the U.S. attorney? That didn't make sense, not after he'd made a sworn statement to his own attorney and provided copies of the confession to Tanner. Palmero couldn't have known he'd been taken to a place near Dallas. Kruger and Castro made sure of that.

Tanner covered every step of his plan, every action of each person, and he couldn't find any flaws in what they'd done up to this point. But the FBI was looking for him, and they'd come too close to finding him.

How?

Sunday morning, after a night of fitful sleep, Allie woke when she rolled to BJ's side of the bed and found only empty space. Struggling to bring the world into focus, she went to the kitchen and made coffee. While waiting for it to brew, she felt the strongest urge in weeks to have a cigarette. She considered for a moment going to the 7-Eleven a few blocks away for a pack — no, a carton — of Marlboros. She closed her eyes and inhaled a deep breath through clenched teeth, fantasizing the heady effect of a tobacco high after so many weeks.

The coffee maker gurgled, interrupting her fantasy. Then she peeked between the blinds of the kitchen window to see if FBI agents were parked in front of her house. They hadn't come as she expected. She wondered which part of BJ's plan had been breached and how the feds learned about it.

She poured coffee, then sat alone at the kitchen table as she had for so many years before BJ came back into her life. Again she felt the overpowering urge for a cigarette. Thank God there were none hidden in the house. Thank God smoking wasn't allowed in the hospital. For a moment she thought of calling Freda as she had so many times to overcome the desperate desire for a drink, then she decided to get dressed and call Lamar Weed to ask about BJ.

She left the house twenty minutes later. The streets were empty in the first light of dawn except for a station wagon driven by a bleary-eyed mother while her son tossed newspapers from the tailgate.

Allie avoided stopping at the convenience store where she'd purchased cigarettes so many times and went to a strip mall farther away. No stores were open, but there was a pay phone in front of the market. She dialed Lamar's cell phone, a number BJ had made her memorize rather than writing it down. He'd admonished her not to use names when she talked to Lamar. When he answered, she said, "You know who this is?"

"Sure do."

"Is he with you? Is he all right?"

"He's fine."

"I want to talk to him."

A pause. "Where are you calling from?"

"A phone booth."

"He's not here, but he's perfectly safe. Nobody will find him."

"Have they been there looking for him?"

"No."

"Haven't been here either. I don't know what's going on. Why they went to the —"

"Careful."

"They went there looking for him but didn't come to my place."

"I'll get in touch with him, see what he wants to do. Call back in an hour."

She replaced the handset, wiped away a tear and shivered in the early-morning dampness. When she turned to the car, she froze. BJ's Cadillac! She couldn't drive his car, not with the FBI after him.

The sky had brightened, but Dallas hadn't yet awakened to Sunday morning. The only sound she could hear came from the freeway a few blocks south. She jumped into the car, drove home and pulled into the garage, closing the car inside, wishing she still had the old Oldsmobile.

She dug the phone book from a kitchen drawer to look up car rental agencies and called an Avis office in a downtown hotel. She arranged to pick up a car, then called a taxi.

▶ 31 ◀

After calling Lamar again from a pay phone, Allie drove the rental car to Ennis. Backtracking between freeway exits and stopping a few times on isolated frontage roads the way BJ taught her caused the thirty-mile trip to take more than an hour.

Lamar assured her that BJ was all right, but she worried about the constant agony he now lived with. She wished she could get him to see Dr. Weiss and start treatment for pain management.

She wondered if he'd eaten the previous night. With no appetite, he'd pass up meals if she didn't insist that he eat to keep up his strength and weight. The high-protein drinks helped for a while, but they were gradually losing their effect.

She felt that, somehow, if she could be with BJ all the time, he'd keep his strength and be all right, but when he was away from her, he'd disappear a little at a time until he was gone. No matter how many people were on the ranch, no matter how much they cared for him, if she wasn't there with BJ, she'd lose him. The thought hurt her heart as surely as if someone had hit her.

Castro met Allie at the cattle auction barn in Ennis, where she left the rental car and rode with him to the ranch. After crossing the cattle guard onto the ranch, he passed the barn and drove across the pastures to the top of the ravine above the bunker.

Tanner and Lamar rode the big quarter horses out of the thicket of trees, sun at their backs, barely visible until they were out of the shadows. Allie leaped from the van and hugged Tanner when he dismounted.

"Are you all right, sweetheart?"

"I'm fine, darlin'."

"Did you eat last night? This morning?"

Tanner didn't answer. Counting heads, he said, "Where're the Krugers?"

Castro tapped his cell phone. "Becky's in the house. Sonny's in the barn, watching the road. He'll signal if anybody shows up."

Tanner turned back to Allie. "Did the FBI come to the house?"

Her brow furrowed. "No. No call, nothing. There's no way they could have followed me either. I did all the things you told me to do while driving here. I even stopped on the freeway, got out and checked to be sure there wasn't a plane or helo flying around."

Tanner gazed at the ground a moment, then looked at Lamar and Castro. "Any ideas about how they got on to me?"

No one had an answer.

Tanner paced another minute, coughing frequently, then headed for the van. "Let's go."

Allie fell in beside him and put an arm around his waist. Castro and Lamar looked at each other. "Go where?" Lamar asked.

"Ennis. I'll call Phillips from a pay phone, see if he knows anything."

Castro drove them to the house while Lamar took the horses to the barn. Tanner asked Allie to wait at the ranch while Castro took him to town.

"No!" she said. "You need me to be with you."

"I'll only be a few minutes, then—"

"You haven't eaten. I won't let you go till you have breakfast."

He sighed and sat down while she prepared fried steak, eggs and wheat toast.

An hour later, with his collar turned up and wearing one of Lamar's Stetsons pulled low, Tanner climbed out of the van and into a phone booth at a service station. He dialed Phillips's home phone.

"Mornin', Phil."

"BJ! Where the hell are you?"

"You're not the only one asking that."

"Then you know the FBI's looking for you?"

"Yeah, but I don't know why."

"The IRS is playing hard ball. Claim you're a flight risk after taking your money out of the company. They sent an agent to your condo, then to the office with a tax bill for your capital gains. Betty told them you'd gone to the Dallas VA hospital, but nobody there knows where to find you."

"And let's keep it that way," Tanner said.

"Your disappearing act gives some credibility to what they say. They delivered a copy of the bill to me and sent the FBI looking for you. The law says I have to tell them where to find you, BJ."

"You don't know where to find me. Who was the agent?"

"Karney. She acted like she'd rather have you brought in dead than alive."

Tanner felt the heat as his face flushed. "That's because I stopped her from stealing a piece of Tanner Systems. I'd cut the bitch's heart out if she had one."

"This is about more than a tax bill. What haven't you been telling me, BJ?"

"Lots of things, but you're about to start learning some of them. Tomorrow I'll send you a copy of a sworn confession of her subordinate, a guy named Palmero. He spilled his guts to his attorney. He developed a bad case of guilty conscience about grabbing taxpayer assets so a silent partner could buy them for a song. Karney doesn't know yet that he blew the whistle. At least I don't think she does."

"He's implicated her?"

"Hell, she's the leader. Forced him into it."

"Any witnesses to back up his story?"

"I'm not sure about that yet. How would you like to take a drive out to Marble Falls? Mr. Travis, my uncle's landlord in the other half of the building with the gun shop, has something for me he won't discuss on the phone."

Tanner gave Phillips the information about the gun shop and Travis's drugstore next door.

"What do you plan to do with Palmero's confession?"

"Be sure he voluntarily delivers it to the U.S. attorney."

Tanner left the booth, climbed back into the van and heaved a sigh. Castro said, "You okay, boss?"

"Yeah, things aren't as bad as I thought."

"Where'd we screw up?"

"Nobody screwed up. Our plan is still running smooth. I have to stay out of sight the rest of the week, that's all."

► 32 ◄

When Tanner and Castro returned to the ranch, Lamar met them in the carport. "BJ, she's been yakking at us ever since you left, telling us to forget the mission. I didn't know you'd told her everything that's going on."

"I didn't have a choice. The attorney for the new ranch gave her the job offer, and she started asking questions I couldn't answer without letting her in on the plan."

"In on it? Sounds more like she's trying to give it a lethal injection."

Tanner gathered everyone at the kitchen table, related what Phillips said about the tax bill and how the IRS considered him a flight risk. He stared into a mug of tea Allie had prepared for him, shaking his head.

"I can't believe the FBI would go along with that line of bullshit. Nothing illegal about what I've done, so far. Phillips figures Karney's run something through without proper approval so she can use the FBI to hard-ass me."

Castro nodded. "All the more reason to keep going with your plans, BJ. Sumbitches deserve everything we're gonna do to 'em."

Allie put a hand on Tanner's arm. "But, sweetheart, what happens when they come for you at home? They'll arrest you. All of you."

Tanner glanced at Lamar before he met Allie's gaze and answered. "I'll . . . have to stay here this week, darlin'. Can't take a chance they'll find me before Friday."

"Then I'll stay, too. I have to take care of you."

Becky went for more coffee, then left the kitchen. Sonny had already disappeared.

Tanner shook his head. "That wouldn't be the best thing for us, Allie."

She spoke with a resolve that told him she wouldn't budge. "I'm staying here to take care of you."

"Darlin', you'll have to answer questions by the FBI first. We have to make up a story. Can't have them following you to the ranch."

She nodded. "Fine. But they'll have to call tomorrow if they want to talk to me, because I'm going to be here after work tomorrow night. I'm taking off the rest of the week. Freda has a good nurse on nights that can handle my shift a few days."

Tanner eyed her, sitting ramrod straight, jaw firm. He hesitated a moment, then stood and offered her his hand. "Come on, darlin'. I have to show you something."

She took his hand, and he led her toward the back door. Before leaving, he said to Lamar, "We're gonna have a look at the new property. Shouldn't take too long."

As they walked toward the carport, Allie said, "What does the new property have to do with anything?"

"I want you to see the place while I tell you some things you don't yet know about it."

Two hours later they walked arm in arm along freshly graded areas through the thicket of mesquites, weeds and brambles on the property adjoining Lamar's east pasture. Allie held onto BJ's arm as they walked, eyes red, her face streaked with tears. He breathed hard after walking and standing so long.

"First, we'll get this property ready to be a working ranch. Then you and Lamar will run both places together as one big ranch. Together they can house maybe forty or fifty vets at a time. While they're here they can be trained in whichever skills best fit their natural abilities and desires. You help them beat their chemical dependencies while Lamar and some good instructors teach them how to work and set goals."

He pointed toward a low area from where they were standing. "Down there will be the main stock tank, a lake, really. Right here will be the main facility and director's quarters. You'll get your wish, Allie, a place in the country by a lake and a way to help vets even more than you do now."

They walked a bit farther, then Tanner stopped at the edge of several acres of newly turned soil where scrub growth had been scraped away but several oak trees were left standing.

He stooped, resting his hands on his knees, breathing hard. "Those trees will make nice shade for the cattle. The rest of the place will be cleared like this within a week. I wish I could see it finished, but there won't be time."

The comment caused her to jolt with another sob. He rose up and held her.

"Darlin', now you know why it's so critical that I get to Austin and go through with my plans. Important to you, to me, to just about everyone you care about. There's a real need here for all that money."

She hugged him tight. "I don't want to lose you, BJ. You mean more to me than anything else. I want to be with you every minute."

He stroked her hair and kissed her forehead. "Neither of us can change what's happening to me. You have to be strong, see that everything else works the way it's supposed to after I . . . go away. That way your daddy and I will both live forever, and the sun will shine on you every day."

He felt weak after the long walk around the property and didn't look forward to stumbling back over the plowed ground to reach the pickup, but the sooner he did the sooner he could rest.

"Ready to go?"

She took a crumpled tissue from her pocket, wiped her eyes and blew her nose, then nodded.

Tanner took a step toward the open ground, froze, then retreated into the brush, pulling Allie with him. The shift in direction surprised her, knocking her off balance. They stumbled along together, holding each other up.

"BJ, what're you doing?"

"Over here." He gestured toward a solid clump of brush.

"What's the matter?"

"Listen."

They could hear a powerful engine rumbling at low speed and very close.

"That's one of the deputies. I saw him coming down the road as we headed for the pickup. Sounds like he turned in through the gate. I can't let him see me, Allie."

"But the truck! He knows somebody's here."

Tanner dug the key from his pocket and squeezed it into her hand. "You go. Tell him who you are, your new position with the new ranch. You came to have a look around and now you're heading back to Lamar's place."

"What about you?"

"I'll go through the brush to the far side and wait by Lamar's fence. Tell him to come for me after the deputy leaves."

"But BJ —"

"No buts, darlin'. Say you got some dirt in your eyes or something. They're still red."

He watched Allie wipe her face and compose herself, then head across the open area toward Lamar's pickup and the deputy's Bronco. As she reached the truck and started talking with the officer, Tanner headed into the brush, directly away from them behind a solid cluster of mesquite. When he'd moved far enough so he couldn't be seen from the clearing, he sat on the ground to rest a few minutes, then turned west toward Lamar's fence line.

His legs felt as if they would buckle, causing him to stop and rest frequently on the half-mile trip through the woods. His lack of stamina angered him as he recalled times he'd crawled farther and faster through the jungles of Vietnam and Laos. Sweat rolled from his forehead into his eyes, making them burn, blurring his vision.

The ever-present pain in his bloated abdomen, the pain he worked so hard to control through mental focus, screamed into his consciousness and clawed at his whole body. He retched twice, then lay down a few minutes, fearing he'd pass out. He hardly noticed the burs and stickers that clung to his clothes and poked his skin.

Tanner had the presence of mind to check the shadows for direction to make sure he didn't wander in circles. He'd count steps, walking and stumbling fifty paces at a stretch, then sit to rest.

He felt as if he'd been walking all day, though his watch said it had been less than an hour, when he heard the familiar engine noise of Lamar's pickup somewhere ahead of him, moving slowly from right to left. He pulled himself up using the tree he'd leaned against and moved toward the sound. In another minute, he reached the fence, but the pickup had traveled two hundred yards south and kept moving away.

Lamar had built his fence too well for Tanner to spread the wires and slip through. He tried to step on the strands where they were stapled to a post and climb over but couldn't maintain his balance, fearing he'd fall against the barbed wire and tear his flesh.

He sat down to wait, certain that Lamar would make another pass along the fence. A few minutes later he heard the truck. He leaned across and waved. The engine revved as Lamar raced toward him.

Lamar backed up to the fence and leaped into the truck bed. His face turned ashen when he saw Tanner. "You all right, BJ?"

"Will be in a minute. Any trouble with the deputy?"

"No, he was a little concerned about Allie when he first saw her, but I think he bought her story about dirt and thorns making her cry."

Lamar slipped a ladder over the fence, steadied Tanner as he climbed, and helped him into the truck. BJ sat on the bed wall to rest a minute while Ike skittered around the truck bed sniffing him. The dog seemed to be aware of Tanner's distress. Then Lamar helped Tanner climb over the side and settle onto the front seat.

As they drove toward the house, Lamar looked at Tanner and shook his head. "You aren't gonna be able to do it, BJ. Go to Austin, I mean. I'll take your place. Ernie and Sonny and I'll do it for you."

Tanner stared at Lamar. Then, in spite of his pain, and anger about his debilitation, he began to chuckle. "Lamar," he said, but a coughing spell stopped him till he cleared his throat. "That's the first really dumb idea I've ever heard from you."

He put a hand on Lamar's shoulder and spoke in a more serious tone. "I love you for wanting to look out for me, but don't forget, there're more important plans for you. If you and Allie don't stay in the clear, then what I'm doing now is a waste of time."

When they reached the house, Allie charged the pickup like a triage nurse. She yanked the door open and examined Tanner, touching his forehead, checking his pulse, brushing burs out of his hair and off his shirt.

"Sweetheart, look at you. Did you fall? You're soaked. What happened?"

He felt better after resting in the truck, but the pain in his abdomen still dominated his thoughts. "I'm all right, darlin'. Little tired, that's all."

He couldn't disguise the pain that shot through his lower back as he stepped out of the truck and doubled over. Castro caught him, then Lamar took his other arm. They helped him into the house and put him on the bed in the master bedroom.

Allie sat next to him, tears streaming. Then her worried expression shifted into one of grim, tight-lipped resolve. Without a word she left the room.

When she returned she brought a pitcher of water and made him drink a glassful, then spoke with the authoritative tone of an experienced nurse speaking to an obstinate patient.

"I'll be back in less than two hours. Becky's gonna see that you drink all this water while I'm gone."

"Gone where?"

"To the hospital. I called Doc Weiss. He wrote a prescription for oral morphine and arranged for me to pick up fifty liters of glucose to give you in IV form. You're dehydrated. And the pain you're feeling is gonna kill you if you don't get some relief."

He shook his head. "No drugs, Allie. Have to keep a clear head."

She closed her eyes a moment as if to compose herself. "BJ, everyone here saw you get out of the truck. You can't have a clear head with all that pain. If you don't get some relief, you'll never make it to Austin, much less do anything when you get there.

"Now, I'm going for medication, and you're gonna take it," she added. "We'll worry about Austin when the time comes."

He started to argue, but his pain and her resolve stopped him.

She kissed his cheek, and he closed his eyes as she left, hoping she'd hurry back with the medication.

► 33 ◄

Tanner drifted fitfully out of a bad dream. He saw himself in his condo. It had become a gray, steel-walled chamber. Several strangers rummaged through his possessions, all humming a weird, droning sound. One faceless person kept pulling at him. He tried to push the hands away, then opened his eyes to see Allie holding his arm.

"It's all right, sweetheart. I'm here."

He saw her through a burning haze, like a picture out of focus, and he couldn't sharpen her image. Where the faceless man of his dream had been pulling on him, he saw an IV needle inserted and taped securely to his arm. Allie stroked his head, then wrapped a pressure cuff around his arm and began pumping the sphygmometer to check his blood pressure.

"Are you feeling better this morning?"

He raised his head and tried to focus, to recognize his surroundings.

"Where am I?"

She touched his cheek and gently guided his head back to the pillow.

"Lamar's bedroom. It's Monday morning. Do you remember when I came back yesterday?"

He stared at her but said nothing. She sat on the edge of the bed and kissed him. Fletcher jumped up beside her. "I started giving you morphine around five yesterday afternoon. Lamar and Becky and I took turns watching you through the night. You slept straight through till a few minutes ago. Over fourteen hours, except when we woke you to take more caplets."

"Why aren't you at work?"

"I'm on leave, sweetheart, the rest of the week. I worked it out with Freda and Doc Maroun."

Tanner's vision improved enough to see Lamar standing behind Allie. He pushed himself up on an elbow and tried to recall his mental list of work for the day, but it wouldn't come to him. He gestured toward the IV line.

"Have to stop this. Can't think."

"No, sweetheart. Not yet."

He reached for the tube, but Lamar stepped forward and put a firm hand on his. "BJ, we have everything under control. I'm leaving in a few minutes to fax Palmero's confession to Mr. Phillips. Allie knows what's best for now. Let her take care of you so you'll be ready for Friday."

Tanner settled back and assessed his feelings, surprised to find the constant pain of recent weeks absent from his body, but he couldn't think clearly, and the sensation disturbed him, left him feeling out of control.

As if reading his mind, Allie stroked his cheek. "It's all right, sweetheart. I remember the first time I ever saw you, how you didn't want drugs. God love you, BJ, you're the dictionary picture of a control freak, but for now I'm in charge, and that's just the way it is."

Unable to battle the drugs that eased his body and addled his mind, he stopped fighting the light-headed sensation, gradually giving up control to Allie. Then he closed his eyes and drifted.

Lamar poured coffee and joined Castro and the Krugers at the kitchen table. Sonny said, "So what do you think?"

Lamar shook his head. "He'll never make it. I'll have to go in his place."

"Not a fuckin' chance," Castro said. "He made the rule right from the get-go. 'Any critical deviation and we scrub the mission.' Hell, man, you're the only one here that has anything to lose. Anybody takes his place, it'll be me."

"Won't work," Lamar said. "You're already in the plan. You can't do two jobs. It'll take another person and I'm the only one. We'll all —"

Sonny rose. "No! Ernie's right. We have to scrub. Send that asshole's confession to the attorney. Let him take care of the crooks in the IRS."

Becky said, "But what about the rest of BJ's plans for later?"

Castro rose. "He's already put in money to get started. We'll have to —"

"That's enough!"

They all turned toward the hall door where Allie stood gazing at them. Castro and Sonny took their seats. She looked from one face to another around the table, then shook her head.

"Don't judge Beauford Tanner by the way he looks right now. I know how he is, and I know what I'm doing. He's going to get good rest for a time. I'll back off his dosage Wednesday night. By Friday he'll be able, clear-headed, and ready to go."

She moved from the table to the windows and looked toward the sunrise. "Never thought I'd agree with what he wants to do, but after being out there with him yesterday, I understand."

She moved back to the table. "Count on BJ to do his part on Friday. The rest of y'all have to get everything else done between now and then. He'd tell you to be damn careful, and if one of you sees anything that doesn't look right, back off and let everybody else know. Lamar, you better head for town and find a fax machine that won't give a return address or phone number."

After returning to the ranch, Lamar sat at the kitchen table with Castro and the Krugers, reviewing every step of Tanner's plan. Allie had cautioned them to be thorough and for everyone to look for weaknesses in each other's roles. The process moved more slowly and with less humor than other times when they'd gone through the steps with Tanner. Still, no one could find fault with the plan, only concern about whether BJ would be able to carry out his part.

Lamar drove Allie into Ennis on Monday afternoon, and she called home from a pay phone to check for messages on her recorder. Even though she had anticipated the call, her heart pounded when she heard a voice identify itself as FBI Special Agent Chapman, calling for Mr. Beauford J. Tanner. She noted the number he left and ended the call. After a moment she nodded to Lamar, who sat watching her from the pickup. Mentally reviewing the story she and BJ had concocted Sunday morning, she took a deep breath and dialed Chapman's number. When he answered, she said, "My name is Allie Killgore. I found a message from you to Beauford Tanner on my recorder."

"Yes, ma'am. Where can I find Mr. Tanner today?"

"Right now he's probably on a fishing boat in the Gulf, and that scares me."

"Why is that, ma'am?"

"'Cause I filled a prescription for him before he left. Morphine."

"Why does he need morphine?"

She hesitated. "Cancer. He's . . .very ill and in a lot of pain."

Chapman's passive tone changed, sounding more concerned. "Ma'am, do you think he's, I mean is he likely to —"

"What, take his own life? No, Mr. Chapman, not a chance. Beauford Tanner never met a problem he wouldn't stand toe-to-toe with and fight. Not even cancer."

"You have a phone number for him, Ms. Killgore? An address where he's staying?"

"No, he takes this trip every spring. Spends a few days camping by himself down on the Gulf. Then he holds an executive retreat with Tanner Systems managers. He won't be holding the retreat anymore since he sold the company."

"When do you expect to hear from him, Ms. Killgore?"

"He's due back at my house late Friday night."

"You don't think he'll go to his home in Austin first?"

"No, he left his car at my house, and his prescription will be running out by then. He'll be back Friday for sure. I'm out of town myself and plan to go home Friday afternoon."

"Would anyone else know about this trip of Mr. Tanner's?"

"His executive assistant — or former assistant — at Tanner Systems would know about it."

Chapman asked for the executive assistant's name and thanked Allie for returning his call.

"Agent Chapman, can you tell me what this is about?"

"Probably nothing, ma'am. Some government tax records need to be brought up to date, that's all."

She replaced the phone with a trembling hand and walked back to the pickup on rubbery legs. Lamar drove Allie back to the ranch as she told him about the call. "I hope Betty covers for him."

Lamar nodded and smiled. "BJ called it perfect again."

"What do you mean?"

"He had me call Betty Wilson at home yesterday, ask her to verify that he always went fishing in the Gulf this time of year."

Allie felt alarmed. "Did you identify yourself to her?"

"No."

"Why would she agree to that? She doesn't even know you."

He shrugged. "BJ said to tell her, 'This is a message from the Angel Gabriel.' All she said was, 'What does he need?'"

At sunup Tuesday morning, Becky loaded avionics equipment and tools into the pickup, along with a sleeping bag and food for three days. She'd ordered the equipment two weeks before taking the Huey from the Oklahoma air base.

Lamar looked in the packing boxes filled with servo motors, wiring, connectors and black electronics equipment cases. "What's this for? I thought the helo was in good shape."

She tapped an equipment case. "This holds part of the gear for the wing leveler, kind of an autopilot for the Huey. Helps the aircraft fly straight and level with no hands on the controls."

Lamar helped Becky cover the equipment in the bed of the truck with a tarp and tie it down. After she left, he went to the property east of his ranch to see the contractor and verify that the work was progressing on schedule. When he returned home, he found Allie watching over Tanner, ready to pounce on anyone or anything that threatened to disturb him. Every time Tanner woke she had nourishment ready and admonished him to eat and drink. He seemed to fight his lack of appetite to get the food down, and he drank all the water and fruit juice she pressed him to drink. "You have to avoid dehydration," she said often.

After Lamar had returned from Vietnam, he'd settled into a passive role for all those years, always leaving control to his dad. But now, after so many days working with and observing Tanner, he moved gradually into a leadership role as BJ's health deteriorated. The others accepted this without question, and he kept them busy.

Lamar took turns with Allie watching over Tanner. Castro and Sonny serviced Castro's van, then left for Dallas after lunch.

Lamar moved about the ranch tending cattle and checking fences, maintaining normal appearances in case Sergeant Conyers or another deputy dropped by. While performing the routine tasks, his mind raced over the details of Tanner's scheme, studying it not as one of the troops, but as a new leader. The more he tried to find fault with the plan, the more he realized what a thorough job Tanner had done, causing him to have even greater respect for the dying man's abilities. If everyone handled their assignments, his plan would indeed change a small but significant part of the world, as he had predicted.

The following afternoon, Castro read a street map and directed Sonny to a downtown costume shop in Dallas, one of two Allie had known about through friends at the hospital involved in drama clubs. The Latino had arranged to pick up a wig of shoulder-length dreadlocks.

"It'll have to be long and full for my part in the play," he told the clerk, who assured him they had exactly what he needed.

Castro tried on the wig, had it packed in a hat box, then drove to the other costume shop in North Dallas near the SMU campus. There Sonny collected a dark-brown wig of shoulder-length hair. After Sonny returned to the van and moved it around the corner from the shop, Castro went inside and bought a beard he'd called about. The cosmetologist took an hour to shape and size the beard to his face and attach it with spirit gum. She guaranteed it would take no more than fifteen minutes to put on each time after the initial fitting.

After getting his beard, Castro drove Sonny back to the first shop to select a beard that would closely match the brown wig he'd bought in North Dallas. No one in either costume shop ever saw the two men together.

While driving back to the ranch, Castro began laughing.

"What's so funny?" Sonny asked.

"We better wear those wigs and beards around the house a couple of days."

"Why?"

"So we don't forget who we're lookin' at later and shoot each other."

► 34 ◄

Thursday morning, as the sun rose above a thin layer of clouds blanketing the horizon, Becky checked the hangar for stray tools and anything that could be traced back to her. Satisfied that she'd collected everything, she loaded her gear into Tanner's pickup, caressed the side of the Huey like a favorite pet, then secured the building and headed for Waco.

She checked the time and figured Sonny would be leaving Lamar's ranch about the same time, riding the motorcycle they'd kept hidden in the barn, to meet her at Waco's general aviation airport. She'd arranged to rent a Robinson helicopter for the final recon flight. She'd rented one of the small aircraft there before, while searching out a place to store the Huey.

She spotted Sonny waiting near the helicopter hangar. He greeted her as she stepped out of the truck in the parking lot. "Mornin', Sis. You get the black box installed?"

She gave him a thumbs-up. "No problem."

"Did you flight test it?"

"I'll have to wait for the first leg of the mission to check it out, make any final adjustments."

They flew under patchy clouds to Mueller Airport in Austin, refueled and departed to the southeast, touring the city at low level, then flying south along the interstate at 500 feet.

Sonny searched the route ahead, gazing down through the plexiglass nose of the tiny helo until he recognized the exit he wanted.

"That's it. Go left. The single-story building."

Becky slowed the helo and banked sharply, examining the building and parking area, checking for overhead utility lines. She leveled momentarily, then moved out for a wider circle, scanning for the best approach, noting trees, poles and wires, and the taller structures in the area.

After completing a wide circle around the building, she flew east, near the air space of Austin-Bergstrom International Airport, then headed southeast for ten minutes at top speed. "See the grain silo dead ahead? That's the northern boundary."

Sonny nodded.

As she crossed over the silo, she banked left paralleling a farm road. "Count five seconds after crossing the silo, then execute."

Becky pulled the yoke back, causing the helo to climb sharply until it slowed to virtually no airspeed. Then she kicked the right rudder pedal, rotating the aircraft 180 degrees into a nose-down attitude and started a steep dive.

She glanced at Sonny, who stared wide-eyed at the ground less than three hundred feet away and racing up to meet them. She leveled the helo fifty feet above the freshly plowed field and banked right toward an adjoining pasture. A few cattle near the fence began running.

Sonny caught his breath and looked at his sister. "Bet you cost that Wyoming rancher a thousand dollars a day by chasing cows and making them run off their prime weight."

Becky laughed as she started a gradual climb, headed northwest, then followed Highway 290 toward Dripping Springs. When she reached a roadside park, she headed north for a half mile, then reduced altitude and slowed until the tiny helo shuddered into a hover.

"There. See the two cedars standing alone? Nice flat clearing right next to 'em?"

Sonny leaned forward and searched the ground 50 feet below. "There's a nice rise between here and the highway to hide a pickup. Everything looks good."

Becky increased power and started climbing. "Let's take this little toy back to Waco."

Allie began giving Tanner reduced levels of medication late Wednesday night. By Thursday afternoon, Tanner's head cleared, and he could maintain a thought without drifting into surreal images. He could also feel the pain in his back and lower abdomen again, though not as sharp as before he'd taken the morphine.

When the Krugers returned to the ranch, Tanner walked to the kitchen with Allie's help, sat at the table and debriefed them on their flight to Austin. Lamar and Castro noted every detail Becky gave about the buildings, the proximity of the Air Force base, and the farmland south of Austin. She drew layouts on the marker board and estimated their dimensions.

Sonny shook his head. "How'd you see so much? I didn't pick up on half that stuff."

"Don't worry. Make a pencil sketch to take along. You'll remember when you get there."

Tanner struggled to put his pain in abeyance and keep a clear head. He quizzed everyone on their roles for the following day. When he couldn't remember details, Lamar filled them in. After reviewing the strategy and contingencies, he gestured toward Sonny and Castro. "You two have your disguises?"

Castro nodded.

"What about refueling plans?"

"Lamar took care of that," Becky said. "I checked it out. Four-oh job."

Tanner nodded. "Sonny, how about lights and power pack?"

"All set, BJ. Packed in one of the boxes with an official government delivery label. My ticket into the building."

"Weapons?"

"Packed with the chair and ready to go," Castro said. "We'll open 'em up in the rental van when we get to Austin."

As Allie stood behind Tanner massaging his shoulders, he examined each face around the table, looking for worried expressions, but saw none. Lamar and Sonny wore poker faces. Castro couldn't suppress a grin. Becky's smile was that of a child on Christmas Eve.

Tanner gazed out the window and across the pasture toward a windrow of trees turned dusty pink by the setting sun. "Lamar, it's time to light the barbecue and grill those big T-bone steaks. Two bottles of Cabernet on the floor in your closet. Let's do it up right tonight. Might be a while before we can all sit down together again."

He felt Allie's hands tremble on his shoulders, then she put her arms around his neck and held him.

Tanner credited an adrenalin rush for the energy he felt Friday morning while he showered and dressed. Allie left the Heparin lock in his arm, taped securely in place with its needle inserted into the vein. She showed Sonny and Castro how to insert the IV line into the lock and adjust the clamp to meter the flow of glucose.

While they had breakfast, Allie looked so concerned that Tanner expected her to make a last effort at begging him not to go through with his plan. Castro made jokes and teased everyone. Becky returned his quips, with encouragement from Lamar and Sonny.

While Lamar, Castro and the Krugers ate ham and eggs and toast, Tanner drank one of the two-dozen protein drinks Allie had prepared for him to take along on the mission. He also ate wheat toast with a thick spread of peach jam, even though he couldn't enjoy the taste of what used to be his favorite spread.

When they'd all eaten their fill, Castro said, "Come on, Sonny, time to saddle up."

He gave his cell phone to Becky, and she kissed his cheek and hugged him. Then she embraced her brother. "Be careful, Sonny. Don't let anything surprise you into a wrong move."

He winked at her. "Take care of yourself, Sis. See you in a few days."

One by one they gathered coats and bags and made their way out the back door, leaving Tanner and Allie alone. When he rose from the table and hugged her, she put her arms tightly around his neck and began shaking with hard sobs.

"Please don't go," she whispered. "If you go through with this, I'll never see you again."

"Sure you will, darlin'."

"You know you'll never get away."

He hesitated, afraid he'd lose control and shed his own tears. "This won't take as long as you think. We'll be together when it's done. I promise. Be sure that you go to work tomorrow morning. I want you to be seen at the hospital when things begin to happen in Austin. Later, you stick close to Lamar. He's as good as they come, Allie. You can depend on him."

She shook her head against his chest but said no more.

He stroked her hair and spoke softly. "Allie, darlin', we both know what's gonna happen to me. There's no changing that. You have to get ready for your new life. That's what'll keep me alive."

He gently eased her away, but she resisted, holding tighter. He started to speak but felt a burning in his nose and eyes, then tears rolling down his cheeks.

"I have to go, darlin'," he whispered. "Please don't make it harder than it already is."

She raised her head after a moment to look in his eyes, then wiped her tears and gave him a long, tender kiss.

"I love you, BJ. I'll always love you."

"I love you, Allie. God's gonna shine the light on you, my darlin'. I'll always be there to see that it's warm."

She turned away from the door.

He left without looking back.

► 35 ◄

Castro drove south on I-35, carefully maintaining the pace of traffic. Sonny sat on cushions in the back of the van, reading a Frederick Forsyth paperback. Tanner, sitting in the passenger seat, punched Des Blaylock's cell number.

"You ready to spread the infection?"

"Glad you called. I've set the clock to start at midnight, but I —"

"Can you back it up, make it today?"

"Sure, it'll only take a few minutes to corrupt the mainframe in Martinsburg. Wanted to tell you that I know how to get into the Detroit and Memphis computers, too."

Tanner pondered Blaylock's comment, gradually absorbing the implication. "You're sure of that?"

Blaylock laughed. "You'd question my ability at this late date?"

For a moment Tanner forgot about the pain in his body and the weakness that slowed him. "That's fantastic! You've set the virus to get all three locations simultaneously?"

"Yep, ready anytime. Want me to do it right now?"

Tanner's heart pounded as he considered his options based on Blaylock's new information. "No, make it sixteen hundred today, and be sure there's nothing left behind that can be traced to you."

"Hey, I'm vapor, boss. There's never been anything but a warm breeze blowing around that sinful computer you leased. I don't exist."

"Be sure the vapor leaves no fingerprints, fancy ties, or stray tools behind."

"Right. When do you want me to send you the system recovery codes?"

"I'll let you know in a few days."

"I don't even know where you are, boss."

Tanner grinned. "You will this afternoon."

Although for very different reasons, Lamar felt more ill at ease than at any time since he'd been arrested at the Circle K in Ennis. He turned into the Love Field Airport entrance after driving Allie from the ranch. Neither of them had said a dozen words during the half-hour trip. As they approached the terminal, she opened a compact, grimaced at her image, dabbed at her red eyes, then applied blush and lipstick.

"Thanks for the ride, Lamar."

"Sorry I can't take you to your house, Allie, but BJ's right. Wouldn't be good for me to be seen there if anyone's watching for him."

She sighed. "BJ's right about everything. A taxi from the airport will support the story I told the FBI."

He set the brake and started to get out, but she stopped him. "Stay put, I'll get my bag."

He felt his face flush. "Uh, Allie, I'm not too good at talkin' about some things, especially at times like this. BJ's now closer than a brother. He saved my ranch and helped me get to be a real person again. I'll do anything in the world for him. You know what he's planned for me, and that's how it's gonna be."

She gazed at him a moment, then a tear rolled down her cheek as she touched his arm and gave him a warm smile. "Thanks, Lamar. He feels the same way about you, and so do I. You can always count on me for anything you need."

"Hang in there. Go do that makeup shift at the hospital tonight just like everything's okay."

She climbed out of the pickup and took her bag from behind the seat. "See you in Doc Maroun's office Monday afternoon?"

He nodded. "If you need anything before then, just call me, you hear?"

Becky checked inside the barn to be sure the motorcycle was still well hidden after Lamar had removed hay bales from the loft. While walking from the barn to the house, she heard Ike barking. Her pulse quickened when she saw a sheriff's Bronco coming through the gate. When the truck turned so that the late-morning sun no longer reflected off the windshield, she recognized Ned, the deputy who lived near the big yellow house a few blocks from Wal-Mart.

Stay calm. Stick with the story.

She waved as the deputy rolled down his window. "Howdy, Ned."

"Mornin', Becky. Saw you from the road and thought I'd stop a minute. How y'all doin'?"

"Okay, but I'm the only one here right now."

"Oh, yeah, Friday. They're all at the VA, huh?"

She shook her head. "Ernie's brother-in-law had an accident yesterday. Nothing too serious, but he'll be laid up a couple of days. Ernie went to San Antonio to help out till he's back on his feet. He'll be gone a week or so.

"Sonny went with him, but I figure he'll be spending most of his time at New Braunfels. He has an old girlfriend there."

Ned grinned. "Sorry about Ernie's brother, but I'm glad to hear ole Sonny has a gal. Tell him to bring her up here sometime. We'd like to meet her."

Becky nodded. "Yeah, me too. Never seen her."

"Where's Lamar?"

"Went to Dallas for something. Said he'd be back by midafternoon." She leaned close and spoke in a confidential tone. "Didn't say what he's up to, but I think he might have gone shopping for new clothes."

Ned laughed and nodded vigorously. "Gonna grill some steaks at my place tomorrow night. Why don't you and Lamar come on over?"

She forced a smile. "Sounds good, but Lamar's going to the cattle auction at Fort Worth tomorrow, and I said I'd go along. Made him promise to take me to Billy Ray's for dinner."

"All right! You're gettin' that ol' boy out of his shell."

"Maybe we'll stop by on the way home if it isn't too late."

"Yeah, do that. We'll want to see how he holds up after a night out in Cow Town."

Becky stayed outside till Ned turned onto the farm road and returned his wave as he drove away.

Castro stopped on the street near the Mueller Airport terminal entrance, let Sonny out, then drove away. He made a U-turn at the end of the block and headed north to the Red Lion Inn. Conventioneers' cars and trucks crowded the parking lot, but Castro backed into the handicapped space farthest from the rear entrance.

He removed a folding wheelchair from the truck, rolled it to the passenger side and helped Tanner seat himself. Then he pushed it to the sidewalk behind the van.

Tanner turned up the collar of an oversized coat. He also wore sunglasses and one of Lamar's Stetson's pulled low, hoping that if, God forbid, anyone who knew him might happen by, they would not recognize him. He sat still, concentrating hard to fight the pain in his body, while Castro unloaded boxes from the van and stacked them on the sidewalk next to Tanner.

After unloading everything, Castro whispered, "See you back at the airport."

He climbed into the van and left. Castro had barely gone out of sight when a bellman came out the door, noticed Tanner and turned in his direction.

"Sir, can I help you?"

Tanner shook his head. "Waiting for a driver to pick me up. Should be here any minute."

"Want me to call somebody? Be sure your party's on the way?"

"No, thanks."

The bellman resumed his trip across the parking area.

Tanner waited fifteen minutes that seemed to last an hour. Several cars had driven by in the crowded lot, looking for a parking space. Tanner glanced up at each car, then lowered his head to shield his face with the hat brim. Another vehicle approached and Tanner looked up, praying to see Sonny, but his heart pounded against his ribs when he saw a midnight-blue Lincoln Town Car inch by in front of him. There couldn't be many such cars in Austin, and this one, or one like it, belonged to Tom Mabry.

After the car passed, Tanner glanced up again, took a deep breath and heaved a sigh, relieved to see the back of a bald head that couldn't possibly belong to Mabry.

A white van, driven by a man with neck-length brown hair and a beard, finally rolled onto the parking lot. The van backed into the handicapped space in front of Tanner, and the driver opened the rear doors from the inside. He looked around to be sure there was no one close by.

"Sorry to take so long," Sonny said. "Couldn't get my beard on straight. Does it look okay now?"

Tanner examined the false beard and hair and nodded. "Load these boxes. Let's get out of here."

Sonny put the cartons in the van, then helped Tanner in the side door and secured the wheelchair. A few minutes later they were back at the airport. Sonny stopped on the street near Castro's van in the long-term parking area. The side door slid open and a man with shoulder-length dreadlocks and a long, scraggly beard emerged. He locked the van, crossed the lot and climbed in beside Sonny, then turned around to give Tanner a good look.

"Well, are we scary enough to be a couple of bomb-happy radicals?"

Tanner studied their faces, shrouded by unruly beards and long hair. "You two could be anything from seventies protesters to suicidal terrorists."

He gestured for Sonny to drive on. "Let's go show some people that we're smarter than y'all look."

▶ 36 ◀

Sonny turned off the freeway and parked half a block from the IRS building. Tanner punched a number on his phone. Theron Palmero answered.

"It's time, Palmero," Tanner said. "Call your lawyer. Be in the U.S. attorney's office with your confession in fifteen minutes if you want to survive the day."

After a long hesitation, Palmero sighed. "Figured this'd be the day."

"I'll be watching for you to turn yourself in. If you don't, one of my sharpshooters will pop the last ear. Better get moving."

Tanner ended the call, and the three men watched the building from the van, waiting, but not for long. Three minutes later, Palmero walked out the front door clutching his briefcase and headed for the side parking lot. Tanner watched through binoculars.

"How does he look?" Castro said.

"Like a zombie in a B movie."

"Want to tail him?" Sonny asked.

Tanner lowered the binoculars, hesitated, then nodded. "Yeah, the way he looks, I don't know if he'll turn himself in or put a bullet in his head."

They followed Palmero to Eighth Avenue, where he parked on the street and paced the sidewalk in front of the federal building. Ten minutes later, a sparrow of a man approached him and put a tiny hand on the IRS agent's shoulder.

Sonny said, "Must be his lawyer. I've seen them together in front of the office on Congress Avenue."

The slight man touched his briefcase, Palmero nodded, and they went inside.

Tanner sighed. "There goes our first shot at the swindlers and assholes in the IRS."

He checked his watch. 1535. "If everything works right, a few minutes from now the information-highway gremlins will hijack a few billion dollars' worth of tax records. That should get the bastards' attention."

Castro held out a hand, and Tanner slapped a high-five with more vigor than he expected of himself. "Let's go, Sonny. Time to show them that somebody's fighting back."

At 3:55, Castro helped Tanner out of the van and into the wheelchair a block from the IRS office. Then he sat a pink cake box on Tanner's lap, and they headed for the building. When they reached the ramp, Tanner watched Sonny turn into the parking area toward the rear of the structure. Castro held the lobby door while Tanner rolled himself inside.

The guard, overweight and in his mid-fifties, stretched to see over the two security video monitors atop the console. He glanced at Tanner, then narrowed his eyes at the man behind him with the dreadlocks and bushy beard. "Somethin' I can do for y'all?"

Without hesitation, Tanner rolled himself behind the guard station and eyed the monitors.

The guard frowned. "You can't come back here."

Tanner checked the monitors. One showed the loading area at the rear door. The other displayed the hallway at the back half of the building overlooking the guard station. He watched as Sonny backed up to the door and stacked six large boxes onto a handcart.

The guard gave Tanner a sour look. "You hear what I said?"

After glancing at Castro, who nodded from the front of the console, Tanner pulled a semiautomatic pistol from under the box on his lap and leveled it at the guard.

"Shut up and do exactly what I tell you if you want to leave here alive."

The guard's eyes widened and the color drained from his puffy face. Tanner motioned for him to turn. "Face the monitors and put both hands flat on the desk."

The man did as he was told, hands shaking, jaw agape. Tanner removed the guard's revolver from its holster, unloaded it and slipped it into his own coat pocket. Then he removed a key ring from a clip on the man's belt. "Which one locks the front door?"

With trembling fingers, the man found the key. Castro grabbed it and locked the all-glass double doors. Then he took the box from Tanner's lap and eased it to the floor next to the security door leading into the office area hallway.

The guard gulped for air when he saw the Claymore. "Good God A'Mighty!"

On the security monitors, Tanner saw Sonny go inside the rear door and approach the guard there. Two other people came into view walking down the hall toward the rear door. Sonny stopped the handcart in front of the guard and searched his pockets until the other people went out the door. Then he pulled an Uzi from under his coat and the guard's hands went up. In a heartbeat, Sonny had lifted the man from his chair and shoved him through a door into the small space Tanner knew to be the telephone equipment room.

Less than a minute later, Sonny's image reappeared on the monitor and gave a thumbs-up toward the camera. Tanner flashed a sign to Castro, who removed an Uzi from under his coat and motioned the guard to his feet.

"Sweet Jesus," the man muttered.

At the same time, Sonny rolled the stack of boxes into the room where he'd secured and gagged the guard, and, if he'd been able to follow their plan, cut the outside voice telephone cables.

Tanner lifted the phone at the guard station, dialed 9 and nodded satisfaction when he heard no dial tone. He nudged the guard with his pistol. "How do I get on the PA system?"

"D-d-dial 85. Y-you'll hear a tone."

Castro grabbed the guard's collar and steered him to the security door leading to the offices. Tanner buzzed the door open from the security console, and Castro positioned the guard inside but kept the door cracked, pointing the Uzi at the man's back.

Tanner lifted the phone again, dialed 85 and listened for the tone.

"Your attention, please. This is security. We've received a bomb threat and there's a suspicious package in the front lobby. Evacuate the building out the rear door. Do not approach the front of the building.

"I repeat. Evacuate immediately. Do not attempt to make cellular or radio calls. The transmission signal could set off a bomb. Exit the rear door. Go to the back of the parking lot. Wait for further instructions."

Before Tanner finished the message he could see people streaming across the monitor heading out the rear door. Most of them appeared to laugh and joke, probably about what they considered a typical April 15 prank call.

Castro peeked through the front hall door and flashed an okay sign. Tanner watched the front of the building, thankful that no one approached, and turned his eyes back to the monitor.

Sonny appeared in the hallway, picked up the guard's phone and punched numbers. The instrument in front of Tanner rang and he grabbed it.

"We're in good shape, boss. Everybody's out. I drilled and bolted both fire doors. Nobody will be able to sneak in on us from the side doors."

"Good work, son. Take the guard to the computer room and do your stuff."

Sonny went into the equipment room where the guard sat bound and gagged. He was the same gray-haired man who'd been on duty the day Sonny had been in the building. Sonny put another Claymore in the hallway 20 feet from the rear door, attached a wire to it and ran the spool of wire to Castro in the lobby. Tanner had the trigger device attached within seconds.

Back in the equipment room, Sonny took another package from one of the boxes. Then he untied the guard's feet and removed his gag.

The man glowered, showing no sign of fear. "Get your hands off me, you tweaker freak. I'll shave that drugged-out head of yours when this is over."

Standing behind the man, Sonny disguised his voice, speaking in a low raspy tone.

"We're going to the computer room. One wrong move will be the last thing you ever do."

He guided the man into the hall and gestured toward the wire on the floor. "Careful. All the people that work here are out in the parking lot. Step on that wire and you might kill most of them."

The guard gaped at the anti-personnel mine, then tried to look at his captor. Sonny held him firm and shoved him toward the computer room.

The guard spoke over his shoulder. "You've been taking too many drugs, boy. There ain't no money in this building. You really fucked up."

Sonny said nothing until they crossed the hall and entered the data center. As he put the package on the floor next to the computer, the guard tried to turn and face him. Sonny put an arm across the man's chest and grabbed his waistband with the other hand, hoisted him several inches off the floor, and held him suspended a few seconds.

The guard lost his belligerence.

Sonny lowered him, then laid him on the floor on his stomach with his face toward the computer. "Watch what I do, but don't move. Understand?"

The guard nodded.

Sonny opened the box and removed a cone-shaped wad of C-4. He pressed the explosive to the outside panel of the end computer cabinet and secured it with duct tape. Then he inserted a remote-controlled detonator.

"You know what this is?"

The guard narrowed his eyes. "Looks like cookie dough."

"It's C-4. This shape charge will wipe out the entire computer system and the outside wall of this building. The man with his finger on the trigger is hiding in one of the offices. You better hope nobody bugs him till you're out of here."

"H-how many of you are there?"

"More than you'd ever believe. You saw the Claymore at the back door?"

The man nodded.

"One in the lobby, another in front of each fire door, and four of 'em on the roof in case the SWAT tries a helo assault. All the mines are set with remote triggers."

"W-why are y'all doing this? There's nothing in here worth stealing."

"Our boss will talk with Treasury and the FBI about that soon enough."

The guard shook his head. "Y'all are crazy."

Sonny grabbed the man's collar and lifted him to his feet.

"Maybe, but the guy in charge of this mission is the smartest man to ever run counterterrorist training for the United States military. I'm betting my life that it works."

Sonny walked the guard to his desk near the rear door and kept a hand on him while dialing Tanner on the intercom. "Computer charge is hot. Claymore's in place at the back door. Ready for me to get rid of the guard?"

He felt the man shudder as he spoke. After hearing Tanner's response, he replaced the phone and walked toward the door.

"Wh-what are you gonna do?" the guard asked.

Sonny turned toward the front of the building to see the lobby guard, hands high, walking toward them on wobbly legs, with Castro standing behind him. Sweat rolled down the man's sallow face. When he reached them, Sonny opened the door and motioned both guards outside.

"Go call the FBI," he said, again disguising his voice. "Tell them what you saw and what I told you. Then go home and have a shot of Jack Daniel's. Tell your grandkids you managed to escape the deadliest terrorist group to hit Texas since Sam Bass."

He gestured for the guards to go out the door. Before closing it, he said, "Good night, men. Y'all have a nice evening now, hear? Oh, and don't plan to come in to work for a few days."

After securing the door, Sonny signaled Castro, then went through the offices closing all window blinds. Next, he dragged a desk into the middle of the hallway and took more tools from the boxes he'd left in the equipment room. Standing on the desk, he removed the ceiling tiles and hoisted himself among the conduits above. Using a heavy-duty electric saw, bolt cutters, and other tools, he cut away layers of wood and metal until he'd made a hole through the roof.

Castro went to a window on one side of the building, then the other, and peeked through the closed blinds. "Some of the cars are gone. I don't see anyone walking along the sides of the building."

Fifteen minutes later Sonny had enlarged the hole through the roof until it was three-by-three feet. He positioned three low-voltage lights on the roof, twenty feet apart, in a triangle. They were wired to a switch and battery in the hallway. Then he set up a Claymore on each of the four sides around the hole on the roof. He attached fuses and wires to them and dropped the other end of the wires down the hole in the roof.

Castro headed for the lobby when they heard the distant sound of sirens. "Somebody must've finally made a call."

▶ 37 ◀

FBI Special Agent Doug Briscoe checked the time when he heard the PA system announcement inside the IRS offices: 1617. The bomb threat had to be a hoax. Friday afternoon, April 15? It might even be an IRS employee who wanted to go home a little early.

Briscoe ran a hand through his silver-gray hair and thought about staying in the IRS deputy director's office to continue his investigation. He decided against the idea since it would violate bureau rules and set a bad example for others who'd seen him enter the office. He locked the documents in his briefcase and took it with him as he headed for the hall and out the rear exit.

Looking toward the front, he saw one of the guards directing people away from the lobby toward the back of the building. The man's ashen face lent an air of credibility to the bomb threat, but most of the evacuees laughed and joked about the exercise, apparently having reached the same conclusion as Briscoe.

The next moment he watched both uniformed guards run from the rear door faster than either of them appeared able to move. "Everybody get out of here. Bombs all over the place. Terrorists inside."

People gaped at the guards; some laughing, others looking fearful. Some of the latter group moved toward their cars.

"Don't go near the building," one guard said. "If they see you out the window, they might start shooting. They've got machine guns."

He gestured toward the waist-high cinder-block wall at the back of the parking area. "Climb over the wall and get the hell out of here."

All laughter faded, and the IRS employees moved toward the wall, slowly at first, then with heightened urgency as the guards rushed headlong in that direction.

Briscoe grabbed the guard who'd been stationed at the rear door and flashed his bureau ID. "What the hell's going on in there?"

"Buncha crazy bastards! They're all over the damn building. I'm getting out of here."

Briscoe climbed over the wall with the two guards and crossed the adjacent parking area till they'd moved around the corner of the next building. Then he stopped them and took a cell phone from his briefcase. While punching in his office number, he said, "Okay, I want to know everything you saw, every word you can remember them saying."

Briscoe called the duty FBI agent, who would notify the Austin police. Then he questioned the guards, taped their comments with his pocket recorder and made notes. Within an hour, the police department SWAT team and other officers arrived and set up an outer perimeter one block in each direction, closed off the streets and had neighboring buildings cleared of personnel.

The FBI and the local police established a control center in the lobby of a building one block from the IRS office. When Briscoe arrived there with the two guards, his boss and the local police commander appeared to be wrapping up their argument over jurisdiction.

The FBI prevailed.

At 1640, Tanner called Des Blaylock's cell number. "Did you spread the infection?" He heard a chuckle from the other end.

"Patient's dead and doesn't even know it. They're still pumping zillions of new records into the bloodstream, but every one of them is trashed."

"You have the recovery data ready?"

"Right, boss. It's packed the way you wanted. Still want it delivered to the same place?"

"Yes."

"When?"

"Wait for a call, then scrub your phone, put it in the package and leave it where I told you. Sure you can find the place?"

"Know right where it is. No problem, long as I can see the marker."

Tanner ended the call, then dialed the U.S. attorney's office and spoke in a pleasant tone to the woman who answered. "Afternoon, ma'am. I'd like to speak with whoever's handling Mr. Palmero's confession."

"I-I'm sorry, sir. Whose confession?"

"Theron Palmero, IRS agent. He turned himself in about an hour ago. Big guy, dark complexion."

The woman sounded confused. "C-can you hold on a minute, sir?"

"Be quick, I don't have much time."

Seconds later a man's voice on a speakerphone said, "This is Deputy U.S. Attorney O'Daniel. Can I help you?"

"You a prosecutor, Mr. O'Daniel?"

"Yes, who's calling, please?"

"Beauford Tanner, former owner of Tanner Systems, presently in charge of the Internal Revenue Service facility in Austin. Are you handling Mr. Palmero's confession?"

A hesitation. "What confession would that be, Mr. Tanner?"

"The same thirty-four-page confession as the signed and notarized copies I have. Now don't dick around. I know Palmero and his lawyer are there. Who's in charge of his interview?"

"Mr. Tanner, we don't —"

Another man's voice interrupted. "Mr. Tanner, this is Derwood Yates, senior prosecutor. How is it that you know about Mr. Palmero?"

"Because he helped Pat Karney rob me and my company — former company — and God only knows how many others. I assume his attack of conscience caused him to send me a couple of copies of his confession."

"Mr. Tanner, we'd like you to bring those copies and come to my office, right now, sir."

"Sorry, Yates, that plan doesn't work for me."

"Make it work."

"Couple of reasons it won't. One, like I said, I'm in charge of the IRS office right now. I and a few trusted men have run everybody out of the building and placed some bombs here and there. Wouldn't be a good idea for me to leave.

"Two —"

"You *what?*" Yates shouted,

Tanner laughed, then coughed. "Two, my copies of Palmero's statement are elsewhere, but I can direct them to be delivered where I want them to go at any time."

Yates said, "Tanner, there's no way —"

"We're staying till you arrest the scum working here and tell the public what's been going on. I'll give you till Monday to expose Palmero and Patricia Karney and whoever else. If you don't get it done, then I'll have to do the job myself."

"And how would you do that, Mr. Tanner?"

"By sharing Palmero's confession with the media."

"That's not the way to handle the situation."

"Neither is sweeping it in the dustpan and quietly sending a couple of assholes out the door. I want the whole world to know what the IRS did to me and some other people. That has to be stopped here and now and never happen again."

"Who else knows you're in the IRS building?"

"Two guards ran out screaming their heads off a while ago. I figure half the city knows by now."

"Tanner, that's stupid. You know there's no way you'll get out of there."

Tanner laughed again. "When you dig around and do your homework, you'll find that I'm terminally ill. There's a damn good chance I'll die of natural causes before the FBI figures a way to get to me. Real good chance

I'll fall on the trigger for all these bombs and level two or three blocks. You think about that while you decide what to do."

Tanner ended the call and grinned at Castro. "The race is on. We're into the first turn and they don't even have their engines started."

► 38 ◄

Agent Briscoe sat in the makeshift SWAT operation center a block from the IRS facility. The lobby of an evacuated building held a collection of folding chairs and tables, phones, a fax machine, PC and printer. Briscoe felt both amused and concerned as he watched Ben Cooper, the special agent in charge, seated on the other side of the table. He'd been impeccably dressed and well groomed every time Briscoe had seen him. At that moment, his collar was unbuttoned, his tie hung askew, and his hair looked as if he'd been walking in a high wind.

Cooper ended a call, laid his cell phone on the table and shook his head. "That was the U.S. attorney."

Briscoe raised his eyebrows. "You already briefed him?"

Cooper shook his head. "He called me! The guy that's taken over the building called him. We have one hell of a situation. I need everything we can get ASAP on Beauford Tanner, former CEO of Tanner Systems."

Stunned for a moment, Briscoe nodded. "The electronics company across town. He's been in hot water with the IRS recently. Did the guy space out?"

"Maybe, but he has an ace that makes Treasury tell us to hold off any action and try to work a deal with him." Cooper related the story about Palmero's confession and Tanner's threat about giving copies to the media.

"Jesus," Briscoe said. "That could rattle the IRS cage all the way to Congress." He rose to leave. "I'll get what I can on Tanner."

Cooper held up a hand. "I'll have someone else do that. I want you here. From what the U.S. attorney says, you may be the one guy who can defuse the situation. Do you recognize the names Palmero and Karney?"

Briscoe nodded. "Palmero's on my list, but I haven't been over his casework yet. Karney's his supervisor."

"Tanner wants those two strung up in a public hanging during prime time. If Palmero's confession goes public, there could be a tax rebellion that won't end till the whole Treasury Department's been flushed. The U.S. attorney wants us to tell Tanner about your investigation. See if that'll convince him to come out."

"How do we contact him?"

Cooper shook his head. "All the phone lines are dead going into the building. He's on cellular, of course, but we don't have a number."

"So, do we wait for him to call, or shall I go knock on the door?"

Cooper snorted. "Yeah, right."

Derwood Yates, chief deputy U.S. attorney in Austin, leveled dark eyes at Palmero, then the IRS agent's lawyer. His thick black hair pointed in several directions after running his hands through it numerous times.

"Mr. Palmero, you're sure Tanner hasn't coerced you into making false claims about IRS actions?"

Palmero shook his head. "There's nothing false about this confession. Everything is absolutely true. Everything."

"So why'd you happen to walk in here at the same time Tanner and his men invaded the IRS service center?"

Palmero shifted and looked at his lawyer, who nodded. Then he looked back to Yates. "I gave the statement to my counsel because I couldn't live with what I'd been forced to do by my supervisor. I waited to bring it to you till I'd put some personal things in order. Tanner called this afternoon and asked me to hurry. Said he wanted to file a claim on behalf of his company before he, uh, before he dies."

"Christ, what's he planning to do? Blow himself up?"

Palmero wiped his forehead with a handkerchief. "He's terminally ill. Cancer. I didn't know a damn thing about him going into the office. Nothing."

"When did you last see Tanner?"

Palmero stared at the affidavit on the desk, clearly reluctant to meet Yates's gaze. "We talked about a week ago. I, uh, called him to say I was sorry for what I'd done. That it wasn't my fault. Patricia Karney forced me to —"

Yates laid a hand on the document. "Yes, I know. I've read your story. Why did you go to him before going to your director, or coming here? Even before consulting with your own attorney?"

"I-I don't know who all might be involved. Karney could be following someone else's orders. If I confessed to the wrong person, they might have killed me."

"Who might have killed you? What makes you think someone higher is involved?"

"Somebody approved her stupid claim to force him to pay capital gains tax now instead of waiting till the required filing time."

Yates leaned forward, eyebrows raised. "Well, as it turns out, looks like she's right. I'd call him a flight risk at this point, wouldn't you?"

Palmero shrugged. "What'd he do before today that made her think that? I'd say she drove him to it."

Yates rose and paced for a full minute without speaking, peering through the fading evening light to the southeast toward the IRS building. "This is a very bad situation you've created, Mr. Palmero."

"What?" Palmero started to rise, but his lawyer put a hand on his arm. "*I'm* the one who's going to prison. What the hell's so bad for you?"

Yates shook his head. "You show up here with a confession of IRS wrongdoing at the same time a terrorist invades your offices. For us to pursue an investigation at this time would appear as if we're submitting to Tanner's demands."

"But that's not how it is. You have my confession!"

"Nevertheless, the situation could be construed that way by the media."

Yates stepped around his desk and stood close to Palmero. "Why are you cooperating with Tanner? Has he paid you?"

Palmero looked to his lawyer for help, but the man stared at Yates, stunned. Finally, Palmero's attorney said, "Mr. Yates, my client didn't come here as a paid informant. He's confessed to crimes that could cost him years in prison. Offhand, I'd say Tanner has outfoxed all of us since the IRS screwed him."

"Allegedly screwed him," Yates said.

"If you don't investigate the allegations in my client's confession, you could face some damned embarrassing criticism at the least. Or, at the worst, the charge that you failed to prosecute. On the other hand, you could suffer with the media, as you said. Either way, my client suffers. He wants due process, and he wants recognition of his full cooperation with the government so he gets the rights he's entitled to. Otherwise, I'll take him out of here and surrender him to federal marshals. Then we'll call our own press conference."

Yates's jaw muscles worked as he clenched his teeth. "There may be a way to sit on this for a while at no cost to either of us. No one else knows about your confession besides Tanner and us, right?"

Palmero wiped his face.

Yates repeated himself. "Right?"

The IRS agent shook his head. "I put two other copies in the mail this afternoon."

"To whom?"

"One to the FBI here in Austin."

"And the other?"

"To the director of Internal Revenue in Washington."

Yates dropped into his chair and turned his back to them, head down.

Sonny worked quickly, storing water in a water-bed-size container in the break room. He set up a generator in an office at the middle of the building. After finishing his other tasks, he reported to Tanner. "Everything is in place, BJ. Water container is over half full so far."

"Emergency doors secured? Heat lamps in the right places?"

"Yes, sir."

Tanner shook his head and grinned. "If they knew what they were doing, the water would have been cut off before we stored any."

Castro dollied a box into the office with rations to last the three of them a week. He carried a large shoulder bag filled with medications Allie prepared for Tanner.

After everything was in place, Castro and Sonny started random patrols along the windows until Tanner called them to the office. For the first time, Castro showed signs of stress. Sweat beads dotted his face, and he breathed in short, fast gulps, reacting to every sound outside the building.

"What're they doin' out there, BJ?"

"Setting up sniper-spotter positions, probably across from the northwest and southeast corners so they can see along all four sides of the building."

"How long till they'll try to come in after us?"

Tanner shook his head. "No hostages, nothing in here critical to citizen safety. And with those space heaters running, the FBI's heat sensors will lead them to believe we have three or four times the manpower we actually have."

"Pure genius, BJ," Sonny said.

Tanner continued. "Their policy is to secure the perimeter and negotiate. They'll use the weekend to try talking us out. It'll get political on Monday, but they won't be risking lives to come in after us, not for a long time."

He laughed, then doubled over from the pain it caused. "I doubt they even know yet about the real problem we've caused."

"Why didn't you tell 'em? That would keep them from coming after us."

Tanner shook his head. "Too soon. We want to get as many of their network locations infected as we can before they know what's happened."

Castro went into the office area near the front of the building. A moment later he returned. "BJ, somebody's calling your name on a bullhorn!"

Tanner rolled into the front office and stopped by the window, where he heard some numbers spoken over the loudspeaker. Then the message was repeated.

"Beauford Tanner, this is FBI Special Agent Briscoe. Please call me on 555-9276."

Tanner noted the time on a wall clock. "Less than an hour since I called the prosecutor," he muttered. "Not bad communication — for bureaucrats."

He called to Sonny as he returned to the director's office. "Getting dark outside. Better kill the lights in here. Don't want 'em shooting at our shadows on the windows."

He waited for his eyes to adjust to the dark and used a red-lens flashlight to illuminate the desk and locate his cell phone. He punched in the number and waited. Briscoe answered on the first ring.

"Congratulations," Tanner said. "You and the U.S. attorney got together in pretty good time."

"Mr. Tanner, there's no way you'll get out of there, short of surrender. Come out now and things will go easier than they would later. What did you expect to accomplish, anyway, if you think you have a legitimate claim?"

"Are you the SAC, Briscoe?"

"No, I'm a special agent investigating IRS procedures in this district. I was in the building when you called for the evacuation."

"What does that mean, 'investigating IRS procedures'?"

"I could explain it easier face to face. Why don't you come on out?"

"I'm not in good health, Briscoe. Would you like to come in here?"

"Can't do that. Bureau policy doesn't allow it."

"Oh, yeah, policy. Well, I tell you what. Policies are gonna be bent and busted before this exercise is over."

"Why is that?"

"You'll figure it out by Monday morning."

"You expect to still be in there then?"

"Absolutely. Y'all can't move fast enough to do what I want done before then."

"What's your phone number, Mr. Tanner?"

"I have your number. That'll do for now. Did the prosecutor tell you about Palmero's confession?"

Briscoe hesitated. "Yes."

"Is that part of the *procedure* you're investigating?"

"It wouldn't be a good idea to talk about that on a cell phone. No telling who might be listening."

Tanner laughed. "Makes no difference. The world's gonna hear the whole story early next week anyhow."

"What are your demands, Mr. Tanner? What would it take to get you to surrender and walk out of there?"

"The IRS defrauded me of two and a half million dollars a few months ago. I want it back. I want ten million in punitive damages to go with it. That's for future income lost because I was forced to sell my company."

When Tanner got no reply from Briscoe, he continued. "Theron Palmero was only a flea on the dog that committed that extortion and a bunch of others before it. The dog that did the real biting is Pat Karney. I want her busted and jailed. I want the whole world to know what she did."

Briscoe chuckled. "I can see —"

"When you put the money in my bank account, I'll have it wire-transferred. Then my men and I will walk out of here and drive away. When we're clear, and certain that no one followed us, I'll call and tell you how to come in and disarm the bombs. Otherwise, I figure you'll lose about fifty or sixty thousand square feet of office space within a couple of blocks in each direction."

"Mr. Tanner, you know we can't meet those demands. The U.S. government cannot and will not be extorted."

"Sure it can. Happens all the time, but usually by some pissant would-be dictator in a place like Panama or Afghanistan. I'm going to ring off now and have dinner, Briscoe. You figure how you're going to bend Uncle Sam's domestic policy so it's as effective as foreign policy. Tomorrow you'll have to give me some solid encouragement. Otherwise, I'll have a notarized copy of Palmero's confession sent to Peter Jennings at ABC. I love his style."

"Mr. Tanner —"

"Get a good night's sleep, Briscoe. I'll call you in the morning."

Briscoe crossed the lobby of the FBI's temporary control center and dropped into a chair facing his supervisor.

"Well?" Cooper said.

Briscoe relayed Tanner's demands.

Cooper snorted. "That old building isn't worth it. The media situation could be a problem, but the spin doctors will kill the story in no time. The guy must have lost it."

Briscoe shook his head. "I don't think so. He sounds too confident. He may be holding an ace or two that we don't know about."

"You think he has hostages?"

"No, something better than that."

"Like what?"

"I don't know, but he created and ran a damn good high-tech company. The man's no dummy."

"Well, he sure as hell's acting like one."

"Maybe that's what he wants us to think. I'd sure like to have profiles of the people in there with him. We need to find out if any of them are his techies from Tanner Systems."

"What are you getting at?" Cooper asked.

Briscoe stood and paced as a fax machine on a table in the lobby buzzed to life. He watched the fax paper feed out, recalling nostalgically that when he'd first joined the bureau, the only information available at an action control center was what an agent could remember and write down.

"Tanner's in there with access to the IRS computers."

Cooper waved the notion away while walking toward the fax machine. "Guard said he'd put a bomb on the computer, but everything on it's backed up at the central site. What could he do with any records he pulled out of there anyway? Tell tales about how much tax — or how little — some people pay?"

Briscoe didn't answer immediately, reflecting on his personal displeasure with the bureau, and some of his own vindictive fantasies in recent weeks.

"Tanner's been wronged — or at least he thinks he's been wronged. He's smart, and he has access to high-tech info. He's also dying. Nothing to lose."

Cooper didn't respond but studied the message on the fax paper. "Jesus Christ."

"What now?"

"Tanner's a retired Marine colonel. Naval Academy. Highly decorated in Vietnam. After that, he formed the Marines' first CT3 command — Counter Terrorist Tactical Teams."

He slammed the message on the desk. "The son of a bitch wrote the book we study at Quantico to manage SWAT exercises in this kind of situation. Hell, he's more qualified for our jobs than we are."

Briscoe grinned and nodded.

"What the hell's so damn funny?"

"He said we'd learn to bend and break rules before this was over. Maybe you should start another argument with the Austin PD about jurisdiction — and let them win."

► 39 ◄

Saturday morning Tanner awoke feeling more rested than he had expected after a night of intermittent sleep on an air mattress. Castro looked calmer than he had the evening before. He nudged Tanner and pointed to the near-empty glucose IV bag hanging on a coat tree beside him.

"Almost out of gas, BJ. I'll get another bag."

Tanner sat up and looked with disgust at his swollen stomach, knowing the nausea would hit him soon. Castro put out a hand and helped him into the wheelchair.

"Stayed real quiet out there last night," Castro said. "Didn't hear a thing after those two helos circled about seven." He held up a small AM radio. "From what's on here, one of 'em must have been a news copter checking on a traffic problem. They blocked the freeway exit onto the street out front."

Tanner coughed several times and tried to clear his throat. "What're they saying about us?"

"Cops haven't told 'em what's happening. Only that there's a problem in the IRS building and the area's been sealed off. I figure they'll get the picture when they fly over in daylight and see the Claymores on the roof."

Tanner shook his head. "They've closed the airspace by now. Any helo coming over will be part of the SWAT team. You and Sonny get any rest last night?"

He nodded. "Two hours on, two off. We can handle a few days like that, no problem."

Tanner went to the washroom, surprised to find the water still on. After sponge-bathing himself, he wheeled along the south windows, peeking out through the blinds here and there. Kruger stood near the corner at the back of the building.

"How's it going, Sonny?" Tanner inquired.

"Nice and quiet, BJ." He thumbed over his shoulder and chuckled. "Bet some of the employees are pissed about having to leave their cars in the lot."

Tanner nodded. "Misfortunes of being in the wrong place when war breaks out."

After passing the north side windows, he returned to the director's office and switched on his four-inch portable TV. According to the news, the entire city knew of a reported bomb threat at the IRS building, but the authorities would not comment, and the news media hadn't been able to confirm the report.

Tanner dialed Briscoe's number. "Seven A.M., Briscoe. Did you sleep well?"

"We were a little busy here, Mr. Tanner. We learned more about you last night."

"Like what?"

"The kind of work your company does. Your background in CT3."

"Then you know that nothing short of your special team from Quantico can get in here, and they won't come because we have no hostages. I figure they'd suffer sixty percent or more casualties anyway. Your local SWAT team will face a wipeout if they try."

"Mr. Tanner, the special agent in charge would like to talk with you. His name is Cooper. I'm going to put him on the phone."

"Is he working on that *procedure* you're investigating at the IRS?"

"Not directly, no."

"Is he gonna arrest Pat Karney?"

"Not unless —"

"Then Cooper and I have nothing to talk about. I'm not coming out till I'm ready. And in case Cooper or some other fool tries to rush the building, we're ready. What does the U.S. attorney have to say this morning?"

"We . . . haven't talked to him today."

"How about Treasury? Are they ready to pay the fine for extorting money from me?"

"Haven't talked to them, either."

Tanner shook his head. "You disappoint me, Briscoe. No contact with the only two sources that can resolve this situation, yet you want to put a negotiator on the phone. Guess I'll call Joan Lunden — always did like her friendly manner — and see if *Good Morning America* would like to know what's happening in Austin."

"That wouldn't be a good idea, Mr. Tanner."

"Not for you, it wouldn't. She won't be on till Monday, but she might invest some time this weekend to get the story."

Tanner paused. When Briscoe did not respond, Tanner continued. "By the way, don't worry about shutting down the cellular antenna for this area. I'm on a radio link to a distant location. You can't disconnect me. You'd only piss off a lot of folks around here with cell phones — specially when they find out I'm still on the air."

Tanner smiled at the frustration he could hear in Briscoe's sigh.

"Looks like you have all your bases covered," the FBI agent said, "but Special Agent Cooper would still like to talk with you."

"Negative, Briscoe. This isn't a training exercise. He'll have to learn by doing and observing. Now, you get busy and contact the people who can resolve this situation. I'll call you around ten."

Tanner ended the call. "Castro, go get Sonny's phone for me. I'll start rotating the calls."

Castro left and returned, handing over the instrument. "What was that about a radio link?"

Tanner shrugged. "Little bluff. I might have tweaked his boss's ego too hard by refusing to talk with him. He could get crazy and decide if we won't talk to him, he won't let us talk to anybody. It'd be a stupid thing for him to do, but then we don't know much about the people we're dealing with, do we? That's the only advantage they have, knowing more about me than I know about them."

Patricia Karney lay awake at 5:40 when she heard the newspaper boy enter her secure condo complex to make his doorstep deliveries. She'd hardly slept, wondering what really had happened late Friday and if the problem had been resolved. She'd heard the radio news while driving back from Houston.

She had called her clerk and an IRS supervisor at their homes. The clerk said that, according to the guards, terrorists had entered the building. The supervisor told her the guards saw a bomb big enough to wipe out half of Austin. "You better do what I'm doing," the supervisor said. "Leave town before the crazy bastards blow everything sky-high." She'd rung Palmero's home number repeatedly till midnight but never reached him.

Karney dragged herself from bed, angry that her weekend had started off so badly. She'd planned to take her daughter and two other girls to Georgetown for the day. The youngsters had been studying stalactites and stalagmites in their private school and wanted to see the real things in the Inner Space Cavern.

After picking up the newspaper, Karney headed for the kitchen to make coffee.

While the coffee brewed, she scanned the headlines: "UNDER SIEGE?" topped the front page, with the subhead "9 block area evacuated; SWAT teams deployed."

She read the story, more concerned by what was missing than by what it contained, little more than the headlines revealed.

"Some jerk had gone too far with an April 15 bomb hoax," she muttered and poured a cup of coffee and headed for the shower. Before she reached the bathroom, a knock at the front door startled her. Who'd be coming at this hour?

Through the viewer she could see two men dressed in business suits. She left the security chain in place and cracked the door.

"Little early in the morning for saving souls, isn't it?"

"Patricia Karney?"

"What do you want?"

One of the men held out his ID. "FBI, Ms. Karney. We'd like to talk with you regarding the situation at the IRS office."

Her pulse raced as she tightened the belt of her robe, removed the security chain and opened the door. "What *is* the situation?"

The agents entered and she closed the door. "You're Theron Palmero's supervisor?"

Karney closed her eyes and nodded. "Don't tell me he's in the building with some crackpot."

"How about Beauford Tanner? You know him?"

Her stomach rolled and she swallowed hard. "What about him?"

"You conducted his tax reviews?"

"Palmero did, why?"

"Ms. Karney, you'd better get dressed. We'd like for you to come with us."

"My daughter's asleep. I can't leave a seven-year-old here alone. What do you want?"

The agent checked his watch. "Get someone to come stay with her, or we'll contact Children's Services to watch her. We haven't much time."

"This is ridic —"

"Now, Ms. Karney. We don't have much time."

Karney stared at the man for a moment, then called the mother of one of the girls
she'd planned to take out today.

As she hung up the phone the thought struck her. "Oh my God! Is Tanner in the building?"

The agent near the door maintained a perfect poker face. The man talking to Karney gave his partner a glance before responding. "That seems to be the case."

"Does he have Palmero?"

The agent's tone flattened. "Get dressed, Ms. Karney."

Karney's daughter came out of her bedroom. "What's going on?"

"Get dressed, Sweetie. Cindy's mom is gonna take you today. I have to go to work with these men."

The child, not fully awake, returned to her room.

Karney was struck by a thought. She turned to the agent. "You aren't taking me to my office if Tanner is there."

"No, Ms. Karney. Now get dressed, or you'll go with us in your nightclothes."

At 9:45, Tanner used Sonny's phone to call Lamar. If the FBI checked phone records, they'd find the call had been answered in the Waco service area where Lamar had been waiting for two hours. Tanner said, "How's it going, partner?"

"Sent the white package where it belongs. No problems at this end."

"Okay, I'll be checking their temperature here in a few minutes. I'm gonna give them another poke to get the fire nice and hot. Should have good news for you soon."

Tanner ended the call after less than a minute.

Castro said, "Time for more pills, BJ."

Tanner shook his head. "I'm calling the feds in a few minutes. I'll wait till after that."

Agent Briscoe's phone chirped at exactly 10 o'clock. He looked at Cooper, wishing the senior agent weren't with him. Cooper lifted the earpiece attached to the phone and gestured for Briscoe to answer.

"I know Saturdays are tough for bureaucrats, Mr. Briscoe, but tell me what you've managed to do this morning," Tanner said.

"We, uh, talked with Palmero and the U.S. attorney. We've seen his confession. If it's true, you have a legitimate gripe, Mr. Tanner, but this isn't the way to handle it."

"What about Karney?"

Cooper nodded. Briscoe said, "We have her in our office for questioning, trying to confirm Palmero's statements. You're making that difficult, Mr. Tanner. We need access to tax files, but we'll have to go to another city for that, unless you'll surrender the building."

Tanner chuckled. "You can come in here — you personally, that is — anytime. In fact, you'll have to if you want to see any tax records."

Briscoe felt an alarm go off in his head, one he'd almost listened to the night before. "Why is that, Mr. Tanner?"

"Contact the IRS's national computer centers in Michigan, West Virginia and Tennessee. By now they'll be able to confirm they've suffered a virus that's put 'em out of business. Service centers all over the country sent records to those locations last night. Now, every damn one of their computers is infected, except the one in this office."

Cooper shook his head and mouthed the word "bluffing."

"Check it out," Tanner said. "I have the only solution key to recover the data. Otherwise the IRS will have to dump everything and start from scratch. The government will go broke before then."

Briscoe watched the color drain from Cooper's face. "Mr. Tanner, nobody can cause that kind of problem, not even you."

"Don't bet your government paycheck on it, Briscoe. I'll call you around noon. We'll talk about Karney's arraignment, and you can tell me when you'll deliver the money. Then I'll let you know how to cure the virus."

Briscoe disconnected and watched Cooper's face grow paler. The senior agent grabbed his phone and punched in numbers. "Get hold of Treasury. I want verification that all IRS computers are on line and working."

Cooper ended the call and shook his head. "There's no way . . ."

Briscoe rose and crossed the command center, his back to Cooper to hide a grin he couldn't suppress. "Maybe, but I'd never play high-stakes poker with that man."

► 40 ◄

Prosecutor Yates watched Karney's reaction as she settled into a chair and read Palmero's confession. All color evaporated from her already pale cheeks, her head jerked, and her eyelids fluttered, as if she were about to pass out. She regained her composure while reading the text.

When she finished, she dropped the affidavit on Yates's desk with a shaky hand, then sat with her arms crossed, glaring like a trapped cat ready to spring. She took a deep breath and sighed heavily. "This is ridiculous."

Yates picked up the document. "You deny these allegations?"

"Of course I deny them! Palmero's a jerk. I tried to help him. Put him on cases that would make him grow, teach him to be responsible. But I knew he had no guts."

She gestured toward the confession. "If any of that's true, it'd be the part that said he cheated taxpayers to help those other people make money. He blamed me to get revenge for my being hard on him. Worthless bastard."

Yates, an experienced prosecutor, said nothing.

"I can believe," Karney went on, "that what's his name — Watkins? — he and the other guy sucked Palmero into some kind of sleazy deal. I'd have found out eventually. Wait till I get back to my office on Monday. Only thing that'll keep him out of prison is if he goes to a mental hospital for the rest of his life."

"You don't know Mr. Watkins?"

"No."

"You never met him?"

"I said I don't know him."

Yates dialed an intercom call. "Set up that security tape for another review."

He ended the call, then went through Palmero's list of taxpayers and asked Karney what she remembered about each case. She claimed to know little or nothing.

"Did you go with Palmero to Tanner Systems to collect their tax penalty payment?"

She held her head high but turned away from his gaze. "I don't recall."

"You don't recall? Less than three months ago you went there to collect a two-point-five-million-dollar check and you don't remember?"

She waved the question away. "I went with him on lots of field visits, but I didn't know the details on all of them."

Yates nodded. "Yeah, well, if nothing else, that would make you guilty of gross mismanagement."

She gave him a burning look that left him feeling that if he were any closer, she'd go for his eyes. "You won't find my name on any IRS documents regarding Tanner Systems."

"Ms. Karney, did you coerce Palmero to extort money from Tanner?"

"No! Tanner's the crook, not me. I've seen dozens like him. They form little companies. Get lucky and make big bucks. Then they cheat, try to keep every penny and not pay taxes."

"Ms. Karney —"

"I'll take care of this." She rose and picked up the confession. "I'll get with my boss on Monday and straighten everything out. We take care of our own, Mr. Yates. I'll bring all the evidence you need for an airtight case against Palmero."

Yates marveled at the steel in the woman, but he believed without a doubt that she was guilty. Four hours of interviewing Theron Palmero had convinced him that the man had neither the brains nor the courage to organize what he'd done. He'd been a good intimidator because of his size and appearance, but nothing more.

"Sit down, Ms. Karney. We don't turn investigations over to the accused. You can make it easier on yourself by cooperating. We don't have access to the files yet, but when we do, I'll check out every detail. If Palmero's telling the truth, then you're in deep trouble. Now, let's go over each one of these cases again. What can you tell me about the Marble Falls Gun Shop? The owner, Ed Wilcox, was Beauford Tanner's uncle."

"I've already told you, I don't remember any of these people."

Yates sighed, then rose. "Come with me, Ms. Karney."

He led her into a conference room that had a TV and video recorder. His secretary stood by the monitor. Yates nodded and the woman switched on the VCR. He watched Karney's jaw drop as her image and that of Theron Palmero appeared on the screen. They were standing in front of a counter looking into a display case filled with handguns.

"This video is from Wilcox's security system. The recorder was in the drugstore office in the other side of the building. The pharmacist sent it to me after speaking with Tanner's attorney. This recording was less than three hours before a Treasury SWAT team shot and killed Mr. Wilcox. Now do you remember being there?"

Karney crossed her arms, then her legs, and seemed to shrink into the chair.

"I want my lawyer."

Gino Zarola, senior Treasury agent in Austin, arrived at the control center at 10:40, his black, curly hair still wet with sweat after a tennis match in the humid spring morning. The wiry man wore a frown of disbelief when he entered, but by 11:30 he'd contacted systems analysts at the IRS facility in Martinsburg, West Virginia, as well as those in Detroit and Memphis.

On a conference call that included Briscoe, the analysts, one after the other, reluctantly admitted that, yes, a virus had infected each of the three network hub locations.

"How the hell did it happen?" Zarola demanded. "Don't you people have protection on those systems?"

After a protracted pause, the Detroit systems engineer responded. "Whoever created this virus is one smart son of a bitch. It's a passive intrusion, like termites taking microscopic bites from foundation beams. The problem couldn't be detected until someone inspected the foundation — or in this case, tried to recall stored data for processing. Each random microscopic bite destroyed a major slice of information. As soon as each host computer recalled the stored data, the main programs and everything in memory were infected."

"What does that mean in terms of recovery?"

After another painfully long hesitation, the Martinsburg analyst said, "It means we probably can't recover anything unless we get the random sequence key from whoever created the virus."

Briscoe leaned close to the speakerphone. "So this guy has hacked into *all* the main computers of the Internal Revenue Service? Corrupted every program? Wrecked every computer that's sent data to the records centers since yesterday? Bullshit!"

"Oh, no," one of the technicians responded. "This was no outside hacker. It was done from inside the system."

"Tanner didn't get into the building till after four o'clock yesterday."

"Then he had help from one or more of our people."

All three systems managers agreed that whoever planted the virus not only had earlier access, but also knew the highest level security codes as well.

Briscoe said, "So where do we stand? How bad will this be for the IRS?"

Zarola shook his head. "It means eighty million taxpayers who expect refunds in the next six weeks won't get them. It means everybody that didn't file on time can say they did. That one little hitch alone could cost the government over two billion in lost penalty fees, not to mention the tax payments owed."

His face turned ashen and his hands trembled as he considered other problems that could arise. "We could come to the point where we'd have to ask taxpayers to prepare and refile their tax returns with a new due date. That could mean the Treasury would have to increase the short-term national debt by twenty-five percent or more till this is resolved."

Cooper looked at Briscoe and shook his head.

Zarola continued. "Worst of all, we could never match up past records with future filings. We may not be able to get new systems set up in time for next year's filing date, not to mention corporate filings due between now and next April. We wouldn't know jack shit about taxpayers next year, whether or not they told the truth about their past carryover deductions or anything else. In a word, the U.S. government could go broke."

"So," Briscoe said. "Tanner wasn't bluffing."

Zarola shook his head. "No. His twelve million is cheap compared to what it'll cost to fix this. Christ, he could've asked for a hundred million. That'd still be a bargain if he really has the recovery codes. He must have some real computer wizards in there with him."

Cooper shrugged. "We don't know who he has in there. My people have verified the whereabouts of every Tanner Systems employee except two women — both on maternity leave. Neither one has the knowledge to do any computer hacking."

Zarola rose and headed for the door. "My boss will be talking to the Treasury secretary. Keep this quiet. The government doesn't pay extortion, not if anybody knows about it."

"Tanner's calling again at noon," Cooper said.

"Stall him."

Briscoe raised a hand. "Tanner doesn't stall. If I don't have something solid for him, he'll contact the media this afternoon."

Zarola spun and waved his hands wildly. "No! That can't happen. Tell the bastard anything he wants to hear, but nobody finds out what's going on here. Never!"

Briscoe and his boss watched Zarola leave the building. After a moment, Cooper said, "You know what Tanner's done?"

Briscoe nodded. "Yeah, he's reached right inside the Beltway and grabbed the United States government by the balls."

At 11:40 Cooper answered a call from Derwood Yates on his speakerphone. Frustration put a sharp edge on the prosecutor's voice.

"The attorney general says to start verification of Palmero's claims right now but not to let anybody know what's going on. I need access to tax records, but Zarola says Tanner has managed to disable every fucking IRS computer in the country. He's created a Catch-22! Made his own demands impossible to meet."

Cooper's face reflected the futility in Yates's voice, but Briscoe raised a hand. "Tanner said every computer except the one in the Austin office. If he's right, the records Palmero referred to are still there."

"That's terrific, Briscoe!" Yates shouted. "How the hell are we supposed to get to them? Drop in for coffee and doughnuts with Tanner and his gang?"

"He's gonna call again in a few minutes. I'll tell him what we need. I figure he'll let me go in and access the system."

Cooper waved a hand. "No way. That'd only add a hostage to the situation."

Briscoe shook his head. "If he wanted hostages, he could've kept all he wanted yesterday. I think he expects me — or someone — to come in and access the files. I bet he's planned on it, because he wants to be there and see for himself, have hands-on access to the evidence."

"You'd actually go in there with that crazy son of a bitch?"

"Tanner's anything but crazy, and, yes, I'd actually like to meet him face-to-face."

Cooper's eyebrows shot up.

Briscoe went on. "How many men can you name that have ever drawn as much response from the U.S. government as quickly as he has? Hell, not even a president of the United States has ever been able to control the IRS the way Tanner is."

Cooper stared at Briscoe in disbelief. After a long moment of silence, Yates said, "I don't have a better idea, but understand you'll be going in there strictly as a volunteer."

"Agreed."

Briscoe's phone rang at exactly 12 o'clock.

"How're those big IRS computers doing?" the voice said.

"Just like you said they would be, Mr. Tanner."

"You have any news for me, Briscoe? Or do I have to call ABC?"

"You're moving the government at mach speed, but I need your help."

"Where's Patricia Karney?"

"In custody of the U.S. attorney."

"When's her arraignment?"

"That'll require either her confession — which we don't have — or corroborating evidence. If the Austin computer's still working, I need to use it to access records that will verify Palmero's statement."

Tanner's laugh gave way to a spate of coughing, then he cleared his throat. "You expect to come in with a typical FBI entourage?"

"No, I'd like to come in alone."

"Alone? You guys don't even go to the bathroom alone."

Briscoe said nothing.

Tanner chuckled. "I said you would break the rules before this was over. Come to the rear door. The front door would make too good a target for your snipers. Stand with your back to the door till you hear it open, then back inside. We'll warm up the computer for you."

Tanner ended the call and gave Castro a thumbs-up. "Briscoe's either a man with balls, or he's crazy. He's coming in. Alone."

A few minutes later, Castro, after making sure the wig he wore covered the scar on his face, opened the rear door. Briscoe, without looking, backed inside. Castro closed and locked the door, then took the briefcase the agent carried and set it aside. He forced the agent's feet apart and made him lean against the door, hands widespread.

After frisking Briscoe and finding no weapons or wires, he steered the FBI man to one side and repositioned the Claymore aimed at the door. "What's in the briefcase?"

"Papers. Access codes I'll need to get into the computer records."

"Open the case but don't put your hands inside it."

Briscoe did as he was told and left the open attaché sitting on the floor.

After checking inside the case, Castro carried it as they walked up the hall toward the front of the building. Sonny stayed out of sight behind one of the office doors cracked open enough to see Castro and Briscoe pass.

Tanner tried to stand but couldn't. He had not been able to get out of the wheelchair all day without help. When Briscoe entered the director's office, his gaze showed astonishment at Tanner's condition.

"Jesus, man, you should be in a hospital."

Tanner recognized the agent from their chance meeting outside the IRS office. "So, you were straight with me when we met before."

Briscoe studied Tanner's face a moment, then nodded. "Yes, I remember. You looked better then."

Tanner smiled. "Guess I could say the same about you, Agent Briscoe. I'd say you haven't slept, showered or shaved since yesterday, and aren't you a little long in the tooth to be the hunter on a case like this? You look like you're ready to retire."

A faint smile warmed the agent's haggard face, and he put out a hand. "I am, but nothing short of a nuclear attack could move the federal government to respond as fast as you have in the past twenty-four hours. I wanted to see the man who did that up close and personal."

Tanner rolled forward, shook hands and took a closer look at Briscoe. "Well, you're looking at him."

Briscoe nodded. "Coming to Austin seemed like a waste of time till you, uh . . . convinced Palmero to help out. How'd you manage that?"

Tanner shrugged. "You might say I captured his ear. We had a heart-to-heart talk, and his conscience got the best of him." He nodded toward Castro. "This is my Number One. He'll keep an eye on you. Nobody will try anything while you're with us, but the other men will keep watching for outside action anyway."

He gestured to the computer terminal on the director's desk. "Is this all right for you? Or do you have a special one to use somewhere else?"

"This will do fine." Briscoe pointed to his briefcase. "I'll need my codes."

▶ 41 ◀

Briscoe called Cooper every half hour to confirm his own safety, but Tanner wouldn't let him give any information regarding the records he had examined. During the afternoon, the two men observed and tested each other with oblique questions at first, then more directly.

"Mr. Briscoe, you don't act like an FBI agent," Tanner said.

"Oh? How am I supposed to act?"

"FBI men don't work alone. They never step into a hostage situation."

Briscoe responded with no sign of stress or concern while he continued examining screens of information. "I'm no hostage. I volunteered, remember?"

He nodded toward the computer monitor. "Everything I've looked at so far supports Palmero's statement. I figure Yates will have enough evidence to pick up your man Bonner along with that guy Watkins in Houston. Based on what I see here, I'm betting they'll want to spill their guts and try to cut a deal by Monday morning."

The afternoon faded into evening. Sonny brought Castro and Briscoe Styrofoam cups of noodle soup heated in the coffee room microwave. He also gave them apples and blueberry-flavored granola bars. Then he attached another glucose bag to Tanner's IV, gave him a fresh protein drink, and two bananas. When he finished, he picked up duffles that he said were filled with food and walked out of the office, saying, "I'll pass this along to the other men."

When Briscoe made his 6:30 call, Cooper's shout projected from the phone loud enough that Tanner could hear it. "Put Tanner on. Now!"

Tanner nodded and Briscoe handed him the phone.

"Yates is ripping my guts out every fifteen minutes," Cooper said. "Let Briscoe give me something. A clue whether there's confirmation or not."

Tanner took a long breath and spoke slowly, trying to steady his weak voice. "Have you arranged to put the money into my account?"

"You crazy son of a bitch! What the hell difference does it make? You know we'll get it right back. You wire it anywhere in the free world and we'll have it back in fifteen minutes. Give it up, Tanner. You're dead."

Tanner waited till the tirade stopped, then he continued in a fatherly tone. "Make the arrangements and let me know when the money will be ready to wire. Twelve million five hundred thousand."

"What makes you so damn sure we're gonna pay? We haven't seen any proof of Palmero's statement. You could be forcing Briscoe to say Palmero's telling the truth."

"If you weren't gonna pay, Briscoe wouldn't be here. Soon as he walked in, I knew we'd won. If Yates is so damned anxious to do something, tell him to write up a press release and call it to me on Briscoe's phone. If I don't like it, I'll send the media one of my own, along with some of the evidence he's found here today."

He ended the call and his laughter led to another siege of coughing. Briscoe jumped to his feet and rushed around the desk toward Tanner. Castro, startled by the swift move, raised the Uzi from its shoulder sling and thrust the muzzle into the agent's face.

Briscoe raised his hands, nodding toward Tanner. "I only want to help. Does he have any medication? Some pain-killers?"

Castro lowered the gun. "Check his left coat pocket."

Briscoe found the Tylenol with codeine, but Tanner shook his head and dug a vial of morphine out of another pocket. He had gone as long as he could. He downed two caplets with sips of the protein drink.

After Tanner stopped coughing, Briscoe went back behind the desk and repositioned the computer keyboard. "You okay?"

"Good as I'm gonna get."

Briscoe nodded, a frown of concern on his face. "What about the money?"

"I won't be around long enough to spend any of it."

The agent gazed at Tanner a moment. "I've been curious about that. Cooper's right. It won't be hard to track it down when you move it out of your account."

"It'll be out of the country."

Briscoe shook his head. "Doesn't make much difference. Just about any country you send it to will cooperate with us. The ones that don't cooperate wouldn't let you have it anyway."

For a moment Tanner gave Briscoe a hard gaze as if he was concerned, as if he feared there was a hitch in his plans. They had talked enough about themselves over the course of the afternoon that they had become BJ and Doug to each other.

"Come on, Doug." Tanner said. "I know how drug dealers wire money into their accounts in one country, then send it to another bank and close the first account. Repeat that a couple of times and it stops the trail cold before anybody can track them down."

Briscoe shook his head. "Not anymore. We can track it all the way around the globe if we have to. The only way you could make your plan work is to have someone standing at the teller window in the bank waiting for the wire deposit to arrive. And he would have to be damned fast at that."

Briscoe shook his head and looked sadly at Tanner. "Face it, BJ. You may get the government to put money in your account, but you'll never get your hands on it."

"You may be right, Doug, but at least we'll have it for a few minutes. We'll also have the pleasure of knowing that we proved the IRS let some low-life in-house bastards commit a ton of crimes and almost get away with them." After a coughing spate, Tanner added, "Go ahead and print those documents. One of my men can bring them from the computer lab after they're done."

Tanner turned his wheelchair toward Castro, away from Briscoe, and gave his Number One a wink. The plan to get revenge on the IRS had worked without a hitch so far, and he felt certain that the government would meet his demands. Palmero, Karney and the others were going to jail.

The last step to make retribution perfect would be getting the money. Des Blaylock assured him that would be the easiest step of all, but Tanner wasn't as sure as the computer expert. He couldn't call Blaylock for another personal guarantee. He had to take the man's word for it.

The medication took over and lowered Tanner into sleep.

"BJ? BJ?"

Tanner awoke and looked up to find Briscoe standing over him holding a stack of computer paper. "This is the evidence to support Palmero's statement. There's enough to put all of them away for years. I'll make photocopies for you."

Tanner nodded. "Two copies."

Castro took Briscoe across the hall where he'd turned on a high-speed photocopier. Sonny was already in the room to guard the agent.

By 7 o'clock Saturday evening Briscoe had copied all the papers. Tanner folded one set into a black canvas attaché and sealed the other in a packing envelope on his lap. "Okay, Doug. Call your boss and tell him you have everything you need. Since he hasn't called, tell him I've written my own press release."

Briscoe dialed a number and Cooper answered on the first ring. "Palmero's statement is all true, but it'll take a few more hours for me to find everything."

Tanner stared wide-eyed at the FBI man. Castro straightened, alarm showing on his face as he looked to Tanner for instructions.

"No, no, they're treating me fine," Briscoe continued. "Even fed me dinner. Only problem is, I don't know how to access all the files I need from the computer. I should be able to get everything I need by morning if I work through the night."

He paused to listen to Cooper a moment, then said, "Yates will need warrants for Bonner and Watkins. I already have enough to show that. Karney's the ringleader, for sure. Tanner wants to know if there's anything yet on a press release. Or the money."

Briscoe listened, made notes, then grinned and ended the call. Before he could speak, Tanner said, "What the hell do you think you're doing?"

"Zarola says the money will be wired from Treasury tomorrow morning at five A.M. local time."

"Sunday!?"

He nodded and gave Tanner a note. "Your bank will have someone at this phone number ready for your wiring instructions."

"This is great, but why'd you bullshit them about not having all the data yet? I want you out of here."

"The closer we get to Monday, the more anxious everybody'll be to get rid of you. As long as I'm in here, they won't lose their cool and try to storm the building or anything like that. Call me an insurance policy."

Tanner stared at the agent in disbelief.

"Yates wants this over and done," Briscoe said. "Wants people to report for work Monday morning like nothing ever happened. Last thing he wants is for the press to know there are armed men in here. If anybody gets a clue that the U.S. paid extortion — never mind that the government extorted you first — it'd mean open season for every terrorist organization in the world that doesn't already see it that way."

"So how does he plan to handle it?"

"He'll tell the press that my investigation turned up evidence against Palmero and Karney last week. They were suspected of leaving a bomb in the building Friday night, trying to destroy evidence. They'll say that the area has been sealed off while we disarm it."

Briscoe laughed heartily before going on. "Here's the best part, BJ. Handling it this way, all the taxpayers that were ripped off will be compensated. That means Tanner Systems will get its two-point-five million back — plus interest." He laughed again. "Damn if you aren't gonna get away with double dipping!"

Sonny peeked in to see why they were laughing. Castro walked him back down the hall to explain what had happened. As they left, Briscoe's smile faded to a somber expression. "There is a major downside to this situation."

"What's that?"

"No way are they gonna let you walk away from here."

Tanner shrugged. "I'll be doing good if I last long enough to call the bank tomorrow. After that . . ."

Briscoe thumbed toward the hall. "What about your men? They aren't on a suicide mission, are they?"

"We'll worry about them when the time comes. Now, what are you gonna do in here all night? We didn't bring a guest bed."

"There are a couple of decks of cards in the coffee room. After you sack out, maybe your Number One will play gin rummy with me."

Tanner shook his head. "The morphine must be kicking in, making my head fuzzy. I know you're a fed, but damned if I'm not beginning to like you."

► 42 ◄

A strong Gulf airflow diverted the rain that had been expected in the Austin area Saturday night, sending the foul weather to the northeast. Special Agent Cooper said a prayer of thanks for the revised forecast as the FBI and Austin Police Department SWAT leaders sat down at his command center table for a 9 P.M. meeting.

Agent Ted Morton, tall, in his mid-thirties, with thinning blond hair and milky blue eyes, gazed at Cooper, waiting for instructions.

Cooper said, "I've talked with U.S. Attorney Yates and with my deputy director in Washington. They want this situation ended before Monday."

Sam Beckton, the Austin Police SWAT commander, sipped iced tea from a 32-ounce McDonald's cup. He ran a hand through thick black hair, pressed down by the black baseball cap he'd been wearing. His intense gaze shifted to Morton, then back to the agent in charge. "Did either one of them volunteer to come lead the charge?"

Cooper ignored the question. "I want a strategy from you two for how we'll get them out of there no later than midnight tomorrow."

Beckton sat back and crossed his arms. "My strategy's easy, but it won't work by tomorrow night. The PD's ready to wait till we starve the bastards out. Going in there would be double stupid compared to the Davidian assault in Waco."

He leaned toward Cooper. "Did you tell those nonparticipants about the Claymores, the C-4, and God knows what else might be in there?"

Cooper closed his eyes a moment. "The situation is more critical than you can imagine."

Beckton glared at the federal agent. "Then tell me so I don't have to guess."

Cooper stood and paced. "There's no need to go into things that don't impact the SWAT action."

"Yeah, right. Like you didn't bother to tell me that the leader of this little band is Beauford Tanner, the guy that invented counterterrorist tactics. Only way I found out about that is because the wife of one of my men works for Tanner Systems."

"Tanner's created a situation outside the building, but it has no bearing on what you and your men have to do."

"You better by God tell me what the situation is. My people aren't gonna make a move till I know every last detail."

Cooper, irritated by Beckton's demand, wanted support from his subordinate, but Morton said nothing while Beckton continued to rant. "We're gonna hold the outer perimeter to keep citizens out of the area for their own protection. Nothing more. You give me a reason — a damn good one — and we'll decide whether to move on the building."

Cooper's stomach boiled. He jabbed a finger at the local police officer. "I'm in charge of this operation! You'll do what I tell you."

Beckton's eyes crinkled at the corners. Then he lowered his gaze to avoid smiling directly at Cooper. He rose, picked up his iced tea and headed for the door. "After you tell me everything, I *may* do what you want. But it'll be *my* decision, no one else's." He stopped before going outside. "If you think you can go over my head with the department . . ." He shrugged. "It could be a humbling experience for you."

After the policeman left, Cooper turned on Morton. "Why the hell didn't you stop him?"

The FBI SWAT leader shrugged. "He's right. We already screwed up once by not filling him in on Tanner's background."

"Then we'll handle the job without him."

Morton shook his head. "We don't have ordnance disposal people.

Beckton's department will have to disarm the bombs once we get inside — if Tanner doesn't explode them."

"He won't set them off."

"You sure about that?"

"I'm sure."

"Sure enough to lead the way inside?"

"Don't get smart with me, Morton!"

Cooper paced a moment, breathing deep to regain control. Morton went after Beckton and convinced him to return and help work on an assault strategy. They agreed that the Austin Police Department personnel wouldn't be asked to join an attack until they had been fully informed of Tanner's actions.

Cooper knew that information would never be shared. The Treasury wouldn't let anyone know about the computer glitch unless the situation erupted into all-out war at the IRS building, or Tanner informed the media, as he'd threatened.

The senior agent kept recalling the bungled ATF action on a remote farm site near Waco not too many years earlier. The situation he now faced in a commercial district of Austin could cost the lives of men and women in Morton's command, not to mention millions in property damage.

Cooper had called for help from the FBI's elite Hostage Negotiation Team at Quantico, Virginia, but he'd been disappointed with their response. "Since there are no hostages, we can only advise you on the situation. We'll have someone in Austin first thing Monday morning."

"Monday will be too late."

"What's the hurry if you have no lives at stake?"

Again, Cooper suffered the frustration of trying to manage a hypercritical situation and amass resources without being able to tell them the extent of the problem.

"I don't blame Beckton," he mumbled. "Trying to run this operation without telling him what's going on makes me look like a jackass."

Tanner and Briscoe played cards and told war stories until 8:30, then Tanner said, "Think I better call it a day. Number One'll put you in the deputy director's office. There's a decent couch you can stretch out on."

While Castro walked Briscoe to the men's room and waited for him in the hall, Tanner breathed deep and struggled to clear his drugged mind, then he called Lamar. "Be ready to attend the going-away party tomorrow."

"*Tomorrow's* service?"

"That's right. The seventh cloud."

"Everything okay?"

"Couldn't be better. Be ready to meet three angels. I'll confirm again tomorrow."

He ended the call, wondering if the FBI had arranged to record all cellular transmissions over the local Metropolitan Service Area antenna. If they had, he didn't expect they could figure out the code he and Lamar used. Even if they did, they wouldn't know what it referred to.

Castro returned a few minutes later. "Briscoe's locked in that office, but he could break out through a window and get away unless you want us to stay with him all night."

Tanner found it more difficult by the minute to keep a clear head. He'd taken another morphine capsule, and it numbed his mind quicker than it stopped the pain.

"No need to worry about the windows, but I don't want him walking around inside. If he wants to leave, he can go out the door."

Lamar and Becky were finishing their second beer at Billy Ray's Night Spot in Fort Worth when Tanner's call caused his cell phone to vibrate. After ending the call, he nodded to her as he slipped the phone back onto his belt clip. One of the energetic waitresses in the gigantic western bar came to their table with two more longneck bottles. She shouted to make herself heard over the din of noisy patrons and the country band.

Gesturing to his phone, she said, "That one of your hounds callin' in to say they treed the possum?"

She laughed and hurried away across the sawdust-covered floor, dodging between tables topped with red-and-white-checkered oilcloths.

Becky said, "What's up?"

"Tomorrow night. Seven."

Becky frowned and leaned closer. "Tomorrow! What's happened?"

Lamar shrugged. "He said thing's couldn't be better."

"But banks aren't open on Sunday."

He leaned closer. "Maybe they are when you have the you-know-who by the balls."

She arched her eyebrows. "Good point."

Lamar dug money from his jeans and tossed it on the table. "Let's go."

She hoisted one of the fresh beers. "What about these?"

"I have to find a pay phone in a quiet place and pray that I understood his message."

They left the Saturday night crowd of happy cowboys and cowgirls. He gazed at the ground, shaking his head as they walked to his pickup.

"What's the matter, Lamar?"

He thumbed back toward the nightclub. "Just thinking about all the years I could have been having fun in places like this if I'd gone to the VA sooner."

Becky put a hand on his shoulder. "Looks like you're gonna get the chance to help lots of other guys. That'll make you feel good. Maybe make up for some of the fun times you missed."

"I never figured I'd ever do the kind of things we're planning, Becky. I owe it all to BJ Tanner."

"We all do."

Lamar's throat tightened and his words came in a whisper.

"God, I'm gonna miss him."

► 43 ◄

Tanner felt himself floating on dark water, lost and disoriented, no horizon. The water became turbulent and waves rolled over him. He couldn't control himself, couldn't stay afloat. He struggled toward the surface for a gulp of air and opened his eyes.

Sonny held a corner of the air mattress at his feet, shaking him awake. "Quarter of five, BJ."

Tanner lay still, gazing at Sonny until he oriented himself. "What's the weather like?"

"Still dark, but the sky's clear. Should be a nice day."

Tanner took a deep breath and sighed, then put out a hand. "Help me up, son. Thank the Lord today won't be the day."

While Sonny helped him into the wheelchair, Tanner said, "How's our FBI friend this morning?"

"Still asleep. Good thing you put him in there by himself. His snoring sounds like an air hammer."

After refreshing himself, Tanner rolled his wheelchair back to the director's office, picked up his cell phone and dialed the bank number Briscoe had given him. The man who answered sounded wide awake, and nervous.

"H-hello?"

"This is BJ Tanner. What's the balance of my checking account? I figure you know the account number."

"Yes, sir. The, uh, balance is . . ." The banker took a long breath. "Sixteen thousand, four —"

"That's close enough. Is your boss there with you?"

"Yes, sir."

"Good. The two of you can authorize a wire transfer, right?"

"Right."

"How many Treasury people are watching you?"

A long pause. "Two. There're two agents here."

"You scared?"

"A little."

Tanner chuckled, then coughed. "Why? You're not afraid of me are you?"

"No, sir, just this whole situation."

"All you have to do is your job, son. You'll be fine. Now here's the deal. You're gonna put twelve and a half million dollars into my checking account. I'm gonna give you a wire transfer account to send my money to another country. Those old boys watching you are gonna try to get it back, but I'm still gonna be here till I know the money's in my foreign account. After you do that, then you're done, understand?"

"Yes, sir."

"You sitting at the terminal where you key in the information?"

"Yes, sir."

"Good. First, put the twelve five in my checking account."

Silence on the line a few seconds, then, "Okay, that's done."

"Now, before we go any further, have a look at the business account for Tanner Systems and tell me how much is there after that transaction. I want to be sure Treasury isn't scamming me."

While the banker found the business account, Tanner dialed a number on one of his cell phones, let it ring once, then disconnected.

The banker reported the company account balance to Tanner. "Are you sure that's the right amount? You didn't take some of the twelve-five from there?"

"No, sir, not a penny. They're all watching."

The cell phone Tanner had used rang one time, then went silent. Tanner grinned in spite of his pain. "All right then, let's get back to my account and make a wire transfer."

No one at the bank made any sound for several seconds. Tanner said, "Are you ready to transfer?"

A new voice came on the line from the bank. "This is Roger Corbin, branch manager. Something weird has happened. Our terminal shows that the money has already been transferred out of your account, but that can't be. No movement has been authorized."

"Are you people trying to pull a fast one? Don't you want to recover the IRS system? You have an hour to get the money back in my account before I start making the damage permanent." He disconnected the call and laughed until a spate of coughing stopped him.

Briscoe's face twisted into a mask of discord. "They didn't try to block the transfer, did they?"

Tanner waved away the question, shaking his head. When the coughing ended, he said, "No, I'm just messing with them a little. The money is already in a foreign account with no way to trace to or from here."

"How could you possibly do that?"

"The IRS can tap any account they want to, right? Down the hall here is the only computer in the IRS network that is working. They put money into my account. I transferred it out, just like the IRS would confiscate funds. The only other thing is that I removed the transaction record so no one but me will ever know where the money went. You can tell them what happened when the game is over."

► 44 ◄

Tanner could hardly stand the pain in his abdomen and lower back. He'd taken another morphine capsule at noon, but its effect wore off in an hour, and he wouldn't take more medication that would slow his mental function until he received word from Lamar. He should have had a call by now. A few minutes earlier he'd called Sonny's phone to make sure the FBI hadn't disconnected the local cellular antenna.

Briscoe sat behind the desk, peering at him. "You need to be in a hospital. You're killing yourself."

Tanner shook his head. "Vietnam already did that. Long time ago."

"BJ, you're gonna —"

Tanner's phone chirped. Castro grabbed the instrument off the desk and gave it to him. Tanner recognized Lamar's voice.

"The florist has wired the flowers."

"Any trouble?"

"No, sir. All verified."

"Excellent! What about Wings?"

"Wings has everything ready. I'm about to fly off to paradise myself. How you holding up?"

"Okay. My guest and I are about to play a couple more games of chess."

Tanner ended the call and gave Briscoe a thumbs-up. "We moved a little faster than your boys. We got the money out of the bank before they knew what happened to it. They still don't know where it went."

Briscoe doffed an imaginary hat, then gave Tanner a serious look. "Congratulations. But now you have to face the other issue."

"What's that?"

He nodded toward Castro, walking toward the door. "Your men."

Tanner dug a medicine bottle from his jacket pocket. "You know anything about the underground facilities to this building, Doug?"

The FBI agent's reaction said that he didn't. Tanner went on. "I'd never have guessed this place had sewer access big enough for men to get out of here."

"You sure about that?"

Tanner winked. "Some of my boys may already be gone. Only had to cross under the freeway to get outside your perimeter."

"Only the two of you still here?"

"Another man at the back of the building. He and Number One will be checking out after dark."

Castro handed him a cup of water, and Tanner washed down two tablets. "Ready for another hand of rummy? I can afford to play for money this time."

Briscoe stared at him like a poker player looking for signs of a bluff. After a moment, he said, "How many men did you have here altogether?"

"Just enough to do the job the way we expected it to go."

Another hesitation, then Briscoe slumped in his chair. "No one left this building. There were never more than the three of you."

"What makes you think that?"

"Guards only saw three men. People in the offices didn't see anybody. Why the hell did you tell me you had more people?"

Castro put a hand on his Uzi, bringing it to waist level.

Tanner said, "Didn't want you to think we came in here understaffed."

Briscoe rose, ignoring Castro. "Dammit, man, you don't have a plan to get these people out of here, do you?" He paced behind the desk, then stepped around it next to Tanner. "Look, I sympathize with what you've done. Your condition will get special treatment, but there's nothing I can do for them."

Tanner said nothing while Briscoe continued pacing, then the agent spun and faced him. "Jesus Christ! You never answered me yesterday when I asked if they were on a suicide mission."

"I didn't?"

"No. What the hell are you gonna do?"

Tanner raised a hand. "Don't worry, Doug. Nobody is on a suicide mission but me. These boys will be out of here and long gone before anybody knows what happened. No bullets, no bombs, no nothing."

"But —"

Tanner tapped his watch. "It's three o'clock. Don't have much time. Deal the cards before the medication makes me too stoned to see them. This'll be your last chance to take advantage of me."

Becky ran into a rain shower on Interstate 8 and slowed the motorcycle, worried that the semis racing past her would blow her off the highway. She cursed herself for not packing rain gear. The huge drops stung, even through the soaked jumpsuit plastered against her skin.

The rain lasted only a few minutes, but it caused her to hold down her speed on the wet highway. The farm road gave her no problems, but she slowed the bike while on the lane to the abandoned hangar. She avoided every puddle, not knowing which ones were deep potholes that might make the bike flip over.

She arrived at the hangar a half hour later than expected, but she'd allowed more than an hour margin. The thundershower probably dumped a quarter inch of rain in the area as it passed, leaving the ground softer than she'd counted on. Would the little Bobcat tractor be able to pull the Huey safely outside?

After inspecting the area around the hangar and finding no signs that anyone had been there, she unlocked the door and rolled the motorcycle inside, out of the way of the helo. She checked the bike for anything that could be traced back to her or the ranch. Then she turned her attention to the helicopter, keeping her gloves on to avoid leaving fingerprints on anything in the hangar or on the helo. She gave the Huey a thorough preflight check, then shoved the Quonset doors wide and started the Bobcat.

Before driving outside, she used a stick to check the depth of each puddle and filled the deeper ones with stones and gravel. The little tractor pulled the aircraft clear of the building with no trouble. She unhitched it from the skid cradle, drove it back inside, then closed and locked the barn. She wondered who would eventually find the Bobcat and the Yamaha that had been sold at auction for cash to a Latino wearing a stocking cap down to his eyebrows and a three-week beard.

The battery power was sufficient to start the engine without using the reserve units she and Sonny had left in the barn. The turbine rumbled slowly at first, rose steadily to a high-pitched whine, then a powerful roar.

Becky closed her eyes and smiled, enjoying the scent of jet fuel, flashing back to the best time of her life when she'd flown the powerful choppers every day. Her memory gave way to reality, and she continued with the power-on preflight checklist.

As she increased rotor speed, the circular wind lifted water from the ground, causing a sparse rainbow around the front of the aircraft where the sun shone through the spray. A moment later the helo lifted and nosed forward, flying over the old runway, then 30 feet above the lake, heading west.

Becky turned north, holding at the low level till she reached the pasture where she'd simulated landing the night she and Sonny stole the aircraft. She set the transponder to a civilian code, climbed to 2,000 feet and headed for Johnson City, west of Austin. After plotting her course into the flight computer and checking her ETA, she slowed the helo to 90 knots to conserve fuel. The sun slipped behind the dark clouds on the horizon, casting a golden glow over the landscape and turning the dark clouds to varied shades of red, pink and purple.

Turning her gaze back into the cockpit, Becky shivered, feeling the chill of her wet clothes. She put a gentle gloved hand on the console, stroking it.

*Too bad I can't keep you, old Huey. We could have such a great time
together.*

Lamar's Sunday afternoon flight from Love Field landed in Austin at
5:50. He shouldered his duffle bag and moved toward the terminal exit,
listening to conversations around him, but he heard no one mention the
mysterious closure of the area surrounding the IRS building.

He followed the instructions he'd written down Friday when Sonny
called him to say where they'd parked Castro's van in the airport parking
lot. He took a deep breath as he approached the truck, wondering if by
some quirk, the FBI had identified Castro and staked out his van.

Using the spare key Castro had given him, Lamar unlocked the side
door of the van and tossed the duffle inside. He checked to be sure the
right tools were in the back, then climbed into the driver's seat and started
the engine. No one came toward him across the parking area.

After warming the engine, he drove to the exit, paid the parking fee
and headed for the freeway. Going south from Mueller Airport, he passed
the exit for the IRS. At the bottom of the ramp, flashing lights marked
a police barricade barring a left turn under the interstate toward the
building. His pulse raced as he continued south, the gathering darkness
adding eeriness to his already electrified feelings.

A few minutes later, he left the freeway, crossed over to Route 183 and
slowed to check side roads. He found one that seemed to fit his needs and
left the highway.

A half hour later, he continued south on 183 to a farm road. He rolled
down the window and peered into the darkness, unable to see in the
fields. Becky had assured him those along the road were freshly plowed.

Three miles before reaching the settlement, he pulled off the road at
the end of a bridge, took out a sandwich and thermos and sat on the
railing. Unable to eat, he took three bites of the sandwich and spit them
into the stream. If a patrol stopped to check on him, he'd say he wanted
to listen to the stream flow while eating his supper.

Lamar listened to the quiet. He could hear an owl in the woods behind him and the gentle movement of the stream. Overhead came the faint sound of a jet in the distance, probably departing Mueller Airport.

After waiting for what seemed like an hour, he checked his watch with a penlight. 6:23. He'd been there twenty minutes and not one vehicle had passed. Becky had done a good job choosing the area.

After setting course for Johnson City, Becky locked the throttle control and engaged the new wing leveler. She made one heading correction to compensate for the crosswind, then observed the helo's performance. She nodded, satisfied that the avionics were performing well.

The lights of Johnson City appeared at the expected time. A few miles south of town, Becky identified Highway 290 by the surface traffic, disengaged the wing leveler and turned east. Her pulse quickened and she couldn't hold back a smile as she reduced power and began shedding altitude.

Hugging the ground will be different here in hill country. Careful. Sonny and the others are counting on me.

Becky eased the helo below a hundred feet and turned off the transponder, flying parallel to the highway half a mile to the north. When she saw the roadside rest area, she slowed to a creeping hover at 30 feet. The moon cast enough light to pick out the triangular space she and Sonny had found while flying the Robinson, so she didn't have to use the helo's searchlight. She settled the Huey and shut down the engine.

Before the rotor stopped turning, she leaped from the aircraft and dashed 20 yards to the clump of cedars where Lamar had stashed two barrels of JP fuel. She moved away the stones hiding the first barrel and rolled it toward the helo. Then she rolled the other one beside it.

Using the block and tackle pulleys and nylon rope she'd attached to the Huey's cargo deck, she hoisted each barrel upright, then inserted a hand pump into the first barrel and began transferring fuel into the helo.

Tanner couldn't concentrate on the cards. His eyes closed, but Briscoe's cell phone chirped. Tanner nodded for the FBI agent to answer the call.

"Briscoe here."

Tanner couldn't read the agent's face while he listened to the phone. After several moments Briscoe said, "Anything more about Karney?" Another pause. "Right. Give me a few minutes. I'll ring back."

Briscoe ended the call and grinned at Tanner. "You win all the way around. We picked up Bonner at his home an hour ago. He'd been in Houston all weekend. When he saw a copy of Palmero's confession, he cracked like an egg. Claimed he was coerced."

"And Karney?"

"Her lawyer is already trying to cut a deal for her, but that isn't gonna happen." The FBI man leaned forward. "What's left is to get you out of here so we can disarm the building and be ready for people to show up for work tomorrow. Cooper wants you and your men to surrender right now. If they testify, the U.S. attorney will go easy on them."

Tanner looked at his watch. Eyes wide trying to focus, he moved his wrist farther away. Castro said, "Eighteen twenty-five, BJ."

"Call him back, Doug. We'll leave by eight."

Briscoe studied Tanner's face. "You aren't gonna do something crazy, are you, BJ?"

"Call your boss, Doug. He and I'll meet in two hours. If *he* doesn't try something crazy, I'll make both of you heroes."

Becky's arms grew tired hand-pumping 110 gallons of fuel into the helicopter. When she finished, she rolled the barrels outside the rotor's area and blocked them with stones. She picked up a canvas bag from where the barrels had been hidden and secured it in the helo with a rear seat safety belt.

Back in the cockpit, she mentally reviewed the preflight checklist, then started the jet engine. The blades turned slowly at first, then gathered speed as the engine whined to a higher pitch. A few more RPM and she'd be on her way. She looked to the right toward the highway and her heart climbed into her throat. Bright lights bounced across the rough terrain coming toward her. The beams were not cast by car lights. Something brighter, like spotlights on a Highway Patrol car.

She looked back to the instrument panel, angered because she'd looked directly at the vehicle lights and impaired her night vision. Had the rotor RPM climbed enough to lift off?

Dust mushroomed outside the tips of the rotor as she pulled up on the collective stick. Then the Huey rose. The beams of light bounded across the ground below but didn't rise to shine directly on the Huey. Looking down she could see that the vehicle was a truck, probably a four-wheeler, with four bright halogen lights across the top of the cab. Some off-roadster must have seen her land and come to see what was happening.

She nosed the helicopter sharply forward, gaining speed while climbing. Paralleling the highway, she headed toward Austin. When she leveled off at 1,000 feet and checked her watch: 18:43.

Perfect! Fifteen minutes to get there.

She turned on both radios and reset the frequencies.

Tanner blinked, trying to focus on the cards. He hadn't taken any morphine for over three hours, and the pain blinded him as much as the drugs. "Whose turn is it?"

Briscoe shook his head. "Why the hell are we still playing cards? You can't even see them. You should be in a hospital."

Castro came to the door. "Ten minutes, BJ. We're about to start setting up for the last supper."

The FBI agent rose. "Last supper? What does that mean?"

"Sit down, Doug. Only means this is the last time we'll all be together for a while."

He gestured toward Briscoe's phone. Castro took it from the desk and laid it on Tanner's lap, then wheeled him into the hallway.

"Wait a couple minutes, Doug," Tanner said. "We'll be right back."

Castro closed the door and rolled Tanner down to the middle of the hall where Sonny waited by the desk and boxes they'd stacked to reach above the false ceiling. Sonny held the portable radio Becky had given them the previous week.

"Sis is on her way. Says she's right on schedule for seven, and she has the package."

Tanner looked from one man to the other. Although the bushy beards hid their features and his vision had blurred, he could make out the disturbed expressions on their faces.

"Don't worry," Tanner said. "Wings'll get it done. No sweat."

Castro shook his head. "That ain't what bothers me, BJ. This isn't the way it should end."

Tanner lowered his gaze a moment, then put out a hand to Sonny. "Better stand by the switch, son. I may not get another chance to say thanks for all you've done. Give Becky a kiss and a cuddle for me. You two stick with Lamar, hear? The rest of this mission is gonna work out perfect. You'll see."

Sonny took the hand and kneeled beside Tanner, tears in his eyes. "BJ, you're the best man I ever had the pleasure to know. I could never thank you enough for all you've done for Becky and me and the others."

Tanner put both hands on Sonny's. "Watch the time, son. Your sister is on her way. Be ready, and don't forget the mail pouch."

Sonny nodded and wiped his eyes. He laid the Uzi on the desk, then climbed to the pipes in the ceiling, staying out of sight right below the hole in the roof.

Tanner watched him climb into position, then turned to Castro. "Did you take care of all the primers?"

Castro nodded and appeared to be near tears.

"You're a good man, Ernie. I'd be proud to serve with you anywhere, anytime."

Castro dropped to his knees and hugged Tanner, his body jerking with sobs. Tanner lifted a weak arm and returned the embrace. Castro leaned back. "BJ, I —"

"She's here!" Sonny said. "Come on, partner. Thirty seconds. I'm turning the lights on."

Castro looked toward Sonny, then back to Tanner. "I . . . I . . ."

"Go, Number One. Get out of here. Stick with Lamar. You men will change part of the world."

Castro put his Uzi on the desk and stared at his boss. Tanner could hear the faint sound of the Huey approaching. He tried to shout but could only manage a croak. "Go!"

Castro stepped onto the desk and spoke with a quivering voice. "BJ, you're the best thing that ever happened to me, man. God bless you."

Tanner's vision blurred as he watched his men climb onto the roof.

Becky leveled off at 200 feet over Barton Springs and headed for downtown Austin. She turned south along Town Lake, then banked over the Holiday Inn. After checking the instruments, she spoke into the radio for the second time. "Final approach. Give me some lights."

Sonny's voice came through her headset. "Lights comin' on . . . now."

Becky nodded satisfaction. Dead ahead she saw the triangular shape of the lights Sonny had positioned on the roof of the IRS building. She banked left a few seconds, then right to line up with the north point of the triangle.

No time to watch instruments now. It's make or break.

She judged the distance to target and sensed the angle. Then she eased the nose over, pushed down hard on the collective stick and reduced power. The Huey dropped like an elevator in free fall, autorotating toward the roof.

She watched the forward point of the three lights flatten in her angle of view as she let the helo dip closer to the roof. When she judged her elevation to be the right height, she added power and pulled up the collective stick. The jet engine screamed and the Huey flared into a hover with the skid rails no more than three feet above the roof.

"Move it!" she shouted into the radio.

Sonny switched off the lights.

Becky eased the skids to the roof without resting the helo's weight on it. First Sonny, then Castro climbed from the hole in the roof and dashed 20 feet for the helo.

Becky looked over her shoulder into the rear compartment until she saw that both men were aboard. Sonny untied the canvas bag from the rear seat, dropped it onto the roof, then gave her a thumbs-up. She added power and the helo lifted, nosing forward at a sharp angle.

The aircraft climbed over the building across the street, clearing the structure by a few feet. Becky could see two men with rifles on the roof, silhouetted against the amber sky, aglow from the city lights. The men rolled away from the edge of the building, ducked and covered their heads as the Huey passed over.

When the helicopter had ended its autorotation and hovered, the building shuddered from the rotor's wind pressure against the roof. Briscoe rushed out of the director's office into the hallway. "What the . . . ?"

Tanner sat beside the desk in the hallway and lifted a weak hand to point to the hole in the roof, then tapped Briscoe's phone. "My team's been extracted. You can call your boss now. Tell him you've secured the building."

Briscoe turned a full circle, a stunned expression on his ashen face. "They're gone?"

"Everybody but you and me."

The agent looked down and pointed at the wires along the hall floor. "These go to the bomb detonators?"

Tanner shook his head. "Never fused any except on the computer. Disarmed it before they left. All you need to do is sweep up and patch the hole in the roof."

He touched the agent's phone again. "You better call somebody, but bring me some water first. I need to take more tablets."

Briscoe stared at Tanner, then shook his head slowly. "Damn if you didn't —"

The agent's phone rang and he took it from Tanner's lap. Cooper's voice screamed through the instrument loud enough for Tanner to hear. "The spotters said that an Army helo landed on the building. What the hell's going on in there?"

A smile spread over Briscoe's face. He started to speak, then lowered the phone a moment to compose himself. "We've been outfoxed. Everybody's gone but Tanner. He's surrendered."

"Are there really bombs in there?"

"Yes, but they're not armed. Send in the bomb disposal team to get the materials out of here. Then you can come in."

"Yeah, I'll do that. And I'll personally put cuffs on that son of a bitch Tanner."

Briscoe shook his head. "Nobody's putting cuffs on Mr. Tanner. Call a MedEvac air ambulance. We have to get him to the Dallas VA hospital, right now."

▶ **45** ◀

Becky headed the Huey toward Bergstrom Air Force Base momentarily, then turned south toward the farm she and Sonny had circled the previous week. She climbed to 3,000 feet, leaned the fuel mixture and set the throttle for 90 knots cruise speed.

Sonny and Castro closed the aft compartment hatches while they dug their gear from large duffles strapped in the seats. Each man tore off his wig and beard and tossed them into a bag. They put on helmets with full-face shields, like the one Becky wore, and Sonny plugged in his headset to talk with her. "All set back here, Sis. Both hatches are open."

"Everything okay with BJ?"

She noted the pause and his melancholy tone. "Good as it can be."

"You two check each other's gear. We have six minutes."

Sonny and Castro shed their clothes, slipped on flight suits and parachutes, and strapped the gear bags to their chests. Then they verified that each had properly secured all harness attachments.

Becky scanned the ground ahead until she could make out the tall white silo she'd chosen as a landmark. She swung the helo wide and turned to the southeast on a line directly over the silo. Then she set the wing leveler and clamped tension on the throttle control to keep it steady. On this course, the Huey headed for the closest point on the Gulf of Mexico. It would cross Matagorda Island and be over water in seventy minutes with enough fuel to fly another two hours.

Becky climbed carefully over the console and into the rear

compartment, shouting so the others could hear her after disconnecting the radio cables from their helmets.

"Remember, jump clear and take a three count before you open your chutes. Ready?"

Each man nodded.

"You first, Ernie. Then Sonny. Then me."

She crouched next to the starboard hatch opening and saw the dark ground ahead where the field had been plowed, a large area that would give them a soft landing. Each man nodded when she pointed at it.

Castro moved up beside her. She touched his arm, and he put a trembling hand on hers, then gave her a thumbs-up. She looked back to the field. As the helo crossed over the near edge, she slapped Castro on the shoulder. He hesitated a moment. She could see his chest swell with a deep breath, then he lunged out the hatch.

Sonny stepped forward and leaped into the darkness with no hesitation.

Becky's heart beat so hard she could hear her pulse pounding inside her helmet. She gave a final admiring look into the Huey's cockpit, then sucked in a deep breath and jumped.

The force of 90 knots air speed caused her to spin backward, but she managed to extend her arms and legs into a spread-eagle position and stabilized, face down. She pulled the D ring and deployed her chute. The rectangular canopy popped open and jerked the harness. It chafed her shoulders and breasts under her damp clothing. She began a gentle descent.

Becky looked in the direction where Castro and Sonny had jumped but couldn't see them. Then she realized they were below her and wouldn't be silhouetted against the moonlit sky. Besides, all three of them used dark-blue parachutes and wore dark jumpsuits to minimize the chances of being seen by anyone on the ground.

The rectangular parachutes would allow a jumper to make a soft landing, about like stepping off a pickup truck moving at five miles an hour. But the darkness made it impossible to accurately judge distance. She flared the chute too high and dropped the last ten feet. When she hit the ground, she rolled to her right and tumbled onto the damp but soft ground.

She gathered the chute and rolled it in her arms while getting her bearings, then headed east across the field toward the farm road.

She still couldn't see Sonny or Castro.

Becky struggled to make her way across the soft loam toward the road, stumbling over plowed ridges, sinking into soft patches of the freshly turned earth. When she reached the fence, she spread the canvas chute pack as a shield across the barbed wire, then climbed over and crouched beside the road.

Lamar heard a car coming along the road from the south. He moved off the bridge and crouched below the roadbed beside the span. The old Ford passed without slowing.

Lamar could hear the sounds of night birds, the rippling of the stream flowing over rocks, a dog in the distance. His heart pounded like a drum in the silence. Any other time he could sit and enjoy the serenity for hours. Not this night. He checked his watch a dozen times in the next quarter hour, then finally heard the unmistakable whop-whop sound of a Huey.

Trembling, he climbed from under the bridge and checked the road in both directions. No vehicles in sight. The helicopter maintained a steady speed and course as it passed overhead along the west side of the road, right where Becky said it would.

For five minutes he scanned the dark sky above the horizon to the north, but he saw nothing. He started the van and crept along the farm road with no lights, windows down, searching the left side and the dark field beyond, listening.

A quarter mile. Nothing.

Lamar slowed, but kept moving. Another quarter mile. Movement next to the fence caught his eye. He stopped the van and flashed his penlight twice. The figure rose, ran toward him and crossed behind the truck.

The side door slid open. Someone tossed a rolled-up parachute inside, then jumped in.

"You all right, Becky?"

"Yeah. Any sign of the others?"

"Not yet."

While they continued creeping along the road, she peeled off her boots, wet jumpsuit and underwear. She found her duffle in the back of the van, pulled out Levis, a pink-and-white western shirt and cowboy boots.

She'd dressed except for the boots when Lamar stopped the van and blinked his penlight. Like Becky, Sonny jogged across the road, tossed in his chute, then hopped in and stripped off his jumpsuit and boots.

After dressing, Sonny slipped into the front seat while they continued driving. They reached the end of the plowed field but saw no sign of Castro.

"Where *is* he?" Becky wailed, gripping Sonny's shoulder. "Did you see his chute open?"

"Yeah, right after I jumped, but I lost him when mine deployed. He had a soft ride down, but he might have landed hard. Crunched something. It's tricky at night."

"That's why we came down on new-plowed ground, so nobody would get hurt."

Lamar switched on the headlights momentarily while turning around, then headed back to the south and crept along beside the field once more. He took long, slow, silent breaths so he could hear in case Castro called out.

Becky crouched in the open side door while Sonny leaned out the front window, peering into the field and along the road.

A quarter mile. Nothing.

They returned to the point where Sonny had been picked up. "Better head back the other way. He left the helo ahead of me. Couldn't have been this far south."

Lamar turned around again.

"Hold it!" Becky said, pointing into the field. "Something out there. Put a light on it, Sonny."

He looked where she pointed and turned on a powerful six-cell light. Fifty yards from the road, they saw Castro give them a weak wave, then drop to his knees.

Sonny killed the light, leaped from the van and vaulted the fence. Lamar's heart pounded when he saw headlights coming from the south. He steered the van onto the road and headed toward the oncoming lights.

"What are you doing?" Becky demanded.

"Car coming. We'll come back for the guys after it passes."

He drove at 30 miles an hour, closing the distance to the other vehicle. As they passed, he noticed that it was the same old Ford that had gone the other way while he'd waited at the bridge.

Lamar kept driving another minute, then made a U-turn and headed back toward Castro and Sonny, increasing his speed. He checked the odometer and slowed as he approached the spot where they should be. Sonny ran into the road ahead of them, holding Castro's chute. The Latino limped along behind him.

Becky threw open the side door and helped Castro inside. "What happened?"

Castro shook his head and laughed, then grimaced with pain as Sonny unlaced his left boot. "First, I got turned around and steered west instead of east. That put me toward the far side of the field. Then I misjudged distance and stalled the canopy too high. Must have dropped ten or fifteen feet. Damn good thing you found us a plowed field. Otherwise I'd probably have a broken leg."

She watched Sonny probe Castro's ankle with gentle hands, moving the foot side to side, checking the toes, feeling for broken bones. "So, what's the damage?"

Sonny shrugged. "Looks like a bad sprain. Ice and rest should take care of it."

"But it's so swollen already," Becky said.

Castro shook his head. "That's from walking so far across that plowed ground. I'll be okay."

While Lamar drove north, Sonny and Becky helped Castro change his clothes, then put their jumpsuits, boots and parachutes into their duffles.

Eight miles later, Lamar slowed and found the landmark he looked for beside the road: a scrub oak with a broken branch hanging to the ground. He turned off onto a dirt road, drove a hundred yards and stopped.

Lamar, Sonny, and Becky hauled the duffles into the woods beyond a thicket of brambles. Lamar shone a light on the ground until he found the hole he'd dug two hours before. A shovel stood punched into the loose dirt pile. They tossed the three bags into the hole and Sonny used the shovel to cover them. Then he tamped the ground level and scattered the rest of the dirt by tossing scoopfuls into the surrounding area. Lamar dragged a broken tree limb over and left it lying across the fresh dirt. After wiping down the shovel, they put the tool in the van and drove back toward the highway. Lamar stopped at the edge of the woods, with the lights out, and listened for traffic. Hearing none, he gunned the van onto the road, switched lights back on and headed toward Austin.

Lamar took a deep breath, his hand trembling on the steering wheel. Then a grin spread across his face and he leaned his head back. "YAAAA-HOOOOO. We did it! We pulled it off."

The other three joined him with hoots and shouts.

"Everything went just like BJ said it would," Lamar added.

The mention of Tanner sobered their thoughts as quickly as they'd begun the celebration. They rode in silence a few minutes until Sonny turned on the overhead light for another look at Castro's ankle. "Better stop at the first liquor store and get some ice. We'll have Ernie in good shape by the time we get back to the ranch."

Lamar nodded. "We'll get a bottle of champagne, too. BJ would want to toast us for completing a perfect mission."

"Yeah, he'd give us the credit," Castro said.

Sonny and Becky nodded, and they all fell silent again.

► **46** ◄

Tanner lay on a gurney in a trauma van headed for University Hospital, where a MedEvac helicopter stood by to transport him to the Dallas VA. Agents Briscoe and Cooper sat across from him while a medical technician checked his vitals and talked with a doctor on the radio.

Tanner blinked hard to focus. "You get the Air Force to shoot down my boys' helo?"

Cooper's jaw muscles twitched. Briscoe said, "Randolph Air Force Base had an interceptor on their tail before they'd gone fifty miles from Austin."

He leaned close to Tanner. "BJ, we know they're headed for Mexico, but they'll never make it."

"Did they get as far as the Gulf?"

"Yeah, but the Air Force will put 'em in the drink before they let them out of the country."

Tanner closed his eyes and nodded.

Cooper said, "Tanner, what about the computers?"

"What computers?"

"The IRS systems. You said you'd help recover the data you destroyed. We searched you and your supplies but didn't find any computer codes."

"Your bomb-disposal boys get on the roof yet?"

The two FBI agents exchanged fast glances. "What'll happen when they do?" Cooper asked, his face pale.

Tanner closed his eyes and smiled. "They'll find an old bank pouch with the code key to kill the virus and instructions on how to clean up the data." His chuckle turned into a fit of coughing.

After he recovered, Cooper leaned close to him. "Why did you do this, Tanner? You sure as hell won't live to spend a penny of what you stole from the government. And there isn't a chance your men will get away."

Tanner struggled to lift his head. He gave Cooper a hard stare. "I didn't steal a damn thing from the government. I just recovered some of what was mine in the first place."

Tanner paused to catch his breath. "Don't forget, Cooper, I still have certified copies of Palmero's confession in a safe place. If the IRS doesn't let the world know what's been done to me, that story will be told my way. Better hurry, too. I don't have much time."

Allie waited with Dr. Weiss on the landing pad at the Dallas VA when the air ambulance landed. No one seemed to notice the sprinkles of rain until the helo turned on its landing light and approached the deck. Wind from the rotors caused the raindrops to sting like tiny darts.

Tanner's face was as pale as the sheet beneath him, and his eyes were closed when they hoisted his stretcher out of the aircraft. Allie cupped a hand over her mouth and bit her lip, fighting back tears. Her breath caught in her throat as she looked at BJ's ashen face, unable to see life in him.

Two men in suits climbed out of the helo. They looked as if they'd slept in their clothes and hadn't shaved for a day or two. One of them trailed behind Tanner while the older man stayed near him, but out of the way.

Allie walked beside Tanner, holding his hand while the emergency response team ministered to him. They rolled his gurney across the flight deck and onto an elevator.

Once they were out of the weather, Tanner opened his eyes and smiled at her. He gripped her hand and whispered, "Told you I'd see you again before you knew it."

She took a deep breath and let out a shuddering sigh but said nothing, knowing she'd cry if she tried to speak.

Allie went to his room and stayed at his side while two oncology nurses and a medical technician set up new IVs and helped Dr. Weiss perform his examination of Tanner.

A few minutes after 8:00 A.M., Allie sat beside Tanner. He lay in the bed near the window of a semiprivate room on the west side of the hospital. The other bed was empty. Two IV containers dripped fluids through electronic measuring devices into his arm. An oxygen tube ran under his nose, and heart monitor wires extended from his chest.

Each time Allie looked at his face, she feared he wouldn't open his eyes again. When he did, they were glazed, vacant, looking through her without focusing.

Dr. Weiss made a note on Tanner's chart, then held it up, looking at Allie over his half glasses, shaking his head. "According to this, there's no reason for him to still be alive. Nothing but sheer willpower making his heart beat."

She gazed at BJ, pursed her lips and nodded.

Weiss put a hand on her shoulder. "Been a long night, Allie. You need some rest. Be real careful driving home. The rain is coming down like a waterfall."

"I'm not leaving." She gestured toward the empty bed. "Maybe I'll lay down a while."

"Wish there was something more we could do, but . . . well, you've seen his chart. You know."

"I know, doc. Thanks for taking care of him."

After Weiss left, Allie went to the nurses' station to ask someone to bring her coffee. The two men in suits that she now knew to be FBI Agents Cooper and Briscoe sat in the waiting area talking with Dr. Maroun.

"They were trying to make it to Mexico," Cooper said, "but their helicopter went down in the Gulf. There were at least three men aboard, maybe more. Any idea who might have been working with Tanner?"

Maroun glanced at Allie, then shook his head. "No, Colonel Tanner came to only two sessions here. He spent a day or two with Lamar Weed, another patient here for a while. Then he went off to work with a couple of other ranchers to help with their money management or something. I think he said somewhere up around Greenville, or Sulphur Springs, but he didn't meet them here."

"You still see this man Weed?"

Maroun shrugged. "Sure. See him all the time. His daddy died a few months ago and Colonel Tanner helped him with the will and some banking stuff. Lamar comes to group sessions once in a while, but that's because I want him to meet some of the men, help decide which ones are ready for the next recovery step."

Briscoe said, "Is he a counselor?"

"Sort of. One of our nonprofit outfits is building a rehab center on a ranch right next to Lamar's. He's on the board and he'll be the ranch manager." Maroun shook his head. "No way he'd be tied up in anything like what you say Tanner's been doing."

Allie moved past Maroun and the FBI agents, stopped for a drink at the water fountain, then returned to Tanner's room. She'd been through the same questions around midnight, and she'd given the same answers as Maroun.

Yes, she knew Lamar, but only because he'd been at the VA. She'd been to his ranch once while visiting the rehab center construction site next to his place. No, she never went to the other spreads north of Dallas where Tanner helped ranchers organize their businesses. Working twelve-hour shifts at the VA left her too little time to worry about anything but spending it with BJ when she could. She said he did not tell her who the other ranchers were, the ones up north that he'd worked with most recently.

Cooper had wanted to ask more questions, but Briscoe said, "That's enough for now, Ms. Killgore. You go back in there. I know you want to be with BJ."

"BJ? That sounds pretty familiar for an arresting officer."

Briscoe shrugged. "I spent a lot of time with him this weekend. He's a fine man, no matter about the IRS thing. How long have you known him?"

Allie stood up to leave. Briscoe rose with her and offered his hand. She gave it a gentle shake, then forced a smile. "Not nearly long enough."

► 47 ◄

Tanner scuttled through thick jungle undergrowth, moving away from the sounds of the unseen enemy that pursued him. The tangle of vines and rough-edged plants scraped against his body, causing pain in his legs and arms, but mostly in his back and stomach.

He moved as fast as he could, but it seemed slow and sluggish, and he could hear the enemy gaining on him.

The grating jungle flora ended abruptly and he found himself slipping into deep, murky water. The jungle pool seemed a safe haven, but only for a moment.

He sank deeper and deeper, unable to swim, then struggled to make his way back to the surface. But something drew him down. He kicked and stroked at the thick black water until he felt his lungs would explode.

Unable to fight the water any longer, his weakened arms slipped down to his sides. Then someone grabbed a hand and pulled him to the surface. He felt his face come out of the water, and he gulped air. He opened his eyes to see a blurry vision of Saint Allie beside him, holding his hand.

She leaned down and kissed him. He tried to hold on to her, to sharpen his focus and see her clearly. She spoke, but he couldn't understand her words. He heard rain and saw it pelting against the window. Then he drifted again.

Now he stood on a smooth sandy beach at the edge of thick green jungle. He lay down and closed his eyes to rest. No sound came from the jungle. No enemies. No animals. Nothing.

Then came a roar, a strange hissing and crackling. He opened his eyes to see a flame-orange fog falling on the jungle. In an instant, the lush green foliage turned brown, then ashen as it crumbled and drifted to the ground like powder, leaving only white skeletons of trees standing.

The burning fog seared his lungs and took his breath away. The sea beckoned, the calm, clear water looked inviting, safe. He moved toward the water but felt searing pain throughout his body. He had to hurry into the water to stop the burning, but his legs wouldn't move.

Unable to stand, he crawled through the deep, coarse sand, then over the packed wet surface at the water's edge, and finally into the water. It felt cool, refreshing.

Then it began to pull him under. Deeper. Deeper.

The water engulfed him and he couldn't reach the surface to breathe. When he knew he couldn't save himself, Allie touched his hand and gently lifted him to the surface once more.

This time he could see her clearly. She smiled, but it was a sad expression, and he didn't know why.

The pain was gone. Saint Allie had healed him. He'd never felt so good! Never.

He smiled at her, feeling a serenity he'd never experienced before. While he gazed at her face, the rain stopped. Then a ray of sun pierced the clouds and shone brightly through the window behind her.

"Thank you, Saint Allie. I love you."

"I love you, BJ. Forever and ever."

He gazed at her as the sun formed a golden halo about her hair. Then the sunlight slowly turned pure white and consumed him.

Epilogue

Patricia Karney was sentenced to eight years in prison and fined $300,000. Full custody of Karney's daughter was granted to her ex-husband, the girl's father.

Theron Palmero was sentenced to two years in prison and fined $100,000.

Doyle Watkins was sentenced to three years behind bars and fined $1.8 million. After paying the fine, he filed for bankruptcy before entering federal prison.

Dave Bonner, upon learning that he couldn't avoid a prison sentence, started his automobile in his closed garage.

Nineteen minutes after the helo carrying Tanner's accomplices left the IRS building, an Air Force fighter jet intercepted and followed the aircraft to the Gulf of Mexico. Because of minimum speed differences, the intercept jet was unable to keep constant close visual contact with the Huey. The helicopter crashed in the water eighty miles offshore. No survivors were ever found. All aboard were presumed dead, and they were never identified.

Tanner's attorney, Phillips, sent certified copies of Palmero's confession to the major TV networks and national newspapers, but the story was never fully or accurately reported.

Agent Briscoe retired in San Diego, California. He works occasionally as a consultant to law enforcement agencies regarding kidnap/hostage situations and terrorist intervention training. He admits to no one but his wife that the better part of his knowledge came not from experience, but from a very long weekend spent with BJ Tanner.

Betty Wilson was promoted to Director of Human Resources for Tanner Systems, a position Tanner had recommended as part of his employee buyout plan. As the company achieved the extraordinary, Betty kept pace with excellent staffing.

Becky Kruger established her flying credentials in the Dallas area. While the nonprofit Veterans Ranch was being developed, she flew personnel and building materials to the ranch. Shortly after the ranch was completed, she became a news-copter pilot for a major network TV station. She continues as a volunteer on the ranch. The old Hueys are still her favorites.

The not-for-profit Veterans Ranch organization that purchased the property adjacent to Lamar's ranch provides free service to the Department of Veterans Affairs. Lamar Weed manages the ranch. Allie Killgore serves as staff director of the facility. It is a working, income-producing cattle ranch, a technical/trade school and physical therapy facility where veterans needing help are rehabilitated and trained to be skilled workers in numerous fields of employment. The facility serves U.S. military combat veterans.

Sonny Kruger and Ernie Castro continued working as ranch hands for Lamar until the Veterans Ranch was completed. They became supervisors, instructors and coordinators for veterans programs on the combined properties. Farm and ranch management programs are only four of the sixteen programs available on the Veterans Ranch, which is designed for personal recovery and development training by three- to six-month programs.

Dr. Maroun, in addition to his duties at the VA, serves as deputy director and screening officer for the Veterans Ranch "guest" selection process.

Allie and Lamar, during development of the Veterans Ranch, spent countless hours together reviewing facility designs, finding board members, establishing donor contacts and generating cooperation with other ranchers and farmers in the area.

They are only two of the many BJ Tanner fans, but they are the two who loved him most. Their feelings for BJ bring them closer to each other with every passing year.

About the Author

Ron Howeth was born in Corsicana, Texas, central to the three main locations in *Final Return*. He served in the Navy in a helicopter anti-submarine squadron, then graduated from the University of San Francisco and worked in data communications in the San Francisco Bay Area. In recent years he lived in San Diego, the central site of his next novel. He now resides with his wife, Mary, in the Temecula Valley wine country in Southern California.

Acknowledgements

I owe a great deal of thanks to many people upon completion of this novel. Joan Oppenheimer recognized my talent and kept me working until I got it right.

Larry Edwards edited this novel and showed me how to turn a long mystery story into a fast-paced mystery thriller. Larry taught me skills that an author needs beyond written words. I'm still working on that and look forward to more years working with him.

For the most technical aspects of the novel, I owe thanks to Mike Nave. I have a fair background in computer and communications technology, but Mike is light years ahead of me. He set things in place in the right time period. I'll never forget our patio lunch at T. G. I. Fridays.

Thanks to the veterans and staff members of the Dallas VA who helped me create the composite characters in *Final Return*. No names are mentioned here in order to protect their confidentiality. I sincerely hope this novel serves them as much pleasure as they gave me while conducting research at their facilities, but on their own time.

The most important thanks of all goes to my wife, Mary. She offered the first challenge and gave me the opportunity to pursue fiction writing. She is my best critic, best friend, best fan, and strongest supporter.

28517524R00187

Made in the USA
Charleston, SC
14 April 2014